CRITICAL HABITAT

TERRENCE KING

Penguins & Ducks Press and colophon are trademarks of Penguins & Ducks Press, Inc.TM

FIRST EDITION

Library of Congress Catalog-in-Publication Data

Names: King, Terrence, author

Title: Critical Habitat / Terrence King.

Description: San Diego, CA: Terrence King, [2023]

Identifiers: LCCN 2023907479 | ISBN 979-8-9881209-2-6 (hardcover) | ISBN 979-8-9881209-3-3 (B&N hardcover) | ISBN 979-8-9881209-1-9 (paperback) | ISBN 979-8-9881209-0-2 (ebook)

Visit terrencekingauthor.com for a peek at new novels, book reviews, deleted scenes, and more.

PENGUINS
&
DUCKS
PRESS
ESTD 2021

ALSO BY TERRENCE KING

The Silent Partner

For Mia

There is a recognition that the current critical habitat arrangement doesn't work, for a whole host of reasons.

— *George Miller*

ONE

Through the frigid night's parting fog, General Speer exited the beaten chopper, ready to take his camp back. The three-day hunt for the rebel hideout had been a fruitless enterprise, and returning to see his Authority camp under siege grated on his nerves. Never had this district been ambushed. Certainly, the numbskull grand regional governor overseeing their camp would cast out blame to the generals, declass them as trench monkeys. Perhaps by quelling the uprising, he would cease to be a trench monkey.

The chopper's engine coughed and died as Speer marched up the scree embankment. He led with a gait of dismissiveness and dread as a tight belt held his protruding belly in place. Fanning loose balls of canvas ambled up the hill ahead toward the main complex like tumbleweeds, bouncing over motionless rebels who could attack and steal no longer. He grimaced as the apprehended rebels crouched on their knees, their eyes downcast in shame, submitting to Authority officers both human and machine. The rebels failed again but had caused irreparable damage this time.

Nearby, low-ranked officers loaded munitions the rebels had poached back onto hovering jeep pods, lobbing them into unstable stacks. Several black-helmeted troopers advanced with a tall, handcuffed prisoner. Speer straightened as he welcomed their approach. Beside him, a gigantic robotic-armed sentry trudged mammoth steel legs forward with profound grace, as if sensitive to its boorish intrusion. All eyes tracked the barbarian robotic soldier's calculated steps, its three-meter height bringing apprehension to everyone except for the slight general. Its titanium-chromed skull resembled a human's in shape and design only, with soft-brained programming dedicated to Authority orders. Dozens of armed sentries peppered the Authority ranks, bias and aspiration among none.

He appreciated the imposing machines despite their technical imperfections, such as their literal communications. Unlike the rank and file, sentries were consistent, precise, and loyal, something humans sorely lacked.

"The highest ranking rebel we could find, General," an adjoining officer said.

"Highest ranking," Speer repeated, inspecting the prisoner. He wore frayed, ragged garments. Another sign of desperation in the rebel ranks. Menacing Authority troopers flanked him, sheathed in armored allegiance, grasping the prisoner tight. Black armor covered the troopers from top to bottom, and their ominous bucket helmets dismissed any remaining humanity underneath.

"Lead commander," the officer amended.

Speer squinted as he searched the dejected raider's face for weakness or other maddening shortcomings. "Explain why you think you can break into my camp, empty our cloud, and wipe our systems clean."

The rebel fidgeted, his eyes hidden behind long strands of hair and avoiding the hard-lined sentry's stone glare. His breath came shallow and fast. "We're scavengers trying to protect ourselves and find refuge."

"Scavengers." Speer studied the disheveled rebel leader: his greasy appearance, gaunt and lanky. A commander who had allowed his rebel comrades to be caught and killed, and still he would lie. How this unorganized pack of dissidents had eluded his forces dumbfounded him. His blood pressure rose. "You think stealing back our intelligence prevents us from finding your headquarters? You stole information you shouldn't have. I've lost many assets to reacquire it." Authority decoders had not had time to decrypt and comb through the data, unable to determine the rebels' location—a regrettable miss. "You have left me a mess to clean up."

"We're starving."

Speer raised his eyebrows and smiled, his temper on a short fuse.

"And we need medicine," the rebel continued, struggling in vain to free himself from the troopers' tight grip.

"Your name," Speer demanded.

"Jameson, sir," the first officer offered. "His people turned him over when they were captured while trying to steal food provisions."

Speer's patience had been tested by the rebels many times, but he cared most about one thing. "Jameson. You have stolen information I want back."

"We're just scavengers trying to—"

"You're rebel thieves, and now, many dead rebel thieves," Speer interrupted. He calmed himself, if only to get his words out. "I *wanted* your bees and food stock, but hand over the download."

Jameson somehow quickly maneuvered out of the troopers' clutches, snatched a pistol from one of their holsters, and fired on himself, doubling over. The armed sentry fixed its weapon on the prisoner swaying on his feet. After interpreting its life reading scan, the machine lowered its imposing steel arm, its beady red eyes turning down as it accepted his self-inflicted demise.

"Another lost asset," Speer said, mostly to himself. "Such impertinence."

It had become common practice, uprisings and pillaging of Authority resources across the region's other forty-three districts, but tonight, Speer's camp had evidently been the weak link. No more would he be the fool. He composed himself to stop his shaking, an erupting rage simmering to a boil. As Jameson groaned at his feet, Speer swift-kicked the dying rebel writhing in the dirt like a defenseless snake.

As if realizing his misstep, the trooper retrieved his loose firearm off the ground in haste.

"Give me that," Speer said, snatching the trooper's pistol. He fired it and the trooper fell, curling in pain as nearby troopers and officers dutifully froze. There was no room for failure. He fired again, the dull blast echoing across the camp as the attempted coup's liveliness died down. Order was restoring, and the rebel gave his last breath. Alarms hushed and spotlights fixed still, as if predawn itself had died. The sentry stood tall and silent and guarded, doing nothing more until it received a new order or, worse, sensed an infraction to act upon on its own.

***

She had always been the faster runner. Faster at everything. It was one of the many things she had on him, confounding her because Y was a half meter taller. *A whole half meter.*

They raced through what had once been a fertile corn field, where overfarming, the war, and then over the years, negligence and waste, had destroyed whole environments. Failed carbon sequestration laced the dead soil. Desperate honeybees had deserted the pesticide-laden and poisoned farmlands long ago, seeking safer habitats. Districts without pollinating bees saw their crops disappear, crops X had only seen in digital images. Apples and almonds were extinct. No one had seen cucumbers, grapefruit, or oranges either. Also, peaches and lemons and limes, bananas and melons and mangoes. Broccoli, cauliflower, and cabbage. Coffee, gone, plus apricots and plums and avocados and pumpkins. Grapes gone, and the wine with them, along with blueberries, strawberries. All berries.

Honey, gone.

She had learned from her elders that human populations first surviving the war and then the radiating aftermath later struggled with infertility and weakened immune systems. Then came starvation and dependence on the Authority for bland but dependable ration deliveries. The honeybees, having been the natural remedy for a dying Earth, and normally responsible for fertilizing the world, had forsaken the sick to protect themselves from ubiquitous poisonous threats and disappeared altogether. All the while, the Authority hunted for them.

"Hurry," she whispered. The rising sun glinted on the dry, furrowed, and contaminated soil crumbling underneath her feet, the dirt clogs crunching apart like crusty sandcastles. In other parts, the rock-hard dirt painted the landscape like cracked concrete.

Y panted, looking like he would vomit any moment, as she monitored the open fields behind them to ensure they were not being followed. She reached into her pocket and pulled out a small tracker spy drone and released it into the distance, hoping to discover a nearby *friendly*, someone who could help them reunite with the rebels. With the quickness of a small hummingbird in the dawn, the spy drone buzzed away, appearing as a small red dot on her handheld sensor. "If our leadership is caught or killed, we were told to get to main camp ourselves. Maybe someone can help us."

"Somehow I don't remember that."

"Maybe because you slept through our Instruction prep sessions," X said, taking one of her insulin-regulating pills out of her small pack, noting she only had a few left: an auto-reg smart med. They couldn't be out on their own for too long or she'd have problems.

4

"I only slept through the boring ones," Y said before vomiting into the dirt.

"Maybe you need to read other things." She tried not to laugh, for it would agitate him more, and he was in no form to withstand much more agitation. Letting loose his guts, and any spirit or enthusiasm with it, would continue to slow them down. No way could she carry him all the way back to home base, nor abandon him to succumb to element or adversary.

She frowned as the spy drone disappeared from the grid and wiped the pesky bangs from her eyes as she peered out after the spy drone's release. The sunrise promised another hot day, blistering, and her hope that the drone would find help dissipated. Rise of the Authority, the new power structure emerging after the war, had segmented populations across the Third Continent into districts during the Dark Era decades before. When it had all started. Greedy political forces confiscated rights and property while feeding dependent populations poisoned foods (regulated foods, really). Armed citizens and factions had had enough, and through a proliferation of mass-scale armaments, chaos ensued, resulting in the annihilation of billions. She tried to shut out the graphic violence she created in her mind: unsuspecting families buried in routine and chores, then, disintegrating skin. Silent screams and haunting images oozed into her dreams.

As she had been told, the new dominant government across the hemisphere disarmed and controlled people in specific, controllable camps housing hundreds, sometimes thousands. Great metropolises, the epicenters of the revolts, particularly during the Great Uprising of the Millennium, were destroyed. Any hope of flourishing or survival, flattened. Elusive rebellious clans grew out of the rubble rather than accepting predetermined, calorie-controlled rations. With impassioned resilience, the kids' clan back home flourished with population growth and expanding hidden farmlands as they grew their own food (and started to outgrow their resources) to fight off the Authority's tyranny.

Y folded his torso over his legs and swayed side to side like a pendulum. His face turned white, or was it green? She heaved a sigh at the misfortune of having teamed up with him. "Great job in losing our backpack, Y," she said, unable to help herself. "Those supplies would have helped us if we're stuck on our own for days."

"You told me to leave it," he said, his face devilishly pale.

"Because I didn't want us *to die*. It's called a *back*pack. You don't drop what's on your back."

"I told you before we left I didn't want to be responsible for carrying all our stuff. I barely even got the data chip. You had to be the last one out of there planting the detonators."

Her mouth agape, X said, "Even with the first unit depending on us, you were late. You just couldn't miss a chance to see the ravaging boll weevils, could you? Remember what happened last time? I keep saving your hide from Sangeeosay."

"You're so good to me," Y said dryly, and he hurled again.

She felt bad for the boy who'd constantly been blamed for slowing down the mission, poked fun at by other rebel scouts. Being an elevated scout leader required more than a fascination with obscure facts about nature and weaponry, the subjects at which he excelled. They had been required to fulfill Instruction's requirements of knowledge in geography, war history, physical endurance, physical limitations, and leadership, all which he disregarded as uninteresting and useless academics and effort. *We can't be seen outside where Authority drones can discover us, so why should we bother running for exercise?* he had asked frustrated instructors. So she had been assigned him as the stronger partner.

Her heart pattered as she noticed a flickering searchlight in the distance—a hazy ball of light, coming and going as if both kind and insolent, unable to make up its mind. *Is it coming closer?* She tried to determine its direction, its will, and dried her straining eyes as they started to tear. In an instant the light disappeared, fading into the desert wilderness and wastelands. Staring did not return its fickle, distant glow. Perhaps the brightening dawn no longer required the searchlight, or she was seeing things.

The spy drone's sensor showed something. Bug-light indicators said dozens of somethings were coming their way. She shuddered. They could not let the Authority recover the data and penetrate its encryption; the hidden rebel camp and all its resources were at risk. The prospect of future generations roaming an unpoisoned Earth would be dead. The sacrifice of a hundred rebels and several supply-stuffed runners would have all been for nothing, and there wasn't enough of either to spare.

"I hope you're done over there, sicky," X said. "We need to move."

***

General Speer toured the Authority camp's main control room, wringing his hands in angst and wanting to strangle someone. His central command was in shambles, and he hated a mess. Firearm blasts had destroyed the mainframe computer, the entire installation's brains. Walls were painted black with smoke, and the control panel's video monitors, metal levers, and plastic knobs congealed into stinking wreckage, incinerated. Surveying the damage, his anger grew. He imagined his private files within the cloud being discovered. Exposed. A dead computer technician lay collapsed in her chair, burnt and singed in a smoldering blanket of fumes. They all should have seen this coming.

"General, no prints," an approaching officer said. "The camera system was disabled, and there is no document of who came in and left Control. We are questioning all prisoners for information about the download."

"No document?" Speer huffed, waving the officer away. "You mean the rebels did not sign in? How uncourteous. Out of my sight."

"I have something, sir."

Speer turned toward the entry, where Major General Leroi stood at attention, her small frame barely raised by her alert posture, elevated by what he thought to be unhealthy doses of aspiration. The sapphire-colored pin holding her hair up was against uniform code, the least of her transgressions. Only in her early twenties, Speer had decades more experience on her, and her last mistake had proven to him what experience was worth.

"What do you have, Major General Leroi?" Speer asked, studying her for weakness: the soft lines of her face and abysmally dark, assassin's eyes that could mock him without a blink. "Tell me you didn't lose more food and armaments to these rebel amateurs."

"No, sir," she said, staying on point. Her stiff, dull, tonal inflections reminded him of stone. In time, she would break. He would see to it. "We secured it all."

"That's refreshing," Speer said, "considering this camp's responsibility in the district. We'd have a mutiny on our hands if we couldn't feed our camp. What else?"

"While questioning the troops, we discovered two children escaped the camp soon after its recovery, sir."

"Children?" The rebels were inventive thieves, indeed.

"Probably twelve or fourteen years old."

"That's young for scouts."

"That's the point, sir. Unexpected and fearless." Leroi pulled up the battered backpack at her side, opening its zippered mouth wide. From across the control room, Speer observed with interest. Of everyone reporting to him, Leroi currently annoyed him the least. She held up a beat-up, boxy device. "A trooper reported they left this behind. It uses obsolete GPS."

"Old technology," a nearby officer interjected unnecessarily, making Speer wince.

"They probably hoped it would work on Authority base, which of course it does not," Leroi added as she rummaged through the backpack. "They had ice sheets to aid screening. But what's most interesting is this." She pulled out a small, amber vial with a stout cork. Loose honeycomb bits. "Honey."

Speer's mouth froze agape. The rumors were true. Clenching his teeth, his chest heaved. Here the rebels were with a stock of bees and stealing armaments from Authority camps across the badlands and wastes. The sole honeybees in the hemisphere, destabilizing everything.

Leroi pulled out a few paper-wrapped packages. "Probably makes anything taste better than the bland rations we provide civilian populations."

The general studied Leroi for impertinence. Her tone, dry like bone, often held a thread of disrespect, fueling his distrust. He stepped over another dead officer. "The children must have the stolen download from our cloud. Send the trackers."

"The soldier who let them pass has been detained, sir. He said he believed they were Loners, which is why he let them go."

"Loners?" Speer scoffed. "Is he blind? Those bloodless freaks don't invade government camps." He grabbed a data entry log reader and, after determining it broken and useless, lobbed it across the room. "Terminate that officer. Useless fool."

"A search team will be assembled," she said, stoic.

"Immediately," Speer added as he approached her, the angry veins popping out of his neck like wormy snakes. He would steal his information back and finally possess those invaluable bees. The more resources in his hands, the more Authority rank and control he could marshal. He stared into her eyes fixed with misplaced optimism and unfortunate naiveté. A downfall he could foresee, a premonition. "I cannot have a repeat of the Mines of Gurth."

Satisfied with her subtle recoil, he could focus on his next move. Speer and his officers started to leave, one of them shamelessly inspecting Leroi up and down as he moved past. Officer Tippler had always had a thing for the major general, regularly toying with her without saying a word. As dashing and strapping as a corpse flower, his dark-buttoned eyes drew too close to his nose, as if pulled together by a drawstring.

Suddenly, Speer popped his head back in, laying out his final words on a platter. "If you want to be a leader in my force, Leroi, get this right. The Authority can't afford to let you fail again."

TWO

"It's so hot!"

"Quit complaining," X said, sitting against the desert rock. She held up her canteen, hoping the boy wouldn't squeal in delight. "Don't waste."

"Well, look at you, Miss '*Always Prepared*.'" Wiping sweat from his broad forehead, Y limped over and snatched the canteen, spitting out the warm, musty water.

"It's what we have."

Beyond the last sloping hill, the desert wasteland's vast emptiness spread out like a dry, tan canvas. The sun's seething rays beat down, warning of danger to come. She checked her video monitor for Authority drones, anything suspicious. Anything large enough (fifty kilos or more) would register as a threat. If only they had their ice sheets, the heat-insulating blankets that shielded drone locaters, but they were gone with the pack left behind. That pack *he* had left behind, with their comlink also in it. She searched her monitor again for the featherweight spy drone, considering the possibility it had been shot down. They were on their own.

It was easier to hide from trackers with hills and tree patches in spots, but those same things also obstructed navigation. She tapped her digital watch compass, which was banged up and barely readable. "It's *kind of* working."

"That's just great."

"We should go that way." She motioned, slipping back up on her feet. "The camp, the water, is east."

"Um, X," Y said, pointing to the rocky terrain. "Don't you think those rocks are more of a threat than an advantage? Who knows what hides there, awaiting lost travelers like us. I think we should go around the rocks first and then whip around."

"It could be much quicker to go over it," she said, discounting the worrywart. "Though this compass keeps changing, going berserk." The dials spun madly as she changed direction. "Geomagnetic confusion, I think."

The foreboding red mounds spread out for kilometers like a vast sea of blood. With the spy drone gone, they could not risk being exposed in the open desert much longer.

"What are you, a mountain navigator?" Y asked.

She dusted herself off. "Weren't you doing computer relations just a few months ago? Which no one knows what that is exactly."

"I study what interests me. Compassing," he said, frowning at the grand rocky terrain. "Could have been valuable now, though."

Suddenly, a land drone approached in the distance, and her eyes popped. She'd only seen images of a relentless prowler scout—never in its true habitat, never the machine's true nature. The barbarous hunter skipped across the desert landscape with its rotating propellers on each side spinning like windmills, helping it balance like wings. Its mechanical legs stretched over the dirt with swift strides and the graceful deftness of a prairie predator. Ensnaring claws grabbed whatever ground they could grapple for momentum and speed, with the uncanny ability to stay upright on unleveled ground. Its balloon-like head rotated as it searched, its telescopic eyes popping out in every direction. An all-directional helicopter drone, definitely the property of the Authority.

X and Y hurried toward the rocks' onset, hiding in the shade as the rebel hunter passed. They waited until the small roar of its hum disappeared before poking their heads back out for a look.

"I can't believe it didn't see us," Y said finally.

X studied the spinning compass now perpetually pointing north. "Probably confused too. One thing's for sure, the Authority knows you stole the download."

"What if we get stuck in these rocks at night? Loners are probably waiting to rob us. Eat us." Loners, the eccentric nomads of the desert, were said to reside in the rocky caves. A depraved devolution of humanity that, supposedly, were not even human anymore. He motioned toward the long, rocky terrain. "It's probably better to hide than wait out here. They won't be thrown off by the rocky jungle for long."

11

"So which is it?" X asked, scanning the empty, rolling badlands behind them, positive the Authority's troopers were tracking their path. "The indecisiveness, Y. We're really going to have to do something about that." Then, dog trackers howled in the distance.

"Dogs. Just go," he said, following her as she scrambled up the expansive rocky hillside.

She crossed through and over the brush-grass cowlicks and rock crevices with trained dexterity and reached the top of the hillside in moments, with only a few scrapes on her knees. She stopped cold at the crest, a sight to behold.

"Hurry up!" she whispered loudly.

Y struggled to climb up the unyielding grade. He cut his hand on a jagged rock, drawing blood, and his foot slipped back. He cursed, embittered as he regained his ground.

"What's taking you so long?" Standing at the top of the ridge, X shielded her eyes from the rising sun's torment.

Y slipped again up the rock-ribbed hillside. "So annoying!"

"Hurry!" she called to him as he finally navigated to the crest. "Think it's abandoned?"

Inside an enormous basin, the rock quarry stretched for kilometers. Each rock summit rose dozens of meters tall, calling up to the sky as if not high enough. Crumbling granite slabs and smaller mounds of rubble surrounded the glorious piles of cut, excavated rock and the yawning mouth into the quarry's belly. To the side, several old shipping containers huddled near the center hub of the quarry near scraps and junk. Except for the center clearing's middling commotion, there were plenty of places to hide from Authority drones, hungry scavengers, and search parties. This was a place someone else before, at some time, must have also used to hide.

Y pointed. "Loners."

Oh, she had seen them, tainted by the poisons, unbroken by their own revolting wraith. The beasts were cast in sullied hoods and layered cloth, attending to a rusted, beaten vehicle that looked nothing like the speed pods they'd grown up with. It proudly displayed an open roof and visible gas tank (ripe for thieves), and its wheels actually touched the ground. "Is that an Old World jeep? What does it use for fuel?"

"Same as the converted cruisers, I bet," Y said. "Modified generators combining hydrogen and methane. Though I don't know where they get the hydrogen out here with no water."

Maybe the place had been abandoned long ago and they could find a hole to be safe for a little while. A pocket hidden within the rock sea. "We just need to find a spot."

"We can't get caught by Loners. We can't. And what if that drone comes back?"

In the distance behind them, what had to be a small search team of armed troops, led by a pack of dogs, was headed their way. If the boy was eaten, torn apart by limbs and bone, she was positive General Sangeeosay would insist it was somehow her fault. "Think anything valuable is in those shipping containers?"

"Well, let's find out," Y said, starting down.

"Look who's adventurous now."

"I don't want to be eaten by dogs out here."

As they scrambled their way down the quarry's hillside, X endured Y going on about how they needed to eat something soon, it was getting too hot, and how she was the one who'd told him not to bother going back for the backpack, *so there*.

They descended a steep dirt road when Y peeled back. "There's something," he warned.

"Where?" X whispered as they hid behind some brush along the path. Had she missed an important detail?

Near the quarry's hub stood a small, dilapidated bungalow, its rusty aluminum roof slanting downward as if ashamed, turning away from certain doom. The shack's rusted siding was decaying, its rough-edged holes on the bottom nibbled by blood rats, the big ones. Her eyes drifted back to several nomadic Loners in grimy cloaks loading the jeep. Probably the battered vehicle had been abandoned at one time, hungry scavengers coming upon it, rummaging and then scattering. Anything that assisted survival was more valuable than gold.

"Loners all right," X said.

"I've never seen them my whole life, just renderings."

"You're fourteen."

From behind the brush a gas-masked Loner, filthy and hideous, rose, raised his staff like a medieval Viking gone mad, and let out a terrifying shriek, alerting others. Stunned, X and Y fell back on their rumps, scrambling backward as the five Loners stalked toward them, weapons raised.

***

Speer reeled, clenching his teeth. Another blathering meeting he had to endure, wasting his time. The Authority's governance of the Western hemisphere and participation in the Global Senate Assembly's concerns sanctioned stupidity. The Authority had already allowed the rebels to siphon off precious resources. Other powers could eventually control these lands. As they placated the Senate's squabbling for scraps and waited for world governments to become healthy, it was the rebels who possessed the sole honeybees, a new lifeline of resources. They needed to conquer the rebels, not appease the Senate's whims.

"We need to do a much better job of protecting our own camp before we can have any advantage over other nations," Major General Leroi said, rigid in her seat at the black oval table next to him. They were surrounded by a dozen generals and high-level officers summoned by the grand regional governor, who again kept them waiting. Dark walls and a short ceiling shrunk the room like the walls were closing in. Only a soft gleam from the table's center illuminated the closeted space like a coffin, but with a table and ominous light.

"Control over the food supply is at risk, Major General," Commander Teek snapped back. Young and slimy, he was a benefactor of his father's rank and cabinet position at another camp. Speer liked Teek, if only for their mutual dislike for the Global Senate. "Too many rebel factions are causing trouble. We need to stop it or our coordination with—"

"Coordination has evolved to independence," Grand Regional Governor Martel, older and gangling, interrupted as he entered the room. His cheekbones and eye sockets were pitted skeletal deep, his face gaunt and emaciated like a starved prisoner's. He glided swiftly to his seat, the top of his head grazing the ceiling, and spoke with confident authority. The air in the room immediately shifted to attention. "The District Council is now providing each Authority district independence for handling rebel interference. It's no longer necessary to seek Council approval to defend our camps against pilfered food and weapons. We are now accountable to only ourselves if we don't engage in *warfare* with the rebels. Being able to respond to attacks swiftly should reduce friction and protect Authority camps across the Third Continent." His haunting eyes zeroed in on General Speer. "That is, if we're able to contain our intelligence from theft by children."

Speer winced at Martel's dig, not expecting this. The shift in the Authority power structure meant power was up for grabs somehow. The Authority's District Council had never relinquished decision-making power at the individual district level, disrupting its own dominion. He gathered his thoughts as Martel's piercing eyes bulged out of their cadaverous sockets, surveying the room.

"Grand Regional Governor Martel," Commander Teek said. "To be clear, do you mean we can defend ourselves without going through lengthy approval processes with the Council?"

Martel's focus bounced around the room. "Correct. In fact, with dwindling resources, combining defensive efforts in the hemisphere has become necessary. We will use our food and medicine to bargain with neighboring districts for defense."

Despite the rebels' possession of the sole honeybees, the crops they would have virtual exclusive domain over—apples, blueberries, oranges, almonds, cucumbers, even pumpkins—wouldn't provide enough food to keep the rebel raiders from risking their lives to break into Authority camps. Cross or hand-pollinating farming had not been reintroduced after the war at a big enough scale to provide most crops a chance to be distributed to hungry populations, so the rebels had exclusive yields on the crops they bore.

The hungry's *impatience* for crops to mature would not allow them to bear much fruit anyway, if they were able to grow at all in their poisoned, pesticide-laden lands. How had the rebels managed to hide their crops from scouting Authority drones? If he had not discovered loose honeycomb himself, he would have believed the honeybees to be mere urban legend, fabricated to build mystique behind the rebel cause.

Commander Salvato grinned through his thick beard. "Our resources will put us in a lead position by default."

"The rebels don't rob us because our rations are plentiful," Leroi countered. "They rob us because they're starving. And we hold all the antibiotics."

Teek jumped on her words. "We're talking about working with other districts, not those pathetic separatists. They succeed at making you look bad, Major General. If the Authority is to build influence within the Global Senate, we need to look beyond your failures within this district. The rebels are just rats. Perhaps your security protocols should be overhauled."

Speer licked his lips, relishing Leroi's failures haunting her. She had been granted a pass, as children often are, for a slight indiscretion.

"You don't oversee any installations, General Teek," Leroi said, raising her voice in defense. "You can't fail when you're leading security of empty prison chambers."

"Major General Leroi," Martel said, "General Speer says you have another mission now." His ghoulish eyes brimmed with calamity, the table center's white light accentuating his pallid, ghastly features. "I expect you will get those stolen plans back."

Speer contained his yawn, bored of Martel's deathly presentation of authority.

"Yes, sir," Leroi said, her eyes downcast as if trying to read through the floor.

Lumpy clogs in Speer's throat disappeared in a single swallow. "As we're focused on stopping the rebels, how do we know neighboring districts won't attack us as their supplies dwindle?"

"Our armament resources are steady," Martel dismissed, "and they rely on us, not the other way around. We will lead the hemisphere through strength as we've done."

Speer frowned. Martel was too soft. The way to dominate districts was to incite fear, not hope.

"Excuse me, sir," Commander Salvato said. "If a group of unorganized rebels can penetrate our camp for vital information and weapons, what makes us think a neighboring province couldn't attack?"

"We'd crush them," Teek interjected.

"Don't think we won't be attacked," Leroi said, bold in speaking up again. "The human condition won't allow people to accept starvation."

Smirking, Teek said, "You need to prevent theft of our resources any time General Speer leaves camp."

Speer smiled inwardly at the jab. It was almost as joyful as a swig of absinthe coating his throat.

"The rebels stole back the information we took and deleted our whole cloud!" Leroi responded. "They would've gotten away with our guns and food if we hadn't recovered our blockade runner. Don't underestimate them."

Teek laughed, somehow causing a familiar, sharp pain in Speer's jaw.

"Okay, enough," Martel said forcefully, quieting the room. "I did not come here to debate but to inform you of the Council's evolution. I'm uninterested in anyone's feelings about the *human condition*." He glared at Leroi as she looked away. "The rebels need to be contained. If populations have unrest, our government has unrest. This is where I want our attention—on the rebels, not our neighboring government districts. Questions?"

The room became still, the air itself afraid to breathe. Martel nodded, signaling it was now Speer's meeting.

He bristled at Martel's appraisal of the situation. Containment was a short-term solution. "Now," Speer said evenly, casually disguising his disgust behind a mask of cursory direction, "the rebels are somehow communicating with each other and moving food and medicine between camps sight unseen. After we first discovered honey in an evacuated merchant vessel and most recently, in an abandoned backpack after this last attack on this camp, we believe the rebels indeed possess a large hive and the sole honeybees in the hemisphere."

"Their own bees?" Teek coughed.

"The only bees," Speer corrected, the soft white light revealing his perspiration. "Unlike our attempts across all territories, they've succeeded at harvesting hives, honey, and the crops bees pollinate."

"This is why rebel populations are growing," Teek said with wide eyes. "Their food isn't—"

Speer shut him up with a harsh glare, his leg bouncing under the table. He was losing patience with this bunch. "Since exhausting our search prior to their last attack on our camp, we believe their hidden headquarters is somewhere in District Forty-Four's forest. They have food and medicinal resources, but they're outgrowing their food production, and that's why they're stealing food.

"They're also especially short on weaponry to protect their fortress. Medicines. Our last intelligence transmitted before our spies were killed indicated the rebels need to expand their crop hectares, but to do so would likely expose their position." He leveled his glare at Leroi. "Of course, we were within minutes of determining their exact location when they stole back all of our intelligence on their base's exact location."

"That district is thousands of square kilometers of forest," Salvato said as he tapped on a small glass control center. A 3D digital topographic image rotated above the table like a halo. Millions of dense lush trees illustrated the scope of the vast woodland frontier.

"Tens of thousands," Teek corrected. "Too many mutations of nature live there."

"You thinking that, General Teek," Speer said, eyeing the rotating geography in colorful animation, "is exactly why they're housed there. Somehow, they've conquered the forest's perils."

"They're hardly an army," another commander spoke up. "No large weapons, no organization."

"And yet," Speer sighed, thankful someone finally made his point, "they've stolen information vital to the Authority's survival." *And to our expansion.*

Leroi spoke up. "We should consider using another mole to pinpoint the location."

"As if we'd never tried that." Teek sniffed.

"Someone who can infiltrate," Leroi added. "Get on the inside. Someone they'd never expect. Perhaps a *non-spy.*"

"From where?" Salvato asked. "They've eluded drones, heat-mapping technology, everything."

Teek laughed. "Every mole we've sent has been detected and killed. We can't keep losing our best."

"Maybe we've been looking in the wrong places," Leroi said.

"Rein in their disruption," Martel declared. The room became still again as he spoke. "The future of our governance within the forty-four territories is at stake. Retrieve our intelligence so we can determine the rebel headquarters' location and peacefully contain them. Rebel colonies must be converted to a satisfied civilian population. This is what the District Council wants—populations happy with their rations."

Speer clenched his fists. If he was in full control, he would deploy the Authority's newest weapons, untested or not, upon the rebels without fear of the District Council's reprimand. He imagined grabbing Martel's throat, digging his fingers into the rough folds of the ghoul's neck.

"General Speer," Martel said, awaking him from his cathartic fantasies. "No more unnecessary deaths, or you will be formally court-martialed to the District Council. Do you understand?"

"Yes, sir." He felt death inside.

"What's your plan?" Martel asked.

Speer traded glances with Major General Leroi. "We will meet and—"

"Not good enough. Tell me you can find these children who have successfully invaded our cloud and eluded your forces."

"We—" Speer started.

"We're going a different route," Leroi interrupted. "We're going to find a standout mole who has the skills to infiltrate the rebels and get us their actual location."

"Now we're getting somewhere," Martel said.

Speer did not like being shown up by Leroi. *Vision and stamina* were required to seriously take on the rebels and win anyway.

"General Speer and I have conferred," she lied as Speer narrowed his eyes at her insolence, "and we determined we will find a skilled candidate with something big on the line. Our spy won't look the same, be the same."

"I'm arguably putting too much faith in you two," Martel said. "We can't afford to lose more of our intelligence assets." He pointed to Speer. "You find our plans and get those bee hives. You"—pointing to Leroi—"find our mole. Succeed this time. The room is dismissed. I want the rebels appeased and on our side. And I want our cloud data back. Get me what I want."

The Authority officers all moved to leave as Speer leered sideways at Martel. He'd been reduced to equal footing with the major general, an unacceptable result of her failures. Speer vowed there would be consequences for Martel, all the while fearing what would happen if his secret files in the download were revealed.

THREE

A contentious Alvarium prisoner up the way jangled small pipes against the bars, piercing Mel Custode's ears as she huddled on her cell's cold concrete floor, trying to hide from the ear-splitting clangs and hoping to get her bearings before she *flipped out.* Rattling vibrations tortured her teeth, stinging the nerves to their roots. Grating bangs echoed up and down the halls like bouncing metal balls, resonating with tinny rings. How had the indignant jailbird acquired the aggravating pipes in the first place?

She sat with her legs crossed as she toyed with a small hive beetle, energetically bouncing within the walls of a small-scale structure. The crude build was one of carbolic soap cakes composed of lessening resources: phenol, lye, and baking soda. It smelled depressing and acidic.

Using her finger to gently flick the insect back within the four-centimeter cake walls worked. The insect flipped off its back, intent on escaping its temporary condemnation. Escaping its trap. Unlike herself, the beetle had a much better place to be. She gave it a pinch as it scrambled and climbed the cake wall only to fall again, exhausted and riled, tossing itself. Like her, the beetle got older and crankier within Alvarium's cramped walls, their cold dominion prescribing helplessness. As young as she was, her strength and faculties would eventually diminish, she was sure. Aged or weak prisoners here had a habit of hiding in their cells, as if they were trying to shrink into their bones and disappear. Her health, too, would decline, and she sensed she would die a little each day as she waned.

"Custode."

A guard stood outside the bars of Mel's cell, holding an invisible pain ray (IPR) baton, the weapon of choice to keep inmates in line at Alvarium Penitentiary—the IPR, the Holy Grail of riot control. Part club, part ray-gun, and light and effective. A crude weapon, and the deadliest one in Alvarium. The guard looked like a bobby from the 1800s in his regimented dark blues, and the cell door unlocked with a sudden clonk.

"Custode," the guard repeated over the clanging pipes. "Get up."

Mel raised her head. *Not again.*

"Up."

She got to her feet. Just keeping her head up took strength. Every time she went through this, things got worse. A bead of sweat crept down her smooth head, producing a small itch down her skin. She tried to ignore it, at this moment hating absolutely all beads of sweat. Back when she had been a free civilian, cutting off mere centimeters of her thick, black hair had made her feel lighter, free of dead weight. But now, a buzz-cut meant her hair could not be pulled during unwelcome prison scuffles. It took no soap to clean when there was little. Also, she didn't have to concern herself with managing unruly curls.

The guard grabbed her and escorted her down the prismatic cellblock, which, unlike common Old World prisons, was not a straight hallway. Instead, an odd zigzag path snaked between the labyrinth of tight chambers, providing a dizzying effect designed to confuse and demoralize anyone forging a beeline escape, then tangling them up in disorientation.

Efficient in its small scale, the remote prison housed thousands of inmates over a few desert hectares. Angular cells of Alvarium Penitentiary lined up row after row. Four to six inmates had a direct view to each hexagon-shaped unit, providing the guards a natural element of monitoring and safety, and assurance any high jinks were thwarted. Enforced sociableness for all.

She shuffled forward through the maze and the concentrated dank smell of sour sweat, the raucous clanging getting louder with each step. Her headache grew.

"Okay, Luther, stop it," the guard called out.

The prisoner leered out his cell as they passed, his cockeyed teeth poking out from his bottom lip like crooked stakes. Mel ignored the grimy inmate's grin, and after shutting out disturbing images of his animalistic behavior, her survival instincts kicked in. Her awareness heightened to a greater purview, threats growing with each reluctant step.

It was like she was awakening from hibernation as her muscles stretched, lengthening like rods as she walked. Her stomach growled, not from hunger but vigilance and alarm. She wanted this nonsense over with.

"Faster," the guard said, kicking Mel behind the knee. She glared back and picked up her pace, if only not to be touched again. "Miss your friends?"

She said nothing traveling through the vestibule as a contentious draft gave her chills.

"I'm sure they've missed you," the guard continued.

They came upon the atrium, the prison's soaring, open-roofed cavity. Brilliant floodlights canvassed the narrow, rectangular dining hall, shards of intense light spilling into the darker pathways in all directions leading to the cellblocks along the perimeter. It was like being too close to the blinding sun in winter: warming rays welcomed, even when reflecting off treacherous snow caps. Beyond the painful lights, the ceiling's mouth and open sky peeked down over the twenty-meter walls, built sky-high to convince inmates they were mere specks on Earth. Insignificant and small. She bet the engineers who built this island's behemoth fortress had bragged about their unattainable heights as they built it, amazed by their closeness to the heavens as they stacked the rebar, steel, and concrete. Seeing the clouds cluster and congregate like roaming beasts above was a constant and painful reminder there was life outside Alvarium's foreboding walls. A life she was missing.

"There she is," a coarse female voice said from beyond the stretch of rusted, off-kilter benches and dented heavy tables.

From among a group of seven prisoners, a young woman—severely tattooed with her hair cornrowed—eased to the front of the two male convicts. Piercing studs threaded her eyebrows, her face soured with ink.

"Custode," the woman continued, her voice rough like sandpaper. "Feeling pretty this evening?"

Mel monitored her surroundings as she always did as dozens of inmates predictably assembled in their polygon cells for the best view.

"She hates us, Chitter," one of the male prisoners said to the leader.

"Is too good for us," Chitter said, having earned her nickname by being the most vocal of the group and often talking too much.

Mel lumbered to the middle of the atrium, tired of being dragged into confrontations she never sought out. Dusk fell, and an orange tint highlighted the night sky over the open atrium. A move to the left, and the prison guard disappeared into the shadows. Not surprising. Something as simple as one of the few tomatoes on the island could get a handful of favors from a rogue Alvarium guard. Any credits would do the trick.

Chitter didn't blink while two more guards fell back into the black, and Mel stretched her wrists, her arms by her sides. Hard to believe, but she would rather be evading the warden's awkwardness right now.

"Get to it!" the guard called. "We don't have all night."

Chitter glared at the guard, a stiff shadow in one of the cellblock aisles, barely in the atrium's sight. "You got the stomach to finally fight me this time?"

Mel was not going to be cut by words. While she could more than hold her own (and living around combative inmates often forced her to do so to survive), fighting had only proven to make her life worse. It solved nothing. Starving without rations and being stuck around the general population were good enough incentives alone to avoid conflict at Alvarium.

Chitter motioned all around. "Our family feels disrespected, you spending all that private time with the warden."

Mel kept her eyes on Chitter, sensing two prisoners slithering behind her. "Have you considered making a quilt or something?"

"Be together—like family," Chitter said, ignoring her snark. "Is all we've wanted."

An aggressive prisoner jumped at Mel, until she swept her leg at him with one swift kick. He fell, wailing as Mel faced another grimacing male prisoner who pulled a shank out of nowhere.

"Where did you get that?" Mel asked, zeroing in on him. He was slight with thin legs and a beak of a head, moving smooth and rigid like a wading marabou.

"Resourcefulness requires skills not everyone has," Chitter said, motioning her head toward Mel.

"I have different skills," Mel said.

The prisoner ran at Mel, and she sidestepped and muscled his arm behind his back. She swiftly swiped the shank and stabbed him in the leg. Instantly he writhed in pain, twisting like cut worms do.

She cast the shank to the side and stood up straight. "No more."

"What makes you feel like this is your choice to make? The warden handing out favors?"

Mel never had any favor from the warden beyond food prep upstairs. Stuck in this place, she'd wished for an easy peace in another time, in an imaginary place of accord and calm. Like the old photo of her grandmother, the one with the single sunflower in her hair. A bright place smelling of clean linen.

Exhausted by this process, Mel motioned for Chitter to get on with it. "What's your move?"

A stocky male prisoner with a faint, wishful beard snuck behind Mel and locked her arms behind her back. Chitter immediately approached Mel and punched her in the gut. Her insides felt squeezed, her diaphragm crushed. Heaving, Mel doubled over, held up from behind until her feet dangled.

"Nothin' to say?" Chitter said, swinging a slap-hook to Mel's face. "You don't appreciate the family you have."

Someone laughed as Mel hung lifeless in the prisoner's arms. Chitter approached her with another slug, Mel quickly dodging to the side. She heard a crunch as Chitter's punch landed on the inmate, his grip loosening as he billowed. A fine distraction, Mel kicked Chitter back onto one of the tables, who rolled over like a kicked bucket. She dropped her legs to the floor and kicked the bearded prisoner's knee with forceful precision, and he fell, churning.

Two more prisoners jumped to the atrium's center and swung at Mel. She moved gracefully out of their reach and swung around, causing one of the prisoner's swings to knock out the other inmate. With a quick step, Mel knocked the prisoner on his back, breaking his nose with her elbow and barely a gram of pity.

"I told you I don't want to fight," Mel said. She peeled off her itchy uniform top, revealing patchy scrapes and scratches across her toned arms and shoulders, which poked out of her loose oyster tank's crude, rough fabric. Alvarium's custom torturous fiber weave. The night's cool air brushed against her skin and sweat. Instantly unrestrained, she felt momentarily free.

"Not up to you," Chitter said, slowly getting up on her feet.

"It's not up to your friends," Mel cracked as Chitter regained her equilibrium. The grounded gang stirred, awakened like by the gentle wind. Others remained knocked out.

All alone now, Chitter balked as Mel rotated her arm, speeding the cramp out of it. Mel studied the ringleader, who turned aside, shuffling in her squeaky, rubber shoes. It appeared the fighting was done. Squinting up through the floodlights, Mel wished she could fly away. The farthest away.

Then, out of nowhere, Chitter ran at Mel, swinging hooks with impressive, skillful nimbleness. Mel blocked and avoided her throws with equal precision, ducking and shifting positions before wiping her brow. After a beat, Chitter went at her again, landing a stunning punch on her lip.

So this was the way it was going to be. Mel jumped at Chitter and tried to sweep her leg but stumbled on a downed inmate's torso, falling into Chitter's swipe against her throat and collapsing against a thick cafeteria table. It hit her like a wall.

"Awwwwww," one of the inmates called out, while others jeered.

"One minute!" a guard called out.

Chitter kicked the inmate up who had run to Mel with the shank. "We got one minute, peoples!" An inmate rolled back over on his back, struggling like a flipped turtle. "Good God, Gilman. You'd think she snapped your back."

After a breath, Mel noticed the blood dripping from her chin, smearing her tank. *Great.*

She ran at Chitter and caught her off-balance, and then pinned her against a table. Chitter shot out her legs, tangling with Mel's until they both fell to the ground as they each struggled for dominance. Mel grabbed the shank nearby, using her knees to pin down Chitter's arms.

"Do it!" one of the inmates called, dozens of them lined up at their cell bars.

Chitter struggled and strained under Mel's strength and control. Mel paused with the shank wrapped in her fist as her opponent transitioned to capitulation, the white flag of surrender in her eyes.

"Kill her!"—"Waste her, Custode!"—"Hurry up, man, I'm trying to sleep!"

She finally threw the shank to the side and stood up over Chitter, exhausted.

"Time's up!" the guard yelled. Blinding floodlights engulfed the prison atrium, more than twice as bright as before, as dozens of guards aggressively moved semiconscious inmates to detention. Hurried medics appeared with stretchers as the guards escorted Mel away, this time without an IPR in sight as hasty routines eclipsed courtesies.

"You're no good, Custode!" Chitter moaned, loaded on the stretcher. "Shrink in your cell where you belong."

"Do you ever shut up?" Mel grumbled as she checked her chin for more blood. Her insides ached. The punches to her abdomen were wallops, the kind she would feel for days. She wanted away from them all. Everyone. She wished away her bad choices of the past, wanting to go to a home she could not. Because home was nowhere.

***

"Well, there ya go," Warden Miriam said, wiping tomato off her chin with a nearby security guard's sleeve. "The one I told you about. You wanted capable and resilient. Ability to improvise when necessary. She doesn't look like your average fighter."

Major General Leroi stared at the flickering video monitor in the security block, trying to determine if this female prisoner would do the trick. The Authority had chartered her to exploit the talent within its grasp, its rich span of resources across the hemisphere. While there were those who used words like *enslave* to describe what the Authority did, she needed someone who could infiltrate rebel communication systems. Not beat down a gaggle of unpolished prisoners who were not even good at being violent inmates.

Someone different.

Mel was being escorted back to her cell, as other security detail peeled knocked-out prisoners off the floor and placed two on stretchers.

"I don't need a fighter, Warden," Leroi said, unsure of the troubled candidate's qualifications. "I need someone unconventional, and smart in their methods. Motivated."

The warden raised her brow. "I'll show you her file. Let's see if your motivation will work."

FOUR

The giant metal door slammed as they were suddenly thrust into the dark, the latch clanking shut. Sullen shock racked X's brain as she tried to reclaim her senses. Stale heat punished her lungs, like she was being sucked into a hot coffin. Would they ever see daylight again? She started to choke.

"I can barely breathe," X said, her lungs drowning as she smelled something reeking of stench and soot. They never should have investigated the stupid rock quarry.

Stupid, stupid, stupid.

Y inspected the walls, pounding them in vain. They were thick, with no ring or hollow. Breaking through them would not be an option. "So glad I'm not the only one whining now."

Recognizing the rectangular storage container from holograms during Instruction, X never imagined she'd be contained in one. This horror was stacked on an Old World eight-wheeler, a mechanized relic that somehow survived the Dark Era after the war. The monstrosity's wheels were absent of rubber, the decaying rims dented, gouged, and egg-shaped, installed with absolute disregard for practical use as a moving vehicle. And configured into a slave transport?

If trapped inside long enough, they would sweat to death. The blighted, rusted ceiling peeled from two corners like well-worn folded paper. An open flap of grimy tarp covered the top, allowing faint light and the occasional breeze to sweep under its wings so bursts of the quarry's hot air could eventually make its way into their lungs. Whatever the opposite of hypothermia was, this was it.

"You're the one who wanted to 'check it out,'" X said.

Y coughed. "They took our water."

"My water."

"Can you two shut up, please?"

They weren't alone. X's eyes adjusted to the scarce light. Her vision separated in a dark prism of empty dizziness. Then she saw him. A young man, slight and no longer optimistic of fortune, curled up in the opposite corner of the container as if resigned to his last breaths. It looked like he'd been there a while, doused in grime and filth and one with it all.

"I can't take it anymore," the young man said, smearing the sweat from his forehead.

X grimaced, unimpressed. "What are you gonna do, complain us to death?"

"Slaves have no one to complain to except other slaves."

"I'm a slave to no one," X said, immediately doubting her words as she said them. Destination unknown, crossings of the rough, would they be sold to the highest bidder? Possibly they were slaves after all. A chill crawled down her spine. "Especially these disgusting Loner *things*. What do you possibly know? You're stuck here just like us."

"Hey," the man said with a hint of amusement. "Control the slave market or it controls you."

She shrugged, her eyes fully acclimated. The young man appeared weak and wounded, an animal caught in a spring-coiled trap. "You don't look able to control any market."

"I'm saving my energy for when I need it," he quipped, as if casting her words to die. "Don't let my current condition deceive you."

Puzzled, she studied him. He looked emaciated, perhaps diseased. Loose skin sagged on his small bones in unexpected waves like he'd at one time been considerably larger, weightier. Hazy, dusty light exposed the blunt contusions on his arms and chest, dark and stolid, perhaps as lucid reminders of what happens to resisters to Authority rule in the outlaw wastes.

"I'm Lootjay. And if you must go . . ." He nodded to the rancid bucket propped in the corner in shame. "Don't make it worse in here."

"Lootjay," X repeated. She could smell his overheated human stink.

"Steal the money, fly like a bird."

Cute. Maybe whimsical, endearing. "How long you been in here?"

"Two days. And when I get out, I'm gonna take back what's mine."

"*What's* yours?" Y asked abruptly, his question laced with judgment as X waited, curious for his answer.

"I take from the world what it takes from me. A very simple transaction to understand."

Suddenly, the container moved. By the way it had looked outside—like a dark hole in a rectangular mound of metal—X wouldn't have imagined that the behemoth actually *worked.* The bumpy ride slammed the container's three occupants against its walls as the vehicle bounced and bumped, its owners having rebuked any need for shocks or tires. Bracing themselves against the corner walls didn't help as X, Y, and Lootjay were thrown wildly in all directions. The pail storing excrement clunked Y in the head.

"This isn't getting any better!" Y cried, falling back and hitting his head against the wall just before the precious box fell out of his pocket. He dove to retrieve it like a wild bird dog. X followed Lootjay's eyes as they tracked the box—just as Y shoved it back in his trousers—and she conceived ways to wring his neck.

"I really should be the one holding on to that," X whispered angrily.

"Nope," Y snapped back as the eight-wheeler's engine roared, grinding and gurgling as its pipes struggled to inhale and the transport wound its painful way around the quarry's mountains of rock. "Like you said, I had one job. I can at least do this one thing right."

"If you say so," she muttered, bracing herself in the corner.

"What do they feed this thing?" Y yelled, shifting off his knees to hug the ground.

After a few minutes of the storage container's unfortunate occupants being thrown around, their bumps and bruises mounting, the behemoth finally came to an abrupt, hissing stop. The back door was thrown open, the sunlight blinding X as she breathed in the dry sunny air, which almost quenched her thirst. Y immediately fell out and into the dirt below. Two Loners hoisted him up.

Outfitted in dusty rags and robes, the leather-faced creatures communicated in a cacophony of grunts and groans and squawks. *Speaking*—communicating between laborious gasps through their respiration tubes like hospital patients. Back when there were hospitals.

Crude body language accompanied the Loners' symphony of peculiar, unintelligible noises, usually involving arm-waving and the beating of chests. One frustrated Loner used his staff to hold Y up against the vehicle until the boy threw up on his shoes. Like a reflex, the Loner quickly brought his staff down and whipped Y's back. An abusive slave master. Other Loners cried out if he'd crossed an acceptable line of Loner etiquette or geometry, and he swiped his staff in a sulk.

X dropped out of the container, staggering and disoriented as Lootjay stumbled his way out into the blinding light. His grime and muck dressed him in layers, and he stumbled into one of the Loners before falling facedown onto the searing desert floor.

"That was awful," she said, trying to find her balance, instead tripping over her own feet into the dust.

A Loner immediately pulled her up to her limp feet. As her world slowed its spinning, she squinted into the sun, finally getting a good look at the Loners' leather-skinned faces, decrepit and browned, their foggy gas masks failing to cover their ghastliness. Meanwhile, two gray, proud women sauntered up and inspected the three prisoners, unaffected by the Loners' revolting stench. The women picked at their clothes, inspecting them like they were at the market choosing fruit. Judging by the potential buyers' calm body language, they had done business with the Loners before. A sand bazaar had popped up across the way. Nomadic commerce commenced under tarps and tents.

"They look like they haven't eaten in days," the first woman said as she and her partner eyed them up and down. She held her hand to her rotund midsection, taking pleasure in her portliness.

"He must have eaten something," her partner said, stepping over Y's vomit, a splattered and quickly evaporating puddle.

"What do you do?" the first woman asked, approaching Lootjay.

"Anything," Lootjay managed.

"Is that so?"

"I've constructed water reservoirs out of scavenged piping and have even dug a well." He smiled at her partner, his eyes glistening with challenge and scheme. "Plus, I take orders really well."

X immediately concluded Lootjay would say anything to get out of anywhere. A distressed primal animal. All while Y held his head up to the sky, thankful to be anywhere but in the storage container, despite the Loner clutching his arm. How'd she let them get into this situation? They needed to get back to rebel camp with that data download, before the Authority troops found them, or these vile creatures discovered the poached possession themselves. The cloud's data would be worth a thousand times more than their three lives combined.

"We'll take him," the first old woman said.

One of the Loners started negotiating with the woman, using an animated combination of squawks and hand gestures, some of which X guessed to be obscene.

As X regained her footing, she smacked her noticeably dry and cracked lips. With nothing to lose, she asked, "Anyone got water?"

The partner inspected X closely, ignoring her question. "Have you worked in the fields before?"

X raised her brow. "Got anything indoors?"

The partner grinned. "I like you. In the fields of Cross, that's where we need the help. It's the most fertile and healthy of any of the desert farms in the district. Or its neighbors."

If there was any way to get out of Loner slavery, she would take it. Y looked to her like he had all but given up; he was probably ready to throw up again. It was up to her to save them. "I can do anything with little rest if I'm out of the sun. My mother taught me no matter how alone we were, we would do what was necessary to survive."

The partner squinted at X, as if trying to figure her out. "Margery?"

"Okay, we'll take her too," Margery said, handing the Loner a small pile of worn bills from the old banana republic of Ferre, the most accepted universal currency among the lone villagers across neighboring districts.

"Okay, c'mon," the partner said. One of the Loners pushed the young man toward her.

"Hey, hey, hey," Lootjay said, taunting the Loner as he stumbled over his legs. His greasy smile gleamed with the confidence of a child who knew he was getting away with something. "You've enjoyed my stay more than I did. But you didn't get me at my best."

"And you're coming with me," Margery said to X.

"Will you take him too?" X asked, pointing at Y. "He's really good with nature and farming. Also best indoors."

Margery shook her head, and she and her partner started to walk away. The transaction was over.

Y raised his head and started shaking. "Oh no, no, no," he said. "You can't leave me here with these beasts!"

A Loner promptly socked Y in the stomach.

"This has gotta stop," Y mumbled, swaying back and forth on his feet.

"He's got' somethin' on him," Lootjay said, pointing to Y like snitches do. "It's gotta be sump'n the way he hid it from me."

The Loner holding Y searched him. Ratty, leather-skinned arms grabbed for his pockets. Y swiftly kicked him in the shin, causing the Loner to scream, catching nearby bazaar busybodies' attention.

X ran up to help, determined to pull Y out of the scuffle at all costs. How exactly she was going to protect the download without getting flogged, she wasn't sure. She wanted to kick herself for having no plan. Then Y palmed the small box to her, undetected, before a Loner's grubby slap pushed her aside.

Margery approached the Loners, her face crinkled. "We like our business easy."

"No regrets," her partner added, her gaze stuck on the curious villagers observing them from a distance.

Margery turned to the head Loner. "We don't want to be on the Authority watch list because of this hubbub."

The head Loner grunted, motioning for Y to be taken away.

"You gotta find the box!" Lootjay insisted. "I bet it's gold. Or silver!"

Margery's partner raised her eyebrows. "We should see what he's got."

After a brief pause, as if considering whether it was a fool's errand, Margery said, "Okay, search him," and a group of Loners grabbed at Y in all places obvious and inappropriate, pulling him to the ground.

"Hey!" Y sneered, slapping one of them. "How dare you!"

Lootjay jumped up and down in delight.

"Leave him alone!" X yelled, her heart pounding.

"C'mon," Margery said, nodding toward the gawking villagers. "We've already gotten more attention than we bargained for with these buggers."

Finding nothing on Y, the Loners left him dusty and humiliated. The head Loner released a grunt.

"Nothin, huh," Margery said.

Lootjay's eyes opened wide, as if a revelation had bubbled up within.

"He's got something, I tell ya!"

Margery motioned to Lootjay. "Search him too."

"What? What ya wanna search me for?"

Lootjay fought off three Loners with gusto, scuffling and pushing at them in aspiring gyrations, punching one in the face. They quickly wrestled him to the ground, rolling with indelicate grabs, pulls, and pin-downs.

Y got to his feet and X palmed him back the box just in time before Margery guided her smoothly to another Loner subgroup. "Search her too."

"Whatchya think I got anyway?" Lootjay screamed. A Loner walloped him in the groin, and he fell on his rump. "Owwwww!"

X patiently closed her eyes and stood still as two Loners patted her down, finding nothing. They shook their heads in disappointment as her mind raced, searching for a way to negotiate herself out of the Loners' hands. Just beyond, a few villagers had taken interest, peering at them in the desert sun.

A Loner pulled out a dull, blunt knife tucked in Lootjay's sock, and immediately the jubilant Loners celebrated in absurd leaps and squawks as X smiled knowingly. Rascals were always rascals.

"What?" Lootjay scrambled to his feet. "That musta been planted on me. Awww, c'mon."

Margery glared at the head Loner. "I don't want to be assassinated by my own workers," she said, snatching the money pile back from the Loner's hand. "Thieves of this world owe the world more than it owes them." She approached Y dead-on as the boy struggled to stand straight. Her sour face made it clear she thought he was damaged goods. "Do you do field work?"

"Yes," Y stammered. "I know the replanting cycles for many crops and—"

Margery interrupted. "Do you understand computer languages for harvesting machines?"

More measured, Y said, "I've worked with the programming for most of the prewar conveyer belt threshing machines."

X motioned for him to shut up.

"*Pre*war?" Margery's eyes opened wide. "Where did you learn that?"

X dropped her head in defeat. Only the rebels had access to old prewar harvesting crop machines, unlike the newer ones provided to law-abiding Authority-controlled populations. Y had learned about the old, recovered ones out of necessity—for repair. Things were going to get worse if they were discovered as rebels on the run.

The farmer's partner spoke up. "We don't want to house someone skilled working on rebel equipment, do we, Margery?"

"Leave him," Margery said, waving Y away as Lootjay smiled.

"No!" X yelled. "You've got to bring him!" She couldn't leave him behind, no way. The lazy nerd was not physically, nor emotionally strong enough to survive arduous field labor. And the data would never make it back to rebel camp.

Margery beamed, amused. "Is that so?"

"I'm really your best option," Lootjay said conclusively to the farmers.

X could feel Y's wide-eyed stare pleading, digging at her like nails. What could she say? To ensure the farmers kept them together, she said the only thing she could think of: "Honey. We have honey."

"Lies," the partner said.

"No way do they have honey!" Lootjay yelled, grabbing more of the local villagers' attention, their heads raised like alerted animals on the prairie. Also, an old East Asian man peered at them in interest.

"It's true," Y said, choking on hot air.

"Why would we possibly believe you, child?" Margery asked, ignoring the boy. "Honey doesn't exist anymore, does it?"

The partner's eyes glazed, unseeing, as if pulled into a dream. "It would be liquid gold around here. Priceless."

"Hmm." Margery glanced again at her partner, who shrugged. She nodded at Y. "We'll take him."

"Okay, okay, look," Lootjay stammered. "You know she's lying, right?"

"She better not be," Margery said as she grabbed the makeshift knife from the Loner, inspecting it before stashing in her belt.

"I'm resourceful," Lootjay said, his voice raising to a desperate pitch. "I don't eat much. I'm good at delegating!"

Margery nodded to the head Loner, who accepted her payment again with an approving grunt.

"C'mon, you two," Margery said, and the Loners pushed the kids forward.

"No!" Lootjay yelled as two Loners pulled him back toward the transport. "Don't leave me with these freaks!" A Loner socked him in the stomach, and he slumped over to a joyous chorus of grunts and cries before being dragged away.

"Kind ladies."

Everyone stopped at the placid, unfamiliar voice to see the old Asian farmer with a priest's Zen approaching them. His long, wiry beard, unkempt and free as expected of the roaming nomads, draped him in gray. The dark-green hooded cloak swallowed his small form like a potato sack, his arms poking out of its mossy sleeves like timid branches. He would be mistaken for a child in adult's clothing, if not for the intimidating scythed staff clutched in his hands, its striking, curved blade an ironic contradiction to his otherwise meek guise. He grasped the staff like one would a cane, leaning against it and appearing too weak to strike anyone if he'd wanted to.

"Mind if Sun Bin interjects an offer?" the old man continued, addressing the head Loner.

"We do," Margery's partner said as Margery studied the old man closely.

The Loner stood expressionless, his crazed wide eyes void of any decision-making prowess as the scavengers squawked with bewildered head cocks.

"Could use two field hands myself," Sun Bin said. "Okay to bid for them?"

X's heart stopped. There could be a way out of this yet.

"Absolutely not," Margery's partner snapped, her eyes on the scythe. "You should mind about."

"Sun Bin looks not to interfere nor contend," Sun Bin said, holding out a small, brown drawstring pouch, weighted by coins judging by the slight muffled jingle. "Sun Bin merely bids for the two farmhands for help with my coops."

Margery narrowed her eyes with suspicion. "Why these two?"

"The young can assist when age is a barrier to progress." The old man's earned wisdom reverberated through each word, at once both kind and sad.

"Our transaction is completed," Margery said, dismissing the old man as the head Loner stepped forward and grunted in boisterous disagreement, thrusting out the money in his hand. "Looks like we have a problem."

"Those who know when to halt are unharmed."

"How dare you," Margery's partner said, eyeing Sun Bin's slight frame and measured demeanor. "You think your weapon scares us?"

Sun Bin grinned, acknowledging his scythe. "Not all weapons must be used."

"May not be a good idea to try to use that one," Margery's partner said, showing a long, sheathed blade on her belt.

Waving the partner away, Sun Bin approached Margery. "Am making an offering beyond rightful compensation to the Loner salvagers."

"Go on."

"For you, two thousand," Sun Bin said.

Margery said, "Why so much?"

"A contribution acknowledging the dilemma Sun Bin laid at your feet."

The Loners jumped up and down in a circus melee as X froze in disbelief. Were she and Y being auctioned?

Sun Bin continued, "No need to make things difficult." He motioned over his shoulders to the occupied villagers who had mostly become disinterested, going about their business. "Avoid any high-profile conflicts."

The partner nodded. No one on the West Rim wanted the attention of government forces. "The honey," she said suspiciously. "You think they really have it."

X tried to figure Sun Bin out. Was he an agent of the Authority, was there a bounty on their heads, or did he know who they were?

"Sun Bin could use help from healthy youngsters," he continued. "If they have wild tales of honey, my generous offer still stands." He grinned between the deep folds of his aged cheeks, something between wisdom and escaping mischievousness. A light flirted to go out. "What have you to lose?"

"Four thousand then," Margery said, crossing her arms.

He handed her two small pouches of coins, and an additional one to the head Loner. Margery and her partner left with more money than they had arrived with, the last Loners departing with a stunned, resistant Lootjay.

"Young ones," Sun Bin said, holding his scythed staff like a shepherd overseeing sheep into the wilderness wastes. "We have a small distance ahead."

As Sun Bin strolled ten paces ahead, X whispered, "Prewar threshing machines? What's wrong with you? You're lucky I saved your hide."

"We have *honey*?" Y retorted in a hush. "How we going to get out of that? You know that's why he bought us."

"I'll think of something," X whispered. "One of us has to."

Sun Bin plowed slowly, caning his scythed staff as he sauntered forward, the blade glistening in the sun like a small moon.

"Did they just fight over us as slaves?" Y asked. "There's a lot of interest in us."

X picked up the pace for them both as the hot orange sun burnt into the hazy desert plains, scorching the land of life and wish. A dying landscape where abled slaves, perhaps strong waifs, would eventually lack resources and resolve. With untold creedless hunters and rogue overlords seeking to merely live another day, slaves were probably easy to come by. "The question is why."

***

"Another attack? The arrogance, in the middle of the day."

"The end of the day," General Speer corrected. Demonstrating his superiority over Grand Regional Governor Martel, even passively, was sweeter than anything he had ever tasted. "During a shift change, sir."

Martel lifted his eyes as he munched on his toast in his dining quarters, a tent not much bigger than a large box. Everyone knew Martel did not like his dinner interrupted, but informing him of another rebel attack on an Authority food facility took precedence over preferences. Speer contained his internal smile, knowing the cramped dining made Martel cranky, the lack of comfort and accommodation often expediting his visits. Also, it got under Martel's skin.

"Your methods of shift changes need to be recalibrated, General," Martel said. "Much more than my definition of time."

Speer breathed in, maintaining his composure. He could barely contain his fury, kowtowing to the aged man who feared war and instead desired unilateral cooperation among districts. Appeasing the Council. Also, belittling him. His mind raced. No way could he tolerate much more.

"This is, after all," Martel continued, "the Authority. Get your act together or I will do it for you."

"Yes, sir," Speer ground out through clenched teeth.

"What else?" Martel knifed stubborn jam from the jar's bottom.

"They acquired ammunition too, sir," Speer said, somehow both dreading and taking pleasure in releasing the information. Rebel attacks and pilfering government targets angered them both, perhaps the only thing they agreed upon.

Martel put his hands down on the table and inhaled. "Mess officer! More jam! Wherever it comes from." Turning his steely eyes to Speer, he said, "How is it we govern tens of thousands of people across zones, all of them voluntarily unarmed, and yet these rebels continue to elude us and build their entire infrastructure at our expense?"

A coarse rag throttled Speer's throat. He had explained this many times before. "The general population's disarmed, sir, I will remind you. Not the rebels. These are the ill of society, using force—"

"I don't need education from you, General," Martel interrupted. "I want answers. These bandits—that's what these rebels are—keep hitting us time and again, and it's a problem."

A mess officer dropped off an unlabeled jar of jam at the table and left, skipping away as if to ensure he wasn't pulled into the verbal crossfire.

"And," Martel continued, "how is it the rebels have a monopoly on the honey? I'd like to have the sweet nectar with my toast at dinner again sometime soon. And chocolate. And coffee!"

"Sir, I—"

"Convince the rebels to play, General. Get my intel back."

My intel. Speer had to recover it before anyone discovered the battle plans he'd devised and hidden on that download. No more of this *rebel containment.*

"Have you a solution?" Martel continued, greedily fanning his toast.

"Major General Leroi has discovered a prisoner from Alvarium in District Seven who may be perfect to penetrate the rebel base. We're preparing her now."

The grand regional governor raised his eyebrows. "Her?"

Speer nodded. "The rebels wouldn't expect a sole female infiltrator."

"And why is that?" Martel asked, putting his toast down. "As I've seen, they've used women and children in their efforts against the Authority. They clearly don't have a problem putting them in harm's way."

"Neither do we, sir."

Martel evidently considered that as he prepared to have another bite. "I expect progress soon," he said finally. "Get those kids who stole my cloud's intelligence and wiped it clean. No more rebel deaths. Do it right, or I'll station you on desert satellite detail like that poor fool Kesselring. Figure it out."

How dare you.

"As you wish, sir." The words pained Speer as he said them, not meaning one of them. The Authority needed to lead and prepare to fight, not acquiesce to the rebels. Martel's plan for progress was one of hope. A terrible plan.

***

Mel's hands fidgeted as she sat in intolerable impatience. Likely she was being observed behind the glass wall, in foil and shadow. Probably recorded, everything uploaded by dutiful machines to a cloud somewhere. She imagined them to be wary, distrustful eyes that never blinked. The isolated interrogation chamber made Mel feel small, like her world was closing in. She had not asked to be here. Alvarium Penitentiary, always intrusive hosts.

Offensive, blazing white lights washed her out of all color—like a ghost, her blood drained. She was prepared to hear again how she needed to get along with her fellow inmates and manage her temper. How she had been responsible for inmates being sent to the infirmary again, and how Alvarium often ran out of beds for the injured. *Blah, blah, blah.*

The warden and an Authority officer paraded into the waiting room, accompanied by two guards, cold and regimented in their firmly pressed wears.

39

"We really need you to get along better with your neighbors, Custode," Warden Miriam said, picking sunflower seeds out of her teeth with a toothpick. She sauntered around the plain table like an angry parent impatiently admonishing a child. "It's expensive, taking care of the injured. I should keep you cooking in my kitchen, away from the crudeness. But you don't really deserve that luxury."

Mel said nothing. Who was the Authority officer staring at her, appearing about to speak but no words escaped? Slight and soft, or was demure the word? She was perhaps ninety pounds, like that of a big dog. Her dark, sapphire-pinned hair wrapped tightly around her head with no loose strands to discipline. Maybe she was tightly wound.

"That was quite a display," the officer said, not taking her eyes off Mel. "Where did you learn to fight like that?"

She was not going to fall into any trap and say the wrong thing, nor be put in isolation again, or worse, planted with the inmates daily.

"Just did what I had to," Mel said before pulling her gaze away, hoping to reduce the tension, not make her situation worse. Moments like these she would be happier back in her cell playing with bugs.

Sitting on the corner of the table, the officer said, "My name is Major General Leroi."

Mel studied the little hand the woman offered for a moment, but didn't take it.

"I'm with the Authority."

The silence was heavy and awkward. The room felt cooler, like wind over ice.

"Of course, you know that," Leroi continued, a forced smile creeping across her face. "The reason I'm here is to recruit you. We need someone with your assets."

"Fighter, chef," Warden Miriam said, reading off a palm-held computer tablet. "Admitted seven years ago? No children, no partner, distanced from family."

"You've got fighter first," Mel said, smiling faintly. "Funny."

"Often reclusive," the warden continued, sighing, "with anger-management challenges. Exhibits both introversion and extroversion tendencies. Warning: can be reckless. Incarcerated for assisting the rebel cause, resulting in the deaths of two Authority troops."

"I know why I'm here," Mel said. She didn't bother to correct the record. Her voice had been shut down by the Authority court. Her mother and sister had been harassed by aggressive troopers, as had all families of the last holdouts giving up their personal firearms, and Mel finally gave up their guns under duress. But then she had elevated the altercation when protecting a neighbor who had refused to give up his guns, leading to chaos and a blood-soaked mess. Troopers mistakenly fired on each other in rage and discord. By the end of the scuffle, her neighbor and both Authority troopers were dead, and she was to blame despite never firing a shot. She had turned herself in to prevent her family's home from being stormed by troopers again. The price for her crime: her family had been moved to an undisclosed district and told she was killed in prison transport.

"The Authority needs you to penetrate a rebellious faction that continues to steal government resources," Leroi said, her smile disappearing. Light to dark.

Mel recoiled. "You want me to help you beat the rebels?"

"Not beat them," Leroi said. "Find their hidden headquarters deep within the district's forest."

"Is 'finding hidden headquarters' listed there?" Mel asked, pointing to the warden's palm-held computer tablet. "You're not asking me to do this."

Leroi straightened up her chin. "This must be where the recklessness comes in. Respectfully, Ms. Custode, I'm not asking you."

"You're ordering me?" Mel glared at the warden. "Can she do that?"

"Yes," Leroi said. "According to the Authority's Service conscription, any civilian requested for classified service must comply or be subject to a formal court martial."

"I refuse," Mel said. "What are you going to do, put me in jail? There's nothing you can do to me, Officer, or whatever your rank is. You think I'm a good fighter and what else?"

"Chef," the warden offered.

"I will cook, even for her. But I'm no spy, sorry."

"Is that your final position?" Leroi asked, eyebrows raised.

After what had happened to land her in prison, Mel had told herself she would never again get in the middle of others' messes, big or small.

She would be the one to lose. Alvarium knew this was her soft spot and enabled manufactured conflicts. Prisoners were toys.

After a moment, Leroi finally asked, "Nothing? So that's your position." Leroi shrugged and glanced at the warden, who nodded to someone behind the glass wall. "Okay."

The grating lights dimmed. A digital projection appeared, emitted from a 3D projector behind the glass. Muted colors dazzled the bare walls as browns and dirty white hues filled digital movements, aged like potent sepia ink. A woman and a teenage child, both imprisoned in their home dwelling, holed up on the floor like chained dogs. A crooked painting of a small family could be made out in the background.

Mel caught her breath. "Mom?"

"And sister," Leroi said without a blink. "Both of whom you abandoned years ago."

Not exactly. "When was this?"

"It's now."

Mel got up and approached the images on the wall. Studied them, searched for clues to their level of pain or anything familiar. Gaunt and emaciated, they were barely recognizable, bony and aged versions of themselves. Eyes empty, void of anything Mel remembered. Their tired faces drowned in a remote stretch, burning with traces of home that seemed reachable but far away.

They were unaware they were being watched by anyone of consequence, readable in tiny moments as their attention bounced from the camera and back to each other, possibly for comfort or answers. Mel touched the walled projection with her fingertips, longing for something she had tried to forget about. They became more distant to her, like people she'd never met. "Can they hear me?"

Leroi watched her closely. "No. They're not hurt. But they're not free."

Mel didn't leave the video images. "You're actually doing this."

"You figured out something Custode cares about," the warden said, immersing herself in her chrono. All-knowing nothing. "I hadn't identified that in the years she's been here."

"Do what we need you to do," Leroi said, "and you can be with them."

"Or?" Mel asked, emotionless. Lost in what wasn't and what was, she fell into a virtual sinkhole, her stomach rising up her throat.

"Or," Leroi said, apparently having been prepared for the question, "we further cut their rations. Until they . . ." The major general didn't finish.

Mel's heart stopped.

"And," the warden sighed, "we can make sure you work in the fields, which you hate, and still cook for me, riling up the inmates' appetites to take it out on you. And you can defend yourself *every single day.*"

Anger rushed through Mel like lightning, and she tried not to shake. Her mother and sister believed she was dead. She had been unsure they were alive, but now knowing they were, a shiver surged through her teeth—a glycerol freeze. "You knew I'd say no," Mel said, her tone indignant.

"We considered you might." Leroi sighed. "And since you've fought Authority rules before, we've got to watch you."

Being watched was nothing new. Every move at Alvarium had been monitored and recorded. Still, she hated the Authority's despicable tactics. Every single one.

"So we're giving you five days, Custode, to find the rebel headquarters and recover a download."

"Five days? A download of what?" Mel scoffed. "You haven't been able to find the rebel hideout for years, but I'm supposed to find it in five days? How many other spies have died following your listless orders?"

"Find them," Leroi said, dismissing her questions, "and protect the Authority's dominion over these lands. We need you to protect your government from those dirty rebels."

"You're the dirty ones," Mel said. She'd never wanted anyone to drop dead before her as much as she did now. "Repulsive."

"We're not dirty nor repulsive, Custode," Leroi said evenly. "We're the Authority."

FIVE

Y discovered Sun Bin's tiny abode was meant to house someone of modest height when, upon entering, he hit his head on the doorway's beam. It was an unassuming stead tucked away into a mountain wall, as if the world had swallowed it up. Nearby farmers resided within a stone's throw, bustling outside their modest rock and thatch-roofed huts, ramshackle and crude. As the sun fell, a few villagers huddled in a closed circle, tempted into illicit and questionable deal-making as they buried themselves within heavy cloaks. Inside, he and X claimed cozy spots by the firepit, the crackling sticks offering a welcoming burn and warming the cramped quarters to an orange glow.

"We're slaves now, aren't we?" Y asked as an eager crackle emitted from the hickory timber's kindling. The gray smoke drifted out of the cage window in easy wisps, possibly alerting someone of their presence. Alerting the Authority.

"Oh, we're slaves." X yawned, laying her head down on a pile of stained rags and brushed sheepskin hide. She sighed in relief as if the makeshift pillow was the softest thing she'd ever rested her head upon. "We've been in worse situations."

He stared at the hodgepodge mound of soiled rags and Sun Bin's tiny cot situated next to the stove. Absorbing the fire's charred smoke, the decaying fabric smelled of death. A lively cloud soon ballooned in the hut, smelling of burnt soot, and he coughed. Was Sun Bin trying to torture them?

"Sun Bin doesn't want to smoke you out," Sun Bin said as he stirred the smoldering porridge. He then opened another meager window, which perhaps only a portly rat could fit through. The stove's cracked damper flue forced the stubborn smoke back into the hut, which somehow then got sucked out the window, happy to be free. In moments, Sun Bin attended to them with two bowls. "Take it hot. Warms the soul."

Y hungrily grabbed the bowl and frowned. "There's almost nothing in there." Larger rations had been provided back home, even in their most desperate times on the run from Authority forces.

"It's hot, though," X said, eyeballing him to shut him up as she stuffed a spoonful of porridge in her mouth, along with one of her last auto-reg insulin pills. Only a couple left now. "No reason to complain. About everything."

Y ignored her glare as he poked his wooden spoon into the thick brown something. Her judgment ate at him like a swarm of locusts. "It's like mud. I can't eat this."

"A combination of tree root, bark food, and water," Sun Bin said, "harvested from the forest greens along the border district. All Sun Bin has until the farmers' bazaar. Or until you two youngsters share any treasured honey for sweetness. Had not expected company tonight."

"Hmmm." X shrugged. "Bark food. Well, we're grateful. Considering where we were, right, Y?"

He struggled to swallow the porridge. It tasted like dirt. "We were bound to be caught by someone," he said absently, admitting they'd been running from someone or something. With X's constant glare, it seemed he always said the wrong thing.

Sun Bin sat down, legs folded, and studied them. "Ones who run must discover how not to run."

"That's amazing philosophy, mister," Y said, rolling his eyes. The old man mustn't have many people to listen to his conclusive observations. "Or should I call you master?"

"Sun Bin is good," Sun Bin said, furrowing his brow.

"Forgive him, sir," X said. "It's been an ordeal."

"Do you think we'd run if we didn't have to?" Y asked. They had always been running and hiding and evading. All his life. When he was five or six years old, during Instruction he'd been taught how to hide in natural landscapes and run long distances without detection. Survival techniques. It was all he'd ever known. "You think you know us?"

"Lots of questions," Sun Bin said. "Sun Bin doesn't know you, nor you me."

"I'm X," X said, "and this is Y."

"Succinct names."

"Well, actually I'm X-G1, X for short. The females are all named X, the boys are all Y. The G was my class division, and I was first in my class, which is how I got the *one*."

"Go ahead, say it," Y said, unamused. She had found another person to brag to about her standing.

"He's Y-H17," X continued. "From the H class, seventeenth in order. He's one year older, too, which you may not have realized with his childish behavior." She smirked, evidently enjoying the words. She was constantly putting him down.

"But I'm the only one left alive in my class since the Authority destroyed our last camp, the only one who escaped," Y said. "So I just go by Y. Unless we're back at home with all the other X's and Y's, obviously. We gave up formal names years ago to keep organized among clans."

"And define our standings in the ranks."

Sun Bin didn't blink. "You're rebels."

"What did you think we were?" Y asked, finally somewhat comfortable sitting up against a rock.

Sun Bin stared into the low fire, tiny embers floating and disappearing as he spoke, as if his soft words scared them away. "The Authority will stop at nothing to find you. Too often populations are caught in the crossfire."

"But you don't know why they're hunting us," X said, shifting on the blankets.

Sun Bin shrugged. "Do you know what you have if you have honey in your possession?"

"Well, I did have some in our backpack at one time," X said, staring wooly-eyed at Y as he tried to forget dropping it, as well as every other mistake she continued to point out.

"Honey is a by-product of life, children," Sun Bin said. "Life sustains life. The bees' pollination provides humanity multiple nutrients so species thrive. Without bees, whole ecosystems collapsed. A serious consequence of war."

"And yet war still lives," X said flatly.

"We studied this already," Y said, frustrated with the old man. They'd learned about everything the bees provided the world—parts of

Instruction he aced. He did not need to hear it again. Exchanging a knowing glance with X, he said, "So you bought us for the honey."

"You surely don't have it on you," Sun Bin said as the kids looked to each other. "But you know where it is."

"We can't take you there," X said. "No way."

"No way!" Y repeated.

"Sun Bin will buy some," Sun Bin said, a glimmer of life filling his tired, deadened eyes. "Sun Bin has coin."

"Not for sale," Y said. "The Authority has always wanted it, but the honey isn't why they're chasing us."

"No questions, no answers," Sun Bin said. "The Authority has sought honey since the cities crumbled and societies disappeared. What else do they seek?"

"This," Y said, pulling out the small beat-up box from his trousers.

"What are you doing!" X yelled, sitting up at the fire. "I'm surprised we haven't been killed yet with you wielding that around."

"The corners scratch me."

"Boo-hoo," X said in disbelief. "We barely know this man."

Sun Bin studied the rebel symbol on the box—a square with a circle in the middle—and the box's dented and tattered corners. It had seen its share of adventure.

"It's this they want," Y said, opening the box. He held the tiny data chip, about half the size of an Old World penny.

"Seriously?" X said, her gaze burning him.

Sun Bin's eyes opened wide, the fire dancing in his shrinking pupils. He stared, mesmerized, as if witnessing a miracle. "This . . . is what they're after?"

"I know what I'm doing," Y said. "You're not the only one who can save us, X. We're already stuck here." He turned to Sun Bin, who had moved toward him for a closer look. "This is a download from the Authority, gathered to destroy rebel installations, before we wiped their entire cloud clean. Rebel data readers think there's compromising information within its contents."

Sun Bin stood up and turned toward the caged window, lost in his thoughts in the desert farms' faint lights. "Compromising information?"

Y nodded. "The Authority wants this back at all costs, we are sure. We've got to get it to headquarters, where it will be safe." He hoped for validation from X but saw nothing, not a glimmer as she hung her head in despair as if she had no faith in him at all. "Will you help us?"

"Experience is the bitterest of wisdoms," Sun Bin said. "Those who appear harmless can cause the most damage."

X and Y shot glances at each other.

"Will you help us?" Y asked again. He placed the red box with the data chip on a flat rock by the fire. The chip's copper edges glistened in the firelight, warming with temptation, as if newly awakened, calling out into the night to its rightful owners.

Sun Bin dropped his gaze. "The Authority is an oppressive government to be feared more than a tiger. All Sun Bin has in the world is in this meager hut with my chicken coop. The jewels of life have left me behind to ponder mistakes, not create new ones."

Y did not understand anything Sun Bin said. "Why did you buy us as slaves then? We need help."

Sun Bin shrugged dismissively. "The other one hollering about honey, creating all that commotion, reminded—"

"You of what?" X asked, stepping on his words.

A weight appeared to hang over Sun Bin's head. His shoulders hunched. His soulful eyes glazed over like he'd been dragged into the depths of despair. "Authority's tricks. Sun Bin was tested and failed."

Y smiled. Ignoring Sun Bin's pensive moment, he felt he may have found the way to employ Sun Bin's help. "Sun Bin," he said, trying to wake him up out of his daze. "If it's really honey you seek, we can help you."

Shaking his head, Sun Bin said, "Sun Bin is just a small farmer. Perhaps tasting honey's sticky texture again is not something an old man like me should hope for. Will get you as far as the next district, an old watering hole. Someone there can help you, get you home."

Y narrowed his eyes, unsure if he trusted the old man. "So you wouldn't try to sell us back?"

"You're not slaves, child," Sun Bin said. "Not anymore. What you need is a low profile as the Authority hunts for you. Too many people have seen us together already."

Six

Leaving Alvarium Penitentiary wasn't freedom, though boarding the sleek ocean speeder for the first time had felt deceptively so. Mel was now enslaved to do the Authority's bidding. Hanging on a promise, a threat. That Major General Leroi had used her words with an IPR's intimidation methods—efficient, disciplined, and charged—all while standing over her, slim as a broomstick. Mel had allowed herself to be coerced into being an Authority agent. A spy.

She felt sick.

Both the captain and the two guards aboard the ocean speeder appeared to be unarmed, and Warden Miriam had been her normal grating version of kind on the dock and had seen her off, monitoring the speeder's embarkment like a forlorn lover saying goodbye. Basic provisions allowed a semblance of peace away from Alvarium inmates and strife as the vessel sped over the calm sea. Unidentified creatures slipped under cresting waves, disappearing into a world unknown, there and then gone like forgotten ghosts. The speeder sped forward, transporting her to a new world, on her mission.

Out of her drab inmate uniform, she was back in her desert linens, which provided a refreshing coolness in the coming heat. Layers would provide warmth at night. Her mid-calf, earth-toned combat boots were functional and comfortable, as was the beige tunic over her base-layer cottons, providing consistent air circulation and slowing dehydration. She was sailing free, if only for a moment.

She stood at the bow, squinting into the sunrise and cutting winds while the boat approached the growing sliver of land's horizon. The fast-moving vessel kicked up the taste of sea salt as it used its sonar sensors to avoid surface collision.

She envisioned holding her mother again, cradling her sister—a reemergence that gave her goose bumps. Eating and sharing, smiles all around. Both of them putting on some weight, filling out. What would she say differently, do better? A small tear filled her eye, or perhaps it was the wind, as the speeder swiftly glided through the brisk chill. A rising sound of flutes and chords filled her consciousness. A familiar and inspiring adagio, music she had enjoyed as a child before certain things in her, like hope, had died. A loneliness she could not explain seized her, tried to pull her under the ocean speeder, but she wouldn't let it, allowing instead the inspiring melody to fill her ears.

To the north, across the dilapidated and abandoned bridge to the mainland, stood the deserted and crumbling remains of the former metropolis, its battered buildings slowly disintegrating, timestamps of a war passed. The Broken Commons. Surviving civilians had been rounded up from devastated cities, pulled from the rubble, and placed in gated and Authority-controlled villages where they would gratefully await ration deliveries. And unlimited Authority control.

Over the years, lone survivors who somehow escaped Authority capture had devolved into freaks, stories told. Restless nomads fed off contaminated soils and water, inhaling wretched air. Absorbing radiation. It was best to avoid the ruins, where the Loners could congregate en masse and spring attack.

Her instructions were simple: *Find the hidden rebel headquarters.* Light provisions meant she was on her own to infiltrate and report exact coordinates. She would travel hundreds or thousands of kilometers of desert and forest lands, with her supply pack of basic accoutrements and foodstuffs, as an unknown agent of the Authority. It was an overwhelming duty, yet independence swelled in her as the ocean speeder skipped over the crashing waves and slowed to a stop over the dirt-brown beach.

"Miss?"

She breathed in the salt and surf and, for one more moment, pretended she had found her freedom.

"Miss?" the voice asked again.

Mel turned to the vessel's captain.

"You wanna find Oasis Marketplace," he said in a gruff voice, taking a swig from his thick drinking stein.

"Oasis," she repeated.

"There's an outpost tavern there where you can find a transport to your destination."

"An outpost tavern. Got it." She tightened her supply strap. "Is the transport waiting for me?"

"You gotta find one."

"Find one?" Mel asked, surprised. "I wasn't told—"

"Oh," the captain interrupted, "you're not on your own." He grinned wryly, his lopsided smile revealing golden, chipped teeth.

A hovering drone suddenly appeared next to her, cooing like an owl. White with black panels on opposite sides of its wiry antennae, the mechanical flying sphere was a quarter meter in diameter with one great eye in its front. Its large, ominous bulb layered with faint prismatic lines allowed light to absorb from many directions at once. She expected to be tracked, but an orbiting ball following her was not what she had in mind.

"All Alvarium prisoners get a tracker when off Alvarium grounds to ensure you don't disappear."

The drone flew a small rotation, proudly introducing itself.

"In case you get lost, Simple Eye will guide you back," the other guard sneered.

"To safety," the captain said, swallowing another syrupy gulp.

"Simple Eye," Mel repeated, eyeing the drone with suspicion as its sole photoreceptor blinked, and it floated next to her, bobbing like a fishing lure. She winced, the flying machine's personality a nuisance already. "Simply so. It blinks."

"Self-cleaning lens," the captain retorted. "Dust and grime and such."

Without responding, she jumped off the vessel just beyond the surf and started up the grade toward the cliffs, the drone following like a trailing eddy, wanting to get going.

"You're gonna want this!" the toothy captain called after her, holding a compact, rectangular device. "This will help you navigate through some pretty hard terrain. Runs into problems around mountain ranges though. No solution for that yet." She grabbed for it, but the captain pulled his hand back, saying, "Whoa, whoa, whoa," smiling as he taunted her, towering over her as she reached up for it. The guards smiled, saying nothing while the captain played. "You didn't say *please*."

Mel didn't utter a word as she jumped again, the captain once again pulling it out of her reach. Fury thrummed through her bones, but she elected not to sock the captain in his protruding gut. No way was she going back to Alvarium before her mission even started. The drone orb beeped in alarm, its antennae shaking as it observed the events, swaying around as if it wished it could do something. She jumped up again to grab it and missed. And again.

"Just say *please*," the domineering captain said as she looked him up and down. "Do the wrong thing, and you're going back to Alvarium. Solitary confinement."

What was the least painful way to get the palm navigator out of his hand? She was not going to be hauled back without getting her family released. She owed them that.

"Don't be stupid," the captain warned.

"Give it to me," Mel said, stoic and cold as she shook off the ocean's stiff breeze. "You weren't ordered to deliver me here without supplies."

"So?" The captain smiled, wiping his chin with his sleeve as he locked eyes with her. Taunting her.

Suddenly, the drone flew up and clonked the captain on the head, catching him off-balance and almost knocking him off the vessel. The palm navigator slipped out of his hands and plopped straight into Mel's like a coin in a palm.

"Please?" Mel smirked. She walked off as the guards looked on, mute.

The captain eyed the drone with disdain, massaging his crown. "You need to be reprogrammed," he grumbled, and motioned to the shipmate guards as they took their positions. The ocean speeder gunned its humming engine and left, bouncing into the waves before being swallowed by the gray-blue sky.

"Simple Eye," Mel said to the drone. "You're no regular drone, that's for sure."

The drone beeped and nodded its antennae in agreement.

"Time to go save Mom and little sister," Mel said, grinning as the drone purred and followed her up the slight grade of sand toward the overlooking cliffs and the desert beyond. She raised her cool linen sleeve, exposing the chrono display on her wrist. The five-day countdown had started.

***

"The Authority is coming! Get up, Y, hurry!" X whispered in a loud hush. Hearing the hubbub outside Sun Bin's hut (those unmistakable trooper voice boxes and the horror behind them), their detection was imminent if they didn't move.

The boy stirred from his slumber, shaking his shaggy hair out of his eyes, and Sun Bin poked his head out from above the burning stove like a mischievous child caught in the act. He had been welding damaged pipes together, using his old, cracked glasses as protective eyewear. He pulled his gloves off and ran to the front door in haste, his baggy robes following his bony legs in waves of rough, tan linen.

"Your chickens are gone!" X whispered, peering out a small window as Sun Bin popped out his door to inspect the coop outside.

"Are they looking for us?" Y asked unnecessarily.

"Um, yes," X snapped. Uncooperative chickens had been loaded onto an Authority storage cruiser, piled in crates, clucking and clacking in boisterous outrage. Next to them were goats and mounds of lettuce and corn husks, crowded in jumbled heaps.

"They're doing a sweep again," Sun Bin said, rushing back inside. "Confiscating the livestock, the crops."

Authority troopers pounded on the door of a neighboring hut and kicked it in before charging in, beating down any insolence or fight. Another trooper knocked down a farmer and pulled a baby pig out of his hands like it was a useless satchel as another set a thatch hut ablaze, resulting in urgent screams. From the corner of her eye, X saw Margery's brusque partner, confronted by troopers, point in their direction. In a clip, they had been exposed.

Sun Bin locked the door. "We've got to get out of here. Quickly now." He opened the damper flue over the stove and revealed an unexpected hidden tunnel, an escape route into the mountain.

"Where does it go?" Y asked.

"Who cares. Let's go!" X whispered loudly. She motioned, and Y held her feet as she climbed on top of his shoulders and flung herself into the rock ceiling.

Sun Bin waved for them to move forward. "Preparation for the worst is knowing the worst is coming. No time to waste."

"Who would've thought you'd be crawling out of here one day, huh?" Y asked, as X disappeared into the hole.

X whispered from above, poking her head down. "You coming?"

"Sun Bin should have known you two would be trouble," Sun Bin sighed as he scaled up Y's back.

"All right, old man," Y said, hoisting Sun Bin up on his shoulders, struggling to climb as the old man's bony pelvis and rump caught on the hole's edge, his legs swinging like clumsy pendulums. "Not sure how you would have gotten up there without me."

"Am not quite as nimble as the future," Sun Bin panted as X pulled him up.

In the dark, cramped escape tunnel, X squinted into nothing as her eyes acclimated to the black. It was dry and stuffy. Cooler than the storage container at least.

"Scythe," Sun Bin said, pointing to his bladed staff below. It leaned comfortably near his cot, as if jeering him for almost forgetting it. "My scythe."

There was pounding on the front door. "Open up! Authority check!"

"Hurry!" X whispered to Y below as he lifted the scythed staff to her. *Pound, pound, pound.*

Y peered up at the damper flue's hole, jittery and distressed. Even with the boy's long, gangly arms, jumping from the ground wouldn't get him up. It may as well have been a leap to the moon. The boy climbed on top of the stove and stretched to reach for the hole's rim, but X's legs were pulled into the tunnel like a vacuum. She couldn't reach far enough to grab him, and she didn't have the strength to pull him up anyway.

Pound, pound, pound. "Open up!"

Clenching her teeth, X whispered, "Anything I can do?"

"Yes!" Y yell-whispered back, glaring. "Shut up and get out of the way!" The ruthless pounding caused the front door to creak and bend. Slices of sunlight and puffy dust clouds escaped through the cracks.

Then her heart dropped. The red box laid carelessly forsaken on the ground, the data chip a couple of meters away. *So clumsy!* "You forgot it!"

Y beelined to the rock and grabbed the loose chip.

"Don't lose it again!" X whispered in plea. She really needed to be the one possessing it.

With one quick move, Y swallowed the data chip and approached the stove.

"Awww, no way!" X backed up as Y stood awkwardly on the stove, making a face as if he had again eaten Sun Bin's porridge. In time, no question the stomach acid would destroy the silicon and precious metals of the chip.

Why did the boy make everything so difficult? "Hurry up!" she whispered as the pounding became more insistent, the door's hinges wavering. They would bust at any moment.

Gritting his teeth and with his eyes closed, Y sprung from atop the stove, his hands catching and gripping the hole's rim. He swung and pulled himself and his long legs up behind him.

As Sun Bin pulled the damper flue back in place, they froze in the sudden darkness as the door below was finally kicked in. Inside the tunnel, X's and Sun Bin's eyes met in silent dread. How did she continue to get into these dire situations? Shards of light seeped from below, landing on their faces in thin strips. She maneuvered for a good view of the room through deep cracks in the flue.

"Troopers and dogs, that's just great," Y whispered.

"Shut up," X and Sun Bin both whispered back.

Through the cracks, X could see several troopers storm the hut, sinister in their dark armor and faceless bucket masks. Zealous pack dogs roamed through the hut, sniffing everything and anything. Her eyes widened when in marched General Speer, scanning the room. She'd seen digital renderings before she and Y had penetrated his camp: haunting and penetrable eyes, his gray mustache. He was a bogeyman in the rebel ranks, ruthless and vile. Instruction taught he had a knack for torturous methods to get what he wanted. His murderous sentry machines were the most advanced on the planet. Accurate and loyal. But he was shorter than she had imagined.

The general inspected rags and hides strewn around the firepit, throwing them down in disgust. He lifted his head, sniffed, and crinkled his nose as if trying to place the scent.

The troopers poked under and around crates, the flimsy table, and makeshift cabinets. "No one is here, sir," one said.

A trooper provided a navigation tracker to Speer. "General Speer, found this."

"A navigation tracker," Speer said. "Those kids were here."

X's temples thumped, her heart hammering. It had to be the data disc the soldiers were after; Sun Bin was right. She wanted to wring Y's neck for getting them into this ordeal. Stealing their intel back, *not just erasing it*, did not seem like a smart decision now. The rebels had sought to grow poison-free foods and provide liberation from Authority rule. Feed and arm themselves, that was all. Perhaps there was compromising information on the download? What kind of information could inspire such a dedicated hunt through vast desert wastes? Such a precarious position they were in, mere meters from Authority troops as one of the hounds voraciously dug into a trash bin below, gyrating in delight at its treasure. She caught her breath as one of the troopers stopped, as if sensing her presence.

"Stop," the trooper said, pulling the dog's attention away.

Still as stone, she didn't move as the hound looked up and around the hut, old cups, dry-crusted with something she was sure at one time tasted like dirt and roots, distracting it.

Speer poked at the smoldering firepit. He kicked a couple of twigs to a sheepish burst of dying embers. "Our arrival was too much of a production. Killing those Loners and farmers, such a waste." He tested the dirt floor with his boot, as if to ensure there was no hidden basement they were missing.

A trooper was on his knees, creating commotion around the stove.

"You sure no one's in there?" Speer asked with a smirk.

The trooper acknowledged the general with a quick embarrassed nod and pulled out the last of the pans and bowls, which fell onto the ground in a clamoring, joyous commotion. The general sighed in irritation.

Meanwhile, Y's face twisted, his hand coming up to pinch his nose, holding back a sneeze. X gave him a pleading look.

"*Please don't,*" she mouthed, her breath caught in her throat.

Unable to hold any longer, Y sneezed violently.

Seriously? X glowered at the boy, imagining them thrown into some torturous Authority jail, perhaps underground where some beastling aberrations would delight in their capture.

"Stop!" Speer commanded, and the trooper near the cupboards froze as a runaway metal bowl somehow rolled around, its circle getting smaller until it eventually stopped. Scowling, he lifted his nose as if his nostrils found heaven. He bent and reached his crooked fingers into the bowl and plucked out something faint. Forensic senses.

"Tree root," Speer said. One of the troopers cocked his head in question. "We've got a traveler. You've got to go three hundred kilometers to get to the forest lining against the desert. Quite industrious."

"General Speer."

"Ah yes," Speer said, snatching the small, empty box, the rebel symbol etched on its front.

X's heart sunk. *Why did Y have to use a rebel-marked box? Of all clues to be bungling.*

"The implausibility of a circle housing a square," Speer continued. "Like the rebel plight itself surviving." X thought the general almost laughed. Speer turned to the closest wall, his fist raised. Instead of punching it, he stormed out of the hut. "Burn it to the ground."

With no words necessary, Sun Bin led X and Y through the tunnel, following the windy, narrow path in brisk silence. In minutes they emerged out the other side of the mountain, filthy and begrimed like they'd been stranded in a coal mine for days. The tunnel's hidden exit was a tight, tapered opening hidden within mounds of rock and desert brush. All was quiet, a world away from where they'd come.

"That was so close," X said, trying not to lose her footing on the uneven ground as they made their way down the small grade. A haze filled her head as she acclimated to the sun's rays.

"The prepared outdo the unprepared," Sun Bin said, using his scythed staff to hold himself upright. "I never thought I'd actually use this tunnel."

"I've got the download," Y said.

"Yes, you do," X said, as she tried not to think of the disc somewhere in his bowels.

"I didn't want to lose it. But I can't keep it in my stomach for long or it will disintegrate."

"So gross," X said. "But you'll cough it up soon enough, you better."

Raising his eyebrows, Sun Bin said, "Unexpected."

"I can't believe what you've got us into," X said. "Now we've got this General Speer chasing us all over the place."

"I took it for the rebels, not myself," Y complained.

"And I don't have my navigator," X said, wanting to kick herself. "Because I had to worry about *you*, Y." In every way possible, it was Y's fault.

"What now?" Y asked.

Dark smoke appeared from the tunnel's exit in airy wisps as Sun Bin's head dropped. "They'll think we'd run to the nearest remote population, try to blend in, hide in caves. Instead, we will go to Vulnus Outpost in Oasis Marketplace."

Fanning his arms like a windmill, Y asked in frustration, "Where?"

"Home," X said. "We're going home, Y."

"I'm so sick of running all over the place, running and running."

"We start at the outpost," said Sun Bin. "Not a place you'll find children normally. Odd sorts frequent this place, but we will find a transport there. Can't act like children though. Make a scene."

Y scoffed. "These children just saved your hide."

"As he saved our hide," X corrected. The dark smoke now billowed from the tunnel, growing in stacks. It dawned upon her that Sun Bin was losing all he owned to help them, perhaps all he had ever owned. "They're burning your home. I'm so sorry." She put an arm around his frail, hunched shoulders. Rebellion costs continued to add up, and in an instant, she carried a new burden.

Sun Bin turned away like a grieving elder. Had it been heartache in his eyes, an attempt to disguise cuts of distress, a flash of a painful past? He turned to the open desert beyond them as if imagining the perils of their journey ahead. "Sun Bin will help you face what we will, get you home."

X hugged Sun Bin tight. "Thank you," she said, and they all started on their way.

"They'll chase us until we're dead, won't they?" Y asked.

"The Authority is not a bunch to give up easily," said Sun Bin.

"I should have stayed in computers," Y complained, kicking rocks. He turned to X. "You didn't leave me back there."

She rolled her eyes, trying to ignore his fussing as Sun Bin's loss weighed on her. New danger had emerged, and they had to get to rebel headquarters before this General Speer exposed them all. "I'd never leave you, I told you that."

SEVEN

"Don't stare. Blend in quietly," Sun Bin said, coming up behind X and Y and speaking with the gravity of lessons learned. "We want a ride, not problems."

Set on a desert plateau a few kilometers from the coast, Vulnus Outpost accepted what it was: a dusty drinking hole where smugglers, pirates, and scoundrels congregated, networked, and did stupid things. Inside the dark, arid tavern, a rogue's gallery of mismatched musicians on stage somehow coordinated strings, horns, flutes, and metal pipes to create a catchy tune of jazz with bluesy roots from the Old World, a diverse smorgasbord for the senses. The mustached man in green velvet picking at the piano contrasted starkly with the long, skinny arms of the woman playing the violin, her floral dress swinging aggressively with each stroke of the bow. Several African men blew horns, swaying in unison, smooth in their rhythm and reverie. A tall beast of a man beat drums, beads of sweat rolling off his brow under the dull, bronzed spotlights as an animated dwarf assisted him on percussion.

The snazzy animated tune rolled on, mostly ignored by the vast spectrum of thugs, criminals in hiding, and offenders to be. No surprise, the goateed transporter in a brimmed hat whom Sun Bin had done business with before he stole two chickens from his coop drank from a rusty mug at the bar. Villainy embraced outlaws at Vulnus Outpost.

The bouncer, a begrimed giant, his overbearing stomach hanging over his belt and fighting with gravity itself, didn't budge. He peered down at X and Y as they gazed up at him with feigned earnestness. "No children. It's *illegal.*" His pained smile showed teeth gleamed in a mix of margarine yellow and stained silver, singing of negligence. It reminded Sun Bin that he, indeed, needed to clean his own teeth soon. They bothered him like an itch.

Sun Bin palmed him a coin, ignoring X's fascination with the bouncer's hanging paunch as if in wonderment of its possibilities. Wary scents of intoxicants, stimulants, psychotropics, and various inhalants and aerosols overloaded his faculties. It smelled like sticky fruit, a tour de force of ethanol infusions. Vulnus Outpost, as he'd been told, was both an escape and a destination. "We'll be quiet in the corner. Sun Bin will drink. They will only eat."

Peering down at the coin, the bouncer looked peaked, like his stomach had problems digesting unsettling things. "Not that type of establishment." He sniffed. "Vulnus Outpost is bona fide."

Releasing a few more coins into the bouncer's hand, Sun Bin said, "Both a relief and gratifying. A bouquet for a calm state of mind."

After a moment, as if the bouncer did the math to determine his new fortune, he waved them past. "Put 'em in the back," he grunted to the willowy hostess, who led them away. "No drinking for the kids . . . or else."

"Sun Bin is impressed they monitor children drinking," he said to the kids, satisfied at his situation-handling. The energetic orchestra got louder as they winded through the tavern, a questionable place at once somber and jubilant as the jazzy blues filled his ears like a brimmed cup. From the corner of his eye, he saw a table of children hoist up beverages to a toast as they walked past, evidently ignoring Vulnus Outpost's bona fide character. Rising voices loaded with braggadocio and threats faded, submerging in the romping tune. With smooth, mysterious grace, the hostess led them to an available elevated booth, more on pageant than he wished. He frowned. Duplicity percolated among the seedy barflies, and he preferred to inquire transporters from a shrouded pocket. Instead, flickering stares followed them, lurking from every corner.

There could be trouble here.

***

Mel and Simple Eye approached the famed drinking hole on the rough outskirts of Oasis Marketplace. Outside, nomads and merchants traded and negotiated business, swindling each other with wrangling persuasion over pelts, skins, and odd potions. Wishful fragrances of copper coin and dusty pouches intoxicated patrons and passers-through alike in the dry heat. Weary farmers in sun-protective ponchos and flap hats spit their tobacco.

"Oasis all right," Mel muttered as a dubious hooligan passer-by leered at the drone with cross eyes.

Simple Eye quickly tried to dive into a small open pouch in Mel's knapsack supply pack, fumbling about.

"You're not going to fit," Mel said as Simple Eye's antennae whirled in circles. "Wait out here."

Two large women wearing long gangster dusters rumbled like fighting chickens. One knocked the other to the ground, and the drone beeped and whirred a small whine.

"You'll be fine," Mel said. The thing had quite a lot of personality. "Keep out of trouble. I won't be long."

Two dark troopers on camels came upon them, studying Mel and her companion from behind their expressionless face masks. Mel stood as unthreatening as she could muster, avoiding their intimidating stares as they strode by. Authority troopers who had taken away all she treasured. Out of nervousness, she held her breath until they steadily moved on, ignoring the knocked-out woman on the ground.

"They're looking for something," Mel said, calming herself. "Or someone more interesting than us."

Simple Eye hummed in sorrow, left behind as she strode swiftly into the outpost and past the foreboding bouncer's eyes following her. Her bald head and toned arms accentuated her warrior-like appearance, a stand-out among the spectrum of villainous characters. Two devilish goons looked her up and down as they exited, and a pack of boisterous men traced her path. Hers was an unwelcome presence among the inebriated, spirituous behavior. She wouldn't linger. Not exactly a first-class trough filled with potential future residents of Alvarium, the place was more a society of vagrants and swindlers strewn together in a hodgepodge of disorder and refuse. She approached the bar, its light blue glow splattering across the multicolored bottles and jars as it splintered off unpolished spigots and taps. Blue light spewed upward from underneath the cloudy glass like it emitted from the earth itself as sanguine luster spotlighted the band. It smelled like old, burnt beer.

The bartender, weighty and tired, inspected Mel. Her thick eyeliner, painted deep around her eyes, successfully accentuated her judgmental glare. "What can I get ya?"

"I need to hitch a ride to the Forty-Fourth," Mel said. Doing anything for the Authority, even to get her family back, suddenly made her feel dirty. Five days could not come fast enough.

"District Forty-Four?" the bartender asked, smacking her gum. Her skepticism grew as Mel nodded. "A lotta choices, but good luck getting that right somebody to take you out to that crazy wilderness."

Mel stared at her dead-on, wishing she could just get a straight answer. "Know anybody?"

"Want me to get on the speaker?" the bartender asked, her words bathed in sarcasm.

Boozing, inhaling, and raucous behaviors bounced around the outpost. Several men hung over their mugs as another flock tried to speak over each other because they, somehow, needed to be heard. Two suspicious beards at a small table took notice of her, pausing their mumbling exchange. Never had she seen so many annoying men in one place.

"No fuss, just an option or two."

The bartender smiled in delight, wry and mischievous. "An option or two." She pawed a handheld speaker to her mouth like an apple. "Attention derelicts," she announced, the loudspeaker jarring any infrequent patrons out of their seats. One drinker spit out frosty foam.

The musical cacophony onstage paused. Tarnished brass horns dropped from lips, the beating drums stopped, the violin strings ceased, the horn swings froze, and Mel dropped her head. Exactly the attention she didn't want. The laughing and forgettable conversations by pirates, degenerates, and petty criminals abruptly came to a halt.

The bartender continued. "This young lady is trying to catch a ride." She raised her brows at Mel as if to say, *Good?*

Keeping her eyes down, Mel preferred to be back at Alvarium where the vexing inmates rivaled. The bartender shrugged, hung up the mouthpiece, the music played, and everyone resumed their bad habits.

"I'm headed that way," a voice said, and Mel turned to see a swashbuckling man, handsome and in need of a haircut. In his mid-thirties, he was gruff with gray hairs splintering out of his beard like needles, and a speech at once deep and kind. He'd probably seen his share of adventures. Conquested too many women too. "Soon." He smiled.

"A good start," Mel said, coy and guarded.

"I'm Beck Holden," he said.

Having gained enough attention, she shook his hand. She could feel his eyes try to penetrate her before they roamed. She'd been in prison for seven years but could still feel a man's crawling gaze.

"Forty-Fourth district, huh? Not a place for the meek." Beck paused as if testing her response.

"I hope not to run into any meek there."

"How much?"

"How much do you need?" she asked, cursing herself for not thinking of this before. How was she possibly going to get to the rebels within five days across hundreds or thousands of kilometers of desert, mountain, and forest terrain without something to trade for transportation?

Leaning on the bar with grating confidence, Beck said, "Different rules across sectors. Trouble can find you fast."

She did not need to be told how difficult her task was by this rascal. A young boy's vulnerability hid under all that facial hair—he was almost pretty. "I'm low on financial provisions but can compensate you when we get there." She had no idea how. That was a problem for later.

Beck smirked as if he had heard this all before. "I don't do charity cases."

"I don't need charity."

He raised his eyebrows. "Were you planning on getting there with your charming personality?"

"I have the resources I have and will have," she deadpanned. "What's taking you up there, anyway? Horse trading?"

"Smart meds. And the perfect converted speed pod to get us there. Recent BV model, not like the Authority's gas-guzzling ones."

"Interesting," Mel said, not taking the gruff charmer for a philanthropist. Or a medic. "So it's slower than the Authority pods?"

"It's not stuck here."

Interrupting them, Sun Bin sauntered up to the bar, using the menacing scythe as a guide. He appeared delicate, as if one slight shove off his feet would snap his thin, brittle bones. "Forty-Fourth district you said? We are trying to get there."

"Who's we? I've got this one," Beck growled, examining the scythe. Pockets of blue light gleamed off the curved blade, twinkling like stars.

Abruptly, Beck turned to Mel and pointed at her accusingly. "Wait a second. You trying to hustle me?"

She rolled her eyes, growing impatient with the swashbuckler. All she'd wanted was to hitch a ride. And *avoid conflict.* "I don't know this man. No one is trying to hustle you, Buck."

"It's Beck."

"I'm Sun Bin. Two children and I are trying to get to District Forty-Four. Can pay you," he said, motioning over his shoulder to the booth where the kids were being accosted by two men holding rusty mugs. "One moment," he said as he left, using his scythed staff to wave the boozy crowd out of his way.

"So *he* is going to pay. Isn't that convenient?" Beck asked Mel. "Wait. *Kids?*"

She was only half listening, her attention drawn to the developing skirmish on the other side of the transient watering hole.

***

X's heart hammered in her chest as she scowled at the men approaching.

"Lookie here. Your parents know you're out?"

One of the men prodded the kids like he was branding them with his finger. Hardy was short and stocky, his droopy eyes apprehensive, carrying the pain of a beaten dog. His grimy helmet of hair was slicked back like cement, and his trousers pulled up too high, showing off his tawdry boots. A gun adorned his side holster as both filthy men smiled through their stained teeth. "Answer me. Should you be at an outpost like this?"

"Shouldn't you be taking showers?" X asked, holding her nose. Both men looked like criminals, the kind with sad stories and bad breath. A rogue's gallery of bar patrons surrounded her around shoddy wooden tables, carrying chipped steins and gathering in packs. It was a collective she quickly categorized as floaters, drifters, hoodlums, bandits, possible heathens, opportunists, felons on the lam, aspiring felons, eventual felons, and at least one bushy mustached mafioso. "I suppose water is especially limited around these parts."

"How precious," said his partner, a taller, buzz-cut man with one arm, an eye patch, and a wooden leg, likely a result of too many bad decisions. "Someone's comin', Hardy."

Not a moment too soon, Sun Bin approached with his arms open in grand style, as if to welcome them home after a prolonged journey, holding up his scythed staff like a beacon. He was surprisingly self-assured, considering he probably weighed half that of Hardy.

"Gentlemen," Sun Bin said, "the young are with me."

Hardy smirked as the eye-patched man turned to Sun Bin, ready to rumble as he eyeballed the staff's curved blade. "Says who?"

If things got out of hand, perhaps they would be discovered as rebels. Or an electromagnetic scanner would expose the stolen chip in Y's possession, despite it being in his stomach or, worse, his entrails. "Says us!" X exclaimed over the eclectic band's tunes. She jumped out of the booth and stood up to the towering one.

"Yeah!" Y added, frozen in his seat.

"Leave us alone," X said to the men, her attention drawn to Hardy's packed holster. She pointed at Sun Bin and made up the best story that she could. After all, Sun Bin held a scythe, not a walking stick. "You won't like what he'll do if you don't leave us alone."

Hardy shrugged, unimpressed. "I've been all over these districts, and no one has ever told me what I could or couldn't do."

"At least not twice," Eye-Patch added.

"Ain't gonna start now," Hardy said.

"Concern of the strength of others is weakness," Sun Bin said evenly. "Mastering of oneself, is wisdom."

Eye-Patch's eye crossed, confused.

"I've put a lot of men in their place, ole man," Hardy said as he sauntered up to Sun Bin, his wide hips waving side to side in carefree locomotion.

A curious crowd gathered, their low profile kaput. Hardy shoved Sun Bin backward, who somehow spun upright and rolled off the shoulder of an unsuspecting bar patron before landing in a flat-foot stance, his scythe arcing outward and toward his aggressor. X raised her brow as the blade spun like a wheel to the crowd's awe, blue light bouncing in a dizzying blur.

"Hey, why don't you try that with me?" a voice said.

Everyone turned to see Mel standing with her hands at her sides, like an Old World gunslinger. X caught her breath at the sudden brash readiness for confrontation. One of Hardy's crew ran at her with a punch, and the woman quickly deflected his arm and flipped it around his back, dropping the crew member to his knees. She kicked him forward with the tip of her boot, and he fell forward on his face and wailed.

X's jaw dropped. The rebels had always relied on guns and speed for protection. They needed skills like *this*. She traded a glance with Sun Bin, who nodded to her as if he, too, had been dazzled. The crowd parted to make room for the spectacle, readying for an all-out brawl as the saloon's patrons traded Ferre bills and the betting began. A strange, hooded woman separated from the crowd. Half her face badly scarred, hard and guarded, she disappeared out of the tavern like a ghost.

Hardy laughed, and a husky, bearded thug (another apparent ally of the Hardy duo) aimed his pistol at the woman.

Matter of fact and grinning with cunning mischief, Hardy said, "You're in the wrong place, missy."

Mel scoffed. "Don't call me that."

Hardy smiled. "It doesn't matter what I call you—"

Click.

A cocked blaster pointed at the bearded thug.

"Not what you expected?" a grizzly voice said, having emerged from the crowd.

"Beck," Hardy said, rolling his eyes. "You don't need more enemies. We talked about this."

"You saying we can't just part as friends?" Beck asked.

Eye-Patch pulled out another blaster and pointed it at Beck, shrugging in delight.

"Looks like we're at a stalemate," Hardy quipped, and Beck reluctantly handed over his pistol to Eye-Patch.

Click.

Hardy turned to see X had somehow seized his pistol and now targeted it at him.

"Not what you expected?" X said, enjoying the comeuppance.

Hardy's smile disappeared as he inspected the red dot on his chest. He shook, perhaps readying for his loose bladder. "Whataya say we part as friends."

"Gimme that," Beck said, ripping away Eye-Patch's pistol and taking his own back as Mel snatched the bearded thug's gun away. Hardy's eyes pierced her with silent rage, the kind of rage that quells last breaths.

"Don't be so sour—this hurts me too," X said, still pointing the heavy blaster squarely at Hardy.

"We better go," Beck said, "before the black helmets are on top of us."

Mel said, "Your transport ready?"

"We can negotiate price when we get outta here," Beck said, keeping his attention on Hardy and his boys as he held both pistols. "Since we settled on how you aren't charity."

Sun Bin wrapped his hands around his scythe in calm relief, like he found peace. "We're all going with you."

"Follow us, kids," Mel said, rushed.

Eyes wide, Beck grimaced. "What?"

"We can't leave them here with these hooligans," Mel said. "You've got room for me in the deal, you've got room for them."

Beck shook his head. "We barely even have a deal! I don't even know who you are."

"My name's Mel Custode. C'mon," she said to X and Y, ignoring him.

"Mel. Short for Melissa?" Beck asked.

"Short for Mel."

"He's with us," X said, motioning to Sun Bin as troopers made their way through the busy tavern.

"Sun Bin is now."

Mel put a kind hand on Sun Bin's slight shoulder. "We must go."

Sun Bin nodded and moved, his aged bones not slowing him. X backed up toward Beck and Mel. The heavy blaster pulled her elbows down like anchors as the thug glared at her with grim uncertainty. She was unpredictable, and she liked it.

Y followed her, looking out for other villainous hooligans who might jump in. Hardy eyed them intently as they backed away. "Anybody else want trouble?" Y asked with new confidence.

Out in back, Beck halted and searched the lot with uncertainty. She knew his look. She had seen it on Y's face a hundred times.

"We're parked over there." Beck pointed.

"You don't seem very sure," X said.

"I'm sure," Beck snapped.

"Then why did you stop?" Mel asked.

X interrupted before Beck could speak. "He doesn't know. He forgot."

Beck stared at X dead-on with disbelief. "I sometimes charge the speed pod on the other side is all. C'mon, before there's nothing to argue about."

As Beck ran ahead, a drone appeared next to Mel, hovering as it bleeped. Its antennae swiveled, as if happy to be in the melee. "Almost forgot about you," she said as it blinked and whirred.

X beamed with amusement at the drone's playful twirling and floating like a round bird as she and Y chased Mel and Sun Bin around the outpost's corner. She touched it carefully, like it was made of razor-thin glass, and it squealed. And she squealed back as they ran.

***

Mel stopped short, shocked to see the fleet of Authority pods sitting idly, awaiting adventure. Authority and civilian pods alike lined up symmetrically like Authority troops in formation, orderly and straight among the desert's dust, parked in uncomfortable precision. The egg-like cocoons had evolved from the crude speed pods she'd last seen before being committed to Alvarium, when they had airy, roofless tops as if they had no concern for exposure or toxic rain. These pods looked more like impregnable, insulated bubbles.

"You have a speed pod?" Y called to Beck, grumbling to himself some twenty paces ahead, while Mel studied the encased vehicles as she rushed by them. They were red clay in color and almost translucent in parts, like hazy porcelain. The grimy, Authority-regulated four-door vehicles looked hardly cared for, with two sad pods missing bumpers and panels, their grills dented like they were crooked teeth.

Then there were the civilian pods. Clear-paneled compartments concealed shipments—veiled contraband—and provided access to critical parts of the pods' bowels. These were the slower, electric-powered vehicles the populace was allowed to possess. Maximum speeds were locked on the civilian pods, ironically called speed pods, but not the Authority pods, so to never be outrun. Each hovered over land with no wheels, no legs, and could be tracked by the Authority.

"Their computer navigation's the best!" Y marveled.

"Some are," Beck yelled back as he led them through the mazed rows. "If you want outta here, hurry up!"

With a huff, Mel cursed herself for complicating things again. Why had she needed to get involved? The confrontation expedited the journey forward, but she didn't know how skilled this Beck Holden was. There were only five days, after all.

Almost four and a half days.

"Do I get to keep the gun?" X asked as they hurried through the vast dirt lot.

"No," Mel said, snatching it. Kicked-up dust clouds tasted like chalk.

"They all look the same," Y complained as they followed Beck through the uniformed vehicle rows.

"Well, they're not all the same," Beck called back, clicking his belt sensor to open the sizeable speed pod's gull hatches, spanning like an eagle's wings.

Mel couldn't believe her eyes. Their escape depended on a grand relic, a transport from another time. A beat-up, black, and dusty beast of a machine with dark, slanted windows, several times larger than the red-clay pods. Unlike the smaller, commuter-fitted vehicles and Authority pods, its stout legs pillared on three sides, holding up the massive vehicle like kickstands. It stood with unbridled pride, unashamed of its outdated functionality, sizable mechanical parts, and things that could go wrong.

"How much fuel does it take to move this thing?" Y asked, as Beck untied the docking station hose and did a quick swipe of a small device on his belt to confirm the charging machine credits.

"I see you like to stand out," Mel said, noticing the pod's front headlights, slanted like angry eyebrows. One of its bulbs hung from a dangling wire. This escape could end before it started.

Beck hopped into the pilot seat and, as if reading her mind, said, "The last model before the hover pods. Good news—it uses less power when charging. Modified hybrid model to ensure we've got speed." He glared at Y as everyone scrambled inside, Sun Bin falling into the third row back seat like a strewn sack. "Even you should like it." He punched some buttons. "Let's move. We'll have the kids' friends here any minute."

"Not our friends," X said flatly.

"That Hardy," Beck said, studying the deck's front display as the pod buzzed on. "Nothin' but trouble."

"You don't clean it, do you?" X asked, swiping at the dust on the dark interior seat in front of her.

Shaking his head, Beck said wryly, "Lemme guess, the black shows the dirt." X shrugged as Beck slapped a couple of switches and read the monitor, furrowing his brows. "Let's hope it has enough juice."

"Enough juice?" Mel asked in exasperation as she buckled up next to him. He gunned the electric/gas hybrid engine, skillfully reviewing his instrument panel, punching switches, and studying fuel levels. He was rough-edged, but she appreciated unrefined methods that exhausted all options.

"Hey, it ain't me who got us into this mess," Beck said, wiping the grime off his panel as he squinted at the dials. "This can't be right. Must be a faulty charger."

"What do you mean?" Mel asked.

"Looks like it barely recharged," Beck grumbled.

"Are we stuck here?"

"We'll use the gas to launch. They don't always update the charging stations—keeps us spending more at the watering hole. Don't worry, we've got enough to get outta here. We'll just need to detour. Eventually." The drone hovered in the back seat next to Sun Bin, emerging like a pop-up surprise. Quick as a whip, Beck pulled out his blaster when Mel, just as fast, held his arm down.

"He's with us," Mel said. "With me."

"*He?*" Beck said, amused and occupied. He looked at the drone squarely. "I don't see it."

"Simple Eye," Mel said, searching out the window for trouble.

X smiled at the drone as it beeped. "Nice to meet you, Simple Eye," she said, beaming as it bowed its antennae and blinked. The playful drone turned to Y, who touched its side panel with curiosity, and the drone twirled and shrieked, moving safely to X's side.

"Tou-chy," Y said, frowning.

"They're coming," Sun Bin said as the thugs raced toward them. "Sun Bin recommends we speed to action."

Beck threw Sun Bin a riled look. "Thanks, I've got this."

"As long as the navigation works," Y said.

"The drone has nav too," Mel said automatically.

"Simple Eye has nav too?" X asked.

"Kind of," Mel said, endeared to the girl.

Beck checked his navigation monitor. "*Airfoil* works, don't you worry."

"You named it?" Mel asked, almost amused.

"*Airfoil!*" X and Y sang in unison.

"Enough back there," Beck snapped.

The mechanical legs of *Airfoil* retracted and the beast's engine roared, spitting out dirt clouds in eye-watering gusts as Hardy and his gang arrived in the parking lot, their shoulders hunched in disappointment.

Back at the entrance of Vulnus Outpost, the hooded, scarred woman pointed in the direction of the speed pods as another pack of armed troopers arrived, their midnight-black armor impervious to *Airfoil's* dust monsoon. One of them spoke into a transmitter as all the troopers watched the modified black speed pod tear away. "We have their location, and know where they're going."

EIGHT

With his hands comfortably interlocked behind his back, General Speer inspected the crude agricultural flying machines resting in the vast silvery aerodrome, to see if his hunch was right. Attentive, empty cockpits and bare display panels awaited instruction. Awaited *duty.* Reasons something could not be accomplished sounded *uncomfortably close* to being excuses, so he listened carefully so as not to miss an opportunity to correct or punish. Silence chilled his subordinates more than anything he could say, and he paused his probing to ensure the team was paying attention.

The grand aerodrome housed several crop dusters—ancient, small aircraft outfitted with large drums and spray systems attached to their wings. They ran on old-fashioned gasoline, the precious resource now largely in the hands of the Authority to prevent rebel theft of aircraft. Such a breach could not stand. The pilot's team followed Speer and the pilot, prepared to immediately make changes on command. All five technicians crept on the soles of their feet like heedful intruders, afraid to make a sound.

"Captain Antonious. These old things still work?" Speer asked, frowning at crunched dents and paint peeling off the dusters' side panels.

"Don't mind their physical imperfections. They've been outfitted with smart technologies to take advantage of their light weight and pilotless operation," Antonious said quickly, defending his babies. His reddish beard covered his round cheeks with an overabundance of ruby and ginger. "Tested only once so far with the new specs." The answer to the question rankled Speer. "The housings are like stomachs of new-grade steel. The poison can eat through almost anything, but not these. Truly amazing technology."

Speer eventually nodded, and Antonious breathed with caution and continued. "Unlike our newer aircraft that require much more fuel due to their heavy loads and are too fast to drop pesticides." He motioned to the pair of muddy-dark jet planes in the corner of the hangar. Sinister and cold, their sharp noses arrowed like pinpoints. "Untested, unready."

"I have concerns these dinosaurs won't do the job, Captain."

The pilot swallowed audibly as his team stood idle. "General, you asked to see what aircraft we used to protect our crops, and how we used the poisons. I mean, *pesticides*. These three beauties are what we use effectively."

Always on the lookout for sabotage, Speer understood his presence itself caused a stir. Nervous energy abounded. Also, everyone was used to his tight-fisted temperament and approach. He feigned patience. More progress better be coming. "Carry on."

"We fly early morning and on calm days," Captain Antonious said with winded relief, "so aerosol bombs don't infect the lungs of farmers or adjacent populations, killing them all like they killed the bees. Fortunately, these self-flying planes don't put our pilots at risk. Our team simply arms and supplies them before takeoff. We do more with less, so we can cover ten times the square kilometers we could just four years ago. The advancement of the pesticide means we achieve greater impact on pests, but unfortunately, it's more dangerous to human populations, doing irreversible damage to the dermis and lungs. Immediate and fatal."

Speer's heavy boots came to a halt at the word *pest,* ringing true of his feelings toward the rebels who stood in his way. The idea of pesticide as a modernized weapon had percolated in his mind despite the Authority's problems with it—an angry geyser, impatient and insolent.

Pesticide.

The team of inspectors froze behind him, waiting for him to move forward before they dared move again. Speer allowed himself the pleasure of having such an uneasy effect on the crew. It kept them alert.

"Say that again."

The pilot fidgeted, peeling at the skin on his fingers. "The old pesticides caused cancers like lymphoma or sarcoma and other soft-tissue diseases," Antonious said, his hand on one of the drums. "This new stuff is like human carcinogens on steroids. Pests can't evade this pesticide, no matter what they do. It kills everything and everyone."

"Hmm."

The ruling class had learned the hard way how civilian populations could reverse progress of the Authority's dominion. Every district, all forty-four of them, were to be controlled and contained. But theft and destruction continued, repeatedly, at the hands of the rebels. Planes were destroyed, speed pods stolen. Once, his troopers had been fooled into a worthless chase through treacherous mountain ranges, following a decoy tracker outfitted on a lone wild horse. He seethed, he itched, certain that his hives were acting up.

He had been outfoxed too many times.

Armaments and food storage facilities constantly robbed was unacceptable. If you owned the fuel, all the transportation and the food supply, then you should be able to control the populations. How content Martel was to merely contain the rebellion of civilians trying to create their own alternative society instead of crushing it. His neck stiffened. So many grand opportunities existed.

Martel could speak and call meetings with the governors, but they were just words. Martel lacked *ambition*. That was his problem. He held back the district's potential for global dominance. The Authority's rule. Prolonging the conflict with the rebels to keep a distracted Authority busy standing still made no sense. Retrieving that developing blueprint of the rebel headquarters was a priority. With the rebels' exact location, the rebel plight would be destroyed. No holding back from expanding to other districts. Only a deserved leader would hold such true ambitions.

"Test this today," Speer said.

The pilot looked at him questionably. "Oh, we can't do that . . ." His voice trailed off as he apparently realized what the general was saying. "Test?"

"Yes," Speer said, greatly disliking the pushback. Having to explain himself slowed progress. He enunciated clearly to ensure he was understood. "I want to test it."

"Oh no, no."

A new resolution rushed through his veins. He stared through the pilot, sensing the fear he stoked. "Are you questioning me, Captain?"

"Too dangerous," the pilot said, a bead of sweat dripping from his brow. "To rid a population of crop pests, we have to alert them to retreat underground for forty-eight hours when we fly and await the poison's dilution. Otherwise, it would wipe out a whole population."

"I see," General Speer said, kicking his leg a step forward, the pilot's team moving forward in cautious proportion. "Continue."

Clenching his fists, Speer bristled at the ignored opportunity for dominance under Martel's nose, and the minions who allowed the Authority to sit idle as rebels proved them to be fools. Unfortunately for Captain Antonious, the failure of complying would cost him. With a wave of Speer's hand, a trio of troopers appeared from the aerodrome's perimeter and the technicians froze in awe as Captain Antonious fell to his knees with whelping cries.

NINE

The speed pod raced over the desert highway with incredible velocity and deft. Such a feat of Beck's own engineering remained largely unknown to the Vulnus factory of hoodlums and drifters. The transport market knew he delivered for each job, every time. That's all they needed to know. Beck preferred to be as enigmatic as the nameless ingredients in Vulnus's Tejvan pain elixir, which he'd always considered suspect being that the golden syrup often brought hazy memories. Second only to his homestead ranch, *Airfoil* was Beck's biggest investment.

Beyond tripling the pod's size, Beck had customized its steering, nav system, speed potential, and storage. Its hidden side panels on the seats stored food or medicine or a paid passenger's contraband. Beck wasn't a pirate (he told himself), as he didn't harm people, he helped them. Paid on assignment, with no agreement necessary to define any transaction as private or confidential or cumbersome. He'd spent most of his time monitoring the pod's comm systems and studying its sensors, upcoming terrain, and power levels. Ensuring he wasn't being followed and the system's encryption was intact required attention to detail. With a wary eye, he'd inspect plaintext messaging that was intended to look ordinary, as Authority trackers were known to trap unsuspecting runners. And Beck suspected everyone.

Through the cracked rearview mirror, Sun Bin in the far back muttered something with his eyes closed (perhaps praying) as X tickled the drone and Y drooped, wheezing, staring out the window. This trip would be like no other.

"Tell me he isn't gonna get sick," Beck said, eyeing the boy in the back seat.

"Beck, something's following us," Mel said in alarm, as her nav indicators woke up in an orchestra of blinking lights.

"I don't see anything," Beck muttered, glancing at his instrument display carved under the canopy glass. Green schematics showed only the desert terrain and a narrow mountain range a short distance outward. After a switch to reboot the nav block, it quickly flashed warnings. "See them now," he corrected. "Something's wrong with the system." He punched another button to widen the detail, and suddenly red bug light indicators swarmed the nav display. "That's a lot of state pods responding to a small skirmish in that outpost."

"You gonna stop?" Mel asked. "We can explain protecting the kids."

Beck had other ideas. A couple of natural rock formations—pink and white and foreboding—stood statuesque like they owned the entire district, laughing at him, as still as stoic black helmets ordering him through their aggravating voice boxes. He didn't do well with confrontations. "I'm not getting hauled in by the Authority today."

Mel shook her head. "What kind of transport are you?"

An Authority shadow pod accelerated next to them, *Airfoil*'s dark windows in the back rows preventing trooper eyes on the cargo. The trooper turned his dark guerilla helmet toward Beck, his oppressive presence suggesting Beck should immediately stop. Instead, Beck gave a friendly wave, gunned the accelerator, and zipped ahead.

"What are you doing?" Mel yelled.

Pushing the steering lever, it seized up. He frowned and shifted the lever hard. Troubling rock formations and uneven terrain could pop out of nowhere in a whip as they raced across the desert floor at over ninety kilometers per hour.

"What's wrong?" Mel asked.

"You ask a lot of questions." He punched the nav. "They're jamming the circuits."

Shaking her pocket nav, Mel said, "They locked mine too."

"I think I can log onto another system." The speed pod's system hummed normally, but the steering lever stuck. "Well, that didn't work," Beck said as Mel eyeballed him. "They took away our eyes."

"Kids, buckle up!" She turned back to Beck. "You're going to get us all in real trouble here, if we even survive."

"How'd they do that?" Beck asked himself, amazed by the system infiltration.

Mel waved her hands in his face. "What's wrong with you?"

"Listen, miss," Beck started, his attention pulled between the displays and the mirrors. He should have known this crew would grate on his nerves. "I was just giving you a ride. Two minutes later, I've got kids and a grandfather to haul and troopers on our tails."

"Miss? Don't call me that."

"Don't forget Simple Eye," X offered, and the drone fluttered in the back seat.

"I didn't get us into this mess," Beck growled, reviewing his digital map on the display block and correcting the steering. "Leave it to me, and we'll get out of it." He punched a sequence, hoping the system would click over to the new settings and allow him to lift the steering and become invisible to Authority trackers.

"Sun Bin not a grandfather, to correct the record."

Beck rolled his eyes as the system half loaded, his live nav returning with emerging landscape details of the mammoth mounds immediately ahead.

"Beck," Mel said dryly, in what surprised him as feigned calm. "You need to hurry."

"C'mon, c'mon," Beck muttered to his system, his steering lever fully frozen.

Sun Bin continued, "While not an advocate for violence, Sun Bin suggests you evade the Authority and get us to rebel headquarters as soon as possible."

"Rebel headquarters?" Beck threw a quick look at Mel as he did the math, computing the distance to the massive rock formation as his nav system loaded. Converging state pods were gaining. It was a lot to concentrate on, but he could make it. "You said the forty-fourth district, but you meant the actual rebel base? You know where it is?"

"If you can get us out of here alive," said Mel.

X popped her head up front, straining the seat belt. "We're going where she's going."

"We're *going* to hit those boulders up there!" Y cried.

"I see 'em," Beck said, punching another lever on the deck. "I gotta free the steering." They rapidly approached the mountain of rock slabs and boulders, more monstrous by the second.

Y moaned as fire shots riddled the pod's rear, and everyone in the back seat ducked. "We're going to die in this old thing."

"We'll make it," Beck said, only able to raise the speed pod up and down a meter or two as it raced toward the giant rock formation, the loading bar almost complete. "And it's not that old," he muttered.

"Steer hard!" Mel yelled.

"It doesn't work yet," Beck scolded, his gaze frozen on the deck display as its loading bar finally flashed bright green. He steered a sudden hard right, and X thudded backward into her seat as the G-force pressed them all against the speed pod's side. Y's face pressed against X, who hard pressed against Simple Eye, who purred as Sun Bin lay completely horizontal in the back. The state pod tight on their tail crashed into the mountainous boulders, blowing up in a violent fireball.

"Whoa," Y said, as the explosion reached the sky behind them.

"Be thankful Authority pods are largely gas-powered, kid," Beck said. "A blown speed pod doesn't get back up."

Mel looked worriedly behind them before wincing at Beck without a blink. "This really isn't good for us."

"There's more of them!" Y yelled, turning greener.

A group of state tube pods arrived flying over the desert floor in a Y formation, sweeping over desert brush and the flat landscape in swift pursuit. The red-and-gray speeders were narrow, pointed cylinders, providing them the aerodynamic benefit of rockets. Their engines whirred ominous roars as they approached more mountainous terrain with grassy patches crawling up the hills like moss. Frantic wildlife scurried away.

"They're serious," Beck said, maneuvering through two huge, irregular-shaped boulders, their bulky noses stretching out to the desert plain like plateaus. They skimmed past them with centimeters to spare.

"Please don't kill us," X said as Y groaned, turning more peaked.

"Do me a favor," Beck said. "Open that small door by your side."

"What door?" X asked.

"Don't you have bigger things to worry about right now?" Mel asked.

He became transfixed on the tube pods mirroring his glide through valleys and spaces within the rocky terrain. Things were getting ugly quickly. How much longer would the speed pod's charge last? Its power monitor was in the red. His temples throbbed as he pointed in the back seat. "The small panel right *there*."

With a small nudge, X popped open the panel, a bag of white pills tumbling into her hands. "What are these?" X asked, her eyes bulging like white marbles.

Pulling his attention from ahead, Beck said, "Not those," and snatched them, darting back to his flight path. The mountainous boulder rushed toward them as he pulled the flight control lever hard, and the pod flew up over its wall. One of the state pods tailing them clipped its bottom against the rocks and rolled before exploding below their carriage.

X pulled out a tidy RID satchel, a lined bag normally used to avoid content detection by Authority scanners. "This?"

Y grabbed it and immediately hurled into it.

"Yes." Beck sighed, relieved until more state pods appeared.

"Ugh," X said to the bag, as she became relieved the data chip had probably escaped the destructive stomach acid.

Suddenly, shots riddled against the back window and pummeled the speed pod's rear, blowing a hole through the trunk. Sun Bin and the kids ducked in surprise and raised their heads to the cone-shaped bullets lodged and marred.

"Bulletproof glass," X gasped, Sun Bin's mouth agape.

"Acrylic," Beck corrected, punching his instrument panel to make it work. His heart sunk, drowning in the pod's gravity as his panel instruments went berserk before going dark. "Oh no."

"Oh no, what?" Mel said.

"Why didn't you think of encasing the computers in the hull?" he asked himself. "You thought of ion cannon shields," he said, disbelieving his own gall. "But not encasing the computers?"

Angry bullets riddled the speed pod. Beck maneuvered the vehicle to the left and right between rock formations, then upside down and back again as an Authority tube pod slammed into flames beside them, shaking their hull. The deck panel suddenly lit back up like the night sky had been illuminated.

"You're a heckuva good pilot, mister!" X called from the back seat as Y continued to hurl into the bag.

Beck flashed a smile to Mel, who was not happy. "Aww, c'mon. Don't be that way."

Her eyes pierced him. "You're trouble, I just knew it."

"Heyyyy," Beck said as he made another quick turn. More gunfire hit the pod's hull as another state pod followed its tail. "That's not nice."

"Two more," Sun Bin said with unreasonable calmness.

"When we get out of this," Mel said, "we are parting ways."

Beck shrugged. "You have faith I'll get us out."

Sun Bin took a notice of Y, who was about to pass out. "He isn't doing too well there."

Through his rearview mirror, Beck saw Y spread against the side window. "Can you grab that now-barf bag?"

X grabbed the stinky satchel from Y's side, his hand limp next to it. She held it up, grossly full, and made a face.

"Hold on," Beck said. He hit a switch and the bottom panel slid open, their cabin pressure plunging as the wind suddenly roared and the desert floor rushed past underneath X's dangling feet. "Do it!"

X winced. "Another problem!"

"What!" Beck yelled over the wind's howl.

"I'll do it." Y sighed. He stuck his hand in the foul-smelling bag and felt around.

Turning around, Mel's face twisted in horror. "What is he doing?"

"I got it!" Y said, pumping a hand covered in bile.

"So disgusting," X said.

"Got what?" Mel asked.

As turbulence filled the speed pod, Sun Bin breathed in relief. "The key to the rebellion."

"The rebellion?" Mel and Beck asked in unison, as more fire shots lodged in the back window like caught bugs and Beck monitored the speed and distance schematics.

He hoped his plan would work. The last time he'd tried something like this, he'd been in the passenger seat himself on a test run in this exact speed pod. Only when it had run out of juice was the pilot nabbed, and Authority escorts allowed Beck to leave the scene. If only Ragstar Lohan could see him now. "Now, X!"

As the wind below lifted her hair up in wild wisps, X dropped the satchel to her feet, and the air sucked it through the bottom floor. The flying satchel rushed behind them as a projectile weapon, exploding onto the Authority pod's front window, blinding the pilot.

They peered behind them, the pod weaving slightly at full speed before crashing into a rocky ridge and splitting in half, exploding in rolling fire.

"Whoaaaaaa," X breathed.

"Who said I was useless?" Y asked through the windy cabin, his face void of color, as he wiped off what he'd pulled out of the bag with his pants.

The bottom door thudded shut, cooling the cabin's air pressure and enveloping them in a hollow calm.

"Very useful," X said.

Beck motioned to the side panel. "Pull out another RID bag if he needs it." No need for the cabin to be as damaged as the outside.

"You do that trick often?" Mel asked, her eyebrows raised.

"Only when I need to get rid of something," Beck snapped, searching his instruments for the last state pod in the chase.

"One can imagine what you've been transporting and dumping," Sun Bin offered.

"I've created a few headaches," Beck said dismissively. He didn't need more judgment. A signal flashed on the instrument deck. "We're losing charge," Beck said, flipping switches. This could only be a bad thing. "They hit the backup power."

"You should have planned ahead," Mel said.

Beck stayed focused on his instruments. "I planned as much as I could at the time. Cutting short our charge. I already get range anxiety."

The hull shook as pellets splattered the side walls. The indoor panels plopped open, bags of white pills spilling out like rain.

"Drugs," X said, inspecting the bags.

"Medicine," Beck corrected as he flipped the speed pod around a monumental rock's corner, jostling the entire pod's contents.

"Medicine," Mel mused.

"Auto-regulating smart insulin. Painkillers. Things the rebels need."

"I take these!" X said.

"Fantastic," Beck said dryly. The state pod tracked them closely as they approached a ravine, narrow and steep-ridged, cut by flooding and hard water currents. Only one thing to do.

"Mind if I take some?" X asked.

"If we make it out of this alive, kid, I won't care."

"I don't see how you're going to outrun 'em if you decelerate," Mel said.

He bounced back and forth between his view of the ravine, his deck nav, and his mirrors. Narrowing his course as they slowed, he accelerated again. "Physics. Hold on."

The state pod stuck to him, using acute reflexes to dodge terrain irregularities and avoid the slip. Beck guided the pod several meters up, as far up as it would allow, and down again, grazing the terrain. He tried bobbing side to side, but the Authority pilot chased him like a tail. Both pods gunned through the ravine, its sides milky from mineral deposits and pesticide runoff, which streaked the ravine like Earth's tears.

"The guy's good," Beck said mostly to himself.

Suddenly, Beck hit the brakes, coming to a complete halt on one of his bobs. The black helmet trooper turned hard to avoid a collision and slammed against the ravine, his pod tripping over the rocky landscape until it finally skipped into an exploding wall of fire behind them. The kids marveled through the marred back window as the speed pod's hum and navigation power faded to black, and Beck smirked, ignoring Mel's hard stare.

"Not bad, huh?" Beck said. "We're not at absolute zero power either. Bet I can fix it."

"I bet the pilot light went out," X said.

"The pilot light definitely did not go out," Beck snapped, his head hung like a heavy cross at what his fading readings revealed. "We've got a ways to go, knowing what I know of this area. No populations nearby."

Then the speed pod shuddered as it floated down the deep, narrow ravine, thudding to its soft landing as its power fell to absolute zero.

Ten

General Speer nested in the Authority camp's control room as the three pilotless biplanes flew in formation across the digital monitor wall. POV camera feeds, true eyes in the sky. Flooded tankers, loaded with tubs of pesticide, hung from each plane's base like bombs as the cockpit cameras and accompanying drones streamed. Speer's famished, steely eyes consumed every colorful moving image on the dozen trapezoidal displays, like each was a juicy red steak.

Then there it was: a blockaded village in the distance, enclosed behind giant, imposing walls. A bastille community of deadened spirit, where voices dared not sing as delivery trucks plowed up the paved highway toward the community's front gates, snaking their way through desert dust.

What were the trucks doing here?

Heavy feet scuttled behind him, and Speer grimaced. Authority troops held an uneasy Captain Antonious at gunpoint, his face wrapped roughly in a wet rag.

"Sir," an ensign officer said. "The biplanes are minutes to their destination."

"I see that. I am paying attention." He squinted at the audacious delivery trucks. They were of Authority origin with hostile barred grills, and beige tarps whipping their backs. He double-checked his chrono and frowned. No ration deliveries were scheduled today. With the stolen assets of late, he was certain that was his food stock.

"Those are my trucks," he said, his blood curdling.

"Yes, sir."

Speer pounded his fist on the control panel. The rebels mocked him, taunting him in broad daylight no less. "They steal provisions from my camp and think they can save civilian populations, do they?"

Many civilians had allowed themselves to be starved. Pumped with opiates and dopamine, hundreds of villagers were no longer interested in food, a too-precious resource to waste on civilians not fighting *for* the Authority anyway. Instead, they waited for life-sapping drugs to feed their starving neuron sensors and addictions, rotting into self-debilitation. Little food resources were provided, the bare minimums of rice and corn. Much of it went ignored by the skeletal, undernourished populace as the crudely manufactured opiates continued to be exhausted. Although the rebels thought they could save them, these people were addicted and listless. *A prime target to test the pesticide's impact.* There were no better test subjects than a disinterested population incapable of running away.

"General."

Speer blinked. "That supply caravan. They will be a part of this."

"Yes, sir," the ensign said, punching buttons on the control deck.

Antonious squirmed with his hands tied, his bushy beard and the mushed gag unable to conceal his fear. Black helmet troopers stood stiffly at attention.

"Captain Antonious," Speer started, his gaze frozen on the digital video displays, committed to his hunt. "Before you go, we should determine something first." The captain focused his wary eyes dead center on Speer. "Ensure that the latest generation of pesticides you so ceremoniously have championed are used with the glory intended." Speer glared at Antonious, hoping he'd see a last glimmer of penance before being dismissed of further service for good. A worthy goodbye. "Don't waste a drop."

Captain Antonious coughed through the rag, panting like a dog.

"I'm relieved we finally see eye to eye, Captain. Commander?"

"General, you wanted to see me?" Commander Salvato said, entering the room. His plump face, normally devoid of any distinctive features, like a dull, gray sky, somehow ballooned. His eyes peeled wide open, surprised to see the arrested and defeated pilot hanging his head. "What is this?"

Widening his arms like a showman, Speer said, "Welcome to our new beginning." He smiled as Salvato studied the room, his mouth agape upon seeing the monitors' live feeds. Salvato would either be an ally, or managed appropriately. There was no room for pesky detractors.

"Commander," Speer continued. "You've often questioned the way Martel has handled things—the Ozmacarta agreement, the rebel outliers. Question is what side you're on."

"Grand Regional Governor Martel calls us in the spirit of collaboration—"

"Martel seeks no collaboration, Commander," General Speer snapped, catching his breath. "While he pacifies populations with our resources, the rebels steal and pretend *they* are the providers. Enough!"

Salvato spoke slowly, as if awakened to the magnitude of the crisis. "Sir?"

Caution in the commander's voice grated on Speer's nerves. "We are going to test Captain Antonious's weapon," he proclaimed, watching Salvato for whispers of movement toward the blaster at his side.

"It's not supposed to be a weapon!" Antonious cried through the stuffed rag, tearing up in anger. Red veins popped out of his head like wormy snakes.

Speer turned to face Antonious, satisfied the black helmets raised their blaster rifles in warning. Committed, aligned. Power surged through his blood. "We cannot put our resources to waste," he said, as the drones streamed the stolen Authority-vehicle caravan accelerating straight for the gated village, the trucks breaking away from each other and scattering like bugs. Perhaps they were aware of the planes' imminent attack. "Let's see if this pesticide does what you say it does, Captain. Test it on the population abusing the Authority's rules." He could taste the throes of victory within his grasp. Rebels suffering. The screams, the horror. "And then, find that rebel base, take their bees, get that download back, and finally wipe the rebels out."

Commander Salvato approached the general as armed troopers intersected him, munitions in hand. "This is madness. We can't kill an entire population."

Tired of running into obstacles within his own detail, Speer seethed. The Authority needed to break rules to grow their domain, crush any dissidents. "It appears you're not interested in quelling the resistance, Commander."

"I am, but not crushing our own populations doing it. It's bad enough we've made them weak and reliant."

"Prepared to engage, sir," said the ensign seated at the controls.

The general studied the commander, anticipating his resistance to progress. "I could use a strong commander for my fleet."

"Your fleet? Martel ordered us to contain our citizens and get our intelligence back in the rebel hunt. This is a mutiny!" With that, Salvato snatched Speer's blaster and aimed it squarely as the armed troopers stood in wait. This, Speer had not seen coming. "Enough of this. Cuff him."

The troopers moved but froze when Speer spoke calmly. "You will not cuff me."

"You are not destroying what the Authority is building," Commander Salvato pronounced, visibly shaken as the troopers did nothing. He shifted his weight from left to right and his hands rattled, his skin white like he'd been drained of blood. His voice cracked. "Cuff him, I said!"

A wicked grin emerged on the general's face. "They get extra rations because of me."

"You will not break the Authority," Salvato said, cool and steady, aiming the blaster between Speer's eyes.

Taking a breath, Speer casually pulled out the truncheon at his side and knocked the blaster out of the startled commander's hand in a flash. He fly-wheeled at the commander as Salvato reached for his own blaster. Adrenaline bursting through his veins, Speer spun the truncheon with ambidextrous reflexes and control as he savagely beat Salvato's head, his torso, his chest, everything. He unleashed the rage of the wild, pent-up frustration and repression, boiling with fire and thrashing down. Each swing released pain. Collision of contact, a cathartic release. First, Salvato had stopped protesting, unable to form words as his blood choked him. Within moments of Speer's onslaught, Salvato barely moved, his blunted nerves no longer responsive to the power release.

"You rely on blasters too much, Commander," Speer said menacingly, catching his breath. Salvato struggled to peer up at him from the floor, his face mangled and frightening as blood trickled out of gaping wounds. Standing tall, Speer kicked the guns to the side. "You've become limited by them."

Salvato gasped as he grabbed one of Speer's boots with his last breath, and Speer kicked him off. Breaking protocol, a trooper turned to the others as if wondering what to do, and, after recognizing their solidarity with the general, the trooper regained decorum.

"Well then, I have my answer," Speer said coolly, ignoring his elevated heartbeat. Back to business. "Ensign Renfro, engage fire."

***

"We're all gonna die out here, aren't we?"

"Shut up!" X insisted. "Honestly, Y, continue to complain and I'll lose it on you myself."

Mel peered down the long, windy ravine as the merciless sun beat down, a forcefield of heat. She tapped her navigation tool again. "This nifty navigation doesn't work." As soon as the words left her mouth, she realized she was holding an *Authority* navigation tool, and she tucked it away.

How had she not thought of that? She was grateful, too, that Sun Bin was meditating by himself a few meters away on a flat rock. Surely he would have been able to pick it out as Authority gear, because anything could and would go wrong on this mission.

"I think it's the iron ore within the ravine's rocks," X said, showing Mel her compass, its indicator stubbornly sticky. "See?"

Simple Eye's eyelid drooped. Its side panels glistened, the sun bouncing off them in yellow starbursts.

"Looks like Simple Eye agrees with you, X," Mel said, "with a terrain reader as useless as a desalination plant out here."

They were exposed, any cover in the shallow ravine erratic and scant. Its narrow, steep-sided edges raised only two meters high, with nowhere to duck or hide. A cursed passageway across the barren plane, the lonesome ravine snaked forward through the cracked desert stretch. Whatever rushing water had carved these scarred craters into the desert floor had not been here in a *long time.* Eventually, someone would pick up on them out here. The Authority would not tolerate their speed pods being destroyed—in controlled lands no less.

"Why don't we start walking?" Y asked, his hand fidgeting the small rope necklace around his neck, as if reassuring himself it was still there.

"Don't lose it," X said.

"Don't be annoying." He found a small stick of brush and poked around. Mel considered her own delight in the kids' bantering, surprised to find herself somewhat enjoying them, despite them being children *from the resistance* on the run with something valuable. And it was on that disc.

A *clang* emerged from within the stalled speed pod's hatch.

Fiddling in the back of speed pod's trunk, Beck worked to repair the damaged energy cell as Simple Eye hovered over him, assisting in a way that could not be helpful. The drone bleeped and blinked its weary eye. Beck's head was buried deep in the pod's hatch, causing his pants to stretch painfully across his butt. Whether Mel liked it or not, she looked away.

"Pass me a smaller wrench?" Beck asked, his muffled voice buried within the pod's innards. "The cabinet is too tight."

Amused, Mel asked, "One of your special modifications?"

"Original design flaw!" he yelled, and another tool clinked and clanked its way through the pod's brains, finally slipping into the ravine's powdered dirt.

Simple Eye hung over the tools at the trunk's base. A mound of dozens of random-sized crescent and monkey wrenches were piled high, and they all looked alike. Simple Eye bleeped as if flummoxed.

"Just pick!" Beck yelled from deep within the trunk. "A bit smaller than the last one."

Simple Eye whirred a dejected groan.

"That's no help. Just decide!"

An antenna in one of Simple Eye's top panels released an extended crane claw. Beck blindly held his hand out as Simple Eye's flexible claw poked clumsily through the tools, grasping a greasy wrench and dropping it into Beck's hand. He immediately went back to work as soon as Simple Eye's arm retracted away.

"This might do," Beck said, teeming with surprise.

Mel moved to a small ridge nearby, keeping her eye on everyone as the dry flatlands surrounded them. Pesticides and war had expanded desert regions into sorrowful death marches, where many journeys came to painful ends.

It was widely known that desperate travelers trying to escape from famine and the Authority's throes often perished in their travels between districts, only to succumb to the earth's elements if bandits or Loners didn't get to them first. Nothing spanned for kilometers in every direction, only mounds of bouldered rock littering the barren badlands. There had to be a lurking cave somewhere, a cavity of rock for shelter. Authority drones and scouts were known to patrol the deserts, sky hawks seeking detractors of Authority law. They could not stay out here.

X was building a small pyramid mountain with bags of white pills as Y scraped the ravine's wall with his stick, curious about the contamination seeping down the wall as Sun Bin blinked awake from meditation. No one had put together what she was doing yet. If the rebels discovered her mission, the crew's futures were uncertain. Would the rebels punish the children for exposing their location, leading the wolf to the feast? Could they be killed? Such a predicament she had put them in. They had already started to grow on her like a pair of comfortable pants she couldn't part with.

"Be careful there, Y," Mel said. "That poison has been gestating for decades into who knows what. It's already killed the soil. Don't disturb it so it kills us too."

Y threw down the stick.

"We won't want to be out here when the sun goes down," Sun Bin said, squinting into the distance. "Loners like the dark. So do night orbs."

"Loners are also active during the day," Y said with a shudder. "They took X and me in as slaves. Remember?"

Mel's face must have shown disbelief, because X raised her eyebrows and said, "It's true."

Scavenger nomads of the desert, Loners had succumbed to disease from the land. She had heard about the devolved humans, their physical depravity unleashed. They congregated in groups supposedly, in ruins. She knew to shy away from the crumbling metropolises, where the worst of the creatures buoyed a framework of haggling and plague. Danger was where Loners and their devolved cousins, the Reavers, were, and she was going to avoid them as much as fighting itself.

"In the dark," Sun Bin added, "they become animals. Their hunger pulls out the worst humanity has seen."

"I've seen the worst humanity brings," Mel said.

"Well, whataya know," Beck said, coming up for air from the trunk with a warped block energy cell. He wiped his perspiring brow with his sleeve. "Melted."

Simple Eye bleeped in happiness.

Beck eyed the drone with suspicion. "A robot can state the obvious, too, I guess."

The drone sang a sour note and scooted next to X as Beck inspected the energy cellblock, pensive. He shrugged. "We'll be walking."

"What?" Y complained.

"What did you think we'd be doing, Mr. Brains?" X asked the boy, petting Single Eye until it purred with a soft hum. "What about the medicine?"

"We'll take all we can," Beck said, lobbing the useless energy block to the ground.

"Tell me more about the Loners," Mel said.

"One should not be afraid of those we know, but of those we don't see," Sun Bin said, a faraway distance in his eyes disappearing as quickly as it arrived. Did Mel imagine it? "No more unsacred of a being than the Loners. Creatures of the muddy deep, not human anymore. Infected by the sins of nature."

"Okay, beware the Loners all the day and night, the whole time," Beck said. "We get it."

"Why'd you do business with them then?" Y asked Sun Bin pointedly.

With a forceful stare, Sun Bin said, "A reciprocal business relationship can keep the evil at bay, even if temporarily."

Mel did not know what to make of the bony old man. He had stuck his neck out to save the children, after *purchasing them*. He meditated and stayed calm, perhaps too calm, considering the pod chase and their serious predicament out here alone. Standing weakly and squinting under the murderous sun, Sun Bin looked like an aged religious teacher swallowed up in his dulled, voluminous robe. Maybe he had foreseen their journey somehow. Would he have the strength to complete the journey? He had to weigh thirty kilograms less than her, and she didn't have much weight to give.

Suddenly, an Authority drone scout swooped past and over them, its light buzz accompanying ominous bleeps as its twin telescope eyes flipped directions to focus on something else scrambling across the desert floor.

"Down!" Mel hushed.

They dove for cover as Simple Eye positioned itself against the pod in a small crevice, camouflage in a pocket. Sun Bin moved to the ravine's wall, his robe blending in with the dirt terrain. If the drone saw them, Authority troopers would canvass the area, no doubt.

"Stay here," Beck said softly. As the drone passed, he climbed on top of the pod's hatch and peered out, a guard on watch.

The Authority normally wouldn't have a problem with her out here. She was, after all, on Authority assignment. Certainly, killing Authority troopers along the way was not part of the deal. Would the Authority believe she did it?

"Looks like the drone was distracted by a wild boar or something," Beck said as he reappeared.

"Is it gone?" Y asked unnecessarily.

"For now."

"Let's pack up," Mel said. "We'll need to find some cover in the mountain range."

"And leave *Airfoil* out here to rot?" Beck asked. "I've invested two years' coin into this thing. No way."

"You think we need more to protect . . . this?" She pointed to the weathered and tortured metal heap. "Or them?"

Beck turned to the kids huddling under the pod's slight canopy. "Walking into the sun's death march ain't my idea of self-preservation, Custode. Now, I might be able to recharge another fuel cell—"

"We can't wait three days to hope it recharges enough for liftoff," Mel interrupted. She was on a time schedule herself. "We don't have enough food or water to make it out here that long."

"Because Y dropped our backpack," X added.

"Shut up!" Y yelled back.

"Wouldn't take three days," Beck said, scratching his beard, "but I need to get this medicine back to District Forty-Four in the next two days."

Mel asked, "What do you mean the next two days?"

"The drugs?" X offered.

"Medicines," Beck said, annoyed. "Some are smart insulin regulators. Others remove toxins and parasites from the body. For those the rebels have taken in."

"You're with the rebels?" X asked, excited.

He shook his head. "No, this is bigger than any of us here. The rebels are out of this medicine, and in days there'll be more deaths. My daughter needs them, or she'll become immobile, I'm told. Things go downhill fast from there."

"You have a daughter?" X and Y asked in unison.

"You're a father?" Mel asked with surprise. Maybe he'd mistakenly fathered the child, disregarded the child's existence until a bounty was over his head. Maybe some unassuming harlot was duped with a taste for volatility, or he was deceived into fatherhood. Probably a swindling he'd deserved. Either way, he was more than he appeared. "So you're not all just about yourself. Shocking."

"Long story. I transport for money, that's it. I just usually know what I'm getting myself into."

"Well, your daughter sounds pretty amazing to me," X said.

"We'll get you paid at the Forty-Fourth. If we ever get there," Mel said.

Beck kicked the side of the speed pod. "Not my fault. But you're right, before it gets dark out here, let's get going."

And with that, the back bumper cracked to the ground with a lazy *thud.*

ELEVEN

Poison mist fell upon the barricaded village like toxic rain. What Speer had hoped for: an unsuspecting populace going about their daily zombie-like routines. Exposed, feeble prey, deserving of what they had coming. A welcome sense of joy escaped his lungs. Emaciated citizens crumpled into themselves and lay still, crying to the vicious skies as their skin burned to a crisp. Awakened from a stupor, the stunned villagers scattered for their ramshackle huts as the simmering poison fell, seeping through clay ceilings, grass, and mud. Those who could not make it to shelter tumbled and collapsed and broke their own falls, disintegrating into dust.

"Again," Speer said as the outfitted biplanes sailed and wrapped around for another turn. The rebels' plan to provide food to the starving people had been thwarted, the envoy wiped out with swift strikes. But he had only just begun. "A complete test. Fly the planes around."

Captain Antonious muffled something through the rag bound over his mouth.

"As you command," the ensign said, slapping the controls.

The muzzled groaning grated on his nerves. "Take off the rag," Speer ordered. Obeying, troopers pulled the rag down around Antonious's neck like an ascot. "What now?"

Antonious gagged on his own saliva. "You're killing a whole population."

Speer yawned, caught between time and space on his own planet. "Anything else tiresome to contribute?"

The captain's attention darted to Commander Salvato, heaped in a blood pool on the floor. An abandoned carcass, left to decompose to the elements. "These planes outfitted with technology are new," Antonious said low, his voice shaking, "but their communication systems aren't ready—"

"Ensign," Speer interrupted, finding pleasure in Antonious's fear. If his tactic worked, he would test large-scale. "Any issues on engaging with another sweep?"

"No, sir," the ensign said, manning the controls with determined proficiency.

"As predicted." Speer nodded, and a trooper fire-blasted Antonious. Speer found fresh air through his windpipes. He almost felt refreshed with one less distracting voice to cloud his thinking.

As Speer turned back to the trapezoidal screens, the planes whipped around the wide blue sky like blackbirds as they prepared to do another ground sweep. Their crude sprinkler heads released the heavy aerosol like heavenly showers. Then, Speer choked. One of the planes overcorrected its turn and descended quickly toward one of the village walls—a diving bird.

"What's wrong with that one?"

"I don't know," the ensign said, pushing buttons frantically as he raced to correct the plane's uncontrollable path. "Communications are corrupted."

"Corrupted?"

The ensign shook his head, defeated. "Collapsed. I don't understand." The towering, barricaded wall jumped closer and closer on the video feed.

"Do something!" Speer yelled as the plane exploded into a grand fireball. Antonious's words about the ill-equipped system haunted him, and Speer clenched his fists. A catastrophic waste of planes, fuel, resources, and weapons.

"The system has bugs, I think," the ensign said.

"Bugs?" Speer snarled in disgust. "No reducing this disorder to bugs." He traced the screens to the last two planes veering off course away from the village in opposite directions, swinging in erratic swoops.

"Sir."

He lacked options. Forget protocol and Martel; he'd be dealt with soon enough. In no way would Speer allow himself to be accused of treason. For his efforts, he'd leverage the rebels' food provisions with the Authority. Lead Authority dominion. The kids, the data, rebel destruction, the honey, the stolen and stocked foods. Everything.

He gathered his thoughts as the obedient black helmets stood guard like dutiful statues. "Get back in your seat and fix them, Ensign Renfro!

Don't tell me you can't do anything!" His blood boiled as the planes swerved toward each other in smooth flight paths, fifty meters over the stretching wasteland.

The ensign shook his head. "We have a communication disorder, sir."

"Shut them down."

"I can't!" Ensign Renfro cried. "Even if I reboot the system—"

"Override them then!"

"They aren't responding!"

Speer braced for the planes' impact, watching in horror as his plan was abolished. They accelerated toward each other in devoted remiss. He held his breath as the planes exploded into a brilliant firestorm in the sky, the drums of pesticide flaring the blast into extreme starburst bangs. Smoldering shards of burning metal and fiberglass pierced the desert floor.

A drone eyed a new rebel caravan arriving from the east, a handful of floating barge pods sweeping in a clean line from the horizon. Before Speer could speak, rebel blasts blew his drones out of the sky, turning the monitor feeds to black.

Ignoring the ensign's empty stare, General Speer said, his voice uncontrollably throaty, "You will speak of this to no one. Everyone out."

Once the harried ensign left with the scurrying troopers, Speer took out his blaster once more. The chamber clicked empty, and he attacked the useless control board, pummeling the levers with his jointed truncheon, an unrestrained chain of anger and hate, a singed madness drowning in failure.

There would be no accusations of treason, no denials. Action must be immediate. Only one person in the hemisphere had the codes for the weapons that could successfully penetrate a hidden rebel base amongst thousands of square kilometers of impenetrable forest. He needed the tree skippers and the bot parkours, but he couldn't command them as things currently stood.

He needed to take care of Martel.

***

The graphic comlink on Major General Leroi's wrist scanned for Mel Custode's whereabouts, its sensors scouring the districts that should have been in Custode's path.

Nothing.

Just a faint clue of the Alvarium recruit somewhere on the digital map is what she wanted. Anywhere. One last time she'd been trusted for this mission. The possibility of being relegated to Alvarium Penitentiary security detail for good made her heart sink.

"Still nothing?" Grand Regional Governor Martel asked, the conference table's soft radiance lighting up his skeletal features in a white moon. "It's unfortunate your defeats have become habit, Major General."

"A temporary difficulty, sir," Leroi said, shaking her head as she sat.

"Perhaps you've been duped."

"Duped," Teek repeated, a stupid grin on his face.

Was the worst to come? Custode running off into the district wilderness, abandoning her duty and leaving her in a lurch? "Sir," she said, as Martel's beady eyes penetrated her soul. "This must be a temporary nonreading."

Inside the cavernous conference room, Martel sat at the head of the gloomy oval table, his disappointment hanging heavy. The officers sat still, their spectral-lit faces shaped like ghosts.

"Where is Speer?" Martel asked. "And that beastly Salvato? I won't tolerate this kind of disrespect."

The compact room splintered into dismal quiet; no one dared to answer. Martel was known for impatience with assumptions and answers that led to more questions. Suddenly, the door burst open and General Speer marched in, fixed on Martel.

"What is this, General?" Martel asked, raising his eyebrows. "And where is Salvato?"

A handful of black helmets abruptly entered, their double-barreled blaster guns held cross-bowed across their chests in bountiful intensity, jointed truncheons by their sides. Armed like canons.

"Many things aren't acceptable, Martel," Speer said. The grand regional governor's eyes narrowed at the deliberate omission of rank. "And Salvato." Speer shook his head. "Tsk-tsk."

Leroi froze in shock. Had Speer finally lost his composure, control of his strings? Whatever was happening, it was like watching a speed pod fleet about to crash.

"What the hell?" Teek asked, standing. Two black helmets immediately moved behind him, stilted and threatening. "Stand down!" Teek ordered. Strong, ominous black menaces: movement nil.

"They don't report to you now, Teek," General Speer said. "No longer is leadership content with rebel containment. We will feast upon their resources, and rebel trash will be hunted down and destroyed. *This is vision.*"

A mutiny within the ranks had clobbered them all, socking them in their guts. At any moment, Martel would call the troopers to detain Speer. Why hadn't Martel done so already? A trooper's holstered side pistol stood out, shining like the North Star. She would fight her way out of here if necessary.

Pounding his fist on the table, one of the senior officers exclaimed, "This is madness!"

A chorus of challenge among the officers was quickly shut down, aggressive troopers shoving them back down in their seats. Leroi stood speechless, unsure what to do. Dying was not the plan today.

Martel remained seated, his hands resting easily on his lap like he was patiently waiting for dinner. The white light fed his deep-creviced, rotten corpse of a face, the sunken caverns carved into his skin. The life sucked out, his eyes piercing. Growing rage behind his ghastly appearance made him even more frightening.

"Speer," he said, steady and calm as anger cut through the air. "Time is running out on reversing course on the treason you are about to attempt." He stared the general down.

"I'm attempting nothing," Speer said absently. "You know I've got you. Otherwise, you would have called your troopers to arrest me already."

Martel didn't blink.

The trooper's blaster pistol. Leroi made her move. Slowly, and with all the stealth she could muster, she moved smoothly like a snake, until her petite frame abruptly deflected off a trooper's armored chest plate, almost knocking her off her feet. She was surrounded. A second trooper domineered over her as she scowled.

"No need to make this more difficult, Major General Leroi."

"This won't work out well for you, Speer," Leroi said. "These are his troops, not yours."

Speer grinned as, somehow, a darker shadow bathed his face. "Martel, are you going to give me the codes so that, once and for all, we can destroy the rebel base?"

"Absolutely not. Arrest him," Martel said.

Leroi's heart drummed. Her footing, stressed and insecure, made her feel as if wobbling tectonic plates shifted underneath her feet as Martel's foggy gaze bounced around the room in search of obedience in a room of unresponsive soldiers.

"I said arrest him!"

"Cuff him," Speer said.

Two black helmets approached Martel as he stood up. Out appeared electrode restraints, known to zap detainees who get out of line. Martel, his head almost scraping the ceiling, quickly shook off both troopers.

"Get off me," Martel said, incredulous. "I don't know what you did to achieve this grandiose idea of who you are. For the short period of time you have left—"

An electrode immediately zapped Martel with a whip of blue static. Both black helmets held him up as he slumped, before letting him fall like a sack of rocks. Then they cuffed him.

"Unfortunate."

"These . . . my troopers." Martel garbled, like he had swallowed his tongue. "You won't get away with—"

"You should have fed them better," Speer interrupted, glowering as Martel's face transformed from jumbled anger to woeful surprise, the air trapped in his pipes. "All this happened under your nose."

As the troopers led Martel out, Leroi dared not move. Speer himself had stolen the food provisions to gain the soldiers' favor, broker their allegiance. The rebels had not broken into all the camps to steal the rations after all, or Speer had used rebel break-ins as cover. No one had seen this coming—using the Authority's own food supply to commandeer an army within an army.

***

"I trusted you, Major General," Speer said. "And yet you failed."

"Even though Custode has been untraceable for a day, she is still an asset," Leroi said, unsure of herself as the musty dungeon's dampness coated her lungs. "I'm sure of it."

The ceiling's dim candescent bulb filled the room with tangerine gloom. She held her head down, wishing she was anywhere else. It was wet and miserable, as slight water trails dripped from hairline cracks onto the cold limestone, settling into dreary puddles. She peeked at Teek and three other dissident officers, bound and chained to the underground cell's wall. Their legs were restrained by steel cuffs, binding them to the stone wall like medieval prisoners. Each strained to breathe through the tattered gags as they melted into the drab rock. Sad, breathing, decomposing corpses. They were doomed. Only she was uncuffed, sitting on a three-legged stool where she'd been ordered to visualize what happened to dissidents. Plopped down as Speer loomed over her, domineering and obstinate like a stubborn weed. Two armed troopers stood by as Leroi avoided Speer's forceful glare.

"You search for the headquarters, I go after the scouts," Speer said. "That was the deal."

"Looks like we both failed," she said under her breath.

"What did you say?"

"We both failed," Leroi said louder. Despite Speer's cruel power, she punched back fear somewhere into the nether. "If you are on some timeline—"

Teek moaned through his gag.

"If you think this is bad," Speer directed at Teek, "I'll send you to detention with Martel where you'll never be heard from again."

Teek shut up.

"My timeline," Speer said as he circled Leroi on the stool, "is defined by need, not wishes. You must track down Custode and those rebel scouts. They took information that I need." He motioned toward the officers curled against the wall. "You're the most capable of this lot, despite recent failures."

"I thought you were leading the hunt for the scouts."

"You must lead both missions. Is there a problem?"

No way did she want to be set up for failure again, as he sought to blame anyone but himself. "Sir—"

"Hunt the scouts," Speer interrupted. "The Authority's forty-four districts rely on us finding and destroying the single factor destabilizing the whole hemisphere. The rebels need to be crushed before they disrupt our plans for territory expansion. I must run a region now."

Our plans? Leroi quickly shunned any lingering insecurities she had in the mission. *Not your fault, not your fault.*

The general had gone mad. How had she let herself get into this compromised position in the first place? Had she succeeded in that last mission, she would have achieved rank, likely moved posts, and never would have had to report to Speer. She wanted to vomit.

Not your fault.

Teek moaned again, and Speer shot him a glare before he quieted back down in a fetal position against the chained wall. Not where Leroi wanted to end up.

The pits in Speer's skin stared back at her, his beak uncomfortably close, making her skin crawl. Penetrating eyes pierced her like forks. She tried not to breathe in his foul scent of warm, rotting mothballs. It was like inhaling decomposing flesh. "There are vital details in that download those filthy scouts stole," Speer said, his voice strident with a hissing undertone. "Hidden communications. If discovered, they can destroy us. Do you understand?"

Us? What details in the cloud exposed Speer? But she nodded slowly, the only thing she could think to do.

"Good," he said, raising his head high like a king. The chained officers turned away and squinted their eyes shut, as if he would forget they were there. "These scouts have proven to be more elusive than I predicted. This plan of yours with the prisoner. Unsatisfying results so far."

"So you want me to accomplish what you were unsuccessful doing." She couldn't believe she said it. A cathartic challenge.

Speer had the angry face of the devil, flushed and villainous. For the first time, she saw a man with untethered power, ready to release it on a whim. "Don't have too much faith, Major General Leroi, that I won't tire of your quips. Or you will end up like these disappointments."

At a signal from Speer, the troopers standing guard opened the heavy dungeon door and Speer prepared to leave.

"General Speer," Leroi said, curious about what would come of Martel's other objectives. "What about the rebels' food and resources? The honey?"

"That's the easy part," Speer said. "I want the intelligence back."

Leroi caught her breath. Now she understood. Getting Martel out of the way had been Speer's intention all along. Speer sought supreme authority over all districts, at all costs, and she needed a way out.

TWELVE

She breathed in the sheltering cave's warming air that ballooned in her lungs as questions faded and underlying fears thawed.

"Let your anxiety sweep through you, Mel. Disappear," Sun Bin said, sitting cross-legged across from her on the spacious cave's dirt floor. She pushed secrets to the back of her mind as they absorbed each other's energy. "No need to run from what ails you, pulls you apart. The travels you ponder."

Did he know what she was planning? She opened her eyes to see him staring at her, seeing through her like she was glass.

"Eyes closed," Sun Bin snapped. Then, calmer, "Repair is in order. Nothing is an obstacle, of this world or another."

Exhale. She tried to concentrate on her mindless meditation and prevent her thoughts from wandering to what Sun Bin knew, perhaps suspected. But she couldn't ignore Beck's commotion. Rearranging, readjusting his pack with absurd rustling about like a wild animal, bugging her to the core. She breathed out, louder this time. How could this guy be so self-unaware?

"Can you?" Mel asked him finally, her brows raised. Even the children weren't causing a racket. Instead, they were conked out, basking in the roaring campfire's glow—the portable, handheld fire lamp's lush emerald light. Dancing green flames coated their serene faces like they were leafy-coated goblins, curled in comfort. Warm rocks radiated welcome heat, transforming the desert cave into a temporary oasis. Nearby, Simple Eye had powered down, recharging for the next adventure. "Please?"

"What?" Beck asked, oblivious and unconcerned.

"Eyes closed," Sun Bin said coolly.

If she could settle herself, she could exist in a world away from the desert plain, hidden within the hillside of the mountain, the steep grade, and covered entryway otherwise buried under wild grasses and scree.

She tried to focus and imagine the elegant fountain's water gently raising the crystal glass ball, pushing it up as everything else disappeared. A soft, filmy cascade off the globe raised the ball higher and higher. The water's breath calmed her. This is where answers would come, Sun Bin had said.

"Well, this worked out," Beck said. With one eye open, Mel couldn't contain her curiosity as she watched him mishandle a few stack packs. "We should have enough to get us to District Forty-Four." The ration bars fumbled out of his hands, the wrappers crinkling as they slipped through his fingers.

"Good god," Sun Bin said.

"If you say so," Beck said absently.

Sun Bin snapped his fingers at Mel. "Back to me. And stay still."

She sat across from him, their palms resting upward. Meditation was supposed to be a place where the world's problems, her own problems, washed away. She tried to shut Beck out, but she was consciously aware of him around her always.

"Conflict has you anxious," Sun Bin said. "You asked for my help. Listen so you may hear yourself."

"It's the fighting, Sun Bin. I don't want to fight."

She felt him study her closely, as if trying to predict her words.

"Not always the solution," Sun Bin said. "But there are times when drawing a sword saves lives. Your own life."

She shook her head. "Nothing good ever comes."

"Outrunning Authority pods is a good start," said Beck as Mel and Sun Bin ignored him.

"Sometimes fighting can help—"

"I won't do it," Mel interrupted. She went cold. "I've lost everything important to me because I allowed myself to be drawn into conflict. Others' conflicts."

"I'll just continue to talk to myself then," Beck said, mostly to himself. "But you *are* welcome."

"Here's how healing starts," Sun Bin said to Mel with a shake, evidently also trying to shut Beck out. "The breathing, the center. See the world through different lenses. Look up, let the light warm you, show you new paths. The water cleanses. You've got the character . . . how you stepped in to save the children."

"I don't need healing, Sun Bin," Mel said, her sense of peace eroding. "Just avoiding the fight."

"Remove your self-doubt. Some of the greatest leaders in history did this to discover healing and develop a process to conquer and prevent wars. Wake what's within."

"Oh, you're kidding me." Beck laid out a small bed, which projected from a small canister the size of a flashlight, somehow transforming into a generous sleeping bag.

Mel smirked, trying not to let Beck's cynicism prevent her desired peace.

"Find yourself, unnaturally," Sun Bin said, his voice soothing like velvet as he and Mel closed their eyes together. "What has been left undiscovered. Become your un-self to learn to become more. What is dark on one side may illuminate and save the other. Here, peace lives, preparing you for when conflict arises."

"What mumbo jumbo," Beck cracked.

She didn't care to understand his arrogance. "It's not the world's fault you don't believe in anything and, it looks like, you love to kill people."

Reclining back on his bag, Beck stroked his beard and said, "Custode, I've just gotta get that medicine to my daughter and the rebels. No meditation is gonna change the kind of healing she needs."

Sun Bin gave a faint smile as Beck laid his head back.

Suddenly, Mel's navigation transponder beeped a high tone.

"What's that?" Beck asked, sitting up.

"Someone's encroaching," Mel said, grabbing the navigation tool from her supply pack, hiding the telltale smoky gray-and-black bars of the Authority's stamp from view.

X sat up, rubbing her eyes. "How's it working in here? The rocks—" She kicked Y to wake him up.

"Ow!"

Simple Eye hummed back to life, waking from its sleep with a few quick blinks.

"Somehow it's reading something," Mel said as she knocked on the reader's base. "Keeps going in and out."

Y trembled as Beck grabbed a blaster out of his pack. "You think it's a helicopter drone?"

"We've been around guns before," X offered. "I learned when I was seven. My grandparents taught me."

The navigation reader beeped again with escalating frequency.

Beck moved to the cave's entrance. "Well, that removes unnecessary concerns because you won't be handling any."

Sun Bin stepped up. "Sun Bin would be remiss not to mention that further mounting a confrontation with the Authority puts us, including the children, in extraordinary and unnecessary danger."

"He's right," Mel said. Any potential calm slipped away as she sprang back into defense mode, as if strangely fighting the Authority on the rebel side.

Stay focused on your mission. And leave this crew as soon as possible.

"I'm not going to wait to die in here," Y said, his voice shaking.

"You," Mel ordered Y and X, "are going to hang back here and wait for us. We don't need to be worrying about you when we investigate who's outside." Even before the current problem of broken-down transportation and the dwindling timeline, being reunited with her family was at risk. Was Beck's boldness helping or not? Getting them out of one predicament didn't mean he could get them out of another.

"Exactly," Beck said. "Let us handle this."

"And me?" Sun Bin asked.

"Pray or something," Beck said, as he approached the cave's exit. Sun Bin soured. "Cross-legged. I'm sure that will help."

"You stay here too, Simple Eye," Mel said as the drone dropped its antennae in sorrow. She joined Beck, crouching outside the cave. Something large moved across the dark valley. The moon's dim light provided little help in determining its shape beyond its colossal size. "I can't believe you," she whispered.

"You wish us to be protecting ourselves with sticks and rocks?" He handed her his second blaster.

"You're trouble. Just . . . trouble."

"When I want your judgment, I'll ask for it."

"You'll get it whether you ask for it or not," Mel said as they peered out. This whole mission had gotten out of hand already.

Beck was too reckless, considering his tendencies for escalation and predicament. Thoughtless, too, despite his quest for his daughter. Abandoning these four had to wait until she found the rebel base in District Forty-Four. Perhaps that would be the best thing to do, while still following Authority orders. The safest for all.

In the valley below, she tried to make out the large, beastly shadow crawling over the vast desert floor, cloud whispers flirting with the moonlight. Whatever it was clunking its way across the valley floor, it couldn't be good.

***

X whispered, huddled near the lamp's warmth and green light. "We can't stay here."

She had to do something. If they stayed, more death would rain down upon them. Y's necklace with the small drive peeked from underneath his shirt, a siren to continental forces. If it was the Authority outside the cave, the intelligence was worth killing them for.

Skeptical, Y said, "Mel just told us to stay here."

"Our plan is different from their plans, Y. I'm still not sure what Mel is trying to do, and the pilot is a crazy person. I don't know what's going on out there, but if we want to get out of here, now's our chance."

Y sulked in doubt. "You mean run past them? I'm not stupid, you know."

She lit up. "That way." She pointed to a dark passageway in the corner of the cave, hidden behind a large boulder like a void of space, narrow and confined hole of darkness, beckoning to them like it had long, crooked fingers.

"You're crazy too," Y said.

"We have to get back to rebel camp and can't let ourselves be caught, or worse, killed." She palmed her last insulin-regulating pill. Her time window was closing before she'd start feeling sick, with blurry vision, etcetera. It was like sanity rolled between her thumbs. With that, she moved to grab a few pill bags from Beck's stash, each holding a few hundred pills. A year's worth of doses meant for Beck's daughter. She frowned.

Beck wouldn't miss one bag.

"We're in danger the more we're with them," X said, stowing the pill bag in her pack. She felt Sun Bin's eyes fall upon her in disappointment. As grandparents scold their children, old sages who saved children had expectations.

However, the old man had led them here, gotten them involved with these two daredevils like a carnivore to meat. He'd also helped them escape the Loners and the horrific realities she and Y would have lived.

"Sun Bin, come with us," X said. The cave exit stared back at her, cold and dark, no Mel or Beck to be seen. Her palms sweat. There was little time. "We can't get caught with these two adventurers with a death sentence. They're reckless."

Sun Bin spoke with the assuredness of hard, falling rain. "Child, recklessness is the dangerous accessory to fear. One can't be bold without fearlessness; it is what leads to change. But this boldness must be calculated." Y moved closer to them to listen. "The plight of the rebels wouldn't exist without strength like this. We will do much better with boldness, but also patience."

"I actually don't know what one word of that means," Y said.

"They will get us killed!" X said in a loud whisper. "We have to get back to base. We'll find another rider."

"Another speed pod?" Y scoffed. "In these parts?"

"How far would it be to walk back to Vulnus Outpost?" X asked. "It would take days, Y. We have to go forward."

"We are not going backwards! And we'd probably get caught or eaten first."

"Y," X said, trying to calm him. "Listen to me." She monitored the cave exit; the other two weren't in earshot. Simple Eye floated their way as if afraid to miss out on anything. "We have to get back to headquarters with the download. The whole rebel cause is depending on us. We stay with them, we die for certain. Do you understand?"

Y's face somehow turned white under the lamp's green glow. White with fear, or he was going to get sick again? "You sure this is the right decision?"

Solemn and patient, X nodded and turned back to Sun Bin. "You said yourself boldness is what leads to change."

The old man sighed. "How can Sun Bin help?"

THIRTEEN

In seconds, the raw, punishing desert night's chill numbed Mel into a shrinking bubble, freezing her insides. They crouched behind the rocky hillside's nettlesome brush, peering down upon the expanded valley passage and the bulldozing thunder. Their elevated viewpoint was militarily strategic, benefitted by distance, surrounding camouflaged terrain, and height. Under normal conditions, they would be able to see passersby trailing across the desert prairie with notice. Instead, the faint moon gazed upon the desolate black, providing cover to daring critters and lonesome, screaming cacti and their long, stretched shadows.

"We can see everything from up here," Beck said, his breath billowing out puffy heat clouds into the chilly night. "Except nothing."

She could barely make out the long, boxy figure in the distance. The old freight truck tore up and down as its gears ground like grating metal, crunching its forward path. Margarine headlights beamed into the desert brush as it scraped and crushed the desert floor, its engine roaring as it plowed, veering farther away. "I don't think their heat mapper is picking us up," she whispered, her flush cheeks now a rosy pink.

Sun Bin appeared behind them. "Intruders?"

Beck jumped, then said, "Not yet," glaring back at the old man. "I see you decided not to meditate them away."

"Paths are lit by the light, but not all can see."

"Really helpful," he cracked, then the large freight behemoth abruptly halted in its tracks, its engine a gasping beast catching its breath. A brisk chill carried through the valley, fueling the exhaust fumes forward into the headlight beams, illuminating the barren desert nothingness in a smoky lemony gold.

"Did it stall?" Mel asked as Beck checked his blaster's clip.

"Loners," Beck said, dismissing her as Sun Bin's eyes widened. "We should go to them before they come for us."

Mel shook her head. "And create more enemies on the road? We need to get the kids to safety."

"Use the dark as cover."

Who did he think he was ignoring her? This was her mission, not his. "Need I remind you I hired you, not the other way around?"

"I'm not going to wait here and wake up to knives on my throat," Beck said. "And don't pretend you've already paid me. This wasn't the deal, anyway, those youngsters back there."

"Kids, stop," Sun Bin said dryly, his attention on the stalled freight truck. Its hulking shadow stood in defiance, like it knew it did not belong on the valley floor, tucked between the canyon's protective hills.

"The old man wasn't the deal either," said Beck.

If only she'd had the patience and the money to find another ride to District Forty-Four, instead of jumping on the first option she'd found. While on a time crunch, she shouldn't have settled for this hooligan who enjoyed confrontation in all forms.

Beck turned to Sun Bin. "We're going to check it out. You can do more up here than down there."

"Sun Bin is coming with you," Sun Bin said, holding his scythed staff up straight. "In better shape than most half my age."

Beck simpered. "You're gonna exhaust me, you know that?"

"It's better to burn a candle cold than to lay still in the darkness," Sun Bin said.

Beck shrugged dismissively as Mel paused. She was trying to avoid getting into more violent clashes, and Beck's reckless machismo was going to pull her into them. "I'll come with you, but if we come across hostiles, we pull back and protect the children."

"Sure," Beck said with a throw of a hat, and she waited a moment before following Beck and Sun Bin down the dark and rocky hillside, in the back of her mind knowing in no way had Beck agreed.

***

Mel, Beck, and Sun Bin approached from its backside, camouflaged by the forgiving darkness. The freight vehicle hummed, its engine burning precious fuel in the cold, otherwise dead of night. Desert wildlife scattered away from the clanky behemoth as if knowing its crude, fiery engine was a mouth of evil and decay.

Their blasters drawn, Mel pointed for Beck to go to the other side of the transport. Beck nodded wryly, as if surprised to be taking orders, from her or anyone.

Mel crept forward, careful her thick boots didn't crunch on noisy dead brush. She listened closely for signs of tremor or horror, prepared to jump. From what she'd heard of the Loners, they ensnared slaves with unexpected fervor. She held the blaster stable in her hand, but she wouldn't use it.

As they turned the corner in the front of the truck, the headlight beams appeared to fade. She held her weapon up to the front canopy bay, prepared yet averse to fire. She strained to see beyond the grimy glass and the golden light's glare, making out nothing.

Sun Bin held his scythed staff tight, grafted to his skin, holding on to the back of the truck as Beck approached the vehicle's front from the other side. Then, like something punched its guts, the engine coughed its last sputter and died.

The three of them stopped as the night's soft wind chill whistled past them like a warning song. The labored headlights faded, faint and muted, struggling to hold their luminance.

In a whip, the truck's heavy gate slammed open and a crazed Loner, bloody and shaken, swung its staff at Sun Bin's head, shrieking with unrestrained rage. A carbide light shone from the mask's lamp atop the Loner's head, like the Old World miners' hats.

Mel and Beck raced to the commotion, drawing their blasters. Awestruck, Mel's mouth opened agape at Sun Bin's dexterity as he fought the erratic onslaught of the wild raider, stick to stick. She lowered her blaster in amazement as the old man struck his scythe out with brisk speed, agility, and aggressive finesse, whipping it behind and over his head like a backsword.

Then, from out of nowhere, two Loners flanked Mel, their arms flailing wildly and knocking her to the ground. Beck raised his blaster as another manic Loner swiped at him as it fired, knocking him off his feet and sending the blaster into the dark desert brush.

Mel jumped to her feet and flipped back a knife-wielding Loner, thrusting the crazed creature over her head like a pinwheel. As the Loner slammed into the ground, shrieking, another quickly flew at her. Out of pure instinct, she dodged its flailing swing and kicked it in the chest. It fell back on its rump and dove to tackle Beck as he scrambled for his blaster in the dirt. In the peripheral light, everything was a blur.

"Mel!" Beck yelled from the ground as he held the manic raider over his head, its head gyrating like a wild boar. "Shoot it!"

She balked, her weapon by her side.

Sun Bin continued to swipe and jab with his staff, knocking frenzied Loners down with swift grace. But she stood idle as Beck struggled, pinned down.

"Shoot it!" Beck yelled again, squirming on his back. The frenetic beast brandished a blade, its head whirling as it wailed.

Mel's whole body stiffened, her feet anchored to the desert floor. A rip current of fear pulled her back. In mere seconds, the Loner's crazed power would descend, perhaps slicing him in two.

While the pinning Loner whipped about on top of him, Beck's clamoring hand finally found his blaster and fired. Like a hunted prey's death knell, its head convulsed with a last piercing shrill, and Beck threw the limp stiff to the side. "Disgusting."

Sun Bin continued fighting the last Loner with inspired grace. Rushing to his aid, Beck moved to fire, as if trying to get good aim despite the fight master's skilled spins and turns in the shadowed night. The badgered Loner shrieked as the scythe's curved blade struck his hideous head. Erratic in self-defense, the Loner swung its staff, unable to land a hit on Sun Bin's twirling form. Finally, with several quick moves, Sun Bin took the Loner down to the ground with the scythe's stick end and plunged it into his heart like a stake. The raving shrieks subsided, and Sun Bin, exhausted and dazed, pulled up his bloody staff and grimaced.

"Well, asking them to leave is out," Beck cracked, dusting himself off.

"Blood still makes me queasy," Sun Bin said, catching his breath.

Mel's eyes bulged wide in awe. How had the old farmer, who often looked like he would fall over, been able to muster such dynamic power?

"A centered mind centers the soul, conquers all," Sun Bin said as if he could read her mind. "Though my back will be sore for days."

"I don't want to fight. It's not who I am." She wished to disappear.

"Thanks for nothing, Custode," Beck quipped, inspecting the Loner carcasses littering the desert floor as he zig-zagged to the vehicle's back end. "Just life or death. No big deal."

Sun Bin went to her. "Let yourself fight for the right reasons."

"You are a great fighter," Mel told him, unable to look Beck in the eye. "I have another path."

Sun Bin nodded, his knowing eyes at ease.

"Let's not congratulate ourselves yet," Beck said, poking around the truck's bed. He tore the gas mask off a grounded Loner and angled its headlight into the back of the beastly truck. A shameful pile of corpses rested against the bed's front wall, heaped and flung on each other like sandbags, their rags crimson red, their limbs hung like slabs on meat hooks. "They're not looking good."

"Looks like one savage eats the others?" Mel asked. A severed arm protruded from the bottom of the stack.

Beck scrunched his nose. "No wonder they wear these masks if they gotta smell themselves."

Sun Bin frowned. "Oh no." The dim light on his face washed him out white as a ghost. Haunted. "Loners don't kill or eat their own, nor stack their brethren in the back of their transports. The Authority must have injected them with the crazed serum."

"Crazed serum?" Beck shook his head.

"Science is used for progress, so the Authority believes. They've been known to keep restless populations docile and obedient. In the case of the Loners' already-contaminated genes, the injections are payback. They are a further exercise of cruelty for the Loners' lack of cooperation. A lesson for others. This, my friends, is the result of a failed search."

"Search for what?" Beck asked absently.

Sun Bin's gaze deadened. "Sun Bin knows this transport. These are the specific Loners who sold me the kids."

"So things keep getting worse," Beck said.

"The Authority will stop at nothing to get what they are looking for," Sun Bin said, his words monotone, as if he were caught in a trance.

"But what would they possibly have been looking for?" Mel asked. A sober realization came over her and she turned to Beck. With the life-

or-death distractions of the wild trooper chases, she had not stopped to put the pieces together. It was the data chip they wanted.

"Oh no," she said.

"Oh no, what?" Beck asked, his eyes wide.

"We need to get back to the children."

FOURTEEN

They rushed back to the cave, the fading fire lamp burnishing the rocks and illuminating the cozy den with an alien green hue. Sun Bin hobbled in late in the chase, holding his aching back. Beck realized Mel's hunch was confirmed: the kids were gone.

"X?" Mel called. "Y?"

Beck hurried, using the Loner's mask light to peek into corners of the cave. He took a breath. "They're not gonna make this easy, are they?" He understood why they all had to escape the villainy at Vulnus Outpost, but what could make the Authority hunt that download with such zeal that the Loners who sold them would be massacred and turned even more crazy? He'd picked up a helluva transport job this time.

Chasing after the kids as they themselves were being chased had not been his idea of a prosperous trip. Some extra money, that's it. Before he knew it, he got a lot more than he had bargained for. *I should not have gotten involved with these people*. He could kick himself.

"I can't believe this," Mel said. "Crazy kids."

"They'll never make it out there on their own," Beck said. The boy would fear the dark before embarking outside. "Not with black helmets and Loner cannibals running loose."

"Don't underestimate the rebels, even the rebel children," Sun Bin said. "While the rain can flood, the wind of the river forms its own mouth and carves its own way."

Beck had enough. "Your sage philosophies are getting underneath my skin, old man. This has nothing to do with wind and rain and mouths."

"That wasn't philosophy. It was advice," Sun Bin said dryly.

"Instead of bickering, can we please concentrate on where they

115

went?" Mel asked, her voice cracking. "We have to find them."

"I bet we only missed them by a minute," Beck said, imagining one less distraction putting him face to face with the rascals.

Everyone stopped to think, and Simple Eye slowly emerged from the shadows, chirping.

"You let them leave?" Beck asked the drone as it whirred a musical sequence of beeps and chirps before sulking. "You should be ashamed then!" he agreed.

"The heat mapper," Mel said, hustling for her navigator to track them. Riffling through her supply pack, she groaned. "It's gone."

Beck stood over his stacked pile of bagged white pills, and his shoulders slumped. He counted. "Oh, come on!" One bag was indeed missing. He'd already been paid for this delivery too. The debt for the delivery would create other complications.

***

"I hate tunnels," Y complained. "And you somehow keep taking us into them."

The flashlight animated the path up and down and all around as they traveled forward, the cave walls tightening and closing in. Damp and musky mountain air filled their lungs, smelling like burnt, dirty water. The tunnel's damp limestone was rich in shiny mineral deposits and overrun with roots, the trees and bushes overhead conquering the mountain as they reached deep into it out of thirst.

"Stay close," X said, her voice not carrying far. The dank, cold rock absorbed their sounds like it was knowingly protecting them, a defensive barrier to the outside world. They were truly underground.

"Don't worry," Y said, following her closely. He kept his long arm on the shoulder of her backpack, which was stuffed with their remaining rations and the medicine bag. They moved swiftly over the uneven ground, Y unsure if they were descending into the mountain or if they were being swallowed up. "These might be natural tunnels," he said, uncertainty filling his voice. "Worn down by water."

"Does it matter?" X asked, guiding them down the dark, bumpy path.

"I should probably be the one leading you," Y said as drizzly walls glistened in the residual light. The harrowing path narrowed as seeping water collected in small pools by their feet, and he had terrifying visions of struggling to swim in frigid cold rising tides in shrinking caves. "Yes, this could get scary. I should be leading."

"What, because you're a boy?" X asked, continuing to move forward. "I'm the one who grabbed Mel's flashlight. That's why I'm leading."

Something dark buzzed past them, a blast of wind in its wake. "What was that?"

X shook her head. "Don't know. Wanna lead?"

"Nah, you got this."

X smiled and they moved forward in the direction of her flashlight's beam. The windy path started to open wide, and in an instant they were in a large cavity, and beyond it, a dim pathway stretched a dozen meters away. They had discovered the opposite end of the hillside, and the rising sun peeked through tiny holes in the rock, making the cave walls resemble a starry sky.

She raised her flashlight's beam up the walls to the clearing's ceiling, and she blinked.

"Bats," Y whispered. "We have to be quiet."

"They don't look like bats," she said softly. "So small."

"They're bumblebee bats," Y whispered. "The world's smallest mammal." The flashlight exposed thousands of them on the walls and ceiling, quiet and calm and still, hiding in the cave like secrets never to be told. The small, hog-nosed creatures were maybe thirty centimeters long, their tiny gray and reddish-brown heads lurched forward on the walls, faced downward toward the cave's sopping, muddy floor. Their ears were disproportionately large, folded forward and protecting their heads, and they were almost as long as their tucked wings.

"They were supposed to be extinct by now, but I guess they're not. A bumblebee bat could fit nicely on one Authority coin."

"They're not extinct," X said with a shiver. "Cute, but not."

Inspecting a small cluster of them, Y couldn't believe they were there. "I read they collect only in small colonies," he said, unaware of his academic tone. "They normally don't roost together like this in thousands. So many in one place."

"Is it now?" X asked as if she did not mean for Y to answer her question.

"Guess I'm not the one who slept through that class," Y said, unable to contain his satisfaction. "It's like nature reversed itself. Evolution doing what it does."

The flashlight shining against the opposite wall of the cave revealed hundreds of thousands of odd, insect-sized bats, perched at ease. Their furry bodies clustered together to create one immensely large, cave-covering mass.

"Wow," Y said under his breath.

"So here's the question," X said, taking a slow and measured step forward. "If there are so many of these things, they obviously have food here. What do they eat?"

"Mostly insects and stuff," Y said casually. "Spiders." The cave was getting colder, and the clearing became larger and grander, opening like a mouth. It smelled like wet copper. "What's crazy," he continued, beholding all around, "is how these little things can rip insects off plants and even in midflight, they're so fast. Never thought I'd—"

"Um, Y," she interrupted, tugging on his sleeve. She kept the flashlight steady across the clearing. Something rustled over a small muddy mound of sticks and brush cradled together into a small, burrowed den. "See that opening?" There was something over the mound. "We need to get out of here."

"Life is recreating itself," Y continued, ignoring her, "like it's going back in time. Wait, what?"

"Are you ready?" X whispered. "We're going to run for that light hole at the end of the cave."

"We can't wake up the bats. They'll lose their minds if we disturb their habitat like this."

X aimed the light at the floor to see thousands of little bugs crawling over each other, carpeting the floor. "I'm pretty sure the bats aren't our problem anymore," X whispered.

"Wow, there's a whole ecosystem in here," Y said, further amazed.

"With everything you complain about, this doesn't bother you?" X asked, her light's sweeping beam revealing that the entire ground floor was moving. "Don't trip this time."

With that, two red, beady eyes slowly rose over the mound. A monstrous spider almost a meter high and two meters wide crawled over the nest's wall, its long legs stretching over the mud and guano with dexterity.

Y froze to stone, his eyes wide. "This is not good."

Ravenous for its prey, the spider thudded forward as it fell over the mud wall like a brick and scampered toward them, its crawling, bristling legs quickly dancing over the bug ocean.

"Now!" X whispered, and she raced for the circle of light emerging from the cave's opening, Y right behind her. "Don't fall behind!"

"Not again," he murmured.

X went for it, her feet crunching on the insects as she ran.

Eyeing the massive clusters on the wall, Y took a few quick steps forward as the crunching and commotion woke the resting creatures from their slumber. His whole being shivered as he raced behind X, positive he heard the chasing gargantuan spider shriek. Their feet slushed through the crunchy floor.

"You coming?" X called back, as they dashed for the light on the other side of the clearing.

"Just keep going!" Y yelled as the dark, shadowed beast horned in on them. He pressed forward, swearing the creepy-crawlies on the floor were making their way up his legs, and hoping they crept up X's legs too.

Then, the bats spread their wings and gave flight, jumping off the cave's walls in brisk swoops, swelling into a swarming vortex. Flapping wings spread as the bats zipped into their wild circular ring with a cacophony of whirring and humming and buzzing. A cyclone of chaos, the thousands of small creatures created a stampede in the air.

Confused by the commotion, the spider tripped up, its sensory detectors confused. One of the wild bats shot into Y's mouth, and he spit it out just as fast as they raced for the cave's exit, the flashlight's beam bouncing a crazed dance.

"Gross!" Y yelled.

"Exactly!" X screamed back over the deafening upheaval as her backpack slipped off her shoulders into a puddled bug swarm.

The spider regained its focus on the human prey, closing in on them. Suddenly, the mother spider's spiderlings departed the nest, springing into the air and catching bats mid-flight with their fangs. The baby spiders thumped back to the ground, clutching the tiny bats with all their baby might.

"I see what you mean by waking them!" X yelled over the pandemonium.

The passageway into the light was getting closer, and they flung themselves out the hole no more than a half a meter wide and crashed to the ground into the morning sun, tumbling a short way down the hillside to stop at several pairs of feet.

"Fancy to catch you two here," Mel said.

"The spider!" Y yelled.

The gargantuan spider showed its gruesome face out the cave exit above, and Beck immediately fired his blaster, missing the beast but driving it back into its abyss.

"Well, it's not coming out now," Beck said, monitoring the entrance with his blaster at the ready.

"What were you thinking?" Mel asked.

Dusting off any loose bugs still hanging on her pants, X turned to Sun Bin, who shrugged and said nothing. "We—"

"You could've been killed," Mel said. "You need to stay with us if you want to make it back to rebel camp alive."

"Have anything to say?" Beck asked.

"It's not just the spider I'm worried about," Y said, and suddenly a swarm of the bumblebee bats flew over them, like they sucked out the air and created a vacuum. Everyone could do nothing but duck as Simple Eye twisted and turned and rolled over midair, its circuitry confused by the flock of hundreds of thousands of the small creatures flying past them in a chaotic cloud. The crew stared in awe of the dark mass traveling past them and away.

"Bumblebee bats," Y continued, astounded by what they had just seen. *An unnatural nest of bumblebee bats. What must happen for a creature to break from its natural instincts over thousands of years, millions maybe, and nest together with so many? What could possibly be happening for nature to evolve in such a way, where it abandons what is natural?* The bats had to know the spider's nest was dangerous, too, yet they had nested there. He looked after them as they traveled over the desert floor. "I think in a weird way they saved us."

"Nature knows its enemies," Sun Bin said, holding himself up with his scythed staff.

"Or sometimes nature just does a fly-by." Beck snickered.

"It's going to be hot again soon," Mel said, looking out toward the sun rising over the desert landscape. "We need to go and we need to stay together."

"You can count on me staying with you!" Y said. No more following X and her harebrained ideas.

Beck noted X's backpack was missing. "Lose something, ambitious one?" he asked, studying her with restrained disappointment. But his tone let it loose. "You know those meds aren't for me. I owe them to the rebels, my daughter included."

"Sorry," X grumbled.

He patted his own pack, and he walked off. "I'll carry the rest. How about that?"

X nodded as Mel leaned down to her. "What were you thinking?"

"I thought we'd be safer on our own. We didn't want you all to die on account of us."

Mel frowned.

X said, "Are you mad?"

Mel pointed to X's shoes caked with mud and guano. "I thought I smelled something."

Pulling out Mel's nav from her pocket, X gave it back to Mel without a look. Snatching the nav back in a huff, Mel's hands quickly covered the insignia markings on its side.

Were those Authority markings he just saw? Y wondered. Four thick black-and-gray bars, horizontal and even. He'd recognize them anywhere. As he'd been quizzed too many times during Instruction, he remembered what each bar represented: discipline, containment, regulation, and dominion. Mel's hand covered the palm nav as her other hand caressed X's shoulder tenderly, like mothers do. She was so good to them. Y's mouth twitched upward as he considered that perhaps she salvaged the nav.

"We're not too far from a temporary rebel camp," Mel said casually. "Just a few kilometers from here."

X scrunched her nose as the evil sun rose. "How do you know?"

"Yeah, how?" Y asked. The nav would not define a heat map settlement necessarily as a *rebel* camp. After all, the rebels' main base would be a week's walk from here, or more, and through some treacherous territory.

"Simple Eye knows the coordinates," Mel said, and the drone blinked and emitted an odd tone, like it had done something wrong. "Signals he's intercepted indicate it's a temporary rebel hideout."

Y nodded, guessing that made sense, and Beck asked, "And get our ride to the rebel base then?"

"Then we're home free," X said, as Sun Bin and Beck shrugged at each other.

"Then we're home free," Mel repeated.

"Then we're home free!" Y exclaimed, looking forward to fulfilling his obligation with the data around his neck. And for this ordeal to be over.

FIFTEEN

One more minute, and she would try the comlink again.

Her barracks were plain and quiet, an isolated, sterile cell without bars. Leroi had slept in her sanctuary for the night, as always. Solitary, like cougars do. The still dryness hung in invisible sheets, cocooning her in a warm pocket, an accustomed truth she accepted as she had gotten older. Sleep hours allowed the world's problems to slip away into relaxed unconsciousness. Neglected tasks haunted her, the unfinished work in her Authority command scheduler's queue compounding into long lists of unfinished business. It had not always been like this, but since her failed assignment she had learned what it took to keep her sanity: waking up her way.

She shut out the thoughts in her head and wished she could go back to sleep.

The sun peeked through the digital blinds across the vestibule-like glass enclosure, as was to be expected this time of morning, and they opened automatically to reveal an alternate landscape. A projection movie reality far away, bathed in sepia and olive hues, bled onto her bare walls and surrounded her in stowed memories of a life past. Hazy pictures from her childhood showed her brother and mother laughing and struggling to grab her as she ran away, a rebellious child with no mercy. The digital images flipped to her holding her knee, bleeding from a fall, her father caring for her. Sketchy flipping pictures showed her playing with an overly affectionate dog, a variety of breeds crafting the hairy mutt that licked her face until she could not breathe. No sound. A silent happiness that Leroi chose to wake up to every day.

Leroi rolled over on the thin mattress to see the boxy, unassuming robot respond to the routine visual display. It grabbed a food ration and placed it on the grill pan. The processed ration baked in an instant and popped open to reveal a hearty breakfast of mock meat, dried biscuit, and melon that was somehow cool as dew, and bland as jicama. Her daily prepackaged meal of necessity. She turned to the warm images that helped her forget the taste.

The night had been a long one. So many routes Mel Custode could have taken to find the rebel camp, and so many things could have gone wrong. Leroi's computer determined 122–152 different combinations of routes, depending on mostly day or night travel. This could be an uneasy volume of problems. The drone provided to Custode had so far proven useless, as neither Custode nor the drone had been seen on the nav map in two days, since Mel had first embarked. Drones were supposed to be trackable, traceable. Simple Eye, so far, was defective.

If Speer knew, the programmers would be terminated.

Leroi sat up, her white shorts and tank sticking to her skin, absorbing her perspiration. Her head ached, the blood in her veins a crawling flow, and she hung her head as if waiting for her body to catch up. A bite of the fake meat proved again to be unsatisfactory, and the biscuit was worse than yesterday: drier to the chew. Only the coolness of the tasteless melon satisfied her need for refreshment and nutrition. On three hours' sleep, she would push through.

The comlink beckoned her. She grabbed it again and held it in her lap. The tiny cylinder was thick and heavy, like a roll of coins had been stuffed into it. A lot depended on what came out of the little microphone/receiver—the fate of thousands or more. Rolling the comlink in her fingers did not ease her mind. It was conceivable Custode had been abducted or changed course and defected, disregarding her family's future. Perhaps she was deceased, since she had fallen off the grid and all heat mapping. Her tracker would have also been destroyed, though. All would have to be confirmed, of course. Speer's eruptions would not settle for theories.

She hit the comlink, and suddenly, something. Distant static, its faint burp. The small plate read movement. Awakened from her daze, Leroi jumped to her computer, a small-lit screen on the wall over her makeshift kitchenette, tidy and efficient. The computer awoke, and its display displaced the childhood images and happiness. The robot dutifully moved out of her way, tweeting its dismay, jarred by its owner. The transmission indicated Custode (or at least, her comlink) was detected in the forty-second district, only a few hundred kilometers away from the forty-fourth.

The rebel district.

Leroi closed her eyes. "Custode, come in. Custode, report." She had to be careful not to provide her identity in the event of a signal pickup. "Custode. Mother here."

Nothing. Only the reserved, quadratic robot blending into the egg-shell white decor like camouflage, moved its box of a head as if to inquire what the fuss was all about. The tempered bot was not used to voices, including that of its customarily quiet owner.

"Custode, come in."

The irony of Speer's lack of faith in her and his insistence she carry out not one, but two vital missions was not lost on her. If he was setting her up for failure, he had provided her two crowning opportunities.

Leroi tried again. Both missions' trajectories could only change if she got a new order to this asset. "Custode. You are overdue to transmit progress. Mother here. Come in."

A staticky, inaudible transmission with white noise came in and out, and blood rushed to her head. Her lightheadedness and sluggishness had subsided, her heart beating so hard in her chest she caught her breath. She waited. All she could do was hope for news of the prisoner she regretted being so audacious to recruit.

Then, a break broke the white noise. Clarity emerged in the transmission. Distant and breaking up again, the words repeated with a pop. Maybe she heard it right. She waited. There it was, unmistakable, and she smiled softly.

"This is Custode."

***

This was not the way it was supposed to happen. In a small, boxy cell underneath the isolated detention center, Grand Regional Governor Martel breathed in the empty dryness as he stood a nose away from thick iron bars. The vast room packed dozens of empty torture chamber cells, each arranged in harrowing order in an obscene parallelogram, his cell positioned in the center of its haunting display. The air was so stale he could choke. Bright fluorescent-inspired floodlights quickly caused brain fatigue. Interrogated before death, this was where criminals gave up everything they held precious. His rank meant nothing down here. He thought he sensed ghosts.

His posture drooping, he leaned against the bars for support, something he quickly regretted as he was zapped by the floating orb hanging above him, sinister in flight. He cursed the sky and backed away from the bars, grating his teeth as he leered upward, wishing it dead. Dozens of tracking eye sensor telescopes popped out of all sides of the hovering globe, creating raised, topographic-like mapping, like a decorated ornament. Dozens of moving cameras were ridiculous overkill, but with Speer, nothing surprised him. Of course, unlike the oft-impaired driverless vehicles and error-ridden sentries, this sinister machine worked flawlessly, gently responding with his slightest movement, waving in the air like it bobbed on water.

He would have considered sitting down just for a second to rest his feet for precious moments, but alarms would wail again, the chamber would shake. The zap orb would be relentless until he stood up. In time he would be electrocuted to death here, where he had sent traitors in the past. He would resist the urge until he could stand no longer.

As a youthful cadet he could have stood somewhat motionless for days, a dedicated statue of discipline and health. Now approaching his seventies, he could perhaps withstand one more hour on his feet, maybe less. Then, it would be the end. If Speer intended for him to relinquish control of the region, he would not. Speer would have to rely on newfound loyalty to perpetuate the lies. And bargain with more theft of Authority resources.

The door to the room buzzed. The lock clanked. Speer paraded in with two security details in tow.

"Outside," Speer ordered them, his voice echoing in the steel-lined chamber filled with aluminum and metal throughout. I'll speak to him alone."

The helmeted guards shut the heavy door behind them. As Speer weaved around the prison cells, he said, "Somewhat ceremoniously, here we are, Martel. At last."

"This is what you wanted? Us alone?" Martel asked, his voice scratchy and contemptuous. He cleared what felt like glass shards in his throat as he tried to make out Speer through the blinding interrogation lights. There was no hiding his disdain.

"I want to see you struggle on your feet in that cell."

"You're incorrigible," Martel said, hardly amused. "An angry child at play."

Speer's voice became uncomfortably closer like a dragon's breath. "I want what the Authority deserves, Martel. Leadership."

Speer moved a step to the side, blocking the blinding light behind him. Martel squinted to see him more clearly as the general glared at him, a mere meter away from the cell bars. A hungry predator about to pounce on its prey, his eyes were gray and ashy like steel wool.

"You are too bold for your own good, General," Martel said, making out Speer's bitter features, his indignant looming intensity. "You're putting the district quadrant at great risk."

"Correction. I'm bold enough to do what needs to be done. I'm mitigating risk."

"You will create war."

"I will create peace through war," Speer said automatically. He moved to the side again, and the blinding lights flared back into Martel's eyes. "Ultimately save lives. If I get my hands on the bees, I have the resources to feed the people instead of starving them to save enough resources for our armies. A noble enterprise, yes?"

Dropping his head to avoid the harsh glare, Martel's hand instinctively touched the cell. The orb zapped him again, an electric current stabbing through his organs. He pulled back like he'd just been bit.

"I'm more thoughtful than your revered District Council," Speer continued, grinning wide and appearing taller. "More generous."

"What do you want?" Martel asked, clutching his chest, the surge stinging his heart like a scorpion pierced it. He'd never felt pain like this, and he gritted his teeth to get through it.

"I'm giving you an option to sit for a while and not be killed by a small toy."

The orb floated ominously above Martel's head, its black eyeballs rotating on telescopic tips, watching intently for infractions.

"You grew up with different toys than me," Martel said as he eyed the orb with unease and suspicion. Then he laid down the hammer, knowing his own fatal future was already written. "Your parents weren't kind providing you nice toys, were they?"

Speer glared at him, motionless.

"Ah, you didn't have a family," Martel continued, gloating he had hit a nerve of his own as he concentrated on his limited movement, straining to not lean against the bars. "Never belonged."

"I'd love to offer you a chair, some tea."

"What do you want?" Martel asked again.

"I want the codes."

Martel's eyes opened wide. "You found something." The general looked away for a moment before reengaging with Martel, like he realized he was giving up his hand. "You *think* you found something."

Silence.

"You think the tree skippers can get you the rebels," Martel continued, making the general visibly uncomfortable, shifting around like *he* was the one being interrogated. "You think you found them and want to destroy them." Martel raised his eyebrows, watching Speer's trepidation with curiosity. No way would the District Council accept Speer's rogue behavior that would kill any chance of unification with outlier rebels. Whatever happened to himself, the Council would most certainly oust Speer from any authority once this mutiny came to light. "The skippers don't have the range to go as far as you need."

Speer exhaled. "Your limitations are self-determined. Mine are not."

"Others, Speer, have determined your limitations without your consent."

Speer smirked, and Martel could tell that stung. "There's always a way," Speer said evenly, "when one is properly equipped."

"The limited power cells require exact coordinates," Martel said, unbothered by the insult. Considering he was in this cell, he had certainly been outwitted already.

"I need the codes."

"The codes can't help you without the coordinates."

"Who said I need the coordinates?" Speer asked, raising his voice as he stiffened. Beads of sweat appeared on his brow. The man probably wanted to strangle him. "It's bad enough, Martel, that you allow the other districts to withhold their weapons. Tree skippers and the robotic parkours, you know how much I've wanted those. You've allowed the districts to withhold resources that would help us beat the rebels. Instead you cower. Give me the codes and live. For a while."

"The parkours are not ready for military use, Speer. Too many bugs. Using unready weapons puts us at risk. Even the sentries are premature."

"Do not dismiss me."

"The District Council believes you to be reckless," Martel said weakly. "I'm doing you a favor by not providing you the weapons. As it is, do you desire to be killed for treachery?" He glanced at the orb above him, its piping eyes repositioning and correcting with every movement he made in the cage, every strained appeal to remain standing straight. It would not be much longer now.

Speer stepped closer to the barred cell, his eyes flashing fire. "Things will get worse for you."

Martel grinned through his tired pain, his legs throbbing to a shake. "Does this mean no tea?"

Sighing, Speer backed away from the barred chamber, taking large strides with his short legs, his arms behind his back. "I won't ask you again."

"You didn't ask me."

"A technicality."

Watching Speer leave, he forced a grin as his legs started to give way. He could black out any moment but shook it off. Repositioning his stance, he tried for a strong realignment of his muscles and joints. Blood rushed through his legs, and he stood tall like the proud robotic AI sentries guarding the main gate. And the door behind Speer clanked shut.

Arming Speer with the codes would change the world stage, challenging the poise and power of district governors and world leaders. The tree skippers and parkour bots could do much peril, but Speer's success programming them would depend on many factors aligning. Speer had become desperate in his quest to destroy the rebels. While he was imprisoned in this torture cell, it became clear Speer was the one pushed into a corner. But different than he had thought.

The general somehow must have what he needed already. Access to the codes. Would he have just made introduction to the process easier?

As the foreboding orb hung patiently above him, waiting to strike, Martel's legs finally tipped and gave way, the sharp pains in his wobbly knees relieved as relentless zaps proceeded till his faint. The last sounds he heard in the empty prison chamber were his own echoing screams.

SIXTEEN

They lumbered through the deepening ravine in succession, at times wavering in fits and starts. Beck wiped his forehead, each step pounding a stake through his skull. The more desert ground they covered, the better off they would be, with nothing to see for kilometers in all directions. Skeletal remains emerged in the sands now and then—a dire warning. At high noon, head coverings did little to quell the cruel sun, their canteens almost empty. Maybe he deserved all of this. After all, his mongoose-like salvaging and betting and haggling and philandering made him few friends.

Airfoil would come in really handy right now.

The ravine's narrowing walls provided little shade, only quick shadows in passing. Maybe the crumbling soil would be cooler on his soles. Climate met consternation, geography, and consequence. Beck grumbled to himself. Two meters down, they were technically farthest from the sun.

It would be hottest the next few hours, and he hoped they'd find water or a cooler place to camp. Nothing was seen alive out here during this part of the day. Wildlife sensed the worst was coming and had withdrawn into hiding. Never had he thought of hard, impenetrable cracked desert ground as body armor.

Looking up ahead, Y led the way northeast through the dry channel with his poking stick. The ravine provided a strange sense of protection from drone sightings overhead, but everyone kept their eyes peeled for them. Then the consistency of the ravine changed, like they'd entered a new habitat, a de-evolution where the ground became darker as if sprayed with ink. Streams of poison runoff dribbled down the sides; still they trudged forward. Sludge pools collected in cracks and gullies, and the crew managed to step and jump without a slip. Sometimes Y's boots would get caked with gunk.

"The only liquid surviving out here, fantastic!" he would cry as he kicked and scraped his boots against banked rocks, silt, and soot, successfully avoiding the contaminated drizzle with precision and luck.

"I'm impressed," X would say every time Y managed to stay vertical.

"I'm annoyed," he'd respond. Sun Bin managed to keep up, his thin sandals caked with muck, his scythed staff both anchor and crutch.

Beck turned back to Mel bringing up the back of their crew as Simple Eye floated nearby, scouting for intruders and distractions. Still, an uneasiness welled.

"We still aiming for District Forty-Four, Simple Eye?" Mel asked to the drone's beeping confirmations.

Beck shook his head. The annoyingly playful thing had been helpful, but he'd never asked why it accompanied Mel. Where it came from. "How do you understand it?"

"More intuition than others?"

He wanted to trust her. She was at once bald, hard-nosed, and lovely, with conviction in her deliberate words and comfortable silence. Soft creases around her youthful eyes carried both kindness and mistrust, like that of a loving but wounded animal. A contradiction, like a dull blade. But something nagged at him, did not feel right. "I don't care what most *people* have to say," he said. "As long as we're going the right direction."

Simple Eye beeped and swirled its antennae with playful acknowledgment.

"Something tells me it just said, 'I told you so,'" Beck said, imagining the drone rotting in a dump somewhere as crazed Loners plucked its broken and unnecessary parts.

"Your intuition is better than you thought," Mel said, smiling under the head cloth wrapped around her head like a beehive.

"Don't fall too far behind," Beck warned as Mel's pace put her ten meters behind them. "Best we're close if we happen upon another drone scout fly-by."

"The signal on the nav is clearing up," Mel called up.

"Must be the distance from the iron ore!" X called back.

Beck stopped, concern meeting suspicion. "So who is guiding us, the drone or the nav?"

"Whichever one gets us out of the sun," Sun Bin said, laboring. "We need to keep moving."

"Hold up," Beck said, turning back to Mel. "You didn't answer the question."

"Simple Eye helps us navigate around threats and can ensure we're going the right direction," Mel said evenly, "based on what we determine off the nav."

"We?" Beck asked sarcastically. "I'm not so sure *we're* going the right direction!"

"Don't be threatened," Mel said, patting his back and walking past him, leaving Beck in awe. "You're still the man."

X snickered. "You like her. Admit it."

"Like her? I can barely tolerate her."

"Hurry up, slowpoke!" Mel called back as she caught up to Y in the front. "Or we'll roast out here!"

Beck shook his head as he followed through the devil sun. Minutes became an hour, the ravine's barren dryness returned as if death stalked them. His temples pulsed. X and Y plodded along as Sun Bin took a rationed canteen swig, while Mel took up the back again, followed closely by the parched drone, whose normally animated antennae drooped and its single eye stared as if glum and intoxicated, withering him further.

Deeper into the ravine, they saw evidence of running water. Deep ridges carved the walls like thick pipes.

"Water flows," Sun Bin said. "Droughts are temporary. Where water is, life is."

"Where water was and life isn't," Beck corrected, grazing the hard brittle walls, rubbing fine dust off his fingers. The sun's arced angle provided the first protective ridges as he sat on a slanted rock in partial shade. "But a tad cooler."

The kids found shade in which to sit.

"How you doing?" Mel asked as she gave out broken rations. The kids greedily gobbled them down.

"How far?" Beck asked. "Damn desert looks the same the more I travel it."

"Close," Mel said. "A temporary rebel camp; it's a large heat map on the nav."

No way would a rebel camp be out here in the middle of nowhere. They'd be too exposed. "Minutes by walk or speed pod?"

Mel checked her nav. "A few minutes north. We can hitch a ride to headquarters from there, I'm sure."

"How do you know?" X asked, her mouth full of rations.

Mel turned to her. "Know what?"

"Know it's a rebel camp?" X asked, swallowing the last. "Authority camps are spread out over the districts too. It's how they keep the rebel camps from sprouting up."

Beck listened in earnest.

"Because the nav says so," Mel said, and Simple Eye bleeped. "It's a settlement with dozens of heat indicators and temporary structures and no large Authority cruisers. So it's got to be the rebels."

X shrugged as Beck squinted, questioning his own skepticism as the ruthless sun shone on Mel in blinding, angelic light. Rebel camps were rare out here, but perhaps she was right.

***

The camp appeared a quarter kilometer away. No walls or gates obstructed their view, dozens of colored tents and canopies sprawling over the desert patch in a carnival of sun-beaten color. From this distance, all appeared okay. No visible Authority pods and, thankfully, no troopers.

"I haven't heard about this camp," X said, tapping her palm nav as Beck eyeballed her. Rebels tended to hide, like secrets and shame, and hearing his own concern in X's voice worried him. Drone scouts were too common in the deserts. He questioned his intuition and slowed his walk forward, cautiously alert.

"As long as they can transport us to headquarters," Y said, pulling at the cord around his neck. "Carrying this thing around causes so much stress, I can barely take it."

"Sun Bin can't wait to bathe in calm," Sun Bin said, limping forward with his scythed staff.

As they drew closer, Beck's heart sunk. The ominous moat surrounding the camp became clearer and detailed: a dark, deep trench brimming with tar. Tumbleweeds and brush debris littered its perimeter, caught in its thick goo. The massive sludge spanned more than a dozen meters across to the camp—a still, silent ocean of death.

"Tar seeping up from the ground. That's a new one," Beck said, inspecting the moat. A dark bubble popped to the surface, gurgling gas.

"The way of Earth," said Sun Bin. "Humankind destroys. Earth exhales, too, its own destructive properties."

Beck shook his words off as nonsensical.

"You think the rebels use the moat as defense against the Authority?" Y asked.

"If they're smart," Beck said, searching the skies. "What do the rebels have, some junk cruisers and old speed pods? Hiding behind a moat alone won't do much."

"Is it hot?" X asked.

"Shouldn't be," Y said. "The tar escaped the earth's crust, but it sits and traps things. Animals, people, anything venturing into it. Their baths turn into tombs."

Sun Bin gazed down into the trench pit as if getting lost in it. "Not my kind of bath."

Straightening to his full height, Beck whistled. "Hey, boys!" he yelled at two nondescript guards strolling casually between tents across the way. As the Authority officers turned to the group, Beck's eyes opened wide, and a pair of black armored troopers appeared behind them. He grimaced, instinctively putting his hand on the gun at his hip. "Not what we'd hoped for."

A pack of Authority helicopters suddenly approached overhead behind them with angry roars. A trooper across the bank called into a transmitter, immediately joined by a half dozen Authority officers, undeniable in their tan fatigues.

Sun Bin appeared dead calm. "An Authority camp."

"I see that," Beck said, glaring as the two choppers touched ground, their propellers sending cyclone gusts into whirling dust devils. How'd they gotten this wrong? Being cuffed would churn his stomach.

"This was not a good plan." Y frowned, his voice shaking over the choppers' propellers.

Fueled by adrenaline, Beck's heart seemed to beat out of his chest. He should have known better than to allow Mel to lead. As several armed black helmets charged them, there was nowhere to run. "Looks like your nav led us wrong," Beck said, glaring at the drone. If only incredulousness could kill. "Or was it this thing?"

Simple Eye hovered silently without a blink, and he kicked himself for having trusted anyone. Being pulled back into the Authority's hand could kill the daughter he was trying to save, a product of a soured relationship gone worse. After another night of him boozing at one of the remaining cantinas (since shut down by plundering Authority troops), the mother had disappeared from his ranch in District Forty-Two.

He had not known she was pregnant. Dericka James, his daughter had supposedly been named. His middle name. (It was odd he'd be honored in that way but omitted from her life.) He'd learned all this mere weeks ago: news of the mother's death, along with the revelation providing medicine the rebels desperately needed could save his daughter's life.

"General Speer has ordered your arrests," an Authority trooper said through his bucket helmet.

"I'm sorry," Mel said, sober and detached as the drone slowly turned its antennae down. "I had orders. I had no choice."

Sun Bin glowered in disappointment, and Beck bit his tongue, tasting a gritty mixture of salt and blood as he inhaled the desert dust. He scowled as Mel's faraway look of sadness swept over her face before it disappeared, leaving a blank stare. Swallowed up in shame. And he didn't care.

"I regret it had to be this way," Mel said, wincing.

His voice choked, disturbed by her distant poise. Had she been brainwashed? Or was she an unabashed heretic from the beginning? The children . . . how she had appeared to care for them. Y's mouth dropped agape, and tears streamed down X's dirty cheeks. Mel had abandoned them all.

"Regret is a casual mea culpa, a weak replacement of amends," Sun Bin said as he was cuffed. Armed Authority reinforcement troopers ran to them in lined succession with their clutched rifles and jointed truncheons on their hips, ensuring no resistance. "Accomplishes nothing."

Mel continued her wooden stare, as if she searched for something else to say, wishing she could read Beck's deafening silence over the thundering choppers.

"Was it you who gave us up or the drone?" Beck asked finally, his hands cuffed behind his back. He should have followed his instincts, learning long ago that trusting himself was the best and only policy. Her enigmatic demeanor and flawless skin had gotten the best of him, her hardened air now reminding him of an empty gold chalice. A lovely exterior with nothing redeemable inside.

"What about these kids!" Beck hollered, as he was whisked toward the choppers.

X cried with anger and fear. "You were our friend!"

"Our friend," Beck repeated to himself, brooding. He stopped abruptly and turned back to Mel, peering around the black helmet pushing at him. "My daughter's counting on the medicine! She'll die without it!"

"Forward," the black helmet ordered him, forcing him back around toward the choppers. "Go."

Mel's eyes opened wide, the hardened glaze washing off her face.

His back against the chopper, Beck shook off the black helmets for one last moment, unsure if his words could be heard at all. "Something happens to my daughter and I'll never forget! Never forget!"

SEVENTEEN

Mel was assailed by a swath of irritating sand, but she marched forward, caught in her own self-perpetuating obligation and doubt. Armed troopers escorted her and Simple Eye through the hodgepodge tent maze, a faded kaleidoscope of the overly sun-kissed. She was sick of the sun, of everything.

At first look, it appeared the isolated camp had been here a while. Tattered canvases, much like her well-being, were overexposed to life's harshest elements, ravaged by the sun, wind, and time. To the side, a makeshift graveyard was filled with stuffed body bags crudely lined up in irreverential rows, discarded like scrapped bones.

Orders had changed from the original plan. In regret, Leroi had instructed her to first bring in the children, Beck, and Sun Bin midway through her mission. Walk them right into Authority hands. No reasons, no explanation. Balking had not been tolerated by that cruel Authority agent who tempted her with the *one thing* motivating her. The apple from the snake. Seeing everyone hauled away in cuffs had made her heart sink. Even Beck.

Black helmets led the march through the faded purple, blue, yellow, and white-hued canopies littering the desert habitat, converging to the camp's ominous epicenter: a dark-gray tent with lazy, black flaps. Why hadn't they let her go? As Mel approached, she stayed focused on the three days left to find the hidden rebel camp or she'd lose her family. Forever this time.

She had to go.

The troopers opened the tent's loose flaps and ordered Mel inside. The sun-sourced cooling system startled, its whipping frigid air slapping her awake. Yes, this was the transitory base's control. Simple Eye hovered beside her, recovering from dutiful excitement. A lanky figure's back faced her as slivers of sun peeked through the flimsy shelter's wavy folds like shards, painful to the eye.

"How was your trip?"

She shivered. *That voice.* A deeper bass than a normal baritone, scratchy, with a sinister rasp. With absolutely no doubt, this was the man who had been responsible for her incarceration. He had taken away everything valuable: her family, her home, her freedom. *Colonel Kesselring.*

"Air cooling," Mel forced with a swallow. "Hope you're comfortable."

"One thing technology gets right," the aged colonel said, his back still to her. He carved a carrot, slowly peeling it with his knife and thumb as if savoring the process. "Air-conditioning. One of the few things not turned into a weapon. Not yet. Then, I hate the heat." He turned to her. "When they said you were coming, I didn't believe it."

Colonel Kesselring smiled wide with the large teeth that had given Mel vivid nightmares, fit in his mouth so full like it was stuffed with forks. Night after night she had awoken to his sneering horse mouth, haunting her dreams. His vengeful promises echoed, ricocheting in her head like her brain was full of marbles. Intent on making her suffer.

The colonel had been in the field too long, seen too much. The sun and the years had been cruel: his skin was weathered and loose, crinkled and tan, with the uneven pigment of sun-worn hide. The result of being passed over for too many critical promotions—stuck in the desert wastelands.

Simple Eye hovered near the cooling system, drawing the chill from thin piping with razor-thin air-blowing vents. The drone opened its door panels, cooling its innards, cooing in a light, high-pitched hum. An annoyed trooper swiped a wand, and the drone fell with a shriek, rolling to a stop on the tent's dirt floor.

"That was not necessary," Mel said, resisting the urge to strike back.

"You can rely on humanity to be the disruptor." He shook his finger like an old man chastising a child. "You, Custode, are a disruptor of gigantic proportions."

"I'm on a mission."

"You humor me," he snickered. He motioned to the troopers to exit as he swallowed a lump of carrot. "It's time you cooperated."

An officer marched into the tent and stood at attention, his chin up, chest out, eyes forward. "General Speer wants an update."

"Tell the pesky general," Kesselring said, his forehead furrowing like thick paper, "we have the elusive child rebels. I'm not interested in what he's got to say. Where is Martel? He's the one I report to." He muttered to Custode absently, "Have never been a fan of this Speer. A bit pompous if you ask me."

"You want me to present all of that, sir?" the officer asked.

"Obviously not," Kesselring said, raising his thick gray eyebrows in disbelief, their angry hairs pointing in all directions at once. He looked to the tent's top as if searching for strength. "Just the first part." He turned to Mel. "You can never depend on the help."

"Anything else, sir?" the officer asked.

Mel raised her own brows in interest.

"We need another ration delivery," Kesselring said. "He can do better than two-week-old crops." He held an unsatisfactory carrot, brown like silt, and scrunched his nose. "Oh," Kesselring added, "and we are preparing to enter the forty-fourth district." The officer nodded and left. "Still not a fan."

"Nice carnival tents," Mel said, bemused. "I'm glad to see you've gotten far in your career, Kesselring."

"Charming, Custode," he said, ignoring her barb with a canteen swig. "The Authority is cautious with its resources from the days we tried to corral the bees, feed the troops. These bright colors, faded now, were supposed to attract the little suckers so we could catch them, colonize them again. Another failure, adding to the rest."

"The bees never came," Mel said, the obvious conclusion underscoring the Authority's failures.

"An elusive bunch," he added. "Appears the tents worked better at attracting your rebel children. The little thieves."

She tried to shut them out of her head, where guilt hid. "I want my family. That was the deal. The original deal. What are you going—"

"They have something the grand regional governor and his marginally useful underling, that Speer, want. What *they* want. Not what I want."

She had three days left unless Leroi changed the terms again. "I have to find the rebel base."

The wind shook the tent's flaps as Kesselring took another careful bite of the half-orange carrot, as if concerned he would chip his horse teeth. Perhaps he was more careful with many things these days. "The Authority is notorious for its deal-making methods, aren't we?"

"I have a mission to complete. Did you hear me?" Mel repeated, wishing the decrepit colonel would choke. He was enjoying watching her squirm.

He squinted, ignoring her question. "So who are the two men? One is older than dirt. I thought I was old."

"One is an old farmer and the other," Mel said, somewhat absently, "some transporter." She wanted to get on with it.

"Transporter?" Kesselring sniggered. "I presume as long as there are populations, we will have those. Weaponry? Food?"

"Medication."

"Ahhhh," Kesselring said, smiling his uncomfortably large grin. "Drugs."

"Medication," she corrected. "Your troopers searched them. You should not have to ask me."

"Where is the data drive?" He became petulant, his eyes glassy as if recovering from a binge. She'd heard stories of him hankering like a peasant for absinthe, the invaluable treasure providing pleasure across district lands. "Their lives are in the balance."

"Maybe it got lost on the way here."

His knowing glare intensified like fire. Seven years it had been since she'd last seen him storming her neighbor's residence. Mel had made the mistake of standing up for the feeble villager clinging to his guns, unwittingly challenging the Authority's power as the rebels had done, making her a co-conspirator. Kesselring gleamed with anger and acrimony, yet appeared deadened, as if his fluids had been drained. Dry, folded skin stared back at her from the crypt, holding a grudge for being commissioned to desert-camp duty forever. She supposed she could not blame him for being surly.

Did he believe she was the young and simple-minded idealist he had incarcerated, or the equally strong-willed, anguished, and jaded woman she was now? He was the same boorish officer.

"You have a chance to redeem yourself. Where is the data file?"

She shrugged. "Send out your search squad."

His body stiffened, his rasp becoming more stringent. "You killed my men, Custode. You challenged the Authority and embarrassed me."

With a steadfast stare, she said, "Your men shot themselves in the dark. It's not my fault they were confused. Made you look bad. Anyway, I did my time for it."

"You did your time for the Authority," he said without a blink. "Not for me."

She said nothing as her heart beat faster. Patrols of the western districts were renowned for going rogue.

"You," he said louder, "were somehow recruited. I don't understand it. We all make bad choices. This time," he said, wagging his finger, "the Authority made a bad choice." Kesselring moved closer. "I run my own rules out here hunting for rebel packs trying to feed civilian populations with their organic crops free of disease, further undermining Authority goals as they populate like rabbits. Do you remember rabbits?"

"I'm too young to remember rabbits."

He gave her a death glare. "What would you say if I told you I was ordered to terminate you?"

Out of the corner of her eye, she saw an open field navigator sitting absently on the table. The advanced kind, illegal on the open market. She did a double take, it calling to her like a song. It was too valuable of a tool to be so noticeably within anyone's reach, especially hers. She immediately recognized it from her years at Alvarium, a guard having showcased it proudly like a crown. It had small-scale geo functions, inclusive of a tunnel reader, used to ensure no inmates successfully dug under the prison. Or any jail. Kesselring's sloppiness continually plagued him with lifelong desert-camp assignments. "Since you put me in captivity like an animal, I believe nothing you say."

A bright glint lit up his eyes. "Death was the order." In an instant, two black helmets marched in the tent and stood on either side of her, stiff like Roman guards. He turned away, as though something provided him questioning. Conflict. When he finally shook himself, he smiled, showing his big wide teeth, which were more blinding to Mel than the vivid colored tents could ever have possibly been. "So many orders. From so many kings. Not so many queens."

Her mouth gaped slightly. "You can't kill me."

"It's your outlook, Custode, that blinds you."

The troopers grabbed her under her arms in restraint. She struggled in vain, their grasps ironclad. At their feet, Simple Eye awoke from its sleep, its single eye half-open as if waking to morning light. The drone suddenly chirped and rolled upright, straightened its antennae, and ticked in small clicks in escalating succession.

Click . . . click . . . click, click . . .

The troopers turned to each other, bewildered.

Mel smiled at Kesselring. The drone continued to be useful.

"I don't believe it," the colonel said.

The drone bowed an antenna toward her as she stood collected and defiant. "Believe it."

Faster now. *Click, click, click.*

"It's a drone, not a bomb," Kesselring scoffed. "Blast it."

Both troopers released Mel and raised their guns at the flying sphere as it fluttered, a loose bird flying the coop. Blasts blew gaping holes through the tent, missing the drone as it bleeped and burped, successfully evading the troopers' gunfire. In the chaos, Mel snatched the palm tunnel reader, drawing it into her pocket. Metal sparked, fire ricocheting somewhere beyond.

"Not me, you fools!" Kesselring yelled. "The drone!"

Simple Eye hovered in between Kesselring and the troopers, out of his reach as he batted at the drone, arms flailing. Missing. Facing him, the troopers lowered their weapons as the colonel glared.

"No words," Kesselring said, disgusted. "Fooled by a machine."

Several responding officers rushed into the tent, and Kesselring waved them off. "It's fine. No more target practice in here." He collected himself as the drone floated next to Mel, whimpering a small tone of approval.

"Sir!"

"What?" Kesselring growled. A new officer appeared.

"The prisoners refuse to assist with the stolen data unless Custode is returned to them."

"Makes no sense. She betrayed them."

"Correct, sir."

"Perhaps we have more use for you than the Authority thought," Kesselring said, his eyes narrowed.

"I won't participate in any of your vulgar methods, Kesselring," Mel said, warning bells ringing in her head. "I'll do what I originally agreed to. I won't help you torture them. I won't."

Simple Eye beeped.

"You brought others into this conflict, Custode," Kesselring scowled, "and you don't have the luxury of hiding in your own cocoon anymore."

"What about my family?" she asked, her one last attempt to negotiate.

"What about them?" He frowned, acknowledging her look of wonder. "Oh, you don't know."

The world shifted instantly, and his words came as though they were spoken underwater.

"Ahhhh," Kesselring said with relish. "They showed you video, and—" He mocked her now, his finger tapping his horse teeth. "You thought . . . they were alive."

Her frame buckled.

"Using old video as a ploy," Kesselring continued, his voice marinated in sarcasm. "Now that is not right."

If Kesselring was right, she had made another poor choice. Could she have known? Did she always know?

"They died last year," Kesselring said with a nod of contrived sadness. "Sick. No doctors, no medicine. Sad, really. Highly uncivilized."

Mel's insides shook.

"They should have used a medicine transporter then," he continued. "One who made *good* decisions."

"You are cruel." Although her emotions welled up, she would show no pain.

"You're helping me this time," Kesselring said, so close she could feel his body heat emitting from under his collar, rising through its vent like smoke out of a chimney. The scent of carrots made her gag. "Or I will make sure your friends suffer the consequences of your actions. They will perish in the Moat of Moorack, more innocent people to die at your hands."

She caught her breath, her anger rising. If she couldn't save her family, she could save the crew and hurt the Authority. Now, on her timeline.

"After all this time, Custode, you still don't understand. Like I said, the Authority is notorious for its deal-making methods. And I'm the authority out here."

EIGHTEEN

Each of the four prisoners nested in the cramped pen like caged animals, claiming their own space. Thick wooden posts lined the square and dusty coop, strapped together with splintery barbed wire. Authority tents flanked it on all sides from about thirty meters, Kesselring's command quarters in eyeshot as several troopers guarded the outdoor jail. Hours had passed, like time somehow stood still. The flaming sun overhead had not moved at all, scorching Beck's world and spirit. Also, he'd heard too many times how Y was sure they'd die out here.

Was there some way out of here? Burrowing themselves under the wired posts would be impossible without adequate tools to dig through the hard dirt, which was packed like concrete. Picking the lock was out. He'd left those tools with *Airfoil,* probably salvaged by Loners by now. Stripping naked, and using their clothes to wrap the barbs and climb the three-meter fence *could* be possible, but he looked to the kids and soured. Then, the barbs were too long anyway.

He wrapped his hands around two of the coop's posts and poked his head through, snapping his fingers to get any trooper's attention. "Hey, can we get some water in here? And something to help with the sandflies?"

Sun Bin slapped a mammoth sandfly dead on his knee. He drained his tarnished canteen dry while sitting cross-legged, his grungy smock shielding his head from the searing sun. Across from him, X pouted as she kicked her boot's heel.

"How on Earth do you not sweat to death in all that armor?" Beck asked. "The cooling system can't be *that* great."

"Quiet," the black helmet ordered. "Get back from the post."

Backing up with his hands in surrender, Beck said, "Just asking."

"This sucks." Y wiped his perspiring face with his shirt. "This is how it's going to end for us."

"There are worse ways," Sun Bin said.

"Worse ways to die?" Beck asked. "Thanks for your sage wisdom. All I wanted was to make a little extra on the trip, that's it."

How could he help Dericka James when her medicine was burning up in the exposed travel packs? There they were, strewn in a littered pile outside a tent across the way, a sloppy pyramid in the dirt ignored by the officers absently marching past. The longer he stayed in this hellhole, the faster his new dream of knowing his undiscovered child slipped away.

"You did this!" Y cried, suddenly pounding Beck on the chest like an angry child. "You led us this way!"

The armed troopers shifted position, letting the disturbance play itself out.

"Whoa, whoa," Beck said, pulling Y's arms down. "Hey, kid. It's not my fault."

"It's not his fault," X said dryly.

"Listen to her. She's smart," Beck said hopefully to the traumatized boy.

"I'm not stupid!" Y yelled, his fists up against Beck's chest.

"No, you're not stupid," Beck said, meaning it. "Just frustrated like the rest of us."

"Look." X pointed.

Outside the pen, two black helmets and an officer escorted a prisoner—a thin, shirtless man shuffling his feet in chains—toward the camp's outer ridge, dust chasing him like ghosts.

Y wiped his eyes, his grubby palms smudging his cheeks. "I can't believe it. Lootjay."

"Lootjay?" Beck repeated.

"Yeah," X said as Lootjay disappeared behind the Authority tents. "We made his acquaintance when the Loners caught us. Total scoundrel."

"I like scoundrels," Beck said, proudly considering himself one. "They're uncompromising in their ability to bargain. And I like bargains."

"Unprincipled," Sun Bin said, narrowing his eyes. "And being in the company of scoundrels can be dangerous for the principled."

"Saving your hide sounds pretty principled to me," Beck shot back.

A group of black helmets approached the pen's gate, dutifully clutching their munitions. One used a gloved palm sensor to open the crude wooden gate.

"Follow us," a trooper said flatly through his guerilla helmet, moving to the side to allow several troopers past.

"Where are you taking us?" X asked, her arms crossed.

"Don't tell us you've got worse detention cells," Beck said, slapping a ravenous sandfly on his neck.

"Put these on," a trooper said, briskly extending thick, dark metal restraints, piping hot from the sun.

"Let us go!" Y yelled.

The troopers skillfully forced the sizzling cuffs on X and Y, their segmented armored gloved hands quick as a whip. The kids winced, restraining their cries in the face of the troopers' daunting intimidation. Burnished black armor gleamed through layers of dust and crud.

"We're not scared of you," X said as Y recoiled from the pain.

Beck moved quickly, avoiding a trooper's slap of the cuffs, and found his face up against a blaster's barrel. He dropped his head and gritted his teeth, eyeballing the blaster's barrel until it was lowered, wishing he was anywhere but here. Then he howled.

"Don't hurt him!" X cried.

"It's okay," Beck said, struggling to keep a straight face. "I won't give them the pleasure. Ahhhhhh."

A trooper approached Beck with his truncheon extended when Sun Bin sandwiched them. "Not necessary," Sun Bin said calmly. He raised his head up to the trooper, who was easily a quarter meter taller. "May Sun Bin politely request his staff? It assists the walk, these old bones."

"Give him a cane," the lead trooper said as Beck clenched his jaws and tried to slide the hot cuffs on his wrists to ease the burn.

"Sun Bin has his own," Sun Bin replied, motioning outside the gate. "It's in the company of our belongings in that tent."

"No scythe," said the trooper.

"Water?" Beck offered.

The trooper returned with a crooked wooden stick, and Sun Bin frowned. "Suppose this will have to do."

Beck's heart raced. Were they being marched to a firing squad, or perhaps an abandoned dark hole to rot? How he wanted to strangle Custode. "I guess that's a 'no' on the water."

The old man extended his wrists for the slap-on of cuffs. He was unresponsive to the blistering black metal, as if his mind somehow conquered the pain, shut it out.

"Come with us," a trooper finally said, waving his munition.

The crew was escorted out of the gate, a doomed family on the march. No one spoke as they dragged past the array of faded canvases draping the tents to the camp's edge. Then they were upon it. Thick, syrupy tar filled the moat, the dark trench circling them like a dying snake, its unseen insides digesting from within. Beck shivered at the thought of all the possible living things within its guts, disintegrating or dissolving or whatever was happening within the dark goo. He thought he heard whispers of silent screams.

Dozens of troopers and a handful of officers in pitch-black sunglasses collected to witness the spectacle. A light, aluminum platform hung over the moat as two desert drones floated nearby, their dual telescopic eyes recording for posterity.

"A plank and a sick observation deck," Beck said. The narrow, makeshift plank extended halfway over the moat, a half dozen meters out. A beaten Old World jeep held the other end of the plank crudely under its tire near the perimeter. Was that the scent of a long-burning death? This was not the first time these bastards had put on a show.

"We're going to die," Y said flatly, trembling.

"Not today," an officer within earshot said wryly. "You will witness payment for crimes against the Authority. The Moat of Moorack isn't kind. The sludge slowly absorbs its prey, becoming one with Earth."

Beck swayed unsteadily, trying to keep his wits as dehydration hit him hard. At his side, the kids frowned—whatever was happening was terrifying—while Sun Bin prayed silently, his cracked lips singing an unknown hymn.

"So this is entertainment in this place," Beck said, leaning over the side of the moat's wall to look at the bloodcurdling pit. The tar's surface was ten meters below—not a lot of time to think after a fateful fall. For the first time he wished he was back at Vulnus Outpost, enjoying

Whipsaw and Franks and the rest of the floating derelicts. Taking in frosty hops and barley.

The officer scoffed. "Here, wrongs are corrected. Slowly."

"Bring him!" an old, gangly officer called out. Beck picked out the colonel with the big teeth and gravelly snarl to be the man in charge as troopers pushed the thin man called Lootjay forward. Dangling chains swung and jerked with jangles and clanks. As Lootjay lumbered, Kesselring's leathery face embraced the blazing rays on his skin with unabashed glory, as if inhaling a religious experience that was soon interrupted.

"Get Custode out here," he ordered a field officer. "Or she starves."

Lootjay, beaten and bruised, bore a swollen black eye as his shoulder bled. He appeared to know his fate, his shoulders hunched as if the sky itself crushed him as he pushed back against his aggressors. He was not going easy.

"Lootjay Wormer, do you understand the charges the Authority has leveled against you?" the colonel asked.

The enslaved young man said nothing as he struggled in vain, surrounded by armored troops. His legs wobbled, about to give way. He staggered to the front and back, exhausted and disoriented, as the troopers nudged him toward the harrowing plank. Halting at the base of the narrow metal sheet, no wider than half a meter, Lootjay's eyes opened wide in horror at the sinister tar pit.

***

In her own loosely canvassed tent, Mel washed from a portable rinse hole, cleansing herself of grit and all the desert had to offer. Wishing the guilt, too, would wash away. The tiny plastic tub was a feat of engineering, with skinny pipes recycling gray water sequestered from exposure to desert heat in a self-cooling tin—a high-tech faucet's filtration system, a robotic arm spinning the square net at high-speed like a drill. She splashed the mild water over her bare dome and down her neck. It was tepid, a chill to the intense heat. The crew was penned up, and she had to face them. Why would they *want* to see her? Perhaps to strangle her to death? Cleansing herself provided a modicum of relief.

For the first time, she missed the nominal accommodations at Alvarium. The freedom of a trickling, full-body shower. She'd daydream under the light stream for a full two minutes before the prison guards hounded her to leave her, still wanting more. She let the water seep down her front and back. It was the cleanest she'd felt since before first laying foot on that boat, and the maddest she'd ever been at herself. Then, thinking of her family, the second maddest.

"Custode," the field officer said, disturbing her first minutes alone.

"So you don't knock?" she grumbled as she dried her face with an available rag, the dribbling stream of balmy droplets creeping down her sides evaporating. Her bare back faced the officer as an arid gust breathed through the tent flaps.

"Sorry, ma'am," he replied, chagrined. "You must witness the reparation."

The reparation? An execution? The Authority's way of punishing criminals in remote districts could only increase dissent among populations.

"Reparation to whom?"

"It's happening now."

"I'll talk to them when I'm ready," Mel said, facing him. "My way."

"Ma'am," the officer said, avoiding gazing at her bare top. "Colonel Kesselring orders you to witness how civilians are kept in line in this territory—or face no rations tonight, and starve like the prisoners."

The prisoners.

She didn't have to think a moment. "Don't call me ma'am. Now get out!" She threw her rag at him, fully exposing herself as he scurried away. "I'm not your servant," she said under her breath.

With a small beep, Simple Eye observed her with a curious and innocent blink. She turned her back.

"Do you mind?

***

"Once again," Kesselring sighed, "do you admit to your crimes?" He spat the remains of a tobacco stogie into the dirt as Lootjay mumbled. "What was that now?"

Lootjay stared ahead into the tarred moat, its foreboding stillness dissolving the graveyard within. Fleeting solace overcame him for whatever was going to happen, dissipating and keen. The swelling

Authority crowd congregated to see him perish. He recognized the cuffed kids immediately. The girl's frown and crinkled face, like she had tasted something sour. The clumsy, lanky boy who looked emaciated, like he'd choked on his own tongue.

"I admit to nothing but taking what was not the Authority's rightful property," Lootjay said louder, his throat coarse, dried to chalk.

"Ahhh," Kesselring said as his officers grumbled. Clearly Lootjay had said the wrong thing. "You believe you are in the right stealing rations. Unfortunate."

Hopefully whatever was happening would end soon. He was thirsty and hungry and tired, and for the first time, wished he was back in Authority captivity. His legs wobbled, his mind hazy. The world spun faster.

"Today, you will suffer the consequences of stealing from the Authority." Eyeing the group solemnly, Kesselring pulled out an unwrapped cigar, a delicacy that few had the means to acquire in these remote parts.

At first, Lootjay thought it might be food the colonel stuck in his mouth, his attention drawn to the cigar like a bull to an Old World matador. He was light-headed and woozy. "I didn't steal, I just took," Lootjay said, anxiously peering down into the pit. An enormous air bubble ruptured at the tar's surface, bursting like a liberated belch. Somehow, the perilous tar pit was alive. Was this his fate? Being devoured in a ghastly stomach of callous digestion, eventually existing only as the escaping gasses that popped?

"I sentence you—"

"What happened to court justice?" Lootjay yelled earnestly, shuddering as his frazzled imagination ran wild. "I thought the Authority protected the people! Food and supplies across districts. Instead our people starve as the Authority hordes!"

Drops of sweat falling off his brow, Kesselring motioned with his finger. "This is justice."

Troopers nearest the moat prodded Lootjay forward onto the plank with their poled truncheons. Horror lay mere meters below. He unwillingly shuffled a couple of steps forward, maintaining a precarious balance on the narrow sheet of aluminum as his skinny, chained legs shimmied, shaking like a drowning fish. Avoiding looking down over the sides, he raised his head higher, as if presiding over a jury rather than being sentenced.

"The world is not silent to humanity's injustices!"

"You stole food and lures," an officer said, followed by Kesselring's nod.

Lootjay's head hurt. An Authority officer had tried unsuccessfully to beat out a confession. Several strong blows to the head and torso had not worked, only reinforcing his belief he was in the right. Earth's resources were for all those in need. He'd had terrible hunger pangs. Why could no one understand? Inhaling merely one ration had provided such overwhelming relief, the chalky substance having descended his throat in satisfying chunks.

As the captive audience gawked at his unsteady awkwardness on the plank, he would have taken the rations again, no matter the consequences.

A light trickle of blood streamed down his shaking leg into a small crimson pool at his feet. The blood began to roll over the plank's side, slowly forming an expanding globule, clutching the plank as it grew.

"Confess!" a female officer with pursed lips called out. She leaned over the platform's rail. "Confess!"

Kesselring raised his eyebrows.

"Confess!" the officers chanted. "Confess! Confess!"

As the blood hanging from the bottom of the plank ballooned, the tar pit below quivered and moved, the thick goo eagerly anticipating the growing droplet's fall. Lootjay shivered in horror as concrete-like, pitch-black walls rose to form a deepening crater several meters across, cresting to ominous heights. Rumbling black waves emerged, boisterous wakes transforming the calm tar into a fierce river of churning sludge. The crater roared below, waiting to be fed. The moat was alive and hungry, hell from beneath.

***

Mel and Simple Eye appeared as the officers began chanting. The ferocious tar river had created agitated storm winds as the spectating officers held onto their hats and sunglasses, gawking in awe from the hovering platform. Both desert drones bobbed in the winds, their antennae spinning as they measured the escalating wind speeds.

Amid the furor, Kesselring's eyes bore into Mel's as the convicted criminal attempted to balance in the middle of the plank while raucous gusts swept from under and around him. She froze, immediately drawn to the scrawny young man facing death. Dutiful black helmets stood their ground as they faced the winds, munitions at attention, holding him to the plank.

Through the howling stood the crew. The children squinted into the wild, dusty flurry, the boy quivering, about to pass out. Mel's troubled gaze met X's, the girl's face quickly turning into a hateful grimace. At once, Mel wanted to disappear.

I'm sorry, she mouthed to Beck. She didn't blame him for hating her. He was no doubt furious, his daughter's life now uncertain. As Sun Bin grasped his cane and leaned into the heavy winds, the kids held onto Sun Bin and each other fervently, using their combined weight to firmly plant themselves on the ground.

Beck showed her his cuffs as he mouthed back, *Who cares?*

The monstrous tar crater curdled and bubbled, its liquified slime walls rising as its center sunk into a swirling whirlpool of muck and oil. Its contention gurgled in waves.

"They've awakened Earth," Sun Bin said into the dusty gusts.

"Not good!" Y yelled over the roaring wind cyclones. "Not good!"

"You're not dying today!" the officer hollered at the boy, fighting the unrelenting gales to stay on his feet.

Mel raced toward the crew, afraid any one of them could be whisked away any moment. Simple Eye raised its eye and reluctantly followed Mel closer to the moat's edge as it fought the winds, swimming in the air like a fishing lure bobber. Greeting troopers raised their weapons in unison. Simple Eye stopped at the presence of the desert drones, their antennae curling toward each other like they were old gossipers.

"Leave us alone!" X cried, shaking her flowing hair free of her mouth.

Guns facing her, Mel stood strong against the wild gales. Seeing the group arrested like criminals—she'd done this, and it had all been for nothing. She had allowed short-sightedness by believing in the Authority, the loathsome institution that had taken away her family, her freedom, and her life. Now the crew faced certain death. Sun Bin peered into the distance, as if he was prepared for the worst. X refused to look at her. Y appeared dismal and dejected.

Mel nudged her head between the stiff black helmets standing at arms between her and the crew, trying to get the group's attention from the moat's horror. "I know I was wrong!"

"You *know?*" Beck snapped back. "You betrayed us!"

"I'll fix it!" Mel yelled, ignoring the black helmets' pushing.

"Back away," one of the troopers said forcefully.

"Watch, Custode!" Kesselring yelled, the winds whipping through everyone like a typhoon. "See!"

The waves of tar raged below the plank as Lootjay struggled to hold his balance, his weak, chained legs swaying like intoxicated stilts. "Make it stop!" Lootjay cried.

"Give it what it wants!" a stringent officer yelled.

The violent moat-ocean surged and roared like the swelling muck below was calling. A shiver wormed up Mel's spine as the monstrous crater with no eyes or teeth anticipated devouring its emaciated prey.

"Reparations!" Kesselring shouted.

In a blink, Lootjay's legs finally gave way, and he tumbled off the plank's side, screaming as he succumbed to the turbulence. He plummeted straight into the middle of the roaring crater's gaping mouth, the swirling, sludgy whirlpool greedily swallowing him up in its ravaging abyss.

The officers all quieted, observing from the platform in awe.

Suddenly, like a switch flipped, the perilous crater dissipated into an eerie calm. Thick, violent waves of black goo settled back down to lifeless tar. The ferocious winds died, allowing everyone's beads of sweat to return, a quick reminder of the fierce sun. A hush fell over the group as the satisfied beast lay to sleep. Two giant bubbles popped up from below the moat's surface in a satisfying belch.

Mel could not believe what she had just witnessed—human sacrifice to the beastly moat, to forever haunt her.

"I've never seen anything like that before," Y said, peering into the canyon below, trembling.

"Earth has a way of feeding off of those who feed off it," Sun Bin said dryly. "Finding balance in an unbalanced world."

Kesselring's boots crunched on the desert floor. "You finally joined us." Simple Eye hovered at Mel's shoulder, its antennae twitching as Kesselring approached. "And witness what happens to those who defy the Authority out here." He motioned toward the drone. "Keep that thing away from me."

"I saw theatrical cruelty," Mel said. She breathed calmly, retaining her composure. She had to find a way to release the crew.

Simple Eye moved closer to her, as if it felt a looming threat in the stillness.

"Friends," Kesselring said as he marched past their lineup, inspecting their conditions and temperaments.

"We're not your friends," X spat. "The Authority is the enemy, and spies for the Authority are the enemy."

The crew's glum faces turned away from Mel, evasive and cagey, as distrustful of her as the troopers. It became clear Kesselring had orchestrated his own cruel retribution.

"Oh, so you're *not* all friends," Kesselring replied, feigning the revelation. "Fair enough." He reached the end of the lineup and sized up Beck closely. "Provide me what I need, and you can leave here and avoid the same horrible fate you just witnessed."

"Whatever you've got up your sleeves," Beck said, "at least let the kids go."

Kesselring spit through his large horse teeth as he leaned into Beck. "Give me the plans, and we won't start with the children walking that plank."

"What plans?" Beck asked, visibly needled, his chest bowing as he eyeballed Kesselring straight on. "You're mad. All you people, what you do here."

Kesselring smiled wider. "You'll go in first then, I promise. You," the colonel said, looking sharply at Y, who shuddered like a quaking bird. "No need to be digested slowly in that muck. Tell me where the download is, and you go home tonight."

Mel had to do something. "Colonel." She felt the crew's glares.

"You had your chance, Custode," Kesselring seethed. "It's a countdown to what you witnessed today."

"I know where the download is," she said, unsure of what she was doing, stalling for time to figure out an escape and in some way make him pay. Then, a glimmer of light sparked in his eye. Of hope, of belief. Or was she just imagining it herself? She kept pressing. "Kesselring, if it's worth something to you, you'll listen to me."

NINETEEN

"General, we found something."

Leroi rolled her comlink between her fingers as she stared into empty space, caught up between two worlds. Dazzling 3D schematics floated above the conference table in a kaleidoscope of color, frozen in time. The dozen officers focused on the perfect rotating projection, topographic and detailed, the room dark but for the terrain's glow and the sun's soft kiss. Leroi blinked, remembering where she was. Resisting being the target of General Speer's ire would require discipline and composure, necessary attributes of a good major general officer, as her attention was pulled to the vivid hologram's intricate variances of wood and soil and rock and treetops.

She tapped the comlink. It was on, but why had Custode not confirmed the children's capture? Perhaps she had not secured the download? Leroi followed Speer's intense interest monitoring the vibrant map, consoled that she owed him nothing. With Martel gone and a mutiny underway, they were hardly bound by customary Authority ranks anymore. Instead, they were connected only by Speer's sinister orders, her tied to a duty she wanted to escape.

Martel. His corpse hung displayed in the compound's core, strung up against a thick acacia tree's twisted trunk. Dead brambles were suspended over Martel's head in a canopy of thorns, looming in threat. This is what happened to those who committed treason. The entire Authority would soon know who was in charge.

"Bring it up," Speer said.

"Here," the control officer said, focusing the dynamic map on a clear strip of land between mountain and forest. The vantage point angled from the ground itself, like someone lifting their head from a nap. "This plot in District Forty-Four is normally hidden from drone flyovers because of where it's situated, congruent with the forest when the map is aimed from above like this." With a repositioned angle, situating the map ninety degrees, the plot of land disappeared. "But from here, without the stretch of forest concealing it. That's something."

A farm. Dozens of rows, vines, and trellises blended into forest vegetation, like they belonged. Something they should have found long ago.

"That is something," Speer agreed. "Go closer."

Leroi's heart raced. An invaluable clue had emerged.

The control officer repositioned the map again, but the controls resisted. She tried again.

"It won't let me, sir."

"That's them," Speer concluded decisively. "The rebel camp is there. Send out our new weapons, and let's see what we're dealing with."

Entering the control room, a lieutenant nervously shuffled toward Speer, wiping his sweaty palms on his fatigues. "Sir, we've received notice the rebel children have been captured. Prisoners of Colonel Kesselring are being held in the District Forty-Two."

"Kesselring." Speer coughed. "Of all people. The incompetence."

"The plans have not yet been retrieved, sir."

"What is Kesselring doing with them if not retrieving the drive? Tell me something that makes sense. Speak!"

"I didn't ask him," the lieutenant said plainly, and Leroi resisted a smirk. No way would the rebel children have walked into Authority camp with the download. That would have been too easy.

The general's face turned stern and cold. "You didn't ask him," he scoffed. "Is there anything else to report, Lieutenant?"

"Mel Custode delivered the children, sir."

General Speer raised his brow as Leroi's heart jumped. Custode *had* followed through, at least on one account.

"Well, I can see we've done one thing right today," Speer said, acknowledging the major general with a nod. "So this Custode is in Kesselring's custody as well?"

"Yes, sir. With two other men."

"Fine," Speer said, massaging his unruly mustache for a moment. "Terminate her."

"What!" Major General Leroi interjected. "We can't kill her. We may need her again." An unexplainable connection to Mel Custode and an explainable disdain for Speer's Authority tugged at her consciousness. Without the stolen download back in their possession, they might need Custode. Was this the right reason? "You're not going after the children too?"

Speer's command became more direct. Defiant. "Do you want to win this or not?"

"*Win?* General Speer," she said, standing as tall as her small frame would allow, "we can't terminate one asset after another. That won't beat the rebels. We're isolating ourselves. You're a general, not an overlord!" She was out of line, but she didn't care.

"Sit down, Major General."

"I will not!" It would indeed be smart for her to sit down. Her chest heaved.

"This installation is in no way a democracy. Sit. Down."

Leroi took her seat, her eyes piercing with anger. In a moment, she had destroyed any sense of alliance with Speer. One of the devoted officers turned his head away, shunning her. There was no doubt Speer was in control, the officers in compliance with any utterance.

But then, the other officers in the room did not carry her regrettable past—that last haunting assignment in remote District Twenty-Seven, in the Mines of Gurth. Her troops had infiltrated an expansive rebel hideout. Only a few rebel children had been tending to the home, half a dozen girls, the adults presumably out searching for resources or meds. With their capture, she would have had a significant prize: a bargaining chip with the rebels to mitigate camp raids. Quite the catch.

Leroi had led with confidence and empathy, setting herself apart from her peers, but inadvertently let the children escape. Those girls had been quick-witted, fooling her into believing they were grabbing dolls and pillows. Instead, the girls had duped her, laying a trail of dandelions (who knew they'd even existed anymore?) her troops could not ignore. While the girls slipped away, Leroi's entire trooper outfit followed the dandelion trails, hoping to discover a secret cluster of the rare flowers and the native, harvesting honeybees. After all, where the flowers were, the bees were, and honey couldn't be too far away. The troopers got lost in the elaborate mine tunnel network and died in the poisoned mine shafts as she waited outside. Silly leadership, having sent the entire outfit on the search rather than a scout.

A painful lesson learned.

The harrowed screams of suffocating officers and troopers preyed upon her sleep, awakening her with agonizing sweats. Obsessed, haunting voices often called for her, the last yells echoing through the mines ricocheting in her head. Family digital replays of her childhood had helped her out of bed at a time when nothing else could. Reflection on loss was more comforting than accepting blame for death. Speer had declared the failed operation a disaster. One fatal mistake and her career up the ranks had been put at risk. Two calamities and, perhaps, execution. Speer had known of Leroi's weakness with children, of her predilection to protect them as victims in an endless war, before assigning her to the mission. Simply, Speer had set her up.

Mutiny with the rogue general would not do her well. Impulse had given Speer ammunition. He had a plan of domination, and she was not part of the equation. She needed a way out.

"The rebels are finally in our midst," General Speer said. "I ordered termination of this Mel Custode, did I not?" he asked, his eyes wide and glazed, drunk with power.

The lieutenant shook like a leaf. Why so jittery?

"Yes, sir," the lieutenant said, his hands trembling as if the wrong words could cost him dearly.

"What is it, Lieutenant?"

"Sir—"

"Out with it!"

"Sir, the grand regional governor outside, pinned up," the lieutenant stuttered, "has got the officers concerned. And, and . . . the reporting officer who received Kesselring's transmission informed him Martel was pinned up like a hunting trophy—"

"A warning, not a trophy," Speer said in response to the lieutenant's apprehension. "What else?"

The lieutenant swallowed the lump in his throat. "Kesselring said you killed Martel and he refuses to report to you. He will take it to the District Council and have you put on trial for treason."

"Kesselring has always hated the Council," Speer said under his breath. "Thought they should be dissolved."

The lieutenant raised his head, braver now. "He said you always were an awful officer."

A pregnant pause hung like thick fog. While Leroi had challenged Speer, she had not denounced him as treasonous. Instantly, the pressure was off her.

"Dismissed," Speer said, his tone dangerously subdued, waving a dismissive hand at Leroi. "Carry forward with the termination. *The camp*. No need to have loose ends disrupt our progress."

One of the officers spoke up. "Sir, are you saying to terminate Kesselring's camp? Kill our own?"

The general paused again, the dozen plain-faced officers hanging on his words. The room's air had been sucked out. "We have to expand, not contract, our dominion. Those who hinder progress are the enemy."

Slow, soft nods indicated unanimous agreement.

Only Major General Leroi blinked, holding her composure and hoping Speer was too furious to notice her. Could she warn Custode? Maybe the criminal she recruited had facilitated progress another way, using the pursuit of the children to deceive the Authority, directing them away from the rebels. If Custode and her troop were terminated, it was conceivable the rebels would continue to elude the Authority anyway. What if Custode had let herself be a sacrificial lamb? Was it possible two children being caught would protect hundreds—or thousands—of others? She did not know this Kesselring, but assassinating an entire Authority camp was mutiny at the highest level. Loathing of Speer had spread to her revulsion of the entire Authority outfit. Its domination, its cruelty.

"We know where the rebels are," Speer declared, his eyes like daggers, daring anyone to challenge him. "Let's get to them before they get us."

At last, Leroi agreed with the general. She would get to them. She just had to figure out how.

***

Sipping from a chipped stein he had salvaged from bombed rubble, Kesselring waited to hear more. The syrupy malt sloshed under his tongue before he whisked it down his throat, his greatest evening pleasure and a rarity in the desert wilderness. Only one flask remained among the stingy allowances of dry-packaged food sticks and a few perishing carrots and eggplant stems.

Several weeks had passed since the last goods shipment, and he had blamed Martel. There had been no answer to any of his urgent communications. But the malty absinthe concoction swished with more pleasure than nights past. With Martel out of the way, he was going to finally dismantle General Speer. He savored the thought.

"Okay, Custode," he said impatiently. "Tell me."

"I think we—"

"I'm not interested in what you think." Kesselring sighed, anxious to reflect on his plan of attack that would finally achieve dominance within the Authority ranks. "Don't waste my time. Staff sergeant!"

"Colonel, wait," Mel said, apprehension coating her voice. Did her hands shake?

"Send Custode in the pen with the rest of them."

"Here." She hit a button on Kesselring's war table, and the 3D holographic sky-view map of the region appeared, hovering over the table like a digital cloud, waiting and ambivalent, at any time ready to disburse.

Kesselring held his hand up, halting the sergeant and black helmets' approach on Custode. Inching her fingers wide, Custode produced a sector on the map's perimeter. Colorful topographics widened and deepened, their shapes brown and blonde and green. Boulders and brush among the mountains were stenciled into the mathematical dimension, amplified as if through binoculars.

"This mountain boulder near the cave," Mel said. "Here."

Skeptical, he grimaced, inspecting the map. The oblong boulder at the cave entrance was unassuming, camouflaged by the surrounding desert gold. "You expect me to believe that, with all the fuss over the stolen download, your rebel friends left them under a rock in District Twenty-Seven?"

"Outside the Mines of Gurth, a former rebel hideout, abandoned for over a year now. You ever look there?"

"I don't want another one of your goose chases, Custode."

"Do you want the plans back or not?" she asked plainly.

Kesselring studied her closely. She was young and her hollowed eyes held pain. She was a young woman who had learned lessons the hard way. "Staff sergeant. Ready a search party to District Twenty-Seven first thing tomorrow. We will recover the stolen cloud data." The young staff sergeant departed in a split, troopers following. "What a coup it would be to have the rebel children *and* the plans back in Authority hands. Your contributions would be plentiful. A refreshing change, yes?"

"Then what?" Mel asked.

Kesselring didn't blink. He took a swig from the stein, letting the malt coat his cheeks, savoring the liquid heaven oozing through his being. With the children and the data chip in his possession, he'd then take out Speer. So much glory would commence in a flurry. The District Council would rejoice, too, he could sense it. His temperature rose with a thrill. "You mean, your friends? There's little help for them."

"Can I at least give them water?"

"Fine." If he did not recover the data chip, he would give Mel's friends to the Moat of Moorack, and the pit's reaction to multiple prisoners lingering over its growling vortex would be a sight to see. He would ensure Custode would follow their hurtling in one fell swoop. "For your sake, pray those plans are where you say they are."

***

The night moon had not yet peered out of the clouds, like it knew of the imminent lawlessness about to happen. Dusk had hit, the first sun lamps illuminating the camp's soullessness, their orange balls of fire emitting angry, warm glows. Fireflies in a barren desert's habitat.

"I couldn't take you in there unless you wanted to be zapped again," Mel whispered. "Not my fault."

The drone turned its head downward in a strong-willed pout. Mel had learned insolence was something companion drones were capable of.

"Come on, now," she said softly as they traveled toward the prison pen. "So what. He doesn't want you in his tent. You're too sensitive."

Mel marched past the masked troopers with resolve. They allowed her to slip past, their approval confirmed by the nod of a nearby senior officer. Simple Eye hovered by her side, its claw extended and suspending four canteens, their small straps clinging to it like hooks.

"Now," Mel whispered.

The drone drifted close to one of the trooper's helmets, and the trooper pushed his arm out to deflect it. In an instant, from its eye receptors Simple Eye snapped an electronic reading of the trooper's gloved palm, as if it was a true biometric scan.

"Move back," the black helmet said, and the drone fluttered with its canteens swinging back to Mel's side.

"Did you get it?" Mel asked softly. Simple Eye responded with a series of soft beeps. "At least we've done one thing right this trip." Simple Eye whirred.

They approached the pen where the crew huddled. Y was being counseled by Sun Bin in a teaching moment, and no one saw Mel press up against the barbed wire.

"Hey."

"How dare you!" X cried as she charged the wired posts.

"Whoa, whoa, kid," Beck said, pulling her back and eyeing the troopers as if expecting them to raise their weapons.

"I know," Mel whispered. "But I can get you out of here."

"We don't trust you!"

"Come on, X," Beck said, smirking at the troopers. "All's good over here," he quipped, turning back to X. "Don't make it worse."

"It can't get worse!" She looked woozy, her eyes rolling back as she stumbled.

"Her insulin level," Y said, moving to hold her. "She's falling apart without her smart meds." He squinted at Mel with hatred.

"I'll be okay in a minute," said X, slowing herself down. "Will rest until . . ."

Sun Bin shook, holding the crooked, flimsy cane firmly as he struggled to stay vertical. "We're getting noticed," he said, nodding to Kesselring looking upon them from a distance before turning back into his tent. "Don't let time get the best of you."

Beck hunched down to X. "We'll get you more."

"We're dying out here, Beck," X said, her words slurring. "Can't you see that?"

"X," Mel said, hoping to break through to the crew. They had to feel like trapped animals. "I can help." She motioned, and the drone swooped over the top of the fence with the canteens.

Beck said skeptically, "One of us won't make it another day out here. Even with water."

"Don't count me out yet," Sun Bin said defensively. "This old man has seen his share of adventures and hardship."

"Believe it, am not talking about you," Beck said.

"I don't deserve for you to trust me," Mel said, monitoring her surroundings for trackers. "I was caught up in something that's not your fault."

"Oh, it's not our fault," X said, her eyes hazy and her cheeks red with fury.

"The Authority knows you kids have the data drive or intelligence about their plans or something."

The kids shook their heads. Sun Bin said nothing.

"Data drive?" Beck asked in disbelief. "Are you telling me—"

"Keep your voice down!" X hushed, somehow finding the energy. "You're creating a scene."

"What—"

"Quiet, Beck," Y said.

Beck rolled his own eyes as X scrambled up to square off with Mel behind the chicken wire. Then he shook his head, disbelieving it possible Mel could do anything. "You still haven't answered why we should trust you."

"The Authority still doesn't have what it wants," X said flatly.

Was it necessary for her to give a lengthy explanation? "They killed my family," Mel said simply. "They used them as bait to get me to find the rebel headquarters in District Forty-Four. When I stumbled upon you, we all became the bait. I won't work for them anymore."

Beck glowered. "You worked for them?"

"Just once. No more."

"We were bait."

"Look," Mel said, wishing her soft voice would get through to them. "I help you out of here, and you never have to see me again. Beck, you said yourself you all won't make it another day out here. I'll come grab you at midnight."

Everyone turned to Sun Bin. "Sun Bin is not weak."

"We don't have timepieces," Y said. "They took all our stuff, remember?"

"Not all of it," Mel said softly, gazing toward his necklace as he quickly concealed it. "The moon."

"We can't tell time looking up at the moon," Beck said. "We look like space farmers?"

"Sun Bin can," Sun Bin said. "Used the moon as a farmer for decades. It does more than control the tides."

"No way can you tell time by the moon," Beck said. "Ridiculous."

"It's true," Y said. "I've read farmers use the new moon and first quarter phases to determine planting and herding. Even times of the year animals bleed less when you kill them."

"You can't be serious," Beck said.

X turned to him, her eyes glassy. "You don't believe in anything but your own nonsense, do you? Outrunning Authority pods, evading the law. You haven't been so handy getting us out of this mess."

"How did I become the bad guy?" Beck asked, his eyes dancing across the troopers, who had shuffled a little closer. Lowering his voice, Beck turned to the kids. "You have stolen Authority intelligence, and you're giving *me* a hard time?"

"What's your plan?" Y asked Mel, ignoring Beck.

"I've bought us some time."

"Us?" Beck growled. "There's no us. This is an escape. That's it."

"There's not a lot of time," Y said, the girl leaning against him.

"That's it," X repeated, "and then we go our separate ways." Stubborn and principled, she was resilient and unforgiving.

Mel inspected each of them. While spirited, they were parched, exhausted, disheveled and grungy with soot, dust, and dirt layers. Familiar guilt churned her stomach again.

"Be ready at the high moon." She prepared to leave, Simple Eye in tow.

"Hey," Beck said, halting her exit. "You can't go back to their side again."

She agreed this was the point of no return. What had started as a mission from Major General Leroi had been flipped on its head, and the Authority was not known for its forgiveness.

"High moon."

***

An hour later, as Sun Bin sat cross-legged and meditated, X gazed up at the blurred moon and hoped the escape plan was a good idea.

" Is it time?" she asked, her question pulling Y's attention from a small desert spider he'd been poking with his finger. Jitters made him restless.

Her head already hazy, the sun-charged tangerine lights flickering like their bulbs were loose did not help matters. Dark, lonely clearings and pathways scattered between pockets of burnishing orange and dying fires. The desert night whispered as dozens of Authority troops and officers snoozed. This would prove to be her most daring escape yet, and she got chills as she peered up. An expansive sea of stars blanketed the sky between ashy patches of darkness, and the moon poked its head out from the black clouds. What if Mel abandoned them, left them here to rot?

"Is it time?" she asked again.

"Soon," Sun Bin said, inhaling the soft desert breeze like it was his last precious breath.

X scanned the hushed tents and temporary structures surrounding them. The lightly flapping, multicolored canvases all looked alike at night, and it was difficult to determine from what direction Mel would come.

"You sure about this?" Beck asked. "We've already been led into a trap once."

"A change in circumstance can lead to a change in perspective," Sun Bin said.

"Damn, you just won't stop saying things, will you?" Beck said, sitting up.

"Not until there's no reason to say them."

"I didn't mean it as a question."

"Shhhh, there she is," X whispered, feeling hope for the first time in days.

Y shuffled to his feet. "Where?"

"There," X pointed, her fuzzy vision clearing just enough to see something. "Between the pods."

Everyone peered into the night, searching for movement beyond the clearing between dark canopies into the stretches of burnished light. Sure enough, Mel crouched between two Authority pods, Simple Eye hovering obediently by her side. X smiled when she saw Mel wearing her overstuffed backpack. She indeed was going to help them escape after all.

"Good eye, kid," Beck said.

They watched on as Mel patted Simple Eye on its head and raced toward the prison pen.

"You all ready?" Mel whispered as Simple Eye emitted a scan signal on the gate lock. It opened with a soft clang, louder than anyone would have preferred.

"How'd you do that?" Beck asked, suspicious.

Mel stopped. "The drone is our friend." Everyone stared, X beaming in a groggy, queasy kind of way. "You wanna stay in the pen or get outta here?"

Y nodded as if that was good enough for him.

"Still mighty convenient, Custode," Beck said, leering at the hovering flying machine. "I'm not forgetting how we got caught in the first place."

"Caged like animals," Y said.

"Uncivilized prisons use uncivilized methods," Sun Bin said.

"Finally something the old man said I agree with," Beck cracked. "Tell us this isn't another trap."

"We've got to go," Mel pled, holding open the fence door.

"Where are we going?" X whispered. She started to stumble but pushed forward. If they were getting out of here, she wanted to stay out.

"Let's get you home," Mel said. "But one quick thing." She motioned across the way.

There they were—their dumped supply packs, carelessly heaped at the foot of a blackened tent in a dark mound of shadow. The smart insulin pills, disregarded packs stuffed with the medicine bags. She was not leaving without them.

"You're thinking what I'm thinking," Beck said, a wry grin tilting up the corner of his mouth.

Mel nodded. "We grab the meds first."

TWENTY

At the thought of recapture, Beck's blood boiled. Thrusting any black helmet over the moat's bluff into the glutinous pit would be a joyful pleasure, the most exuberant he could ever be around the sludge stew. With his med packs slung over his shoulder, he searched. The coast was clear. No ordinary exit this time. They could not afford to set off alarms.

The camp was eerily quiet. The sky cleared into a vast blanket of open sky. There was moonlight to see where they were going, but more light to be exposed themselves.

Sun Bin hobbled toward the parked speed pods, his cane poking and dragging across the desert floor as the drone led the way.

A blind man led by a dumb drone.

Why had the cosmos picked on him? Was it a poor draw like in cards and you just managed the circumstances you'd been dealt? Whatever higher power there was or wasn't (he'd never invested his true feelings in either), he could really use some fortune now.

Then it hit him: getting their hands back on the medicine packs—and his blaster on the storage tent's floor—was indeed fortune. No god or deity had helped him. He was managing his own fate out of this place.

The crew huddled, desert dust crusted on their skin like paste. Except for Mel, who glistened as clean as a shined medallion.

There was no god. There couldn't be.

He hated this plan from the beginning. Escaping the camp undetected was an absolute impossibility. Canvassed tents provided no cover from sound of the crew's endless bickering. There were too many of them, extending into a train of escapees. Worse, the old man was excruciatingly slow, a rising liability. And Beck couldn't bear slowing down further to respond to Sun Bin's philosophies and platitudes. Getting mixed up with this crew meant he'd forever be on the run.

"Is this really gonna work?" Y whispered as he stuffed the last of the loose medicine bags back into the pack. X quickly palmed a smart pill into her mouth, swallowing her dose dry.

"It has to work," Mel said softly as X strapped on her pack. "Simple Eye can unlock the pod and we can be hours ahead of them before anyone realizes we're gone. He jammed the other pods' ignitions."

"I'm glad *he* has got it figured out," Beck said. "Everyone ready?"

They nodded.

"Let's go."

Rushed and hushed, they raced to the Authority speed pod. The kids jumped in on either side as Sun Bin fell into the back seat like a lumpy sack. The front doors opened, and Mel slid into the pilot's seat, surprising Beck.

"You're kidding me," Beck said.

"No time to argue," Mel said. "Get in."

Beck ran around the pod to the passenger side, cursing under his breath. "Keeps getting better."

The doors clicked softly shut, and Simple Eye plugged into the digital dashboard deck. A ten-point code sequence was necessary to start the Authority speed pod's ignition, and Beck winced as the dash code numbers and symbols on the light-up display bleeped and spun in a blur.

"It's tight back here," Y complained, Sun Bin squashed against him.

"Bigger not always better," Mel said, and Beck frowned and turned to the back.

"X, can you see if there's anything we can use in any of the side panels?"

"No panels," she said, searching around. "Nothing back here."

"You mean the Authority didn't outfit our getaway pod with food or sunscreen?" Beck asked with a huff. Mel ignored him, no surprise, trying to tune him out. This was the best plan?

The display sequence spun. One number hit, nine indicators to go.

"That's a lot of combinations," Y mumbled, and Beck regretfully had to agree. They could be here a while. He thought back to a six-point sequence he'd tried to figure out when trapped in a salt mine once. It had taken three days to get the conveyer capsule to eject a hundred meters up. He'd almost gone mad. A ten-point code was exponentially worse.

And this was numbers *and* symbols. Who knew how many? His eyes narrowed at the drone.

"I'm on the record," said Beck. "Running away in an Authority speed pod that doesn't start ain't my idea of a smart getaway."

"Know your direction and you're not getting away," Sun Bin said. "You're leading the chase."

The old man wouldn't quit.

Outside the speed pod, it was deserted. Kesselring's entire outfit rested in their tents, their regulated-temp cocoons. Burnishing sun lamps glowed in small circles of flickering orange dust, and a small, dying fire rested under smoldering firewood, crackling its last faint pops.

Then Y said, "We've got company."

An officer aimlessly waffled across the clearing with unwieldy, irregular steps like a drunken pirate. Dressed only in Authority-issued white shorts and an undershirt, the officer mumbled to himself as he shuffled, and his heavy boots kicked up billows.

"He's sleepwalking," Mel said.

"Even the sleeping don't sleep in this place," Beck said, the hairs on his skin rising. "But the moat, that thing wakes up."

"Wait," X said softly. "I found something."

"Nobody move," Beck said in a hushed voice. The heedless officer moved toward them in his bumbling stupor. "He may see our shadows move through the blacked-out windows."

"I thought—" Y started to say.

"*Shhhhhhhhhhhh.*" Everyone shushed in unison.

X carefully shut the discovered compartment door, but it popped back ajar, its metallic contents falling into her lap. Beck's heart raced as several tools bumbled down her legs, clanging against each other in excruciating slow motion, finally tumbling to the floor with clanks and bumpy thuds. He froze, his eyes following the officer. His temples pulsed like rockets.

The officer stopped in his tracks, peering around to both sides, then behind him. His attention was drawn to the speed pod, hovering above ground cold and still. He stared at it for a moment. With something perhaps registering, he awkwardly cocked his head. No one in the speed pod moved as the combination display continued to turn. A whistle dangled from the officer's chain necklace, clumsily swinging around like it, too, was intoxicated. From the corner of his eye, Beck saw a combination symbol hit. Eight to go. This was definitely Beck's worst attempt at a breakaway ever.

"He heard us," X whispered.

"He heard you," Y corrected.

"Oh, it's so my fault. I've barely got my wits back," X retorted angrily. "We can happily return to when this started."

"I'm really glad you're starting to feel better," Y shot back sarcastically.

"Quiet, kids," Mel whispered.

"Don't make us come back there," Mel and Beck said softly in coincidental timing, recollecting themselves as the officer careened their way.

Another combination symbol hit with a light *ting*. Seven to go.

The officer straggled toward the speed pod, if only to hold himself vertical. His was the awkward gait of an intoxicated brute, despite nary a bottle or any visible contraband.

"No way can we just wait to be captured again," Beck said, about to pop open the side door and retrieve the munition on his belt. That whistle wasn't going to be blown if he had any say about it. "Before he calls the alarms."

Mel held his arm. "Wait."

He focused on her. "I'm not dying here."

"Wait," Mel insisted, hushing him.

Two numbers hit on the combination display, Simple Eye staying duly focused on starting the ignition. Floating in front of the deck, its claw attached to the main sequencer churned to the left and right with buzzes and soft clicks.

"Hurry," X whispered.

Outside, the officer peered about as he approached the vehicle. He stared into the black space of the pod's windows, seeing nothing. X studied him from the other side of the dark glass, mere centimeters from his face. From the officer's relaxed expression, it was clear to everyone he was relieving himself on the side of the speed pod. X made a disgusted face.

"Nobody move," Mel whispered softly.

The drone continued its pursuit of the combination, and another symbol hit.

Y tried not to laugh as the officer muttered unintelligibly, perhaps relieving on himself. Beck eyeballed Y and shook his head slowly in a warning.

The officer finished his deed and shook it off before stumbling away, kicking and dragging his boots.

"I can't believe he didn't see us," Mel said, and another symbol hit the display.

"Obliviously," Beck observed, taking his hand off his blaster as the officer disappeared behind a dark tent. Maybe there was a god after all.

"Some are unaware of opportunity or peril," Sun Bin said.

"You're not kidding," said Beck. "Not a lotta time before another one of those clowns comes upon us."

Another combination symbol hit. Four more to go. Simple Eye blinked at Beck, who was not impressed.

"When you gotta go, I guess," Y said as another number appeared on the front deck. Simple Eye kept drilling its claw to the left and right, working the ignition sequencing as another number hit.

"This thing may actually work," Beck said.

"You've never liked Simple Eye," X said. "He knows it too."

"What are you talking about?" Beck asked over his shoulder.

"He knows you don't like him."

The drone blinked innocently at Beck as his claw worked another combination. Only two left.

"If *he*," Beck said, paining himself, "gets us outta here, I'll forever be grateful."

"He's coming back!" Y exclaimed in a hushed tone, and everyone turned to see the underwear-dressed officer bumbling his way back to the speed pod, this time holding an axe, which he cradled like a delicate baby.

Beck's eyes bulged as he pointed his finger in Mel's face. "Enough of your way. *No* way am I going back into that pen or getting hauled into that death pit."

"We're almost out of here," Mel said unconvincingly as another symbol stuck on the ignition's sequence panel. One left. She punched a switch, locking the speed pod's doors. *Click.* "We're not ruining this now."

"You're locking me in?" Beck asked, exasperated. How had he let this happen? "What am I, a child?"

Then Sun Bin closed his eyes and took a breath like the world was washing over him. "Kids," he said with stoic resolve.

"He's coming!" Y whispered.

"Kids, he's talking to you," Beck said, uninterested in what the old man had to say. Meanwhile, he adjusted his blaster as the officer stumbled toward them, raising the axe like a flag.

"Kids is all of you," Sun Bin said, somber and contemplative, like a grandfather on his deathbed. "You must make it to rebel camp. The resistance needs you to follow through on what I didn't do years ago."

"What are *you* talking about?" Mel asked, as the last symbol almost hit on the ignition's combination display but kept on spinning, now slower.

"Ask my Sangeeosay," Sun Bin said.

"Let me out," Beck said, unable to wait anymore while the indicator struggled to spin. Dying here tonight was not happening. Not any how, not any way.

"You know Sangeeosay?" X asked.

"Let Beck out!" Y whispered, quivering.

"Open the door!" Beck yelled as the axe-wielding officer charged them, mere meters from the pod.

Mel glared at Sun Bin. "You're not going out there either."

"If this junk doesn't start, you've gotta let us both out if we're to have a chance," Beck said, done with this routine. "Open the doors!"

"We're in this together," Mel said, straight-faced.

With a heavy breath, Sun Bin said, "Don't let me down." He lifted his head back and poked his staff onto the front button of Mel's side door, unlocking the doors with a whack. All the doors popped open like a bird spreading its wings.

"Sun Bin!" X called out.

Before Mel could secure the doors again, Sun Bin popped out the back hatch and slammed it shut in one smooth maneuver. With one last wave, he raised his cane and greeted the axe-wielding officer with a swift lash to the abdomen.

As Beck leaned out the pod and raised his blaster, the sage pierced him with determination, his eyes red and stormy—how Beck imagined an alien's eyes would look. It was like Sun Bin had been saving his energy for one last fight. "Leave now. Get the children home."

Beck paused in shock as Sun Bin took down the officer with two quick swipes of his cane.

"Go!" Sun Bin hollered, and in an instant, caustic officers and troopers were upon him.

"Crazy old man," Beck said as the sage fought with impressive skill. Beck fired two shots at the troopers before diving back into the speed pod, successfully taking them down.

"We can't go!" Mel yelled, as two fire blasts almost blew off the pod's top. "Give me your blaster!"

"You're not getting my blaster!"

Sun Bin swung his cane with quick spins, slamming blasters and Authority opponents to their knees. With a sudden blinding switch, luminous spotlights replaced the burnished orange glows, turning the officers and troopers into an intensely brilliant, colorless assembly of aggressive undead. He turned and spun and swiped, striking his foes with the agility of a young martial artist, avoiding fire shots with unpredictable twists, spirals, and strikes. Sun Bin lashed another trooper in the neck with his cane before a trooper's truncheon smacked him down.

The last symbol hit on the pod's display, finally unstuck, and the deck lit up as the ignition fired. A soft whir filled the cabin as the pod hummed to life, and the activated illuminating headlights fanned out toward the desert darkness.

"I can't believe it, the flying pile of metal isn't completely useless," Beck said, as Simple Eye leered back at him in displeasure.

Mel switched off the ignition, and the lights faded out as the power coughed dead.

"We can't leave without him," she said, crouching by her open door as fire shots whizzed by.

"We're going!" Beck yelled, punching back the ignition fire and the doors shut. He tried ringing through to her. "He wants us to go or we'll get thrown in that pit, all of us."

An alarm blared in the Authority camp, and an army of troopers descended upon Sun Bin at the ready.

"We have to get Sun Bin!" X cried as Sun Bin took a blast to the shoulder, throwing off his equilibrium. He swung his cane at an advancing officer and missed, then missed again, struggling to stay vertical.

"Let's save the kids, save my daughter, okay?"

With a solemn nod, Mel frowned as fire blasts tucked into the pod's back window like splattered bugs and ricocheted off its sides.

A surprise blast pierced through a blown section of their pod and hit Y's shoulder. The boy slumped in pain. "Owwwww, ow, ow, owwwwwww."

X tended to him, using his own shirt to stop the bleeding.

"Move!" Beck yelled, and he slapped his window down, firing at approaching troopers.

Blaster fire knocked Sun Bin down to one knee. He swung his cane erratically like he'd been blinded, missing his opponents as they circled him, encroaching like famished beasts.

"No!" X cried, as Sun Bin wielded one last swing before falling flat as his cane broke in half.

Mel gunned the accelerator, and they sped off into the desert night as Beck killed the lights. They'd use the terrain nav. After checking behind them again, he leaned forward to the pod's display schematics, ensuring no Authority pods had given chase.

"Looks like you did kill the charge of those other pods," he said in the uncomfortable silence.

Soon, the pod's cabin was as dark as it was quiet, filled only with the engine's hollow hum. Beck peered out over the dark desert void, caring to see nothing. Indeed, the old man had sacrificed himself. Precious moments had allowed them to escape.

Simple Eye plopped next to X in the second row and blinked hopefully, but she emoted nothing as Y sunk into X's lap, breathy and pale. The drone frowned.

"We'll hit District Forty-Four shortly," Beck said, studying the instrument panel, a soft light emitting from its intricate display. "If I'm reading this correctly . . ." he said, trailing off. This Authority model was outfitted with some pretty fancy tricks. Its elaborate sonar display provided an uncanny ability to fly at night. Neither exterior lights nor labor-vision (which required the participation of a human being) was necessary. The nav panel provided longitude and latitude specs, as well as indicators of other Authority pods in the region.

This was good. He'd see trouble before it saw him. Quite likely the Authority pods could easily find them on their navs too. Out here, far from any Authority installation past Kesselring's post, they could be good if they kept moving, but they didn't have much time. Eventually, they'd have to dump the pod unless they ended up near mountains where the signal faded. They were a good fifty kilometers out from their destination district, and the pod's battery was fully charged. He was newly optimistic.

"Looks like we may get there after all."

As the speed pod sped quietly over the desert floor, no one replied. Mel wouldn't look at him, and he understood.

TWENTY-ONE

"Colonel Kesselring's speed pods are in flight, General."

What could Kesselring possibly be doing in flight? At this late hour his pods should be sleeping and his camp as desolate and dead as the desert around it. "Get him for me now," Speer instructed the pilot.

"Also, sir," an ensign said, appearing beside the pilot at attention. "I have the decoder."

Speer turned to see a wiry young cadet, perspiring and pale-faced as if he'd never seen the sun. His skin gleamed with a white sheen, like a jellyfish reflecting light. "What is this?"

"A trained decoder, fresh out of prep," the ensign said, responding too quickly to Speer's ears.

Eyeing the decoder up and down, Speer was looking at a child. Reluctant and acquiescing, he was unable to understand the magnitude of his duty yet aware of his doomed circumstance should he fail, like a suffocating fish caught between nets. A youngster was incapable of the task at hand.

"What are you, twelve?" Speer asked. "I don't want a *human* decoder. I want a loyal, capable decoder machine that will work all hours until I have my codes."

The pilot stepped in. "I have the colonel, sir," the pilot said, punching Colonel Kesselring up as the ensign and decoder left in defeat.

Appearing scrappy and unhinged, Kesselring's garish face filled the control room's screen. Deep shadows found their way into the tired folds of his face as he stared back at Speer with brazen contempt.

"What do you want, Kesselring?" Speer asked, his chin raised.

"Why are Authority speed pods coming from the southwest toward my camp without authorization?" Kesselring countered. "You're up to something again."

"Do I need permission?" Speer sneered, throwing a knowing glare to the grinning pilot. Everyone knew he despised the colonel. It was as universally accepted as the casualties of war and the scarcity of spices. Besides, doing all the right things did not lead to assignments in key districts' outer rim.

"I'm asking why Authority pods are attacking my camp."

"Attacking?" Speer asked in a huff. "Why would I order Authority pods to attack your outpost? I have better things to do running this district."

"You're overstepping your bounds, General Speer."

"Why are any of your pods in flight in the first place, Colonel?" Speer asked. He'd seen the Global Senate do this, their questions bouncing back and forth like a ball zeroing in on its target. Supreme gamesmanship and posturing Speer often regretted as more time wasted. "You've circumvented protocols again, though readings show most of your pods have zero power charge. How is that?"

"Custode escaped, and we have recharged fuel cells at the ready." Kesselring sighed, fatigue washing over his face. "We have two pods in flight in pursuit of all four prisoners."

"Four?"

"Custode, a male companion—I think an assistant or something— and the children all escaped."

"Escaped," Speer repeated dryly. "Did you locate the stolen cloud files?"

"If I had the stolen files, I'd have alerted the higher ranks. Again, why am I being approached? I heard Martel is dead."

"Yes."

"I heard you killed him," Kesselring said. "This won't be good for you. I will ensure the Council court-martials you properly. This is not your dominion."

"You're probably right," Speer said, satisfied he had gotten under Kesselring's skin. Exactly what he had wanted, except he had miscalculated the colonel's ineptness in letting the elusive rebel children escape—*with* the stolen cloud files. Unforgivable.

An awkward silence canvassed the transmission.

Speer nodded to the pilot, and with a button punch, the screen went black. There was a shrinking window for Kesselring. No longer would he tolerate those who got in his way. "How long before arrival?"

"Less than an hour, sir. Daybreak."

TWENTY-TWO

It would not be long before General Speer's henchmen would appear and take her away, likely never to be heard from again. Authority officers and troopers had evolved into accomplices to Speer's mutinous power grab. If he was going to take over the district and the region, no doubt the continent was next.

Leroi's pristine bunker had been untouched. The small hair she had placed on the thumbprint identification for her computer remained, only visible with specific angled light—an indicator that her space had not yet been violated. Her personal belongings appeared to be in order. No food rations had been poached.

Stuffing her travel pack with compressed food stuffs and travel gear, she had an eerie hunch she was being watched. She determined there were no obvious camera feeds after she examined the walls, ceiling, and her miniature kitchenette.

Ill at ease, she sat on her bunk, the white sheets wrapped tight the way Authority officers are trained to make them. She rolled the comlink in her fingers. She could reach out to Custode again, warn her of the Authority troops this time. Find her and escape the district's dominion and Speer's hold on her. Ascending through the ranks had always been the goal, not elevating the rise of a crazed, power-hungry madman intent on destroying anyone in his way. She'd enforced the Authority's laws since her family had been killed in the war, imposing the laws of the land. This was not the Authority for which she had invested her life and avenged her family. Never had she had empathy for anyone running counter to Authority leadership.

"Custode, come in," Leroi said to a static reception. Again. "Custode, Mother here." The reception went in and out, static. *Was that a male voice?* It surely was not Custode.

She turned to the mini-boxed bot, its square head frozen still, a powerless piece of sleek furniture. Normally reserved and sedate until called upon with installed programmed orders, the suitable machine knew to respond to movement, a wave of her hand. She motioned her arm wide in front of it. Nothing.

"Em, four, three, six. Power on."

The servant machine stared into nothing, its dual-lenses as unresponsive as a dead wire, and she slid up the simple bed next to it for a closer look. M-436 was a hard-brained domestic companion with limited duties, known for devotion to its owners and incapable of self-derived thought like the soft-brained ones. With no ability to leave their homestead, limited-range domestics like the M-436 were the only machines allowed in officers' barracks in Martel's district. Unlike the progressive coastal districts, where mishaps were known to happen from time to time.

Curious, she unsnapped M-436's meager squared top, less than half a meter wide and long, and caught her breath. Something obstructed the little machine's lens, and she quickly reached for it. A transmitter camera feed had been installed, corrupting the limited ability of M-436 to do much of anything. Recording. She was being watched.

Speer.

Who could help her? Really, she had only one option. Being surveilled, she could not make the call here. First, she tried Custode again on the comlink as she stood up and snatched her prepared travel pack, not realizing she had left her Authority badge behind.

***

A ghostly hush followed Leroi through the open concourse toward the camp's transit hangar, the aerodrome's nucleus. Typical morning mist hung in the air, thin and dewy, awaiting the sun's promising arrival to burn it off. She kept her ears open for the comlink's next crackle. If Custode was not alive, someone had her comlink.

Head down, she wished for the light fog to provide more cover. It was quiet, nary a soul about. Still, Leroi felt like all eyes were on her. Ahead stood a towering, armed AI sentry guard standing post at the silvery aerodrome's entrance, shifting its large metallic frame as she approached. Its beady red eyes studied her, a laser on her brain. It was an intense examination, machine to human. She stopped and forced herself to remain unruffled as she tried to ignore its attempts to see through her.

Frantic, she rummaged through her travel pack, her heart racing. Did she really forget her identity credential? She could imagine it there in her barracks, abandoned, calling to her. The sentry's cold presence felt heavy, hanging over her like it could crush her in an instant. She took a breath and held out her forearm in preparation for the scan, the secondary authentication process, its updates often amiss. She didn't blink as she waited, trying to halt suspicion and calm herself down. It wasn't working.

Programmed to detect rising heart rates and impropriety, the sentry moved toward her slowly, creeping like a prowler, light buzzing sounds accompanying each deliberate move of its well-lubricated limbs. Its wiry brain read a diagram blueprint as it sorted through a mountain of data.

Breathe.

The comlink in her pocket crackled, the startling, staticky, unintelligible words coming through in bits and fragments, bringing unwanted attention to her as the sentry's mechanical head repositioned like it was raising its eyebrows. She grinned in embarrassment as she clicked the transmitter off, and the sentry paused before continuing her register.

"Your business?" the AI sentry asked, its digitized, impersonal voice smooth and direct.

"Maintenance," she said without thinking.

The sentry aimed its piercing red eyes as if to intimidate the truth out of her, the crime. Sensory readings commenced, and the sentry's gargantuan buzzing legs shifted to the side. She nodded as she ambled in relief, grateful her credentials somehow had not yet been revoked. The whole recalibration process, or cleaning of Authority detractors, removed humanity in whole. All unpleasant, she had heard.

After entering the mammoth hangar, she picked up her stride and managed to get out of the sentry's sight. In the corner she saw them: several sleek jets, their pointed noses green with white tips. Martel's experimental longer-range fliers—untraceable, low-flying, high-speed jets powered by compressed hydrogen, the only known plentiful gas resource left on the planet.

Clicking the comlink back on, she whispered as her boots scuffled across the vast varnished cement floor. "Custode!" The soft echo bounced around the aerodrome, so loud it was like she screamed. "Custode, are you there?"

Static erupted from the transmitter, undecipherable and louder than she preferred. The gigantic sentry faced her from the entrance, monitoring her activity. Its beast of a head was one of the soft-brained machines she hated, doing what people often do: reaching their own conclusions.

"Hurry up," Leroi said under her breath, and in a quick moment her visitor arrived. Once the sentry guard read his credentials, Officer Tippler sauntered across the hangar floor, grinning widely.

"Major General," Tippler said, inspecting her up and down as he got uncomfortably close. "Have you finally come to your senses? Sneaking by the sentry. Of all places though."

Leroi appealed to him, pushing her hand against his chest. "Tippler, enough of that. You know we are never going to happen."

He frowned. "I would have preferred to finish my rations—what little there is—if I knew it wasn't urgent."

"It's urgent, Tippler." The sentry faced away from them, on guard. "I need your help."

"That display with the general. It was like watching a speed pod crash."

Tippler gave her a look that was something between trouble and innocence, like a boy with a ball. He'd grown into the cockiness, his handsome looks. Rugged, lovely somehow. With the severe drought of fertility, though, procreation wasn't happening around here anytime soon.

"Help me," Leroi said, her pleading brown eyes trying to do the convincing. She needed to do more. No time to play. "He's a madman, Tippler. You saw what he did to Martel. Any of us could be next, put up on sick display."

Tippler paused, most likely considering the consequences of turning on Speer. "Why would I help you?"

***

Bombs, blasts, and combusting fires erupted in Kesselring's camp, smoke plumes rising into the morning sky. The sun burnt through the scowling clouds as the Moat of Moorack awakened, curdling into dark waves and crests. Authority speed pods had overwhelmed the camp, and the blast fire calmed down as the last of Kesselring's troopers and officers were killed.

Under a ravaged tent, Colonel Kesselring had scrambled inside a covered speed pod, the colored tarps camouflaging him within the carnage. The speed pod needed charge before its ignition would start. He'd been put in a situation of such unacceptable mutiny and overreach, fighting for his own life to escape Authority forces. The one thing he did not blame was Speer's obvious contempt and disregard for Authority rules. He should have seen this coming.

Those fools.

"C'mon, c'mon," Kesselring huffed under his breath, anxiously waiting for the crawling charge level to rise. Beyond the veiled tarp and dark glass, obedient Authority troops marched past. Speer's troopers, in cleaner armor, better maintained, with no grime clogging their joints. Searching for more members of his unit to terminate.

Speer.

The troops would kick a body on the ground to ensure it wasn't alive before verifying with another blast to the chest. He had lost his whole camp in mere minutes. Annihilation unsanctioned by the District Council would have its consequences. They would pay.

As quiet as he could, he tried the ignition switch to no avail. It needed more time as he sweltered in the hot box like in a coffin.

Winds gyrated wilder over the moat as the wave crests grew among enlarging whirlpools. A deceased officer lay on the edge of the moat, killed by his own. Resting at its ridge, a hand dangled over the dark, roaring waves below. Torrential winds didn't budge the dead officer, gravely enticing the moat's appetite. Soon a black goo wave, impatient and quenchless, soared upward to the ridge and slopped itself onto the officer in thin mucky ropes. Two, then four, duplicating quickly to eight and then sixteen. The black muck pulled on the body like hooks, dragging it over the edge until eventually a much larger glob swept the officer down to the hungry river below. Officers on the nearby Authority cruiser's observation deck watched in horror and awe.

Kesselring sighed under his breath, waiting for his speed pod to charge. A trooper pointed his direction, presumptively posing a question if anyone had looked under the pile of fallen tent canvas. Two troopers nodded and marched toward him.

C'mon, you damn thing.

Sweltering in the hot pod made Kesselring's heart flutter. God, he hated the heat. He stared in anticipation at the deck's charging display as sweat crept down into his beaten skin's folds, the beads sinking into them like they'd found gutters. Since being relegated to remote camp assignment, he had committed to a day of reckoning, never imagining his whole camp would be obliterated.

Months before, he had come upon the Moat of Moorack by happenstance, his entire installation plowing forward over the desert crawl to find a camp halfway to the adjacent district's forests. It was a strategic place where supplies could be acquired yet provide geo-coverage for the unrelenting rebel search. Upon their approach, the deaths of two unsuspecting scouts were the most horrifying he had ever witnessed.

It was here he nested and set camp, their new satellite hub. The protective moat would defend against rebel aggressors, an unnatural boundary. If Authority leadership would come after their own, he'd be prepared. He was proud of his inclinations of distrust of Speer's Authority, a rogue general with his own tactics, regardless of Authority sanction. Instead, it was he who should be leading this district. All districts. With Martel gone and Speer going rogue, there was much business to be done.

Through the hidden crack of tarp layers, he could see the probing troopers were mere meters from discovering him, their blaster rifles in hand. The charging display finally signaled green, and he hit the ignition. In an instant, the speed pod hummed and the air-cooling system initiated, blasting his dripping face with relief.

"Finally," Kesselring mumbled, and he accelerated the speed pod, flying into the troopers before they could fire their blasters. In flight, he surveyed the camp, his eyes wide in shock. Stunned officers and Authority speed pods were being sucked and pulled into the moat by the aggressive muck hooks, slinging and hurling tentacles, curling and aggressive like whips. Doomed troopers fired their blasters to no avail as they were dragged over the ridge, screaming on their descent to their horrifying sludgy graves.

An Authority officer peered curiously over the large-capacity cruiser's observation deck, a bead of sweat courtesy of the newly rising sun falling off his forehead into the violent, mucky pit below. Ravenous waves soared up with a tempestuous force to grab the body fluid drop and its owner, reveling him in swirls.

In mere seconds, dozens of the moat's suckers shot up and clung to the bottom of the cruiser, octopus tentacles overwhelming its prey. An uproar filled the Authority cruiser as it tilted upward, the ruckus of officers scrambling for balance as the hard-angled vessel was pulled down toward the moat, a capsizing shipwreck in the air.

Men and women screamed and clambered as dark, mucky globs gripped and hooked over edges of the deck, dragging the cruiser's pull. A horrified officer tumbled off the cruiser's side, promptly disappearing into the moat's stormy abyss. In desperation, a daring officer at the cruiser's tip had his sights on jumping off the cruiser's end to the camp side of the moat. As the cruiser continued its descent into the earth's bowels, he jumped, only for muck ropes to promptly grasp and pull him into the gnarled, raging river.

The cruiser was finally gobbled up by the violent sludge, whirlpool currents attracted to the feast like magnets, assisting the beast's ingestion. The last of the terrified souls ingested, the turbulence soon calmed.

His whole camp and the aggressors had been wiped out.

Kesselring shook his head as he raced away, superior once again to the Authority ranks who disregarded his adeptness, his loyalty, and left him out in this desert hellhole. He would have told anyone, should he have been asked, not to test the Moat of Moorack.

"Idiots," he mumbled as he set the course for District Twenty-Seven, hoping the hidden stolen cloud data was indeed where Custode said it was. The price for Speer's betrayal had not yet been paid. After acquiring that download, he would have what Speer—what *the Authority*—craved in his possession. The superior bargaining chip.

TWENTY-THREE

The nav reader told Leroi the location of the comlink was District Forty-Three, in the middle stretch of open desert wastes. If she could get to Custode and the rebels, she could escape Speer's clutches. Clearly the former convict was elusive, slipping through everyone's fingers like sand. Tippler stood back, negotiating with the armed sentry patrolling the aerodrome hangar's main entrance. From the white-nosed jet's cockpit, she could make out that he was distracting the towering robotic guard, its head scanning, testing his sensory impulses for any sense of violation. There wasn't much time.

The thought of getting hauled in front of Speer made Leroi sweat. Apprehension at the thought of a firing sentry marching forward and firing its iron hand could cause anyone to itch under their government-issued wears.

She studied the plane's foreign controls as her nervous hands shook like vibrating throttles. The gauges were cryptic, minimalist in detail. Several switches were unmarked. Why did nothing seem to be where it felt like it should be? She'd been trained to fly the latest Authority planes (though they had recently moved to East camps for supply transport), not a relic like this Old World hydrogen-fueled jet.

She punched the plane's silent ignition, slowly maneuvering toward the hangar's wide-open exit. The rippling tires crinkled over the cement floor with a light squeal. She flinched and gritted her teeth. Any doubt the AI sentry had of her intentions within its harebrained circuitry would soon be confirmed. She was indeed stealing an Authority WR-97.

As she lowered the cockpit's hatch door, she slowly accelerated forward, holding her breath. After hitting what she thought—hoped—was a cabin pressure control, the jet stalled. In a huff, she flipped it back and the engine rumbled awake. She clenched her jaw as her cabin shook.

The sentry guard raised its towering head high as its flaring eyes burned in bright beams. In condemnation, the steely beast abruptly shoved Tippler aside with its straight steel shoulder, knocking him to the floor as it stomped toward the escaping plane. It was coming after her.

"It thinks," she mumbled, bracing for any firepower coming her way as she thrusted forward out the hangar's barn doors, quicker now. She'd need to get airborne soon. The jet's boosted power rose to a deafening roar. She acclimated to the controls, like piloting a speed pod perhaps. One that cruises higher, faster, and uses a lot more fuel. This could be a one-way trip. "I learn too."

When Tippler scrambled to his feet, jumped up, and slapped an inconspicuous lever down the sentry's back, it raised its robotic armament at the plane and its unlawful occupant. With a clack, the sentry froze mid-step, powering down to a stop into a halted menacing statue.

Leroi gave a quick wave to Tippler as she accelerated down the runway, her lifeline from the aerodrome's crushing repression, promptly taking flight like a freed bird from its cage. *Hope it's worth it,* Tippler had said. While he had finally tired of his fruitless advances, no doubt he had been happy to take the rations she left behind.

***

"There's more, sir."

"Spit it out then," General Speer said, reading District Council correspondence text. Someone had notified them of Martel's passing, and a hearing was being requested to determine what was underfoot. After securing the governorship, then came dealing with the Council. The Councillorship would be wide-eyed. He could taste liberation on his tongue.

"Kesselring also escaped."

Speer paused, buried rereading the transmission, studying the initial questions in the Council's inquiry for clues of their next moves. Their scrambling. The curt language suggested a formal investigation had already started. *Good. A waste of time and resources.* But hearing Kesselring's name infuriated him, and his nostrils flared. He felt a tug on his throat. The name rang in his ears, a banging echo.

"Unfortunately, we lost over a hundred personnel," the lieutenant read. "Two dozen speed pods, one cruiser."

Speer finally looked up. "What?"

The officer was equally absorbed in the tablet transmission, squinting as if trying to decipher the incredible details. "A passing freighter reported it. Death by natural causes, that's all it says."

Speer scoffed. "We've got a mutiny on our hands, Lieutenant. I don't accept natural causes as the reason for elimination of an entire Authority-manned cruiser. I want our deserted major general hunted. Kesselring hunted. Custode, hunted."

"The children, sir?" the lieutenant asked straight-faced.

The world spun in his head like a mad top—vibrant, blurry colors boiling over. He grimaced, his stomach churning. The rebels, breeding with each other and undoubtedly entertaining other jarring pleasures. Each more repulsive than the next.

"Of course, the children!"

A petty officer arrived. "Sir!"

"What!" Speer cried, his threshold for bad news shrinking. Any moment he would shake the life out of every living being in sight.

"The deployed drones confirmed location of rebel farmers in remote District Forty-Four. Also, the decoder you requested has broken the code sequencer. Your request is available at the ready."

"Finally some good news," Speer announced, his heart releasing kilos of pressure.

"The drones were destroyed but not before confirmed location data was transmitted."

"They know we found them. Prepare immediately for the invasion."

The lieutenant readied to transmit. "I'll inform the Council."

"You'll do nothing of the sort," Speer said, eyeing the lieutenant with iron resolve. The District Council was slow and obstructionist. Impotent and weak, wilted like dead flowers. He had other plans now. "We don't have time for negotiation as the Council tries to convince us to abstain, despite it being unnecessary. They mustn't know a thing. And the rebels will abandon their base soon."

He took a breath. This was it. He said it again.

"Prepare immediately for the invasion."

***

Their speed pod sputtered its last breaths as Mel piloted the crew slowly toward a lavish, ivy-clad hidden wall tucked in District Forty-Four's forest, causing a stir among the rare bustling wildlife alerted to their arrival. Enchanting sights pulled the speed pod forward, swallowing it inside nature's living nucleus.

Stunned frogs, deer, and beavers stiffened, their faces stone cold as the humming speed pod cautiously floated through the dense, green overgrowth. Filtered daylight eased through the magnificent umbrella of trees like it, too, was awakened. The forest welcomed them in its way, opening like heaven's gate.

"Almost there," X said, leaning forward from the back seat. She held Y's head, pale and sickly, in her lap. "There's a hidden port. Go slowly."

The impaired speed pod stammered forward, Mel piloting with painstaking caution as warning lights flashed on the control deck. She was grateful they were close. "It's on its last legs."

"We gotta make it," Beck said before turning back to Y. "He's gotta make it."

What was it she felt, exhaustion or relief? Different circumstances emerged since learning her family was dead. What she would do next she didn't know, but she was delivering the kids. "How is he?" Mel asked, peering back through the rearview mirror.

Y's face was sweaty and colorless like broken glass, and his eyes peered out at nothing as X held him. "The blood has stopped. His heart hasn't."

"Let's give him what he needs," Mel said. She powered down the marred, bullet-laden windows, ushering in the forest's calming scents—damp earth, pine, eucalyptus, and old fallen leaves. Tumbling streams fell in lazy waterfalls over statuesque lush ridges into small splashy pools, misty droplets dancing onto quenched leaves and stems. The saturated air was sticky and rich. Nature's palace. "Amazing, this place."

"Breathe in," X said softly. "We're home."

"Is that a monkey? I think I saw a monkey," Beck said in astonishment, forcing her to smile. The nimble ape jumped from tree to tree, and Beck frowned as Y moaned, his eyes closed. "Looks like the smart pain meds are wearing off."

"I just gave him another without telling you," X said, her face surly. She petted Y's hair as he grasped the data disc around his neck. "Look. Over there."

Mel floated the pod toward the ivy wall, in which two huge thick, steel doors opened. Abundant ivy clasping them tumbled free as the entrance widened several meters. A great white light greeted them as they entered, the flaky rust on the massive steel doors breaking. Oxidation thrived in a place so dank.

She caught her breath, astonished by the magnitude of the port inside. Beaming lights fell upon hundreds of bubble-shaped metal pods, reflecting like white suns. Rebel pods like the Authority pods, but mostly rundown older models with faded paint and older hardware. Yet, a real fleet.

"Quite an operation," Beck quipped, as the ragtag pod marshaller guided them with torn flags to park between two equally damaged pods.

"We make good with the resources we have," X said, glaring as if to remind him her words were a favor and she was still not talking to him.

"Don't embarrass us," Mel said. "Let's not get kicked out before we arrive."

"In case you forgot, missy, I helped get us here."

"Don't call me that," Mel said flatly.

The pod doors popped open, and Y was immediately pulled out on a stretcher, taken by scrappily dressed rebels presumably to medical care. Mel exited the pod and was greeted by a bearded rebel, stocky and built and probably too masculine for his own good.

"She's with us," X yelled back as she chased the medics down.

The bearded rebel shrugged in acceptance. "What about him?"

"I'm leaving," Beck said, handing his packs over. "My daughter, Dericka James Kane, is she here?" The rebel nodded and left.

"You're leaving?" Mel asked with pause. What would he do, swindle more suckers out of their money back at Vulnus Outpost? Misfire quips at any available woman who made the mistake of happening upon that wretched place? "Your daughter."

"Don't pretend you want me here, Custode. I've gotten nothing but conflict from you since day one."

What was it with this guy always bickering? "We had to get here. You were our ride."

"Risking my hide," Beck said, approaching her closer. "Abandoning my pod, almost thrown in a roaring muck pit. Taking on fire from how many Authority pods? Unimpressive, right?"

"I don't know what you're talking about."

"What impresses you, Custode?"

"They have food here," she said with a nervous swallow, as the med bags were whisked away by attendants. "Replenish. Spend time with your daughter. I'm sure she'd love to see you."

The words came out of her mouth like dry chalk. What was she doing trying to get him to stay longer? A familiar sense of steadfast affection and doubt crowded her senses, like a bad taste you can't shake.

More than a year had passed since *he* died—a love she had only started to explore, surprisingly discovered in Alvarium Penitentiary's food line on a humdrum day she'd expected to be bookended by days exactly like it. A brash young man, his heart had been hidden behind sweltering smiles and sorrow, having the kind of confident swing to his gate that attracted strife in such a place. Inmates respected him as a loner; so had she.

Many a night she'd imagined leaving with him one day, often falling asleep visualizing places they'd go, and how he would cradle her without gaping Authority guards interfering. He was her hope chest of dreams. Then she'd see him the next day sometimes, caught up in immature talk with other prisoners, like unfledged birds debating whether to leave the nest. And she'd go about her duties until they came across each other again, and the cycle continued.

Soon it became as predictable as lights out, thoughts of him comfortable like a favorite blanket. In the day, her eyes always drifted to him in the atrium or when passing through Alvarium's labyrinth of dim passageways. Then one night, theft of rations from the prison's kitchen had led to a riot and several deaths by the deathly IPR baton. In a flash, he succumbed to his injuries after defiance and screams. Her uncharted flame burnt out, a flame she did not want to relight.

Beck gave her a long look that she could not decipher, as if he were trying to read her, each nerve firing. Penetrating eyes trying to see beyond her horizon, a place she herself didn't really know. Just when she thought she couldn't take it anymore, he said, "Tell me you want me here."

She stuttered. "I— They—"

"Exactly," Beck said with a shake of his head. "After I see my daughter and get my money, I'm gone."

***

He'd had to descend a steep, bright, fluorescent lit tunnel to get to the shadowy cave. This was the medical section, a crude waiting area Beck discounted as light on resources, but he hadn't expected much from the rebels anyway. All he wanted to know, finally, was his daughter.

In a couple hours' time, Beck had learned more than he ever wanted to know about the rebels' latest triumphs and challenges with farming, feeding, and keeping control of curious rebel children anxious to explore outside headquarters. The most interesting thing he'd learned was how an air ventilation system protected against breathable poisons known as an Authority go-to weapon called AirNet. The underground generators pumped air through a hybrid thick-meshed carbon and photoelectrochemical oxidation process before using water screening for the massive network of tunnels, shafts, and caves. Transporting resources from multiple entrances within the forest helped the rebels keep their hideout within the mountain concealed from the Authority's drones and heat-mapping technologies. All quite impressive, actually.

"Beck Holden?" The rebel nurse stood before him, solemn, distanced, and unimpressed. She looked him up and down with judgment he was used to. "You are here for Dericka James Kane?"

He nodded. As he had known, his daughter carried his middle name, not his surname.

"I'm sorry, Beck," the nurse said in a dry cadence, and Beck sensed his name had been hard on the nurse's tongue. What was she saying? Things didn't compute, it couldn't be. His forehead crumpled as he discerned what the nurse was communicating. Dread washed over him. This had to be a mistake.

"I—"

"Again, I'm sorry."

Her words had the desired effect if it was blame she was casting. Anchors weighed down his legs as he shuffled backward, powerless, like swallowed in a vacuum, or drowned in the deep. The fighting he'd persevered through, the escapes and near deaths he'd survived. Had he manifested this? A wave of emptiness made him dizzy as he wrestled his twisting emotions in slow motion. He'd let time and *choices* get the best of him, eaten by his demons of arrogance and play and swindling.

"What happened?" he asked, lightheaded now.

The nurse abruptly turned away. Befuddling. Had she even known what he was asking? He fought so his knees wouldn't give way, crinkling and bending to the loss of the daughter he had never met.

This is what he'd heard about the rebels sometimes. They could be cruel too.

***

Dozens of mechanical tree jumpers pounced across the treetops, careering their way in closer toward the rebel farm, Speer's determined location for the attack. Springing forward like methodical jumping spiders, the pack of monstrous weaponized machines, controlled remotely from base, stretched across vast blanketing tree canopies in their purposeful hunt. Their long spindly legs bounced from tree to tree, covering large stretches of forest without the hindrance of navigating through the dense wood.

Forest tree jumpers were staunch weapons Martel had safeguarded through development. He had believed remote districts would have surplus notice of advancing troops trudging through deep forests, and that the rebels would have ample time to hide from an air approach. Slippery rebels had eluded them at every plundering. The tree jumpers would remedy such a problem.

Speer savored this assault and did not blink as drone cameras flew over the spiders' pursuit. It was a moment to behold. He oversaw the invasion from the camp's control room, attended to by multiple officers and tree jumper controllers. Two dozen trapezoidal screens from as many lenses outfitted the multiple tree toppers, lighting up the control center, the largest two-meter screen in the center and the general's focus. The rebels' downfall was to be enjoyed by every eye available.

Tree jumpers could achieve great distances in forests in little time, leading surprise attacks. Elusive rebels required ingenuity to catch, which Martel had lacked, nor had he had the backbone to use the weapons, even test them. They had been Speer's idea to develop in the first place. It would take time to discover the jumpers' weaknesses, Martel had complained, yet never lived to see. Speer had been impatient to use the dangerous machines.

Now, finally, the jumpers' elongated, flexible legs pounced over sprawling canopies, their meaty claws grasping onto leafy limbs before leaping for the next. Their weight never fully realized on the trees, like skipping stones on a lake, they fearlessly bounced forward in brisk bounds and breakneck speed.

"Sir?" a controller asked.

"Go."

The pouncing tree jumpers reached the border of a sea of trees, ending dramatically at the mountain's foot, where a farmed clearing stood. The spider-like machines cascaded over the canopy's end in a mechanized waterfall, landing with soft thuds into the lush heavy grasses. Two jumpers plopped into the calm brook, stretching out their elongated legs onto the field and immediately pulling themselves out. They licked their chops like conquerors. Without stopping, dozens of remote-controlled infiltrators surged through and over the rows of tomato-laden trellises, trouncing and bashing through the feeble rebel-built constructs.

Frenetic video feeds filled the control room. Then, he saw a small crevice in the mountain, a conspicuous boulder largely blocking it. "Zero in," he said, heeding the opening. It was big enough to allow rebels to slip through. Supplies to ship through.

Jumpers attacked the entrance, their eyes transmitting their foray into the passageway, searchlights atop each of the jumpers' metal craniums lighting it up like comets. They searched and hunted, seeking their prey and redemption, coming up empty in the dark, hollow cave.

"Nothing, sir."

"Keep going," Speer growled.

The tree jumpers maneuvered through the narrow passageway, their spindly legs climbing on top of each other as they scuttled and foraged forward, eventually congregating in a vast, empty cavern and standing in still, shallow puddles. Only a few lonely, wooden pallets in the middle of the large, abandoned space remained.

"What is that?" Speer asked, pointing to one of the feeds, curious if his hunch was right. He'd never seen one, big or small, before. "We have eyes. Do we have ears?"

"Yes, sir," a controller said, confirming on her earphones and activating a jumper mic on the control loudspeaker as the feed skipped in static. The signal weakened within the mountain.

Another controller mobilized the jumper toward the enormous dome-shaped mound, strewn carelessly against a cave wall like scraps. "A discarded beehive, sir." One of the jumper's sharp legs poked the mound's wall, quickly cracking it in half, exposing a deserted mass of dried-out honeycomb and disappointment. Its crackling hisses could be heard through the control speakers.

"No bees," a controller said. "Perhaps it's all a lie, the rebels having bees."

"They have them," Speer said grudgingly. "They're just not here."

Suddenly, the boulder in front of the cave opening rolled shut, a computer-generated forklift within the ground elevating the two-ton hunk of rock over the crevice, blocking the entry with the spindly tree jumpers still in the cave, black as a bat.

"What was that?" an officer asked as the video feeds died.

"The tree jumpers are trapped," Speer quipped. He took a breath. He should not have used his whole fleet of tree jumpers at once. *Rookie mistake.*

"No exit, sir," an officer said, reading the blank jumper feeds across the monitors.

"They mobilized their evacuation quickly," a controller concluded.

"Too quickly," Speer said, mostly to himself. He had underestimated the rebels' prowess. They'd succeeded in eluding the Authority. *Again.* "Their communications are efficient."

"How did they move their headquarters so fast?" another officer asked.

"This isn't their headquarters," Speer said, it paining him to say the words. "It was an ancillary farming site, also serving as a decoy. They were ready for us. What we've learned is they can't grow everything where they are. And they could never transport hundreds or thousands of people through the forests quickly. They're underground. And they took the bees with them."

"How do we find them?"

"How we would flush out rats. We pick an area nearby, they can't be far. And we drown them out."

TWENTY-FOUR

"Rebel defenders," General Sangeeosay said with a sharp command, so potent that Mel felt like she had hit her head on a bell. Dozens of rebel fighters, adults, and precocious adolescents scrambled to their seats. Mel sat amongst them amassed in the hollow meeting center, their safeguarded shelter deep within the mountain's cavernous belly.

Something was different here at base, where hazy ambition and the process of living had worn everyone down. Haggard conditions eroded even the most committed through time, untreated ailments the never-ending struggle. Rebels appeared with red bumps on their skin, probably from yellow flies or biting midges. The oldest adults looked like dead walking, their wiry gray hair falling over their heads in wispy sheets. Children, too, lots of them. Some were adult-like with their ripened seriousness and secure demeanors. Babies and toddlers fussed and scuttled. Abundant fertility abounded, unlike in the dreary civilian populations overexposed to pesticides, poisoned soil, and rationed diets. Caretaking mothers looked as ashen as clay, drained of color, and the young men looked at the ground as they trudged. The rebel plight had taken an exhausting toll.

Beck plopped down next to her, contemplative and cold, lolling in the chair like he had merged with it. Had he not found his daughter? Had she refused to see him? Her own loss of family left her directionless, unsure of where to go, how to feel. All she knew was her fight was over, and she would soon leave this place.

General Sangeeosay, the elder stateswoman of mixed Asian descent and leader of the rebellion, commanded the room's attention as she stood next to an impressively translucent diagram. She was graceful and confident, her movements smooth and flowing like a constant breeze.

Posture solid, she pointed. Ghostly white lines sketched out their hidden mountain in an aurora, a triangular hologram with spatial recognition of the woodland terrain canvassing them like a tarp.

"The resistance's stolen data has been recovered with the Authority cloud's complete download," Sangeeosay announced to the huddle of about eighty rebels. "Many of our own perished in acquiring it, only X-G1 and Y-H17 made it back, though Y-H17 is now healing in our infirmary. We installed tracking information into the data before it was stolen from us. Fortunately, we've discovered Authority forces did not have time to mine the data and determine our location."

Many rebels nodded and murmured in welcome appreciation of this good news. Out of the corner of her eyes, Mel saw Beck remained pensive and grim, staring into space, possibly not hearing a word.

"But"—Sangeeosay sighed—"we decrypted intelligence suggesting a brewing mutiny within the Authority ranks. What we believe to be plans for destruction of the Authority grid of power. How it affects us . . ."

A blueprint appeared on a blank cave wall behind her, serving as a screen for the topographic map with sections of district regions painted in toxic yellow.

"What does it mean?" someone asked as Mel watched, contemplating what to say to Beck.

"Destroyed rebel sites." The room became still—not a foot shuffle, a cough. "A document of kills against orders from the District Council. A rogue general has disregarded Authority protocols and has been systematically killing rebels, not governing them as ordered. This sole general has killed thousands of our brothers and sisters over the last four years alone. The entire cloud's download has revealed plans to destroy Authority camps, one by one, with targets on specific Authority leaders. We have here a rogue regime with a hunger for power and a disregard for rebel or human life."

Everyone hung on Sangeeosay's words.

"According to this record, our location has not been discovered. However, it's still become necessary to facilitate an evacuation. It's been brought to light the Authority discovered our ancillary tomato farm, presumably the notorious General Speer, who is hunting this specific location with a vengeance. Three tribes tending to the farm's acreage were forced to evacuate quickly. Authority forces may be able to decipher our location within hours, if not minutes. Our time is short to respond. Our entire operation, our families, are at stake."

The mumbling in the room grew louder, as if a nest had awakened.

Mel leaned over and finally whispered to Beck, his face empty and vacant, "Did you find your daughter?"

"She didn't make it," he whispered back as the general continued her address.

What? His daughter is dead?

"I'm sorry, Beck," she said, holding his hand delicately. His eyes lowered and his face stoic, the man looked like he'd been stampeded over. Chills swept across her skin as she caressed his arm, an odd tingle that she did not understand. For a moment she forgot where she was as Sangeeosay's voice disappeared into the background, like in a distant echo chamber. What does one say in such a circumstance? Beck's empty gaze tugged at her, as if he was trying to pull her closer. For the second time, she saw a young boy behind his bristly face.

"The Authority has evolved into an evil institution now looking to erase our whole society," Sangeeosay said, Mel barely hearing it.

"I thought I had time," Beck whispered. "The world, everything, looks different now."

"Money doesn't cure that, does it?"

Beck yanked his hand away, pointing his finger at her in anger. "I don't need you to point that out." He got up and left, leaving Mel stunned.

That had to sting. Probably shouldn't have said that.

"Simply," General Sangeeosay continued, "our natural defense lines in the forest will stall but not thwart an Authority attack. We need a two-pronged approach: those of you who will lead the counterattack and those who will lead the tunnel evacuation. Follow your assignments. We have trained for this moment."

A chill shuddered down Mel's spine. As if to distract herself from her own dejection, she raised her hand to the general's curt nod. "No assignment yet, General." She regretted the words, hanging over her like a weight of obligation, as she said them. Nothing right escaped her tongue.

"We need you to assist the tunnel evacuation. There's a lot to do there." She raised her brow to the attentive assembly as she monitored her chrono. "Any questions? You're dismissed." The room stood and spilled out. "Wake what's within."

***

After a harder than desirable landing, Leroi tumbled out of the cockpit like a scrapped sandbag. The sleek hydro jet fanned swirling gales until the engine died and it descended slowly to a stop. Her tracking sensor said Custode was here (or at least the comlink was), and she searched the grounds. Jumbled tents flapped lightly in the wind, others having rolled over the camp's ridges and now floating on top of the dark, murky moat.

Deceased officers and troopers littered the middle of the camp like debris. *Kesselring lost this fight.*

"Custode, come in," she said into her comlink, hearing herself faintly nearby. Again. "Custode, Mother here."

Something moved within one of the angled tents, and she drew her blaster. An old beaten man emerged, swallowed in his tattered robes and holding himself up by a scythed staff. He hid his battered, bloody face behind his feeble hands, trembling.

Leroi lowered her weapon. "I won't hurt you," she said as she moved toward him tenderly, afraid she might push him over with merely a breath.

He leaned against the scythe, his weight bending as his knees wobbled. His eyes narrowed in suspicion as she moved nearer, appearing shaken inside as much as out. She handed him a flask off her belt, and he gulped the water down carefully between his dry, blood-crusted lips.

"Thank you," he said softly, his voice coarse and throaty. "If only the moat was made of water."

She smiled faintly, trying to be patient with him as he raised the flask to his lips again. "I was directed by a comlink to this location."

The man revealed his grisly, well-baked fingers, dark blood oozing out of broken sores. "This is what you're looking for."

The comlink.

"Where did you get that?"

"From a friend who said she did not need it anymore," he said, his breathing labored. He closed his eyes as if to dig within himself for strength. "Upon her duty, she suggested Sun Bin share that she was appreciative for being tracked into desert hell."

"Custode." She had to hand it to her. She had been outwitted.

The old man repositioned himself, his bloodshot eyes swollen, deadened. "She wasn't going to lead you to the rebels."

She smiled, believing that to be true. "What are you doing here?"

"Amends," he recounted, "for mistakes Sun Bin made years ago. Found peace through the violence getting me there. Got this back." He acknowledged his scythed staff as if it were an old friend. "No easy task."

"Amends?"

"Are you an Authority inquisitor?" he asked.

"Used to be, but I've given that up," Leroi said, further surveying the camp's damage. Torn tents, pierced and scourged in battle of some kind. Scattered bodies and weapons, disarranging the landscape. Things didn't add up. "Kesselring's troops, they wouldn't have abandoned this camp."

"The earth took them back," he said, his eyes turning distant.

"Custode. You know where she is?"

"Sun Bin knows where she was going. Not to be found by the likes of you."

"I know what the Authority, or the lead general, is trying to do to her and the rebels. He'll stop at nothing to destroy her . . . everything."

The old man stared at her through the bulbous swelling around his eyes. "What do you offer, so I know there is no horseplay here?"

"Horseplay?"

"I am Sun Bin and shall provide you an open door to lead yourself, and should not need to as teacher."

She would be hunted by the Authority and better off with the rebels than out on her own, than disguising herself in various outriggers or villainous outposts, surviving hosts of dangers as a solo woman in the wastes. "I have insight into the plans General Speer has for Custode, the children, and the hemisphere. There's a mutiny in the Authority, of which I am a part of no more. I know how he works."

"You would share this why?"

Pausing, she then said flatly, "To live."

After a moment, his eyes twinkling, Sun Bin said, "You must pilot us."

***

After a while, X's weary eyelids grew heavy from no sleep in days. She held Y's hand as he lay on the recovery mat, a crude infirmary with dozens of patients arranged on the cave's floor, many hooked up to IVs. Dim fluorescent lights in the damp cave's corner provided enough darkness for those who wanted to sleep and enough light to remember they were still alive. A woman nearby wrapped with sullied gauze turned away with a sheepish frown.

The blast wound to Y's shoulder was wrapped and compressed with dressing and tape. She was careful not to disturb the trauma as she caressed him. Robotic caretakers scurried, moving the sick and semi-ambulatory onto their feet, some into primitive wheelchairs.

Y peeled his eyes away from her as he fumbled to sit up. "Thanks to you, I'm alive."

"Getting the cloud data was really gutsy. Now, we must evacuate the mountain. Authority forces are coming."

"All for nothing."

"Our intel was protected," X said, the gravity of their circumstances hitting her. There were a lot of people to move, and some could be left behind. Families were crying, forcing their last hurried goodbyes. "Look at me," she said, trying to connect with him as he pouted.

Beck poked his head in. "Hey, kid, I've got something for ya."

She recognized Beck's growling voice immediately. "Go away."

In a whip, he threw her a pack of smart meds, and she caught it at her chest. "I had some extras stowed away. Always keep some extra for yourself," Beck said. "Should last you half a year. How you doin' there, young man?"

Y motioned to himself on the raw mat.

"You'll heal in no time," Beck said, a pained smile escaping from around his whiskers.

"What about your daughter?" Y asked, unable to contain a cough with his laugh, and X finally glanced up at Beck, interested in her fate. The man, rough and unrefined, had a *daughter.*

Beck's gaze darted around, like he wished he was far away. "Not so good, kid. She didn't make it. I can't believe after everything—"

As if hit by a hammer, X instantly ran up to Beck and wrapped her arms around his torso, almost knocking him off his feet. "I'm so, so sorry."

"It's my fault," Beck said, his hand hovering above X's shoulder before he awkwardly patted her. "I should've . . . made her more of a priority."

"What now?"

"I take my money and leave." Beck sighed, and X pulled herself from him. "Nothin' for me to do around this sinkhole." He turned to see the rebel attendants whisking anguished patients away as an unexcitable robotic nurse helped Y stand.

"You could help us evacuate," X said, looking up at him hopefully. "It's a thin herd."

Beck shook his head. "If I stick around, I'll probably end up dead like the rest of them, thrown into a mass grave somewhere."

"So you're gonna just go," X said, her frown full of contempt.

"This ain't my war, X. I've already gotten myself into more trouble trying to get here. I've got a homestead to manage. A job I owe."

"Leave now then." No sense in her allowing herself to think their trouble getting back to base somehow made them family.

"X—"

"Leave now then!" X cried, alarming the emptying recovery room. "Leave us here to fend for ourselves."

"Kid, I—" he started.

She stared him down, feeling anger and other things she could not define. Wanting him to go.

Beck raised his hands and backed up. "Okay, okay," he said, all eyes on him, including the robotic nurse who froze. She watched Beck leave in what she hoped would be the last time, as she tried to forget him in whole.

***

Beck cursed to himself as he rushed through the narrow, lamp-lit passageway in a huff, the hell he'd been through to get to this place hunching his shoulders. He'd found himself anticipating meeting Dericka. Dericka *James.* A total letdown; at least the rebels could use the meds.

As he approached the beat-up pod he'd arrived in, technicians scrambled about shifting carts of battery cells and preparing to transport necessary tools, assembly joints, and transformer parts. The mighty evacuation had been employed and was underway. He inspected the pod and shrugged, impressed that the damaged hull was welded together and the bullet-ridden glass had been replaced. Before going anywhere, he poked his head in the back seat to confirm the delivery of the bags of currency he'd been promised.

"The general triple-paid you for your trouble," an attendant said.

"In Ferre currency?" Beck asked as he counted the bags. He hadn't expected that.

"For your delivery plus Custode's fare. We repaired everything we could."

"We swapped out batteries. You're charged up," said another, and Beck plopped in the pilot seat. Sensing movement behind him, he turned to see Simple Eye hovering in the far back, its sole photoreceptor eye blinking, curious and spirited.

"Miss Custode wanted you to have him," the first attendant said.

"Him," Beck repeated, shaking his head. She must have thought he needed the company, or had hoped he'd take the responsibility off her shoulders.

"She said you needed to be looked after."

"She did, huh?" Beck asked as he buckled himself. To the drone's sad purr, he quipped, "Well, you tell her I can't wait to sell him for scraps when I get back to Vulnus. He'll be a hit with the ladies at Reggay Bunker, too, I'm sure." The drone would surely cause a stir with its gawking stares at the outpost's backroom pleasures, no doubt stunned and abashed by the garish costumes and absinth-infused concoctions' aromas alone. Its single eye frozen awake made him chuckle. "I promise I'll be good to him."

Hadn't the drone been property of the Authority? What was he going to do with the drone out in the flatlands once they could read its geo-tracker? He'd be toast quick.

"His tracker was already disabled," the first attendant said as if reading his mind. "His insides were filled with sand, like from a sandstorm. When's the last time you've cleaned his insides?" he asked accusingly. "He'll be most valuable only as a nav tool companion."

"Will he now?"

The attendants shut the pod doors (Beck thought rudely), and Beck was off. In moments, the pod was out through the hangar's rusted doors, and he steered slow and steady into the wooded green. The ivy-clad doors thundered shut behind him as if to say, *Good riddance.*

A familiar hollow hum filled the pod, both disquieting and causing him uneasy contention. "Enough of these people," he grumbled as he set the nav course back home. Back to where dismal chores and subverted dealmaking, haggling, and inventive libations at Vulnus Outpost awaited. Plus, a job that needed to be done.

Simple Eye bleeped in agreement.

"Let's avoid the black helmets, shall we?"

Simple Eye murmured.

"Not sure I see our future together," Beck said to the drone's whirring soft moan.

It would be two solid days of pod travel to get back, enough time to think about who he lost. From the corner of his eye, he saw something move in the woods. He jumped. Clawing figures, shadows. Then, through his mirror he saw them. *Was that—*

He turned to get a better look through the rear's back glass, around the pesky drone bobbing unhelpfully in his face. There they were. A small group of trooper scouts, sifting through thickets of foliage and approaching the rebels' wall.

The Authority had found them.

TWENTY-FIVE

Six Authority trooper scouts had reached the base of the rebels' wall, the only accessible entrance to the mountain's rebel fortress. Some ten meters from under the hangar's floor, the scouts prepared to climb, grasping with their thick segmented gloves around the fat jungle ropes as faint thunder rolled. One inquisitive trooper peered upward, as if anticipating intense rain until the ground began to rumble not far underneath their chasm.

Outward to the forest, nothing conspicuous moved. Time stopped. No birds flapped their wings. The landscape was a frozen portrait, a still heartbeat. The trees stiffened and breezes died down, as if alarm had caught its own breath. Only the small babbling brook and trickling waterfall interrupted the silence as the ground grumbled awake.

"Something is com—" the trooper scout announced through his helmet as wild, monstrous bears suddenly descended upon the group, unleashing their ferociousness and tearing at them with long, sharp fangs. Two ruthless bears pulled on either side of an unfortunate scout, ripping their victim apart into ruptured halves, and then halves of halves, their jagged gnawing teeth refusing to surrender their prey.

From the control room, General Speer observed the gruesome feed across his trapezoidal screens, where the lead trooper's helmet streamed. Speer stayed glued to it, witnessing nature's abortion. A barrage of black, aggressive bears sped at the cam from afar, massive in sight and scale, destroying all backwoods vegetation in their path. They plunged over trees and thickets, their uproar rising in cries and wails. The cam bustled as it tried to move out of the crazed beasts' path before tumbling, its rustle roiling and deadening to a stop.

"Our scouts are being taken down by wild bears," an officer stated obviously, punching up an alternate cam stream that provided a peek at the roaring animals. The gargantuan beasts were four to five meters long, trampling over his troopers in snorts and grunts.

Speer sneered. "That's their weapon?"

The wild beasts had been trained somehow, perhaps provided for as pets. Nature itself was corrupted from radiation contamination, but the rebels had harnessed its power? Their brazenness and overconfidence in the bears as a shield made him chuckle.

"So they got a few of ours," Speer lamented. "We know where they are. Their days are numbered. Find the power grid."

An officer nodded as she controlled a drone hovering near the grisly carnage, the wild bears on their hind legs desperately reaching for it, their serrated paws flailing unsuccessfully to bring the device down. The detection drone hunted for the power center.

"Too much moving water, sir," the officer said. "And iron ore. It's throwing off the reading."

Speer was about to rant when she amended herself.

"Wait," she said as the drone sensor's signal strengthened, then faded, near the wall's base as the bears continued to clamor. She skillfully navigated the orb around the bears' claws and jaws and smiled with satisfaction. "The grid appears to be at the base of the mountain. The density can deflect the sensors, but it's imperfect."

Suddenly, another bear jumped from a nearby rock and ripped the orb from the air, stomping on the detector as the screen feed fizzled and broke up, and all the cam feeds died to black.

"What now, sir?"

"The rebels relied on the bears to deter us," Speer said. "Launch phase two."

***

"General Sangeeosay. A hostile Authority jet approaching," a young rebel guard said from behind a ramshackle monitor deck. Its shoddy shelving clung to thick wire cables fastened to slight wooden panels.

The general zeroed in on the monitor. An Authority hydrogen jet hovered in the forest, its base blasting gales into the foliage as the bears curiously watched the monstrous machine maneuver over them before disappearing back into the trees, leaving mauled trooper carcasses behind.

"What's it doing?" Sangeeosay asked, recognizing the sleek jet's white tip. Who knew the antique hydrogen jets were still in use?

"Requesting admission," a female voice said over the staticky comm system.

"How much firepower does that jet have, General?" the rebel guard asked.

"It's nothing we can do anything about," she said. The jet's twin rocket barrels could blast the mountain's walls to smithereens this close, burying caves and tunnels along the perimeter. How did the Authority know of this entry to the fortress's port hidden this deep within the forest? Because the power grid was the most vulnerable if discovered, it was encased under the fleet's rich iron-ore floor. She had ensured their camp had been necessarily covert, maneuvering pod shipments through the elaborate tunnel system so to not expose it.

"Rebels," another voice said.

Sangeeosay froze, immediately recognizing the weak voice over the static, disbelieving this moment.

"Inform General Sangeeosay her husband has arrived," Sun Bin crackled through the speaker, and her heart warmed. Time rushed through her like she'd been knocked over by an ocean wave.

The hangar doors widened, breaking more ivy as dozens of rebel pods spilled out on either side as the jet gently landed in the fortress's port. Sangeeosay appeared as attendants assisted Sun Bin out of the jet and the remaining rebels continued to scatter in evacuation. Her heart hammered upon approaching the bruised sage, his limbs heavy, his face a bruised patchwork of red and purple. She caught her breath as she met Sun Bin's eyes.

"You've not aged well, Yong gan." *Yong gan:* her pet name since they were young. Her brave man. Before he had been foolish.

Sun Bin smiled through his pain, and the Authority-clad woman braced him as he held his scythed staff straight, much as shepherds hold their non-scythed staffs. The hangar doors thudded shut, startling everyone as if the air had been sucked out of the room.

"Standing before you as one who learned," Sun Bin said, "to achieve greatness within. With attentive instincts to your relocating habitats that Sun Bin cannot shake."

Within. Her creed. Where all progress starts. His words had always jolted her soul awake, much like the sun on ice. She saw her past as she studied him, searching for the younger man behind the years and the skin folds. Also, she remembered the mistakes. Gazing at him, Sangeeosay saw a much older and humbled man, like a starved harvest welcoming rain. Hopefully he was more principled.

"He needs medics," the woman said.

Sangeeosay raised her brow. "You are with the Authority," she said, confident the woman no longer was. No Authority officer would approach in such a sympathetic manner. Sun Bin would have known better than to navigate her as such.

"Francine Leroi, formerly a major general with the Third Continent Authority forces. I now join you."

Suspicion quelled, Sangeeosay nodded to the alert rebel lieutenants at her side. "We can fully investigate you when there's time, which there isn't now. Sun Bin," she said, her voice gentler. Seeing him filled her heart to the brim, but she had no time to revel. "Why now?"

"Sun Bin did time and more, Lingdao," Sun Bin said, using his affectionate recognition of her rebel rank.

"Much time away, Yong gan," Sangeeosay said, painfully aware ignoring a rebel order has high costs. An order of exile, banishment from their prior rebel home she'd not wanted to give. But he had given her no choice. "How did you know—"

"An ear always to the ground. Missed you much from afar."

She cocked her head, recognizing his hurt from the pain, touched by his warmth and the softened spirit within his frail, battered bones. Regret and sorrow showered her like the reemerging of last rites. A refusal to leave his ailing mother behind in an Authority raid many years before, despite orders, was his cross. His mother had been confined to a gurney and perished in a last-ditch effort to escape, but her dutiful son had survived. He had not left her side, inspiring others in kind. The rebel location they'd been procuring as a new base had been discovered, and rebel losses were plenty. As punishment, Sun Bin had been vanquished from the rebel plight.

Their eyes were glassy, but Sangeeosay interrupted the moment she'd wished to come for over ten thousand nights—seeing her Yong gan once more. "There is no time to address your untimely return, Sun Bin. The Authority's arrival is imminent. We need to evacuate. Listen this time."

***

In the twitching orange light of the caved passageway, Mel led a group of twenty rebels, mostly children, mothers, some older men, and adolescents, assisted by a young girl using an old pen light on a worn and creased canvas map. The deeper Mel traveled into the tunnels, the sharper her realization that she was being pulled deeper into the rebels' fight. She suddenly felt lost and weary.

"You're probably used to your nav reader, aren't you?" Adrian asked. She was all of thirteen, freckled, and precocious like all rebel children. Mel shrugged. She had not bothered to pull her nav out since arriving. "Nothing will read here in the mountain, so we've resorted to old-fashioned communications."

Right away, it felt like the child was parroting what she'd heard rebels say over the years.

"Old underground sensors mapped out this mountain before they were destroyed during the war," Adrian continued, leading the group farther into the mountain's belly. "These readouts have proven invaluable." She opened the wrinkled canvas, revealing an elaborate and intricate map of underground tunnels within the fortress, some going for kilometers until ending in spatial underground bases. "We use the tunnels to transport resources among separate, small farms to keep headquarters safe. When we're not evacuating."

They approached an uneven fork in the tunnel, congealing with another group of rebels from within the mountain. Instantly, their mass tripled in size. Everyone moved swiftly and orderly, leading Mel to believe they had done this before.

"We'll go this way," Adrian said. They melded into another group trekking through a wider-mouthed tunnel leading to a large cavity, where no less than two thousand rebels congregated.

Dozens of automated subterranean vehicles (ASVs) that had been modified for long-distance traction underground with mud tires and side-tunnel sensors were stuffed with food supplies and munitions at the ready. Anxious rebels lined up before the three specific passageways, mumbling and murmuring as they followed their drills, getting into specific spots in the spacious den. X and Y followed their recovery unit, many on transportable gurneys. X beamed and waved at Mel when she saw her.

Natural sunlight seeped into the surprisingly large cavity, and then Mel saw it. A gigantic bee's nest hung from the cave's soaring ceiling, vaulted like a cathedral, as majestic rays beamed from a hole at the top. Laborious bees worked as others waggled in a mating dance. They collected in the nest, deep in its soulful womb as if they knew of the danger coming their way—a hair-raising, breathing beast.

"An enormous bee hive," Mel gasped.

"A nest," Adrian corrected. "We transport them to and fro in hives, then bring them back here. What you see isn't human made. We protect them."

"There have to be tens of thousands up there," Mel said, astounded.

"Hundreds of thousands," Adrian said, grinning at Mel's wide-eyed amazement. "This is what we've hidden from the Authority. The last known bees' nest on Earth. How do you think we got those?" She pointed to an ASV, its back door crammed with fruit crates.

"Are those apples? And peaches? I've only seen holograms—"

"The only ones on Earth," Adrian interrupted.

"A large number of children too," Mel said, amazed by the hundreds of children under twelve clad in worn, drab clothing, playing and teasing each other as they assembled in impressively straight lines, coordinated like crows.

"There's healthy fertility among the freedom fighters," Adrian said with honor. "With an aversion to poisoned diets."

Mel nodded.

At that moment, General Sangeeosay reappeared and spoke above the din. "Reminder, people," she said sternly, specifically monitoring the children, "no talking through these tunnels until you get to your evacuation site. From there, a transport will pick up each of you before departing for the temporary rendezvous point."

Two young boys giggled until they met Sangeeosay's hard-nosed stare.

"Parts of the tunnel's channel sounds like an echo chamber, detectable over soil," Sangeeosay continued. "No talking. The entire rebel cause is in our hands. Carry forward. You know your roles."

From the corner of her eye and beyond all the bustle, Mel thought she saw Sun Bin emerge from the shadows across the cave, a prevailing lily-white spirit emanating from the darkness. Then, she blinked, disbelieving her own eyes, as he moved slowly, his scythed staff twinkling small stars from the cave's soft golden light.

How . . . how did he escape? How did he get here?

Bruised and beaten, there he stood, his shoulder loosely dressed in gauze, undoubtedly slapped on with haste during their evacuation. She shivered, and her heart overflowed as the old man crept forward, his knuckles tightly grasping his scythe. Two assisting rebel adolescents held him up on either side, one watching the blade carefully as if fearing decapitation.

"Sun Bin!"

He immediately recognized her, a soft grin cracking his blood-crusted lips as Mel noticed the major general accompanying them. She froze, confused by Leroi's presence, the one who had recruited her, tracked her, and changed her orders.

What the hell is she doing here?

Her heart raced. The enemy was in their midst.

Then the enormous mountain grumbled. Low-light burnishing lamps down the passageways quivered as the ground beneath everyone moved. In one quick moment, everything went black.

TWENTY-SIX

"The power grid has been eliminated, sir."

Speer's eyes focused on the drones' digital feeds coming to light, awakening through walls of smoke. Static and the shaking feeds canvassed the wall. He mused over how the rebels had outwitted Martel and the District Council, hiding in a *mountain*. They'd outwitted everyone.

One feed twitched, but he could still make out the detail. Somehow the defiant heavy doors stood, fastened within the immense side walls, taunting him. "Pry them open."

"Pry them open!" the controller ordered into his headset.

At the ivy wall's entrance, two tall, weaponized android sentries balanced on hover-disc platforms, floating up to the hangar doors with ominous grace. They holstered their blasters in metal-piping sleeves and gripped their steel segmented fingers in the huge wall's crack. Their fingers pried like vices, scraping metal screeching through the wood.

He turned his attention to the other streaming monitors displaying parkour bots aggressively jumping through the forest's thicket, attacked by the bear beasts until the parkours' swipes broke them on their backs. Speer watched technology triumph over beast, then smiled until two of the monstrous bears tore one of his parkours in half. *Another untested weapon unready for battle,* he could hear Martel say. He seethed; there was no time to spare. The rebels were within his grasp.

"General. You won't believe this. We've located a hydro jet in the rebel camp."

"One of ours?"

"It's a WR, so yes."

The controller punched in a new video feed, the sentry's outfitted headcam providing sight into the hangar as the doors widened, morning forest light filtering in, exposing the sizable rebel port. It was empty of speed pods or ASVs, revealing only the jet's lifted back end, its white-tipped nose crushed headfirst in the demolished power grid below.

"And we just discovered one of our hydro jets is missing," the controller continued.

"Leroi," Speer breathed, his blood pressure rising. She was conspiring with the rebels. He should not have given her a chance to redeem herself. "Snuck right past us. How is that possible with its power exhaust?" He slammed the control board, getting madder by the moment.

"Sir, it's an incomplete prototype."

Speer grabbed the controller by the throat. "Does that look like an incomplete prototype?" he sneered as the controller gasped. Speer's eyes bulged as he threw the controller to the ground. "Blind bats."

Suddenly, aggressive rebel pods rushed out of the hangar, blasting gunfire in streaming flares at Authority troops. Armed troopers fired back with a barrage of overwhelming firepower, and within seconds, a dozen airborne rebel pods disintegrated in burning heaps of metal, their fiery smoke threading through the forest's green.

"If that's their fleet, I'll have honey with dinner," Speer said. He stayed glued to the monitors, searching for clues of reprisal. Burning destruction billowed in stacks, several of his troops dead in a junkyard of both rebel and Authority parts. Getting his data back was the priority at this point, but the bees . . . they would change the power landscape. Handling the District Council was one thing. He would need the bees to take on the Global Senate. "I want my bees and my download *back.* How long for me to get there and finish off these traitors myself?"

"Four minutes at Mach Five, sir," another controller offered, punching the calculations.

"Get the jet ready." He wasn't losing the rebels now.

"General," midlevel officer Cabello added, perspiration beading across his forehead, "the ion cannons are approaching the targeted zone. We are about to withdraw the troopers in preparation for the fire."

The heated general stared down the officer who dared to insinuate his decision required more thought. Or, with the power grid down, ion cannons. "Withdraw no one. I want those plans and those traitors at all costs."

"Sir," Officer Cabello said dutifully.

"Withdraw no one," General Speer repeated to himself. If he lost some of his own infantry in his bid to destroy the crafty rebels once and for all, so be it.

***

Sounds of shuffling feet filled the deep chambers, led by primitive fire torches and illuminated headlamps in a shuddering mass of hurried distress. Children who'd been teasing each other just minutes before had become solemn and resigned, as if the worst was coming. Misplaced denizens realized the seriousness of their plight.

Mel led X, Y, and hundreds of freedom fighters forward as Adrian ensured they followed the correct path.

"We need to go this way," Adrian said, as they came upon another fork in the tunnel network.

"I'm not sure we should take any more steps forward with her here," Mel said, motioning to Leroi. She sized up Leroi quickly: short, reserved. Was *demure* the word? The Authority officer was still a threat.

"She brought me here, Mel," Sun Bin said, his weary eyes woeful. "Saved me from dying alone in that dreadful camp."

Mel studied her. "So she could find us all here."

"And report us," X added.

"I'm no longer an Authority officer," Leroi said.

"What are you then?" Mel asked flatly, aware she was holding everyone up. The swelling, anxious crowd of rebels fidgeted, anxious to move forward through the narrowing tunneled chambers.

Leroi paused as if she had not thought about that. "Custode, I had to escape the new Authority, their—"

"The *new* Authority?" Mel choked.

"The new, the old, it's all bad!" X interjected to Mel's satisfied nod.

"I'm here to help," Leroi said. "I'll prove it."

"You will," Mel said, her green eyes penetrating Leroi with steely resolve. No way did she trust this defector, this *liar* who had used her dead family as bait. One mistake would end it for Leroi.

"We need to go," Y complained.

"What direction?" Mel asked, hardly tearing her eyes from Leroi as Adrian pointed to the map's canvas of squiggly lines.

"This one," Adrian said, "leaves the mountain and goes under the forest, with air tunnels in some of the roots." She motioned to the large group of anxious hundreds behind them.

"What do you mean?" Mel asked.

"Forest creatures burrow into the tunnels," Adrian said. "We have dedicated tunnel repair workers exactly because of them. The tunnels on the south side, they sometimes flood, collapse from the weight of water. We collect the clean water on that end; that's how we've survived. On this side, the tunnels have been known to have their problems."

"What kind of forest creatures?" Y asked. "Like the bears?"

"Do you kill them?" X asked, Mel sensing her slight quiver.

"Curious burrowers," Adrian said, "moles, rats, etcetera. Some are protective of their nests though. Like the bees. We don't kill them."

"Leroi, come with me," Mel said, sure to keep an eye on her. "Let's be a step ahead, clear the path."

"I'm not leaving him," Leroi said, Sun Bin's frail arms holding onto her and his scythe for balance.

"I'm going," Sun Bin said. "I'm old but not helpless."

"Fine," Mel said, not in the mood to argue. "How much time do we have before the Authority finds the tunnels?"

"It depends how distracted they are by the bees," Adrian said.

"We're leaving the bees behind?" X asked, wide-eyed.

"We can't take them, X," Mel said. They couldn't haul the monstrosity of a bee's nest through the narrow tunnel walls. Transporting it, they'd have to squeeze it like a sponge, break it in fragments.

"But that's all of them!"

Adrian nodded solemnly. "Yes, but look around you." Weary freedom fighters leered at them, their eyes heavy like lead, awaiting direction in the hope they weren't being led to slaughter. "They're looking to us to save their families."

"But the bees!" X insisted. "We've lost so many of our own trying to save them."

"Child—" Sun Bin said, his weak voice crackling.

"If all the bees die, the world dies!" X cried.

"Be quiet, X," Y said. "They're just bees."

"Just bees?" X whispered harshly. "We've built up our forces to protect them for generations."

"No time to argue, X," Mel said, softening her tone the most she could manage. "We'll do what we can to save the bees, okay? But first, we must save the families behind you."

"But—"

"I promise," Mel said, tilting the girl's chin up. "We'll die trying. Okay?"

"Okay," X said. She nodded as Mel's mind raced thinking of a way.

Holding the fire torch forward, Mel's arms ached like she'd been holding it up for hours. Her shoulders stung, too, as her mind drifted to the possibility that there would be a lot more pain to endure before they escaped this place.

The restless rebels sweltered in the congestion, the dank earth closing in. The tunnels made everything feel smaller: their long path forward, the train of rebels in waiting. Her legs shook. Hundreds of rebel freedom fighters depended on her to lead them forward. How'd *she* earned this position? Stress was building: rapid breathing, stale air. Random coughs filled the tunnel. Their situation had become dire, and she felt the rebels watch her for clues to their survival. Then she remembered. From her pants, she pulled Kesselring's stolen nav.

"What's that?" Adrian asked.

"A field Authority nav," she said, palming it with her one hand as she struggled to hold the fire torch in the other. "If it reads desert tunnels, maybe it can read these."

She held her finger to her lips with a forceful glare to ensure the group stayed quiet as she stepped forward. Leroi and Sun Bin followed her closely, flanked by the kids.

"The others need your help, X," Mel said.

"I'm staying with you," X said, forcefully moving past her and grabbing the torch. "And giving you back both hands."

Mel acquiesced, immediate relief welling in her shoulders as if she had dropped a burdened cross.

"Take my headlamp," X said.

She snatched the headlamp and crowned her head. They'd have to move forward carefully without disturbing the tunnel's integrity, but how? She turned back to the swelling group of rebels, their feet shifting impatiently, their eager eyes awaiting clearance. *So many of them.* It was a growing populace that must frustrate Authority forces.

They needed to ensure there was some distance between everyone. The weight of all of them could disturb the tunnel's integrity, its lining. And were those distant explosions she heard? They needed to move. One quick adjustment to her headlamp band and she thrusted forward, haunted by the massive shuffling mass behind her. It was like being chased by an enormous, breathing boulder.

***

As dusk fell, the remaining six grand regional governors across the Third Continent paraded through their routines, aloof in their expectation of the ordinary life. Simultaneously, at the strike of ten o'clock, black-masked figures positioned in wait as the unsuspecting government officials lay reading in their beds, sat at lonely dinner tables, and strolled out of home bathrooms. Lucid moments became masked in perceived safety within their placid nets. Soon dark gloves cupped silent screams as they stabbed and sliced, leaving their victims to fall into their own curdling pools of blood. Tonight, General Speer's mercenaries broke the District Council's dominion.

In her night robe, Grand Regional Governor Lee finished making her night tea as she streamed with Ambassador Mahoney.

"Thank you, Ambassador Mahoney," Lee said into her nexus, clinking her spoon and preparing to settle in for the night. "The District Council exists for this exact reason, quality control. I'm not entirely surprised that this *Speer* has created such problems. The Third Continent is not his to corrupt."

"Time frame?" Ambassador Mahoney asked. "This must be swift, or you'll be dealing with other powers stepping in."

"How much time do we have?" she asked, sipping her tea with both hands, a soothing warmth embracing her soul.

"Global Senate rules require immediate response. In the next day, I need something to take back."

After another swallow of her tea, Lee said, "Tomorrow's eve I will provide authorization from the District Council to reprimand General Speer. Not merely censure, but incarceration. Everyone will be on board. Unfortunately without Martel, but the remaining will approve. Count on it."

"Thank you, Grand Regional Governor. I trust that the Authority does not prefer reduced standing on the world stage. The Global Senate will be satisfied when he is mitigated."

"Good night, Ambassador."

She took one last sip of her tea and switched off her night lamp with a touch. The glistening moon spilled through her intimate quarters as a cloaked executioner then slipped out of the shadows, ambushing the governor from behind with an Old World ninja's invisible grace.

Lee fell to her knees at the foot of her bed in a praying position as her head fell into her blood-soaking sheets, her last gasps inaudible as her mouth opened and closed like a dying fish until she moved no more.

**

To the west, the sleek hydro jet hung over the clearing near Rebel Mountain as Speer monitored his chrono. Rebel Mountain was its name, Speer reasoned, until it was destroyed, at least. Roaring gusts dusted up over indelicate ground crops and debris as he landed. He peeled himself out of the cockpit and dropped to the furrowed ground, landing in a hidden field of . . . *Are those strawberries?* The honeybees couldn't be far from here. He would indeed have it all: destroy the rebels, jail and terminate the treasonous Leroi, and possess the bees. All was within his grasp, he could smell it. Recovering the stolen data would mean nothing now with the District Council obliterated. He *needed* those bees.

"Sir," an assertive voice on his comlink reported. "A drone scout has located the underground cavity likely housing rebels on the west side. The result of a ping from an old model field navigator." A pause hung, as if there was confusion in the newfound information. "Colonel Kesselring's, sir?"

"It's not Kesselring," Speer said. "The fool is sloppy, but he's not here, and we'll deal with him soon enough. This is more obsolete technology in rebel hands. Fire the cannons on the north, south, and east sides," he ordered. "We'll force them out as we also destroy the western wall. Shock and awe."

The commander gave the order, and the cannon-outfitted speed pods promptly launched missile arrows of fire, hundreds raining upon the sprawling mountain's forest green, igniting pockets of overgrowth in rage and fury. Eager kindling embers quickly spread into combusting blazes, devouring the wood with abandon.

"Third wave," Speer ordered into his comlink, his leather boots crunching on the plowed soil as he beelined toward the rebel cave. He was to witness the massacre personally, at any cost. Dozens of black-helmeted troopers and armed infantry officers descended with him upon the cave wall as he kept his distance, observing with cover. Two troopers installed an explosive device on the mountain's base, attaching it to the jagged rock like glue as they prepared for the blast.

From beyond the forest, shelled missiles resounded through the region with roaring echoes. Troopers searched the smoky skies in surprise as whistling missiles pelted them. A clash of loosened rocks and boulders cascaded down, crashing into grounded speed pods and trapping unsuspecting troopers, crushing them in an instant. Flying embers swept into the hull of the rebel port, and dark smoke swelled into the mountain as troopers were sucked under the heavy rubble like a vacuum.

"Fire when ready," Speer ordered into his hand comm from a safe distance.

Today will be the day.

And the day's last hours' light broke.

***

Shell blasts above shook them as they hurried through the expansive underground tunnels, humid and forever winding. Gravel and silt rained down in a flurry of rubble as Mel coughed, finding it harder to breathe. The wet air could make her lungs collapse. Sunlight crept through the tunnel's clay/mud ceiling as the ground shook, tiny streams of light seeping out of pinholes, like a starry sky. Not much daylight was left; it would soon be gone. The tunnel tightened as hastened rebels shuffled behind her with rapid gasps. Stuffy, moist air weighed on her, sinking and nauseating, smelling like a dank grave of roots and copper. Old, wet death.

"This tunnel becomes straight soon," Mel said, studying the field nav, "like a path through rock. Or we're out from under the mountain."

X stayed close, her flaming torch spilling light against the tunnel's walls as Adrian called up to Mel. "Where'd you get that field nav?"

"Swiped it from an old foe," Mel said off-handedly as she marched forward. "And when I say old . . ."

Adrian stopped. "Wait. It's not by any chance an Authority field nav, is it?"

Soon another blast above them shook the ceiling's stability before the tunnel behind them gave way, collapsing on Adrian and drowning her in an angry mud avalanche. Mel watched in shock as her eyes met Adrian's, a quick glimpse as Adrian's horror disappeared in the overwhelming sludge wall of roots and wood. Mel tried not to panic as she shivered, now separated from Y and the rebels.

"Y!" X cried.

With relief, Mel could hear the muffled yells beyond the wall in the earth swallowed. Sun Bin leaned into Leroi, burying his head in her shoulder. Getting them to safety would be a struggle in every way.

"Y!" X screamed, holding tightly to Sun Bin and Leroi behind her. "They are alive on the other side."

"We'll meet you there!" Y yelled faintly through the debris wall. "We'll go another way!"

After stomping on the field nav and crushing its core, Mel took a breath, clutching Sun Bin's lessons to her like a shadow. "Let's go forward," she said as X held on to the collapsed wall, its muddy grave adjacent. "We'll meet him at the rendezvous point. Not a lot of time."

X nodded and followed her.

Frustrated and tired and knowing of no other option, Mel pushed on, relieved Sun Bin's weak legs had not yet buckled as he held onto Leroi. With X lighting their path, Mel lurched forward as another blast hit. She pulled X to her as the tunnel collapsed, the crusted wall of mud and thick tree roots raining down, sodden and packed. More bombs blasted overhead. As the wall settled and the ground fell upon them, heavy and wet, she coughed and choked as the earth swallowed them into its tomb.

TWENTY-SEVEN

Y realized the freedom fighters were immobilized and likely to be crushed. Grungy faces had changed from semi-disciplined dismay to terror, some despondent while others yelled with confusion and hysteria. Concern about being captured had devolved to staying alive. Among the group of four hundred, they had three fire torches and five headlamps between them.

"Go back, go back!" Y yelled, and they turned to escape the way they'd come. The condensed horde of bodies shuffled forward in an impatient, bulbous mass. "Meet the other group, keep going!" Y hollered over the panicked murmurs and shouts. The tunnels had not been tested for a mass exodus. Any moment they could disappear into a dying underground crater. If they got cornered by Authority troops, it would be a massacre. They needed to make it to the larger tunnel.

Pushing through, Y managed to get midway through the group, wielding the torch he'd seized from a younger boy, a much less-deserving manager of the flame. He held it up like an Olympian, his other arm in its sling hanging like a useless appendage. He ignored the bumps against his delicate shoulder wound and the needling pain pinging his senses with panic.

"Move it," he said, shoving aside the freedom fighters, who were virtually all shorter than him. The prodded rebels roamed like the domesticated animals he had read about during Instruction—slow, herd-like, and in need of leadership. They needed to get to the other group, then the transport.

A sense of being left behind agonized the forward march. Could Mel and X isolate him any more? An empty pain panged in his stomach, a sense of queasiness like he had not eaten for days, and his stomach was eating

223

itself. A migraine emerged as his breaths stifled, the air becoming stuffier, like it was too dense for his lungs. Or perhaps there was just less of it. His chest tightened as rage built and grew like a mountain. He should have challenged Mel. He should have fought her, Sangeeosay, whomever, to ensure he was not separated from the group in the first place.

This was their fault.

He clenched his jaw. Of course, with his lack of fortune, Authority fire had hit him and not X. As always, she walked away unscathed. A slow burn singed through his veins as he ignored any concern whether she lived or not. Anger roared through him.

"MOVE!"

***

Cut off and boxed in, Mel's heartbeat hammered as X's single torch slowly died out. Her headlamp bounced around the collapsed chamber. It was five meters wide. She examined the dirt-rock ceiling, searching for a way out. They would suffocate shortly. Missile explosions had unsettled soggy roots and captured water in the earth, further compromising the precarious tunnel's walls. Collected rainwater trickled down the rock's hairline cracks, quietly seeping into their shrinking cavity with the promise of drowning all within.

Then, a glint of light through a bundle of roots peeked through the ceiling. Was she seeing things?

"I don't know how long before it fails," Mel said, tugging lightly on a root to test the ceiling's sturdiness. "There are small air pockets within the root system, which means we might be able to break through."

"It's only centimeters deep in some places," X said, her brow dripping sweat. "They've said that certain parts needed to be reinforced."

"We could use a shovel about now," Leroi said, straining under Sun Bin's meager weight.

"I wish we'd climbed the top of the mountain rather than going under it," Mel said. She frowned as Sun Bin wobbled, his weak legs giving in. He looked pale, even in this light, like he'd lost all fire within. Leroi laid him down gently, easing his head down onto the dank dirt floor.

"Unintended," Sun Bin said, coughing. "This old body has little fight left in it."

X crouched next to him and grabbed his hands, teary-eyed as she gazed down on him. "You can't give up now, Sun Bin, you can't!"

"Child, you've given Sun Bin more new life than in seven lives," he said, struggling with his breaths, his sweat beading.

Examining his shoulder under the blood-soaked gauze, Leroi revealed his gaping wound, blood spilling in a ceaseless flow. "His wound's opened again," she said, as she petted him.

Further inspecting the roots, Mel shifted her headlamp sideways to search for holes of light through the darkness. "We'll get you out of here, Sun Bin. All of us." Though she was unsure how. Fatigued, her arms and legs had lost all steam. Her breath felt shallow, her lungs empty and tight.

"The earth is more delicate than it seems," Sun Bin said, faintly wheezing, as X held his head in her arms. "Do not fail yourselves. The answer is to always look up. You will find light there."

With that, a slate of tunnel rock gave way and a burst of water gushed against their feet—a disturbed natural rainwater reservoir unleashed. Leroi struggled to hold up Sun Bin's head and torso as the caved-in tunnel started to fill, the spouting water jolting them with a rush of ice-cold fear.

"Help!" X cried, her face filled with panic.

Leroi joined her yelling pleas as Mel searched the tunnel's root-ceiling, newly awakened to her own desperation. No way was she letting them all die here. She pulled and tugged and tore at the roots' ends, trying to break free a small patch of earth. Just enough to have hope for sunlight, air. Life. Her hands screamed as they bled, the roots slicing her skin. Frantic now, she became erratic, pulling at everything her bloody hands could grasp.

"Help us!" Leroi and X yelled. Sun Bin began to float as they held him.

"Pull the roots down!" Leroi yelled. "Hoist up!"

"I'm trying!" Mel cried, gritting her teeth and using her boots against the wall for leverage as she pulled with all her might. Then, she discovered some give as the icy water rose to her knees.

"You're doing it!" Leroi said.

"I'm pulling more of the roots into the cave, not getting us out!" Mel yelled as her hands oozed red, ripped and torn. She thought she felt herself pulled upward, confounding her equilibrium. She became confused. Had she really been pulled up?

"Look up!" X yelled. "Look up!"

"What the—" Mel said. She pulled the roots a few centimeters. That's all it could be. Then the roots heaved her toward the ceiling a bit more, unexpectedly boosting her up with an abrupt lift under her water-heavy boots.

Suddenly, a thin metal rod poked through the twisted root bundles, a small camera eye on its tip. The camera head twisted cockeyed.

"Simple Eye!" X yelled, hoisting herself above the gushing rainwater. "Hurry!"

"Not simple at all," Mel cracked, unsure what the drone could do at this point. "C'mon, get us outta here."

"We're gonna drown!" Leroi screamed.

Mel turned back to Leroi, steely-eyed. "It's okay if the kid yells and screams, but get ahold of yourself. I'm working on it." She turned back to the drone. "Pull the roots. I'll push!"

Ignoring her pained hands through her adrenaline surge, she pushed upward as Sun Bin bobbed, the bone-chilling water almost submerging him. There was no time. She strained to thrust upward into the muddy ceiling when the root system abruptly pulled up. Broken light blinded her. A welcomed hand grasped her arm, and she was pulled up until a small sideways tree clogged the exit.

Her drenched blaster drawn, she raised her hardhat to see Beck poking his head over the hole, now a quarter-meter wide. She lowered her weapon, never happier to see him.

"Whatcha doing down there?" Beck asked, grinning widely.

"Hope you're not expecting a damsel's welcome," Mel quipped, wanting to strangle his handsome, gritty face. "Hurry, it's flooding."

Using muscular claws and grasping onto the thick, muddy roots like vices, Simple Eye tugged and widened the opening. X squinted into the sun as she and Leroi held Sun Bin's head up as he buoyed, about to succumb to the well's gush.

"Sun Bin first!" X yelled. Beck ignored her and abruptly grabbed and hauled her up out of the tunnel, sodden and soaked. "Hurry!" she yelled again, wiping mud out of her eyes.

"I *am* hurrying," Beck said, lowering his arms for the old man. "And don't yell—troopers are everywhere."

Mel wrestled underwater as she held up Sun Bin, the gushing, icy current thrashing them both about, chilling her bones. The flooding flow transformed into a rising muddy whirlpool. Images of her being pulled from her family and institutionalized moved through her like lightning as the water raged. Haunting thoughts interrupted her need to breathe as her temples pulsated. She raised Sun Bin, fighting against the current to keep her feet on the tunnel's floor. Soon she felt the relief of Sun Bin leaving her arms, his hands clutching his scythe like a lifeline.

She heard her name over the water. Was that X? Unable to see anything from under the muddy tow, she thought of the erratic speed pod chases as she struggled to get to the surface, the horror at the Moat of Moorack, and, oddly, Beck holding her. Then, the revelation her family was dead, getting the children home to safety. If there was such a thing. Sun Bin. *Do not fail*, he had said. Exhaustion was getting the better of her, while the need to breathe crushed her insides.

Leroi struggled next to her, and Mel inhaled a pocket of air before diving back under the rushing whirlpool and thrusting Leroi upward. Leroi was lifted out as Mel sank to the floor. The frigid cold cramped her legs, the bitterness piercing her body like knives. She thrust upward with all the force she could muster, tiring, gasping at the surface as Leroi, Beck, and X grabbed for her over the edge as the rising water brimmed. The frigid air made her shake, but she could breathe. Everyone had made it out, and she lunged forward a step, becoming light-headed. Familiar Simple Eye bleeps registered in her consciousness as the drone twirled with glee.

"We got you," Beck said as they pulled her out fully. Mel coughed and spat out the filthy, rusty-brown water as Beck laid her down, carefully laying her head back. Eyes up to him, she had never imagined him from this angle. He looked down upon her, studying her condition as if ensuring all her parts were in order, and attached. Perhaps he managed everything (and everyone) like they were speed pods, or *Airfoil*— mechanized tools that could be repaired. At once powerful and tender, which she would normally consider suspect, Beck smiled as he wiped grit from around her eye.

"You made it!" X beamed.

"Quiet," Beck said, monitoring their surroundings for the invaders and pointing to two half-submerged dead troopers. "Black helmets have bosses, and they'll be looking for these guys soon."

Mel leaned upward as she got her bearings. "Surprised you came back."

"The drone wouldn't shut up, knowing you were in trouble," Beck said. "I almost deactivated the thing for salvage. How's the old man?"

"He's dying," Leroi said tersely as she and X tended to him, having moved him above the overflowing crater as the well's water rolled downhill.

Soaked and parched, Mel crawled to Sun Bin like a shiftless snake, shaking him to wake. "I'm sorry," she said softly. His eyes were serene, distant.

"You looked up," Sun Bin said knowingly, grabbing her hand. "The land will always take back."

"If you let it," Beck grumbled, surveying the grassy and muddy landscape.

"The Authority did this," Mel said, the lump in her throat making her voice coarse. She held his frail hand firmly, a hand she couldn't let go.

"The Authority," Sun Bin wheezed, "is a symptom . . . of a poisoned land." He set his eyes firmly on Mel, as if trying to see through her as he moved farther away. "You have to stop it, Mel."

"You want me to fight."

"You must not run."

"Sun Bin," Mel said, her eyes starting to flood. "We need you."

"Oh, child," Sun Bin said, catching his breath as if his lungs were punctured, "lead as you will, like fire. I'm with you at your call."

"I don't want—"

"You . . . must," Sun Bin said, interrupting her as the light touch of his fingers receded, "wake what's within." He took his last breath, and Mel paused as she closed her eyes, sinking into a chasm. She lowered her head near his, breathing in his spirit as a fevered chill went down her spine.

Simple Eye whimpered a sour note. The sun set. X wept in the quiet moment before jarring blasts echoed close by. Darkness swelled, falling over them like a black sheet. A sudden explosion hit Beck's speed pod at the trees' perimeter, blowing off the roof into a blaze of burnt metal.

"Awwww, no!" Beck said. "My money was in there." He fired a couple of shots, and one trooper fell as another approached. Bristling, Beck fired two more blasts, but the trooper successfully ducked them. "I told you we needed to be quiet!"

"Excuse me!" X said, her face streaked with tears. "Not an easy day!"

The black helmet fired several rounds and hit Simple Eye, frying the shrieking drone into a charred sphere of burnt panels.

"Simple Eye!" X cried as the drone hit the muddy, uneven ground with a *thud.*

Seeing the trooper raise a wrist to prepare to call control, Beck steadied his hand and fired, finally taking down the last black helmet. "I knew this wasn't a good idea."

***

As the dawn glimmered orange in the east, Mel stepped back, drenched in Earth's paint, plastered with the mire's filth and struggling to see through the caked muck. Before her, Sun Bin's body was entombed in a mound of mud, much less than he deserved. She would not leave him here forever, forgotten in molded soil as life often is. At least Beck knew better than to try and stop her from burying him.

Despite Beck's uneasiness, he let her continue without interruption, anxiously monitoring the grounds, routinely turning in circles, his blaster drawn. Her tired bones hurt, and her eyes stung from covering Sun Bin's corpse with mud and dignity. His death was her fault, and she had insisted she bury him alone. It was she who had agreed to take him and the children from Vulnus Outpost. It was she who had sucked him into his last hours of struggle on the run.

And yet she had never thanked him.

Sharp pangs of exhaustion pierced her back. Her wounded hands burned and her neck strained, an exhaustion she ignored. Whatever happened now, how could she ignore the rebels' plight?

As she covered Sun Bin's grave with the last mud clumps, his scythed staff laid to the side, its curved blade in the mire, lonesome and calling. As Beck, Leroi, and X let her be, she ached as she carefully bent down to inspect its muddy blade, the rising sun's yellow and orange glimmer bouncing off its spotty shiny parts. She held up the staff, its thick, round wood solid, ample in mass. It had more heft than she imagined Sun Bin could have dragged across the vast desert prairies.

She thrust the staff forward, the weighted blade at its tip inside her unseen opponent. She gripped it still and held her breath. Her strength and balance returned like a welcome memory. She let herself breathe in calm. The pain in her hands dissipated like desert dust, and she swung the staff around like a bokken, its blade spinning in calculated rotations as she thrust it forward and then backward, spreading her stance as she lunged the staff with grace. Again.

Her mother and sister, dreams really, seared through her as she twisted and turned, their remembrance and love swirling in a fight dance with the twirling blade. Loss and pain, solitude and death. No tears, the pain would be gone now. She grounded center, handling the scythed staff as both a javelin and a baton. Her breathing evened out as she crossed her hands and wielded it with a windmill of speed, ignoring the astonished stares of X, Leroi, and Beck as it spun through her hands faster and faster, her reborn rage providing her focus and determination to become what she needed to survive. To go forward. To embrace her other side.

The warrior.

Twenty-Eight

Speer approached the decimated cave wall. Blasts ricocheted against the mountain rocks, echoing across the sky with jarring clacks and booms. Relentless barrages continued to strike the mountain's perimeter, pounding the rebel fortress. Speer kept his eyes on the prize: he would capture and kill Custode and Leroi. With the District Council dissolved, he would set his sights on delivering a death knell to the Global Senate—a time of reckoning the rebels and global powers would never forget.

From inside the mountain, Authority forces had reported the capture of no one. Tiny floor beds and movable trundles, frayed linens, and empty cupboards indicated a growing rebel populace had inhabited the maze of meager caves and surprisingly oversized rooms. A smattering of littered garments, cleaning rags, and crude stoneware indicated they'd left in a huff. Only a few inactive transporters and ASVs remained in the main hangar, since pulverized from the power grid's annihilation.

Speer and his band of troopers entered the cave, stomping over the crumbled, shaved rock. There were no supplies, no rebels to be found. His nostrils flared. The evasive rats had successfully departed with resources. Many, they had stolen from his camp.

Again.

Making his way through the mountain's main artery to a clearing, he clenched his fists and stopped. *Think.* The power grid had been destroyed, and yet they found a way time and again to communicate. *How do they always know we are coming?*

"Commander Adie, who is responsible for this pathetic offensive that gave them time to evacuate?"

She swallowed, her eyes drenched in fear. "I am, sir. But I take direct orders from—"

A quick nod, and the black helmets fired their blasters. Commander Adie stammered as she fell into a lifeless heap at his feet. He watched her, curling and gurgling as her eyes met his, wide-eyed with shock and the reluctant realization she shouldn't have been surprised. Too many times he had been let down. So far, only the machines had not shown such ineptitude. His orders were not vague; instead, they were definitive and impatient.

A black helmet approached him. "Sir, we have uncovered an elaborate tunnel system."

"You don't say." Speer sighed, his eyes rolling up and around as he continued to move forward. "I don't want to hear—"

"They must have evacuated—"

"Enough!" Speer said, throwing his palm to the trooper's face without taking his eyes off the ceiling. Overhanging the top of the cave, the magnificent sight of a bees' nest up above greeted him like a brilliant chandelier reflecting rays of glittery gold. For the first time, he almost believed in God. "The treasure of all treasures."

The troopers awkwardly gazed upward through their restrictive helmets. "Shall we destroy it, sir?" one of them asked.

If he looked close enough, he could see the massive nest was alive and heaving, its massive belly moving like a beating heart, quivering inside like a massive womb. "No, we'll take it."

**

"They were right behind us, somewhere around here," X said, hoping she was right as she maneuvered around furrows and craters in the churned soil, trying to imagine where Y and the rebels would be. If only they had a working field nav reader. Her heart sunk as she imagined the worst. Hopefully Y had made it through the other exit tunnel, and then the rebel rendezvous. Mel, Beck, and Leroi followed her and poked around, searching for a clue.

"So you don't know if he's trapped but think he might be?" Beck said incredulously.

"I think," X said, staring him down. She allowed herself to bother talking to him at all, accepting he had indeed saved their lives, before focusing her attention back below her feet as Mel peered over her shoulder.

"We can't stay here for long," Mel said. "Can you feel that?"

"Feel what?" Beck shook his head in disbelief. "We have to work off facts, not feelings."

"More troopers I bet," X said as she tended to a wounded Simple Eye at her feet. The drone's eyelid blinked in wounded earnest, as if enjoying the attention.

"No," Leroi said, poking Mel's shoulder.

The mellow hum of the large transport encroached upon them, almost covert. X's mouth opened wide in awe as the behemoth, as colossal as an ore barge, rolled over the landscape like a rumbling gray cloud. It was twenty times larger than the rebels' stolen blockade runner had been. Grungy, rebel faces peered out at them from hundreds of oval portholes. Hovering like it came from another planet, the gigantic ship held no less than two thousand rebels along with much of their supplies inside. The imposing rebel cruiser was multilevel, its hull and crawl spaces restricted in height and expanded in width to fit its expanding rebel community within its walls. The vessel's burners were encompassed within its leg pillars as it landed, its steel claws expanding to evenly grasp the uneven earth. It landed with a gentle boom.

A rebel captain popped his head out of the cruiser side door as rebel fighters stood prepared with arms. His frazzled hair overwhelmed him as much as his tattered, threadbare clothing. "Want a ride?"

General Sangeeosay appeared behind the captain, searching. Her hopeful gaze stopped at the mud mound laying atop one of the craters.

"Is that—"

X interrupted. "We buried him." Mel stood next to her with pledge and resolve, holding up Sun Bin's scythed reclaimed staff. "She did, actually. Did you know him?"

"Thank you," Sangeeosay said, ignoring X's question. A cloud of sublime mourning washed over the general, regrets of a life now absent.

"General, Authority troops are advancing," the captain said. "Fuel levels are lower than originally thought, the gauges are corroded. We must find a place to harbor and scout for reserves. There are two nearby possibilities. We need your direction."

Longing for Sun Bin and stricken, Sangeeosay nodded slowly and retreated inside the transport without saying another word.

X beamed back up at the rebel captain hopefully. "Did you pick up Y?"

"If you mean Y-H17, we picked up most of his outfit. Y-H17 and a few others stayed back to protect the nest."

X coughed. "What?"

"He said, 'If no one protects them, the Authority gets them,' and he refused to board. No words got through to him. We had to depart."

"Them?" Beck asked.

"The bees, of course," X said. She pictured the bees' home abandoned in the dark cave, alone and quiet save for the bees' buzzing.

"The Authority would kill for that honey," Leroi added, somewhat out of place as a recent rebel convert. "And will."

"I'm not going to keep getting dragged into a war that ain't mine," Beck quipped. "I've got business to tend to back home. I'm done with this party."

"We can't leave him!" X pleaded. "You can't pretend Y can save himself!"

Mel turned to Beck as Simple Eye let out a soft whirring moan from X's cradling arms, its claw repairing itself with a tiny sparkling wand.

Shaking his head, Beck opened his arms to the landscape like a showman as Mel's steely-eyed gaze stared him down. "Who's stupid enough to go back to that mountain?" Beside himself, he fidgeted. "Aw, I can't believe this!"

"That's what you get for coming back to save us," X said, beaming up at him.

A rebel officer said, "We've been detected. We must find safe harbor. Plan to depart in T minus twenty seconds."

"On board now," the captain said as Mel nodded at Beck.

"My speed pod's gone, so we're going for it on foot, because that's the smart thing to do," Beck said sarcastically, starting to walk in circles, resigned.

"I hope we can come back for you," the captain said.

"Not counting on it," Beck said, as Leroi and X shared a grin, and the barge's side door shut with an ominous whoosh.

Through the windows, fatigued rebels glared with interest and distress, as if wondering why the crew was being left behind. A little girl waved at X. She smiled back faintly as the barge departed abruptly, and her mind wandered back to Y and the bees' nest and what would befall them all.

***

Y and the other young rebels hid around the cave's wall corner, sight unseen, like rebel ghosts. They could see troopers congregating in the cave's clearing, swiftly executing their orders. Under the nest above, they dropped piping that expanded into a system of parts, starting as one-metered aluminum poles and extending into colossal thirty-meter ladders. A digital schematic read the distance necessary, and the poles flipped upon each other, multiplying to the desired length. Just as Sangeeosay had feared, the troopers were planning to take down the nest. Stealing the honey was one thing. Stripping down the nest, though, would be a much bigger ordeal.

"Y-H17, what next?"

He grimaced. Every time he heard his rebel signature, he weirdly preferred X's nickname for him. She did not acknowledge his last-in-class designation, just as he didn't acknowledge her first. As "X" and "Y," they were on equal footing. He turned to the three young freedom fighters, heroic in their quest.

After a long night of evasion, their grungy faces were pasted with dread. They'd soon regret staying back if they didn't already. "We can't let them take the bees or find the honey. You ready?"

"If you can do it wearing your sling, we can," X-R9 said, motioning to Y's sagging arm wrapped in gauze. "Without slings." She was slight, but her tone was powerful.

He ducked back in the dark as a pack of armed troopers marched by. He caught his breath, stunned they hadn't been seen.

"Why did we do this?" Y-M5 whispered, a beefy and brawny fifteen-year-old who appeared to have eaten more than his fair share of rations. With genetics on his side, he had more muscle in one of his arms than Y did in both legs.

"Because no one else would," X-R9 said.

"No diddle-daddle," Y said, holding his mini-blaster and preparing to assault, aware he had no plan outside of protecting the nest.

"Where did you get those?" Y-N14 asked, pointing to Y's munitions, the mini-blasters strapped to his ankles under his boxy, frayed pants: half-pint munitions with a fraction of the firepower of regular barreled guns. The inquisitive young boy had long lashes that softened his brown eyes, which were dark like wet river rock.

"I took them from the fast box. Stored them on my legs for backup."

"I want one," the boy retorted.

"Me too," X-R9 said.

"I've got one, but I'm short on ammo," the older Y-M5 said. "My dad will lose his mind though."

"Of course," Y said, disappointed to give them up. Mini-blasters would have limited impact on the troopers' armor anyway. They were meant for target practice within the young ranks, not destroying Authority troopers. But an Authority gun—he'd be more effective with one of those.

A trooper climbed the ladder extender uncomfortably close to the bees' nest. Scaling its rungs, his heavy boots fit each step snugly as two troopers held the ladder's base steady. Getting anxious, Y's limbs went numb, his legs aching as he crouched down. What to do as the trooper neared the ladder's top, carrying hefty shears on his belt as stray bees fluttered and flurried about?

"Um, look," young Y-N14 said, pointing.

An ASV hauler hovered over the crushed rocks at the cave's entrance, backing in with its gate down, like a mouth prepared to load the poached prize.

"They're gonna take the nest," Y-M5 said. "If they can get it down."

Y's attention was pulled to the black helmet atop the ladder, the shears gripped and unsheathed like a weapon. Thousands of bees crawled and descended upon the nest's crown. He gaped in wonder, reflecting on the horror he'd seen at the moat. Was nature itself an aberration? Perhaps it evolved to its next normal, what was natural. Maybe nothing was natural anymore.

The trooper hesitated upon the ladder's peak, perhaps knowing he was about to disrupt an ecosystem of seismic proportions. This was no small feat, taking down a nest of hundreds of thousands of bees. Then, as if he'd made the abrupt decision to get the job over with, he hastily moved to clip the stem. Working to get his footing as he leaned in, the bees clung to his armor and gathered upon his helmet. His arms flailed as stray bees attached to him in moving clusters of gold. He tried shaking them off, a useless exercise.

"You sure we shouldn't just use a drone for this?" one of the officers called from below.

"Don't rock the ladder!" another officer yelled as he ran to assist at the ladder's base, peering up at the teetering trooper. "Just clip it! They can't hurt you!"

Both troopers glanced at each other through their faceless helmets and shrugged before turning back to the trooper, one arm pressed against the nest as he struggled to snap the stem.

In the cavity's shadows, a spare ammunition clip fell out of Y's pocket, tumbling down his side to land at his feet with a dull *clang*, unheard above the commotion in the cave. He sighed, imagining X balking at him. Hesitating. Careless. He would demonstrate he was not useless within the ranks, even if he died proving it. Everyone would see.

"Okay," he whispered to the other three. "The mini-blasters don't have enough firepower to take down the troopers, so we need to go after the officers first."

"That's the plan?" the girl sneered.

Y glared at her, a precocious X in the making. "I was getting to that."

"I can't believe we have baby blasters," the older Y-M5 said, frowning.

"They're training guns, you know that," Y whispered, conscious of another trooper outfit coming their way lugging a giant, empty storage bin. The Authority must have believed food resources had been abandoned during the evacuation too. Rebel plans for evacuation had been prepared from the beginning, and he'd sat through Instruction learning more about the tunnels' blueprints than he had ever wanted to learn. Now, just the bees' nest hung precariously from the cathedral ceiling, as the trooper wrestled the giant sheers.

"Hit the officers, not the nest," Y continued. "Mini-blasters could destroy it."

"Baby blasters," Y-M5 muttered.

He scanned their faces to gauge their readiness. "Don't aim high. If I take down a trooper, grab one of their blasters. You remember their armored weaknesses?"

"The neck and knees," all three said in unison.

"Okay, let's go," he said, leading the charge into the cave's clearing, the small clan firing their mini-blasters. From one segmented corner, a firestorm emerged.

Surprised by the assault, several troopers and officers immediately took fire. Y-N14 struggled with his mini-blaster's clip as his sister, X-R9, successfully fired, missed her target, and ran for cover. Adolescent Y-M5 held mini-blasters in each hand near his torso and fired at the troopers with reckless and excessive abandon, his face wide with excitement, his face red and swollen like a strawberry. Then he frowned, disappointed he missed everything he'd aimed for.

"What are you doing?" X-R9 asked him as they ducked behind a pony wall of crates and blocks stacked like bricks.

Y-M5 frowned as the ammunition depleted and his mini-blasters died.

"This way!" X-R9 yelled, and both boys ran for cover. From behind a cave wall, she fired deliberate shots as they hid, grazing an officer within a growing crowd of firing troopers that congregated en masse in a firing inferno.

"What now?" Y-N14 asked over the clamoring blaster fire.

Y continued to hit and miss troopers as the fire blasts intensified into a deafening barrage. His clip emptied, and an eruption of fire forced him to slip behind nearby giant storage containers.

He stewed. Was X with Mel and the crew aboard the *Catharsis*, the savior rebel cruiser, while he was here alone trying to be *a hero*? The bees' nest, its draw, had pulled him back here like a calling beacon, a magnificent buzzing knell. Why had he allowed X to fool him into thinking leading a team of young rebels with minis could stand up to Authority forces? Or had he just fooled himself?

It was her fault.

After slapping his empty clip down, frustrated nothing was working out, he looked up to see a trooper peering down at him like he was trampled grass.

"A child," the trooper said through his black helmet, his mournful tone projecting disappointment.

"Unless," Y said, his mind racing for an option, understanding his dire situation. "Pretend you never saw me?"

He stared up at the blaster's barrel. This was not at all how it was supposed to go. Behind the trooper's menacing black-eyed glass was a face he'd never see: the nameless, faceless executioner he'd never know. If only X could see him now, facing his demise as she cozied up to Mel and Simple Eye. She was probably being celebrated while he was again ignored, the unknown savior. Acquiescing as he swallowed the dry lump in his throat, he counted the beats to his end, down on his knees like a thirsty vagabond wishing for that first and last precious drop.

Then, something pulled the trooper's attention: two fire blasts preceded a vacuum breeze sweeping through the cave's mouth as the mountain moaned. At the cave's entrance, dry forest leaves and sagebrush skipped across the cave's floor, sweeping it with dust and debris as smoke billowed behind it in puffs of white and gray, as if a new season had arrived.

Rubble and gravel slipped off the walls in sheets as the earth settled, and the black helmets turned to the clouds of smoke, their blasters drawn but restrained. They bounced looks at each other, bewildered at the disturbance's gall to intrude. Another gale blew through the cave, a long gasping breath as the earth burped crumbles of rock. The leaves and debris danced, and the dust twirled. Y's eyes strained wide in anticipation. What was happening? His heart hammered in his chest, the drumbeat pounding his ears.

Suddenly, two figures appeared in the demolished wall's entryway, the backlighting masking them as dark shadows. Was he seeing things? He poked his head out farther to see black helmets responding, revealing the hellfire aimed at both Mel and Beck. Warmth rolled through his veins like a powerful ASV. Beck's blaster fire mowed down the firing troopers one by one as Mel, caked with dried mud, struck at them with a scythed staff, swiping them off their feet before she plunged the blade through their chest plates. Was that Sun Bin's scythe?

A smattering of gunfire sparked off the cave's walls as Leroi and X appeared, a second wave through the ghostly smoke. Like the arrival of the cavalry, Simple Eye, too, swam through the air, weaving and bobbing and distracting trooper gunfire that instead penetrated the mountain wall, ricocheting into nothing. Y's blood quickly burned as a symphony of chills rose through him like an orchestra. They had not abandoned him after all. They had come back.

Y rose to his feet and wrestled with the distracted trooper, caught up in his own frenzy and exhilaration, endorphins blazing under his skin as he punched and kicked with all he had. His eyes glazed with new, euphoric power as he caught the trooper flatfooted and startled. Seizing the moment, he snatched the trooper's blaster and the trooper dropped, hit by fire, before the blaster jammed. Y threw it down, incensed.

Meanwhile, a sly trooper slipped behind Mel and blasted her arm. She dropped the scythed staff in pain, her arm singed a burnt-black and emitting gray smoke like she had been branded. A wounded Simple Eye extended a claw to pick up the scythe in a feat of painstaking and uneasy balance.

As Y peered out in hopes of finding another blaster or load clip, Beck prepared to blast a trooper until Mel crouched and swept her leg out, knocking the trooper off his feet. She dropped to the downed trooper's side and elbowed his neck, knocking the wind out of him. Simple Eye passed her the scythe, and she knocked the trooper out cold. Who knew she had it in her?

One of the last standing field officers aimed his weapon at Mel, but Leroi fired at him as Simple Eye launched a free blaster weapon in the air. Mel skillfully snatched it with her good hand and shot at another trooper firing at Beck. The black helmet fell back on his rump.

"Good job there, missy," Beck said, taking down two troopers trading fire with him.

"Don't call me that," Mel said, shooting at the firing troopers at the ladder's base. "Good shots yourself." She elbowed a stealthy officer sneaking behind her in the abdomen and, with another swift move, broke his nose.

As Beck crouched to avoid fire blasts, a shot ricocheted off the wall and sliced through the officer's side. He fell with a *thud*.

"Where'd you learn that?" Beck asked, his eyes wide.

"Nothing to worry about," Mel said as she tore down another aggressive trooper with one shot.

"We'll have more Authority gifts soon if we stick around," Beck said.

"I'm here!" Y yelled, relief washing over him.

"Y!" X beamed, her head poking out from behind the cave wall.

With an adrenaline rush, Y raced through the decreasing gunfire and grabbed the downed trooper's blaster. He shot and missed a black helmet, who turned to him and fired, hitting his leg.

"Awwwww," he wailed, dropping the blaster as Beck fired and hit the trooper from behind. Y crawled as shots ricocheted, nodding to the kids hiding behind the corner wall unhelpfully. He peered out to see Beck fire on another combative trooper. Two of Beck's missed shots ricocheted and hit the bees' nest, disturbing the protective home and causing a frenzy. The belly of the nest started to heave and growl, a beast awoken. Like a switch had been flipped, the bees swarmed in a buzzing, golden wave.

"Oh no," Beck said.

Meanwhile, the trooper atop the ladder struggled to snap the stem's final thread as the troopers at the extender's base fell to blaster fire. The aggressive bees swarmed the trooper, covering him like thick, yellow dust.

"They're in my helmet!" the trooper cried, struggling to strip his helmet off as the bees wormed their way under his armor. He wavered at the top of the ladder as it shook, troopers dead at its base. In shameless rage, the horde of bees relentlessly blanketed the trooper and he screamed, falling the twenty-plus meters to his demise.

X's eyes bulged as the bees took flight, emptying the nest in a well-communicated tussle. "Hurry, this way!" she yelled as she led Mel, Beck, and Leroi to a hidden tunnel nearby.

"Well, taking the bees with us is out!" Beck yelled as the bees' humming amplified into a roaring, thunderous buzzsaw, bewildering Simple Eye into a tizzy, twirling in flight. The drone bounced and clanged on the ground, its sensors thrown off by the swarm's chaotic order.

Y watched them leave longingly, separated from the group by the resounding, moving wall of bees. He met X's gaze and she stopped, as if she didn't want to leave him. Was it sibling love? Sibling rivalry and also love?

"We have to go!" X-R9 yelled, and Y dragged his foot as the kids hauled him into one of the side caves as the bees flew through the great room in a raging cyclone.

Over his shoulder, he saw X had finally left, and X-R9 and the boys pulled him into another sealed compartment. Simple Eye, a fraction of

241

itself (as its side panels were bent inward and an antenna was missing), squeezed through the cave's door before it slammed shut. In a flash, Y's hope of being reunited with the crew had been snatched as quickly as it had arrived.

***

About twenty meters outside the cave wall, Authority forces collected as Speer arrived, wide-eyed and alert. He was going to win today.

"This is the west entrance to the disturbed nest, sir," the commander said in what Speer thought was a cautious tone, unsure of how he would react. "We think it was Custode and Leroi that entered and—"

"Annihilated our entire outfit," Speer finished. "All was good when I was here ten minutes ago."

"I understand they had help and—"

"The nest has not yet been preserved?" Speer interrupted. There was no need to hear the rest.

"No, sir," the commander said, his voice cracking. "The bees have taken flight but have not left the main complex. It's as if they refuse to leave."

Speer was not amused. "Bees fly. What do you mean they refuse to leave?"

"There's another entrance a mere twenty meters up we think the rebels used to—"

That was it. "Blow the wall," Speer ordered.

The commander paused as if he didn't agree this was indeed the smartest thing. "Kill all the bees too, sir? We don't want to collect them before—"

"Commander," Speer said, squinting as he lost his remaining patience. *Push me one step further.* One more casualty today was not a problem; they'd been adding up. "I said blow the wall. Do you disagree with this particular tactic?"

"No, sir," the commander said, and he left in a huff.

An Authority sentry, giant and sinister, held its artillery cannons on both pipe-woven arms, loaded with ammunition. It stood alert like a hunter, eavesdropping on Speer's words.

Finally, someone who will listen to me the first time. "Check the entrance and work our cannons to destroy it," Speer said. "After I search it, we'll destroy the mountain rock by rock."

"Destroy the mountain rock by rock," the sentry repeated, its red beady eyes reading Speer in a trance.

"That's what I said . . . until it's done," Speer said, shaking his head. The robotic machine was not technology at its best, but it didn't argue. At this point, he was done with everyone and everything. "Idiot."

The sentry nodded and followed Speer as Authority cannons outfitted on deluxe Authority pods fired above the cave's mouth, their assault guns thrusting forward like pistons. Instantly, the mountain's cave entrance collapsed in a mighty rock and sand avalanche.

"Destroy the mountain rock by rock," the sentry repeated to two other machines, agreeable and compliant. "Rock by rock."

***

Y and his clan of young freedom fighters traveled through a narrow passageway as the mountain shuddered, rattling pebbled sand. Grit and silt rained down in acquiescence to the Authority, more than he ever would. Living through this, Sangeeosay would have to acknowledge Y's heroism as he fought off Authority troops, wouldn't she?

And what about X? Concern for her, trapped within the mountain's crushing walls, haunted him. Had she really come back but left him behind again?

"You've got not one gunshot wound but two!" Y-M5 said in awe and echo as they shuffled through the side tunnel, flipping on the headlights, which lit up the kids' faces like ghosts.

"We can't take on those troopers by ourselves," Y said, blood drenching his pants. "What would we do even if we could get out of this place now?" His knees felt weak.

X-R9 didn't blink. "Now you say that? After we got ourselves stuck here?"

He felt sick again. "I thought—"

"You *thought?*" Y-M5 said, his face flushed and rosy red within the hard light.

Y-N14's eyes pierced Y like daggers. "We didn't follow you so you could back out halfway through."

"I—" Y tried again.

"Don't," X-R9 interrupted. She went up to him. "We trusted you going against Sangeeosay to save the bees. We don't have them now, do we?" Her misty eyes welled with tears as her voice shook.

"My mom's gonna kill me," Y-N14 growled.

"We're going," Y-M5 said. X-R9 backed up as the three kids prepared to continue down the rattling tunnel. "You should do the same."

Y's spirit withered as he watched them go. Any sense of command and self-resolution dissipated, and he suddenly questioned everything. Was this really his fault?

The mountain grumbled louder and the ground quaked, his bloodied knee jarring as he fell back against the tunnel wall. Now he didn't care about being buried in the unstable rock, unable to get up.

"Just leave me," he heard himself say.

"We've got to get out of here," X-R9 said out of nowhere, kneeling down to him. She held out her hand. "Use all you've got. If the Authority doesn't get us—"

"The mountain will crush us," Y said as she pulled him up.

To the side, Simple Eye lay, struggling to power up with its single eye fading. Clumsy on his feet, Y dragged his leg as he fought the pain to run faster behind them as they got farther away through the shifting, claustrophobic tunnel, the natural light far ahead.

Behind him, the drone's eye opened as it started to bumble toward the exit, as if fearing to be left behind also. Rolling in fits and starts, the drone rolled forward as larger rocks started to crumble from within, clunking its head and jarring it awake.

TWENTY-NINE

Inside the hidden and jolting cavern, Mel could not believe her eyes. Rubbing them in the glistening blackness, she looked again. A massive heart-stopping honey pool, twenty-meters wide and filled to the brim, encompassed most of the dark space. Only a meter-wide walkway bordered the golden glow, surrounding it like a saucer.

How deep could the honey possibly go? The rich, heavy syrup sank into the cradling rock. Soft light beamed through the cave's peak, revealing the massive storage of liquid gold in a canopy of white haze. Disturbed walls of rock grumbled like a hungry beast as the pool swayed in elegant waves and splendor as if in slow motion.

"Grab onto anything!" Beck yelled, his eyes bulging as his blaster slipped out of his hands into the shifting pool, its golden waves shimmering light into the deep's darker copper. He scowled. "No other exit out of here, huh?"

Another cannon blast rocked the mountain's core, unsettling it. Information/weapon systems were to be destroyed. Anyone left behind would be finished.

Staying close to X, Mel grappled crevices into the wall of rock with one hand as she leveraged the scythed staff as a javelin to keep her propped up against the wall. Leroi and Beck held onto whatever they could within the jagged rock, everyone just steps from each other as dust and debris rained from the cavern's unstable lining.

"I bet that's not an earthquake," X said, her hands grasping both a rock's ridge and Mel's torso as the ground beneath them shifted like unhappy tectonic plates.

"Don't think so, kid!" Beck hollered. For a flash, like in an odd dimension, the room calmed as the sun's rays eased through the rock ceiling hanging over the golden pool in white, soul-stirring light. "So we left one collapsing cave for another. What we need is an exit!"

"It's real," Leroi said, her eyes wide. "That's a lot of honey."

"Way too much honey," Beck said, his eyes darting uneasily around, looking for a nonexistent back door.

Mel's mind raced. Was there a way to transport even part of it?

"Supposedly eighty-thousand liters or more," X said, as if she could read her mind.

Mel searched the pool's edge for a tool, a pole, anything to get them out of here. The mountain grumbled louder, punches of anger in response to each ferocious bomb's hit.

"Too much of anything can't be good!" Beck yelled over the mountain's roar. It quaked louder as they held on to the walls for dear life. "I heard the stuff is overrated anyway!"

Mel blinked. There, piles of hive collectors and storage vats were strewn to the side, holding up a corner of the shaking cavern. Maybe something to help them escape? As she gripped the scythed staff, she scooted away from the honey pool. Perhaps she needed forty steps.

"They were working on a plan," X said, dusting herself off as the cave settled—intermittent relief. "Maybe broker peace? I don't know what we're going to do if it's in Authority hands."

"Well, we can't take it with us," Beck said. "I say we go back how we came in."

A few more steps and Mel could make out the pile of tools. *Are those fighting sticks?* Abandoned batons lay next to the storage vats. She moved closer.

"I'm staying outside of tunnels and caves for a while," X deadpanned.

Mel paused. Authority jointed truncheons. She recognized them immediately, piled and forgotten, perhaps acquired during rebel raids and hidden away from rebel hands, the children. Stolen from the dead?

"Hiding, I see," a man said, suddenly appearing through the cave's door, his gun drawn. A hunkering shadow lurched toward them, as if to witness their execution, as reflecting pieces of mountain rock behind him smothered the cave in slivers of natural light. "Always hiding."

A towering sentry bumped backward clumsily, unable to fit through the tight entryway. Behind it, a parkour bot blasted a sensor on the wall, slamming the cave door shut. The cavern dimmed again to a ghostly hue as they became closed off from life and death outside of this cave.

"Damn robots," he mumbled under his breath.

"General Speer," Leroi announced, "the self-appointed regional governor of the forty-four districts. You are hardly in control of one."

Mel could sense the evil sneer crossing his face.

"You," X gasped.

"Much more than that," Speer said flatly.

Mel's blood curdled. *He's the one behind recruiting me.*

He moved toward them, Mel aware of his intent of accomplishment, of death.

"No one thought of locking the door?" Beck cracked.

"So this is where you've kept it," Speer said, transfixed on the profound and haunting golden honey pool. From the delicate light seeping down from the ceiling like a chandelier, the general appeared aged and worn, absorbed in the spectacle. An old critter, his eyes bugged out of his face like yellow beetles. "As the bees settle back in their hive, you hide in here with *this.*"

"Their nest," Mel corrected.

"Why don't you put the blaster down," Beck said. Mel wondered under what conditions Beck thought he could order Speer.

Speer shook his head. "I don't take orders from rats."

Beck raised his brow. Of all the names he'd been called, Mel suspected he rarely had been referred to as a rodent.

Mel moved slowly for the truncheons.

"You," Speer said, aiming his blaster at Leroi. "You're a traitor."

"I'm—"

Leroi fell, the shot echoing in the cave like a hollow cannon. He immediately aimed the blaster at the other three as Leroi recoiled in pain. Her weapon slipped and disappeared into the golden, copper goo.

"We'll kill you here," Mel said, squarely aiming her blaster at the general with her good arm, her blasted shoulder in stinging pain. The blaster jammed.

"You," Speer said, unflinching, as if unsurprised by the weapon's limitations. "You are Custode."

Mel struggled to unjam the munition, readjusting its clip as Speer fired again, hitting her in the groin. She fell, dropping her scythed staff precariously over the honey pool's edge. Her blaster stretched a meter out of reach.

"You're famous?" Beck asked, keeping his eyes on Speer's barrel.

"You have been a nuisance since they released you from Alvarium," Speer said calmly, moving dangerously close to the pool. "Released on my assignment. A disappointment." He abruptly fired at Beck, hitting him in the shoulder. Beck hunched in agony.

Speer crept forward, on his own mission. "You're a difficult one, Custode," Speer said, stepping over Leroi as she lay still, holding her gushing wound. He fingered his mustache with his free hand, his glare moving to X. "So the girl here. Are you involved with the stolen download from my camp?"

"You won't get it," X said flatly.

"No bother," Speer yawned. He moved toward Mel as she struggled for her blaster, the gash in her leg bleeding into a crimson puddle. "The rebels will be hunted down. Every single one."

"This isn't how I imagined going," Beck said with exasperation, appearing faint as he hung over the pool. The thick honey reflected golden light into his eyes like fire. Speer fired a shot at his leg, and Beck retracted in pain.

"Beck!" X cried.

"I know about the carnage left in your crew's wake," Speer said, menacing in his slow stroll to Custode, reveling in his prey's anguish as he picked up her scythed staff and inspected it. "Now, I'm here to take what's rightfully mine."

Sun Bin's words rolled through Mel as she lay by the truncheons, contemplating her next move. *The land takes back.*

"It's not yours to take," she said, seizing two of the truncheons as she scrambled to her feet. She tried to ignore the throbbing pain in her leg and shoulder, becoming lightheaded.

Speer threw the scythe end of the staff at her throat, and she clumsily blocked it with the truncheons, her arms and shoulder scalding in agony, her head hazy. Blood loss ignored, she determined she'd battle with all the power she had.

After a grimace, he swung again. As Mel spun and struck Speer, he swiftly blocked her tepid strikes with skillful staff handling, maneuvering it like a swordsman. He struck her in the shoulder and pummeled her back as she wailed.

"Who's gonna stop me?" He slapped the staff at her leg, knocking her back to her knees. "The bees will burn in this mountain, every single one."

"You can't!" X yelled.

"Oh, child," Speer said, wagging the scythe. "Your precious bees have been locked in your little mountain by my cannons. They had the chance to leave. They're a quite fussy bunch." An evil grin washed across his face as X turned white. "But don't you worry. The world will be fine without them."

Mel rushed with swings of the truncheons, a surge of released rage roaring. Blocked by Speer's reflexive dexterity, she drove one solid hit on Speer before he struck her again. He spun the staff around and thrusted the blade at her midsection, which she narrowly blocked before he struck the side of her head and she fell backward onto her rump.

"Fine without all of you," Speer said defiantly, standing over her with authority and fury. His nostrils flared.

Mel eyed him, his feet on the edge of the pool. The man behind the deaths of her family, behind the lies. Her body twitched in pain. Her insides bled. She was exhausted, her body surrendering, her vision blurry. The milky light brought her to another time, digital hallmarks of her mother and sister. Ghostly images clouded her vision, and the general's voice started to fade.

"Each of you," Speer continued, "will remember this day when your precious bees were taken. If I can't have them, they will be eradicated. Then, the end of the resistance." He held the staff over Mel, preparing to plunge its end through her chest as the cave rumbled. His attention drew to the shifting cave's walls. "Those damn machines weren't supposed to continue to pummel the mountain with me *in it.*"

"The bees aren't yours to destroy," X said, holding onto the wall as the cave seemed to roll back and forth in its own wave of consciousness.

"Yes, they are, honey."

With that, Mel drove a truncheon into Speer's knees, stunning him as she pulled the scythed staff toward her and spun and thrust the blade into his abdomen.

Mouth open in shock, he staggered around the pool. More jarring blasts shook the cave, heavy artillery pummeling the adjacent great room. The cave's insides started to finally collapse on itself, rock and slate crushing down upon them. Speer's eyes wide, he fell back into the boisterous pool, inhaled by its rich splendor as a massive boulder fell from above, pummeling him farther and completely into the wavy, golden deep. He sunk, pulled down by the sinking rock as he disappeared, and the goo swallowed him whole.

"Don't call her that," Mel said under her breath as the ground convulsed from side to side like an angry behemoth.

Beck struggled to stand, and reflexively caught X with his arm as she almost fell into the pool's swishing and lapping.

Catching her own breath, Mel leaned toward Beck. "Pull it out of you, Beck."

"I've always got it in me."

"This way!" X yelled, and Beck somehow threw Leroi over his shoulder, scowling in pain as they all stumbled through another hidden passageway. The mountain shook and shivered, unsettled and unnerved, as they ran. They shifted left to right in the confined tunnel, bouncing off the walls to stay vertical.

"You have tunnels in tunnels?" Beck yelled as they raced toward the distant circle of light, which seemed to get farther away, X sprinting out front. The mountain groaned as it fell into itself, its voluminous caves and tunnels falling within its crumbling outer layers of broken rocks and boulders and silt. As Mel brought up the rear, Beck struggled to run as Leroi bounced in his arms.

"Run!" Mel cried as Beck sweat and Leroi's face went white, her eyes barely lucid.

As the mountain imploded, X, Beck, Leroi, and Mel popped out the exit, spiraling down the charred, grassy, and jagged hillside, tumbling upon themselves, jarred and rattled. Mel landed last, scuffed and bruised, her back broken maybe, as she lay on top of Beck, facing him. She moaned as she tried to shift her weight, amazed at their daring escape as the mountain collapsed like a deflating bag. Tall, wavy grasses and burned tree patches surrounded them like painted camouflage.

"Keep moaning and people will get the wrong idea," Beck said dryly.

"Oh, you don't have to worry about that, cowboy," Mel said as she writhed off him to the ground, jolting Beck with her elbow as she tried to ignore the stabbing pain all over.

X smirked. "Never getting along."

"I don't understand your problem, I'm not that bad," Beck said as he and Mel managed to their feet. "Ya know, in certain districts, I could be the perfect catch."

"We haven't found those districts yet," Mel said as she stood up straight, strained as her wounds ached, and pulled out the palm reader falling out of her pocket.

"That thing still work?" Beck eventually asked.

"In and out. We need to get to the transport. It's close."

"Simple Eye!" X yelled as she ran to the drone lying still like scrap metal across the way in the furrowed soil. She picked it up delicately, its eye blinking slowly. "How'd you get here?"

Mel frowned. "You don't think Y left—"

"Why would he have done that?"

"I bet the drone found you," Beck said. "These machines, they know where their owners are."

"The transport, we must find," Leroi said weakly, as if awakening from being drug induced. Color started to return to her face.

"The sentries will find us soon if we don't," said Beck.

"We will," Mel said, careful to twist her torso. Somehow, her back wasn't broken, but it throbbed like it had its own heartbeat. She searched outward, monitoring the drone's blink and its weak bleeps. "Simple Eye's nav says the cruiser is idle. Looks like they found a haven while they search for fuel."

"Safe enough for a nav to find them as easily as you just did," Beck said. "And I have no idea how you can understand that thing. But let's go. No sense in staying around this crumbled heap." She didn't blame him for wanting to get out of here. Drone patrols and trooper sweeps were probably imminent.

"You understood him enough to find us," Mel said, eyebrows arched.

"Didn't need to understand much, I just followed *him* and all his sulking."

"Can we fix him?" X asked, cradling Simple Eye like a precious doll.

"We'll do whatever we can do," Mel said, brushing X's disheveled hair out of her tear-filled eyes.

"Please!" X begged as they moved farther into the smoldering landscape, away from the dissipating Authority cannons and settling rock.

"A couple of bad hits," Beck said to the drone. "Not such a great day you're having, heh?"

Mel blinked, spotting a small group a short distance ahead. Y and several rebel children unobtrusively traveled through the prairie grasses as the curling smoke from the patchwork fires splattered across the charcoal sky.

***

Kesselring stepped out of his absconded speed pod and peered around and under the unassuming rock. Finding the data chip would be like discovering gold. Tired and haggard, his whole being ached like he'd left his entrails behind at the Moat of Moorack. The pod's charge was about depleted, about to turn to zero. Still, he was here.

En route to this remote part of the district, he had come across severe irritants. Recounting the turn of events leading up to Speer's assault of his base camp, Kesselring scoffed. He'd floated past nomads, Loners, a team of bandits, another team of bandits devolving into cannibalistic Loners, and at least one witch.

After lifting a couple of rocks and finding nothing, he checked his data reader, confirming he had it right. This was the place, just outside the Mines of Gurth. Maybe, but there was nothing. He checked again, peeking around the oblong boulder, then got on his knees and picked at the dirt and brush, searching for the disc like a hungry scavenger, finding the whole exercise degrading. This was how Loners searched for treasure, the desperate heathens.

Could it be attached to something? He knew not its size or color, but he'd know it upon discovering it. Then a dark calm filled his lungs, as if black tar blanketed his innards.

There never had been anything. Custode had tricked him. She had known Speer would not relent in his pursuit of the download and would certainly not let him be the hero in its recovery. Speer would attack, and she and her friends would be gone. And he, Colonel Karl Kesselring, would be banished from the Authority for deserting his camp under fire.

Duped again.

His rage boiled over, overwhelming him as he shook. Veins popped out of his neck as he pounded the hard, rocky ground until his palms bled.

"Cusssstoooooooodddeeeee!" he screamed, only to be heard by curious wildlife in the desert highlands, their heads perking up and then becoming as disinterested as the passing wind. His surreal dream rushed in fast-forward. He'd stop at nothing to find the woman who deceived him, for her part of the impetus for Speer's obsession to take control over all forty-four districts and destroy his camp.

He would seek and annihilate everything the Authority had built and everything they thought about building.

THIRTY

Aboard the *Catharsis*, Mel strolled up the aisle with Beck and Leroi toward the weary, grateful rebel officials awaiting them. For whatever reason, the ship's occupants had not wanted to wait more than two days to acknowledge their heroics, no matter how their unwanted attention. All eyes were on them. Did she belong among this family she did not know? A familiar anxiety pulled at her like strings.

Her bandaged shoulder ached, crimson oozing through the gauze over her begrimed clothes; she had no others. Fatigued rebels glared at her with suspicion, a questionable welcome. Did these people want her here? She had resisted receiving the honors that Sangeeosay had insisted they accept. Leroi saw it differently, so as to not offend their hosts (as if Leroi understood the rebels most). They had indeed saved two thousand lives, after all. They had kept the download. But in the end, she had agreed to go along with it.

The ornamented award ceremony was as elaborate as it could possibly be on a retreating rebel barge cruiser's deck, modified from its Authority-owned specs to provide for thousands. Like vast Old World cruise ships, the rebel cruiser housed hundreds of cramped, efficient cabins and possessed the utility to handle immense quantities of food and water. Advanced hydroponic gardens thrived in the bottom hull. Here, the main cabin hall was outfitted like an ancient temple, adorned with worldly artifacts from the rebellion's start, its post-war beginnings after metropolises were flattened and technologies were destroyed. Treasured platinum and green tapestries from centuries before hung from the ceiling against the dais—colors that used to represent a modern, clean future.

Hundreds of rebel freedom fighter families—men, women, and children—stood at attention in their grubby clothes. From the makeshift dais, X stood tall next to Sangeeosay, raising her chin in anticipation of the honors they were about to bestow. Tired, reluctant dignitaries observed with feigned patience, anticipating the next stretch to the rendezvous point.

Critical dangers remained ahead, questions unanswered. Where were they to go after the gathering with other rebel populations? What challenges would face them en route? Despite their hydroponic resources, without the massive bee colony, how would they manage with their limited food supply?

Mel, Beck, and Leroi made their way through the cluttered, silent crowd, an eerie quiet blanketing the deck. Triumphant trumpets in Mel's head provided her calm, giving way to a sweet adagio. She had helped save lives. Was Sun Bin looking over her, a hovering spirit from beyond his muddy grave who helped her understand all she couldn't see? She would visit him again someday, provide him a proper marker. A new world called to her now, a place where she had never searched for but always longed to find.

What was she doing here?

She stole a glance behind her, and the former Authority soldier smiled back proudly, as if they were in a celebratory grand ballroom during peacetime. It was as if Mel had found her own inner peace and home although they were at war with an unforgiving force. They would be chased down, despite Speer being gone. With an unknown future, smiles would be short-lived.

She caught a glimpse of Beck at her side as they strode forward, surprised by his poise as they managed the embarrassment of being stared down by the disheveled crowd. Sangeeosay may have meant to honor them, but it was tension that laced the deck—a rug to be pulled from underneath her feet any moment.

The three heroes arrived at the dais, a platform normally used for the handout of food rations since the cruiser was modified from its Authority origins. A few steps provided height and access to hungry hands. X smiled brilliantly at all three of them. Behind her, Y stood, appearing a bit shorter somehow. Stymied and stoic, his shoulder and leg were wrapped in bandages and gauze.

X dressed Mel with her medal, its thin chain holding the platinum clay medallion emblazoned with a feather and a knife crossed over each other—symbols of strength, wisdom, and restraint. A balance of power, the center of competing forces, ignoring the known rebel insignias as if they were unnecessary and outdated. As X prepared to place the medal around Leroi's neck, it hit Mel. Sun Bin's spirit had provided her sight if she were to accept it. His voice called to her, saying only her name with more meaning behind it. The sense fell over her like water. A fighting spirit unleashed upon her, and she was a prisoner no more.

***

Many miles away, relentless crunching steamrollers flattened what was left of the rebels' mountain in a vast, rolling field of broken rock. The automated steamrollers, refurbished to be cruel, pilotless land levelers, crushed and compacted the stubborn rock into surrendering foothills of mashed stones and dust.

Armed AI sentries waved their blazing flamethrowers as they strode, the towering pipe-woven machines spraying the ground with fiery river flows as they scanned for remains of life within the rebel home's destruction. Nothing was to survive.

Armed robotic parkours raced and jumped over rocky obstacles with springs in their jumps and weights at their feet, continuing their search for anything to kill. Timid wildlife, having endured the barrage of missile bombs and fire across their habitat and sensing the clamorous, leg-pounding machines, disappeared like dissolving dusk into the burnt woodlands.

***

As Beck received his unsought honor and forged a smile back at X, she, for the first time, did not glare back at him with disdain. He met the sorrowful eyes of the overseeing Sangeeosay, and the long fight, the toll. His loss quelled now-forgotten hopes. His pain oozed deeper than the ten or so years without his daughter, something medals and ceremonies could not cover up.

The Authority invasion had reversed post-war progress and could have destroyed a civilization. He wanted to leave this place and embark on a vague form of retribution, payback of his own. Wishing for the peace of his homestead ranch, it called to him like a bell, missing him. He owed an employer a delivery, but did that matter now anyway? With his daughter gone, there was no reason for him to stay here, but he accepted the medal around his neck with reverence, aware of Sangeeosay's distrustful eyes watching him with eagle eyes that sought to be one step ahead.

Oh, I don't trust you either.

***

Y's crucible got heavier as he avoided eye contact with the unlikely heroes up front. Regenerative effects of the synth-flesh covering his wounds had not yet taken, and the heavy burlap-like cloth felt itchy. Roiling goose bumps fanned under his coverings as the regal proceeding cast doubt upon the esteem provided to the medal bearers. Why was X appointed as the hero to adorn? Also, he should have been situated next to X rather than behind her, providing honors to those who had assisted the rebel cause. He had saved rebels too.

Precious rebel lives. A restless sneer crept across his lips.

The girl's bossiness never changed. Her perceived leadership hovered over him, haunting him like a stain that won't come out. He could not help but stare at the back of her head, wanting to cause pain of his own. He had been the one to swipe the download in the first place, the one bold enough to acquire the intelligence that initiated the evacuation.

But General Sangeeosay would have none of it. The honors were bestowed upon honorable rebels who had *followed the indisputable orders* of retention and evacuation. Rebel children's lives had been put at unnecessary risk, and with the reported death of the entire bees' nest, the boy's self-determined burden had been established as a noble but grave miscalculation.

No one understood him. *Let the adults handle it,* he could imagine Beck saying, admonishing him like he was still a child for trying to save the bees on his own. Had not the adults fled, abandoning the bees? Instead, hadn't he faced the Authority's wrath on behalf of the resistance, focused on responsible, long-term sustenance? Instead of running? As he saw it, his priority was in the right place, and here he was ignored. The download had confirmed rebel detail, but had not been decrypted before it was recovered, but the Authority had discovered their home anyway. There had been an uncelebrated accomplishment in getting it back.

Even Sangeeosay had come around to appreciate X as a leader.

Restless and twinkling, Simple Eye rose from the side staging in a technician's hands to float by X's side, and Y winced. He had thought the drone would never survive the crumbling mountain. Restored, polished, and rebuilt with refurbished panels, its antennae spun in excitement as X beamed at the heroes as the crowd hushed.

Of course, even the drone is distinguished with repairs.

Her head high, the general held her hand up for the weary rebels to acknowledge Mel, Beck, and Leroi as Y stewed. Silence filled the crowded deck. No applause, no acknowledgment. Weary freedom fighters stared at the heroes in silence, the sea of grungy faces and leering gazes remaining still, without a blink.

Was it judgment or simply exhaustion? Perhaps the rebel assembly was questioning why he was not properly acknowledged, after risking his life as he did, or they were indignant because the bees had all perished, and they were all now on the run without a home. Chills worked their way up his spine as he felt invisible, like he had disappeared into the ornamental dais, discarded like a useless prop. Anywhere else would be better.

He did not belong here.

***

All the while, sweeping fire over the leveled rock had left a desolate ocean of stillness and singed death. Satisfied with their savage demolition, the steamrollers, sentries, and Authority cleanup forces withdrew, leaving stunning destruction in their wake. A crushed and demolished rebel mountain, a crater of its former existence, called for nothing or no one. Its physical presence had been erased like a forgotten bad dream, a long sigh. The eradication of the rebel lair had been time-stamped.

It was absolutely still as the sun went down, save for an airy wisp rising out of the slate's wiry crack, finding its freedom as it reached the sky, a hand from the grave. Chilling silence met with a muffled crumble somewhere down in the nether. Then, from within the kindling rubble, an exhausted and unnerving queen bee slowly emerged, unsettling a tiny trough of pebbles to behold the fading slivers of light, content to be alive.

* * *

About the Author

Terrence King lives in San Diego with his wife, his bonus children, and their Bernedoodle. His website is terrencekingauthor.com where you can find supplemental materials, book reviews, and more.

Message from the Author

Thank you for reading my novel Critical Habitat, more than six years in the making. I hope you enjoyed it. If you would be so kind to take a moment and add a review, I would be especially grateful! Reviews and referrals are key ways for a new author to compete in a crowded marketplace, and your voice is powerful.

If you do write a review, don't forget to email me at terrencejking@gmail.com so I can forward you a special deleted scene from Critical Habitat, that may or may not be included in the upcoming follow-up. A special "Thank you."

Milton Keynes UK
Ingram Content Group UK Ltd.
UKHW041604071123
432058UK00023B/60